**Praise for The World of Hetar series and *New York Times* bestselling author**

# BERTRICE SMALL

"Readers who enjoyed the first in [this] new series will devour Lara's latest adventure."
—*Booklist* on *A Distant Tomorrow*

"Small's newest novel is a sexily fantastical romp."
—*Publishers Weekly* on *The Sorceress of Belmair*

"Rich in colorful characters, brimming over with Small's unique sense of erotic passion and a plot filled with mystery, the fourth title in the series is another masterpiece."
—*RT Book Reviews* on *The Sorceress of Belmair,* Top Pick

"Small is not only a queen of erotic/adventure historicals, with the fifth book in The World of Hetar series, she is a grand mistress of erotic fantasy.... With this newest story, the author demonstrates that we can 'have it all.'"
—*RT Book Reviews* on *The Shadow Queen,* Top Pick

"The final volume in The World of Hetar delivers a fantasy lover's delight."
—*RT Book Reviews* on *Crown of Destiny*

**Also available from**
**Bertrice Small**
**and Harlequin HQN**

*The Twilight Lord*
*A Distant Tomorrow*
*Lara*

**Watch for more titles in The World of Hetar series,**
**coming soon!**

*The Shadow Queen*
*Crown of Destiny*

# BERTRICE SMALL

# THE SORCERESS OF BELMAIR

HQN™

ISBN-13: 978-0-373-77690-0

THE SORCERESS OF BELMAIR



This edition published by arrangement with Harlequin Books S.A.

For questions and comments about the quality of this book, please contact us at Customer_eCare@Harlequin.ca.



www.Harlequin.com

**Printed in U.S.A.**

For all those readers who love Lara and her world.
Thank you.

# THE SORCERESS OF BELMAIR

# Prologue

THE OLD KING of Belmair was coming to the end of his days. He sensed it. And as he had lived over eight hundred years it did not seem to him like such a great matter. But he was leaving his world in even poorer condition than he had inherited it. He knew what needed to be done, but he had never quite been able to bring himself to do it. Now, however, as the purple sands in the great hourglass representing his life that sat in the king's chamber ebbed away to almost nothing, the king knew he must act before it was too late. If it was not already too late.

"Send for the dragon," the king said to the chief footman who stood next to his throne.

"Send for the dragon!" the chief footman said to the second footman who repeated the command to the third footman, and so on until the order had reached the last footman in the line within the chamber.

Opening the door the last footman called out, "Send for the dragon!"

And then they all waited in silence. After some time had passed one of the dragon's servants, dressed in bronze-gold livery, ran into the room and up to the king's throne.

"My mistress is sleeping, Your Majesty. It will take some time to awaken her for it has been a long while since you have sought her counsel," the servant said.

"Are you a servant of the first rank?" the king asked.

"I certainly am!" the servant assured the king. "My mistress would allow no one of lesser stature to speak to Your Majesty. Though she sleeps, the protocols are always and ever observed."

"How long will it be before she is awakened?" the king asked.

"I'm afraid it will be several days, Your Majesty," the servant answered, his tone holding just the proper amount of regret. "She tends to sleep heavily."

"Time enough," the king replied pleasantly. "Send to me before she comes."

"Of course, Your Majesty," the dragon's servant said, and then bowing, he backed from the chamber.

As he did, he was passed by a beautiful young woman who hurried into the king's presence. She was tall and slender with the grace of a willow. Pale as moonlight, her long hair, which was worn loose, was as black as the night, and her eyes were as green as spring. She was dressed in a flowing gown of violet silk.

"You have sent for the dragon, Father?" she said as she came.

"I have. It is past time, my dear Cinnia, that I did so," the king told his only child.

"You know what she will say," Cinnia responded. "She has said it before, but you would not listen. Will you listen now, Father?"

The old king sighed. "I have no choice now but to listen," he admitted.

"But will you follow her advice, Father?" Cinnia persisted.

"I fear I must," the king replied, and he sighed again. "My time is coming to a close, Daughter. Look to my glass. A successor must be chosen to follow me. It is the dragon's duty to choose the next king of Belmair, and it is your duty to wed my successor."

Now it was the girl who sighed deeply. "I do not know," she said, "why a queen cannot rule Belmair, Father. I am as good a sorceress as any male sorcerer."

The king nodded. "It is true, Daughter, that you have strong powers, but tradition dictates that a king rule Belmair."

"Can tradition not be changed, Father?" Cinnia asked seriously.

"Tradition, Daughter, is what keeps our society civilized," the king reminded her. "Remember our history, my child. The last of our kind to challenge tradition, to cause dissent among our peoples, were sent from Belmair. We do not want to be like them now, do we? Their lives were shortened when they left here, and they have been gone for so many centuries now that they have forgotten their own history. They do not remember from where they came, yet in their overweening pride believe themselves superior to all others in the world in which they live. Worse, they have changed little. They are still contentious." His eyes began to grow heavy. He slumped in his chair. "I am weary, Cinnia. Leave me now," the old king said.

"Are you all right?" she asked him anxiously. "Shall I call the physician?" Her small hand felt his forehead to see if he was feverish.

A small chuckle escaped him. "Nay, Daughter. I am neither ill nor quite ready to die. Look to the glass. There is yet enough purple sand in it giving me the time I will need to speak with the dragon. To meet with my successor. I am just old and tired."

Cinnia moved closer to the old king, and bending, kissed his withered cheek. "I'll call Samuel, and he will help you to your bed, Father. The king of Belmair should not sleep upon his throne. It takes away from your dignity."

"As you will, Daughter," he answered her. "As you will." And his gnarled old hand waved her from his presence.

# I

THE DRAGON FINALLY opened her eyes. Turning, she found her servant standing by her bed, waiting. She yawned and stretched lazily. "How long have I slept, Tavey?" she asked her servant, yawning again.

"A little over a hundred years, mistress," Tavey replied. "The king has called for you. He is in need of your counsel. The purple sand in his hourglass is almost gone."

"Humph," the dragon replied. "How typical of Fflergant," she said. "For all his bleating about tradition he has never done anything in a timely and correct manner. Now as his days end he calls for me. I have advised all the kings of Belmair since time began, but never have I dealt with one such as this king."

"Perhaps," Tavey ventured, "it was meant to be this

way, mistress. Have you not always said that everything happens for a specific reason?"

The dragon arose from her bed. Her name was Nidhug, and had she allowed herself to appear in all her glory she would have stood higher than her own castle. For simplicity's sake she used her own magic to stand no taller than eight feet. It allowed her to enter the king of Belmair's residence easily as the chambers there were only twelve feet high. "You know me too well," she said. "How long have you served me, Tavey?"

"Since the beginning of time, mistress," he answered her with just the faintest smile touching his thin lips.

"Humph," Nidhug responded. She stretched out her paws. "You have kept my claws nicely trimmed," she noted. "And my scales are quite supple."

"I have oiled them weekly, mistress," Tavey said. "Sleeping should not negate your need for maintenance. You are the Great Dragon of Belmair, mistress."

"How long ago did Fflergant call for me?" Nidhug asked her servant.

"Five days ago, mistress," Tavey responded.

The dragon stretched again, opening her delicate gold wings and extending them briefly before refolding them. She was a very beautiful creature, her scales an iridescent sea-blue and spring-green. The crest upon her head was purple and gold. She had beautiful dark eyes swirled with both gold and silver, and thick, heavy eyelashes that clearly indicated her gender. "Tell Fflergant that I will come to see him in the third hour after the dawn tomorrow morning," she told Tavey. "But before you go to him, tell the cook I will have two dozen sheep, a dozen sides of beef, a wheel of sharp yellow cheese and six cakes soaked in sweet wine for my dinner. Oh! And a nice salad, too, Tavey," Nidhug said. "I am in the mood for greens tonight."

"At once, mistress," the servant said, and hurried from the chamber to first speak with the dragon's cook. "She's awake," he said, entering the kitchens and giving the cook the order for his mistress's dinner.

"Is she ill?" the cook wanted to know. "'Tis scarcely a mouthful."

"It was only a nap," Tavey said. "Add a few dozen roast geese and capons to the order if it pleases you. She could very well discover she is hungrier than she thought, and will thank you for thinking of it," he said. Then he slipped out the kitchen door to cross the dragon's gardens, which led into the king's gardens and into the king's castle. Before he could find the king, however, he met the king's daughter, the sorceress Cinnia.

"Is she awake?" Cinnia asked immediately upon seeing Tavey.

"Yes, my lady, she is."

"When will she see my father? The sands seem to be moving faster," Cinnia said.

"Come with me, and you will learn the answer to your question," Tavey said.

*"Tell me!"* Cinnia demanded.

Tavey turned and looked at her. "You are not the king of Belmair, my lady, and my message is for the king, not his daughter."

Cinnia's green eyes narrowed, but the dragon's servant stood his ground. "I should be Belmair's next ruler," she said darkly.

"Belmair has never been ruled by a woman," Tavey replied quietly, and he began to walk toward the king's chamber once again.

"Does that mean it shouldn't?" Cinnia said.

"It is not our tradition, my lady," her companion replied. "The dragon has always chosen Belmair's kings. When there has been no son as has happened in this case the dragon chooses a suitable man, and if there is a king's daughter and she is unmarried, then she weds the new king so that the blood of the old king continues on as will happen for you, my lady. It is a good and sensible tradition, and has kept peace on Belmair."

Cinnia said nothing more. What was there to say? Her fate had suddenly been taken out of her hands. She was Belmair's most respected sorceress, but she no longer had any control over her own life. If she attempted to defy tradition she would be punished. The dragon's magic was far greater than was Cinnia's, and she was more than well aware of it for it had been the dragon who had taught her.

Reaching the king's privy chamber, they entered. Fflergant looked pale, but seeing Tavey, he seemed to perk up.

Tavey bowed to the king. "My mistress has just awakened, and, learning of your need, has told me to tell you she will be here in the third hour after the dawn tomorrow."

"Thank her for me, and tell her I eagerly await her coming," the king replied. Then he fell back among his pillows, and his eyes closed again.

Tavey looked to the great hourglass. The purple sand was almost all gone now. When the last grain of it dropped from the top to the bottom it would turn silver, and the king would die. He bowed again, and backed out of the chamber.

Cinnia went to her father's side. "You cannot die before this is decided," she said. "It is tradition. And you cannot die before you have passed your authority to your successor. That, too, is tradition on Belmair."

"I have almost waited too long," Fflergant said weakly. "My pride could not admit to the fact that I was getting old, Daughter. But my time is very close now. I heard your mother singing again in my dreams last night. She is waiting for me."

"And you will be with her soon enough, Father," Cinnia said softly, her eyes welling with tears. "But do not leave me until you have met this man who I must wed and who will be Belmair's next king."

"There can be no delay," the king told his daughter. "Once he is chosen and brought to the castle, the marriage must take place. My last breath as king will be his first breath as king. That is also tradition, Cinnia."

The young woman nodded. "I chafe against it, but I will not break with tradition, Father. I will not be like those exiled from us so long ago," she promised him.

"I am relieved to hear it," the old king said with some small humor. "I know how difficult it is for you, my daughter, for you are not a woman to sit by her loom weaving contentedly. Nidhug has taught you well, and you are a great sorceress."

"I show promise, the dragon says," Cinnia responded with a chuckle.

"I wonder who she will choose to follow me," the old king said. "What are your thoughts on the matter, Daughter?"

The young woman considered, and then she shook her head. "I can name no one I would choose to follow you, Father. Unless there is someone in one of the three provinces I do not know of, I can think of none. Its dukes are ancient, and long wed."

"Memory fails me, Daughter. Do any have sons?" the old king asked.

"Only Dreng of Beltran," Cinnia answered, "but he is long wed."

"How odd," the old king said thoughtfully. "In a time when a king is needed it would appear there is none to be had."

"Perhaps tradition is about to change," Cinnia suggested mischievously, "and a queen will follow you."

"If that be so," replied her father, "the queen still needs a husband if she is to produce the next king. Even all your sorcery cannot give you a child without a man."

"We can make all the suppositions we want to make," Cinnia said. "Only the dragon can tell us what is to come, Father. Even I acknowledge that. I am sorry she did not come tonight, but I know how hungry she is after one of her little naps. She must eat before she can consider the solution to our problem."

And Nidhug was indeed enjoying her evening feast. She praised the cook lavishly for her presence of mind in including the poultry offerings. "No one, Sarabeth," she said to the cook, "can roast a goose as you do." She popped a whole bird into her mouth, crunching down upon it, her thin tongue whipping out to lick her lips. "Delicious!" Nidhug pronounced as she swallowed the goose. "And capon, too! Is it stuffed?"

"Of course, mistress, and with that apple and walnut stuffing you so like," the cook replied, forgetting entirely that it had been Tavey's suggestion to include a bit of poultry. "I only did two of them, but I roasted two ducks in the plum sauce you favor, as well," Sarabeth told the dragon.

"Excellent!" the dragon said. "I shall need all my strength tomorrow, for the king is not an easy man to deal with, I fear."

When the dragon had finished her meal she went up upon the battlements of her castle and stretched to her full height. Then unfolding her delicate wings she rose up into the night sky. Belmair possessed twin moons. One of silver, one of gold. Their phases were identical, and tonight they shone in their first quarter, lighting the landscape below her as she flew. Peace flowed through the dragon's veins as she looked down.

Belmair was not a large world. It consisted of four islands of varying size set in a great sea. The largest island, which bore the name of Belmair, was the king's land. The three provinces were the smaller islands of Beldane, Belia and Beltran. Beldane was a lovely land of valleys, gentle hills and glens. Belia was mountainous. Beltran consisted mostly of great tracts of forest and meadows. Each province was ruled over by a ducal family, and each duke answered to the king.

The kings of Belmair did not always follow a familial succession. From the beginnings of time as far back as the Belmairans could remember, it was a dragon who had chosen the king from among the ducal families. And if the preceding king had a daughter of marriageable age the new king was required to wed her.

Once many centuries back, a king designate had been betrothed to a woman he loved when he had been chosen to be king. The betrothed maiden was willing to step aside for her beloved's sake for no one chosen by the dragon to be Belmair's king could refuse the honor. The previous king's daughter was willing to give up her place for she saw the love the king designate had for his betrothed, and she was a maiden with a kind heart. The dragon settled the matter by sitting both maidens in a pen filled with peas. Somewhere among the peas was a pearl. Whoever found the pearl would be the king's bride. The rumor was that the princess, finding the pearl first, surreptitiously pushed it into the other girl's view thus giving up her place. The dragon, who knew all, saw the princess married to the young duke of Beltran, who was also in need of a wife, and blessed her with healthy children and many happy years with her husband to reward her for her good and thoughtful heart.

The dragon stopped to rest herself upon a mountaintop in the duchy of Belia. It was spring, and the snows were melting. The sea surrounding the island, visible from her perch, sparkled in the dappled moonlight. She closed her eyes briefly and breathed deeply of the fresh mountain air. There had been but one Great Dragon of Belmair before her—her father. And when her time was over there would be another Great Dragon, but as she had yet had the inclination to raise a hatchling, she knew she would continue her watch over Belmair into the distant future.

The problem before her was to choose a successor for King Fflergant. But there was no successor here on Belmair. She knew each ducal family, and she knew all the men in those ducal families. But none of those males was the next king. She might have changed tradition and chosen Cinnia to be Belmair's queen. But Cinnia, while a great sorceress although Nidhug would never tell her so, was not capable of ruling Belmair no matter what the girl thought.

"Greetings, Nidhug. How beautiful you are in the moonlight," an elegant voice said, and then Kaliq, the great Shadow Prince of Hetar, laughed as the dragon's eyes flew open with her surprise to see him standing before her.

"My lord Kaliq, I greet you in friendship," Nidhug told him. "What brings you to Belmair?" Indeed what did bring him to Belmair? She had not seen him in at least a thousand years. Kaliq of the Shadows did not come casually. There was a purpose to his visit. And to come at this particular time? He had intrigued her as he always did.

"The purple sands in Fflergant's glass are almost gone," Kaliq began. "You need a king, and there is no king at this time here in Belmair, is there?"

The dragon shook her head. "Nay, there is no one, my lord Kaliq."

"That is because Belmair's new king is in my palace, Nidhug," the prince said.

"He is Hetarian?" This could not be!

"He is my son," the Shadow Prince surprised the dragon by saying. "His mother is called Lara. She is the daughter of Ilona, queen of the Forest Faeries in Hetar, and of a Hetarian called John Swiftsword. Lara has always believed that Dillon was the son of her first husband, Vartan of the Fiacre. We were once lovers long ago, and I told her that we Shadow Princes no longer reproduced. But how could I deny myself the joy of having a son with her for she was perfect. I left my seed in Lara, and when she was ready to give Vartan a child that seed bloomed. I saw to it that the boy had Vartan's coloring, and when people looked at him as a boy they saw Vartan through the magic with which I surrounded him."

Kaliq chuckled. "Lara has always thought Dillon gained his magic through her and her faerie blood. But he has my blood, too. He came to me for training when he was twelve. He is now twenty-two, and a great sorcerer. The perfect king for Belmair, and the perfect mate for the fair Cinnia, the sorceress of Belmair."

"She is a great sorceress," Nidhug said proudly. "I have taught her myself. But a Hetarian as Belmair's king? I do not know, my lord Kaliq."

"He was not born in Hetar, nor has he ever lived there. He was born in the Outlands into the Clan Fiacre. He was raised by the Fiacre, and later in Terah by his mother and his stepfather, Magnus Hauk, its Dominus. And for almost half his life he has lived with me."

Nidhug nodded, but then she said, "For all its lands with their differences it is still considered the world of Hetar, and the boy's grandsire was Hetarian."

"With faerie blood in his veins, as well," Kaliq responded. "Trust me, Nidhug. Dillon is meant to be Belmair's new king and Cinnia's husband."

"Show him to me," the dragon said quietly.

The prince held out his palm, and blew into it until a large iridescent bubble had formed itself into a perfect sphere. Then he gently waved his hand over it.

The dragon peered into it and saw a handsome young man with dark hair and blue eyes. He sat on a bench in earnest conversation with a lovely young girl while three young children played about them. "Who are the others?" Nidhug asked.

"The girl he speaks with is his sister, Anoush, daughter of Vartan. The other three are Magnus Hauk's offspring. The older girl is Zagiri, and the twins are Taj and Marzina."

"The twins are quite dissimilar," the dragon noted.

"Yes," the prince replied. "Kol, the Twilight Lord, caught Lara on the Dream Plain, and implanted his seed within her. As her husband had just gotten her with child that seed quickly took root, and the children were born together, and assumed to be twins."

"I thought Kol was imprisoned," the dragon said.

"He is now," Kaliq told her. "And he has been forbidden from the Dream Plain for what he did there."

The dragon nodded. "This is an interesting family whose blood you would mix into Belmair," she said drily. She peered more closely. The young man was fair of face and sturdy of form. Was he strong enough, however, to rule both Belmair and its sorceress? "Can he wield the power of a Belmairan king firmly? He looks to be a gentle man. But he cannot be! You are asking me to introduce a stranger into Belmair as its new king. The ducal families will not be pleased by a decision such as this."

"Only Dreng of Beltran has a son," Kaliq said. "And he is married."

"But all three dukes have grandsons," the dragon pointed out.

"Most are not old enough to be king, and the two who are could not control Cinnia," the great Shadow Prince said quietly. "Fflergant's sands will be gone in less than three days, Nidhug. Do you think I did not know this time was coming? I did not give Lara my son on a purely sentimental whim."

"Does he know?" the dragon asked candidly.

"He will before he comes to Belmair," Kaliq answered her. "I believe he has suspected it, though, for the last few years."

"And his mother?"

Kaliq smiled. "In time, Nidhug. Lara has only partly fulfilled the destiny that was planned for her. In time she will, but for now it is Belmair's future we must concern ourselves with. Have you seen enough?"

The dragon looked a final time into the bubble. "He is loving," she said. "Tender with his three sisters, and thoughtful of the little boy. I can only hope you are correct, my lord prince, and that your son is strong enough to master Cinnia. If he can then he will rule Belmair well. She would be queen of Belmair in her own right, you know. Swear to me that your fatherly pride has not blinded you."

Kaliq blew gently upon the bubble and it dissolved. "I love him well, I will admit, but he is strong, I promise you, Nidhug. He will be one of Belmair's great kings." Reaching out he placed his hand on the dragon's forehead between her two eyes pressing the heel of it firmly against her skin. "Here is all the knowledge that you will need to know," he said. "We will speak again soon." Removing his hand from her forehead, he disappeared from her sight.

The dragon stood for a moment longer, absorbing the knowledge the prince had transferred into her head. Then she looked up at the star she knew as Hetar. It was a crystalline-blue, and it twinkled coldly in the black silk night sky. She would be fortunate not to have an insurrection on her hands when she announced that the next king of Belmair was a Hetarian. While Hetar had lost the history of its beginnings, Belmair knew that history well. Those who called themselves Hetarians were not originally of that world. They had been Belmairans once. But they had chafed against tradition, and caused such trouble among the world's people that the king of that day had gathered them all up, placed them into a bubble and sent them to the world of Hetar.

She had never bothered to consider exactly what had happened to them because it didn't matter as long as they were no longer able to cause trouble for Belmair; Kaliq had given her that knowledge when he had touched her forehead. For centuries in their arrogance and pride, the Hetarians had existed in another bubble of sorts, believing themselves the only denizens of their world but for a people they called Outlanders.

The Outlanders and the Terahns were Hetar's original inhabitants. Like the Hetarians, the lord of the Dark Lands had come later. But now all knew that the other existed. The women of Hetar were in revolt against the government that kept them subjugated because of their sex, as their ancestors had once been in revolt against the ruler of Belmair for wanting change. And from this madness the next king would come.

Nidhug shook her head. She had to trust the great Shadow Prince, for of all the creatures in the Cosmos he was the one who stood highest in the Originator's favor. If he said Dillon of Hetar was to be Belmair's next king, then it must be so. The dragon unfolded her golden wings again and rose into the night sky to fly back to her castle. The dawn was just beginning to pull at the edges of the sky when she gained her own battlements. As her large, clawed feet touched the stone roof she shrank down to a more manageable and less frightening size.

Watching her come, Tavey marveled at the beauty and the magnificence of his mistress. He stepped forward immediately as she landed, bowing. "Your oil bath is ready, mistress. And Sarabeth has prepared a small breakfast for you," he told her.

"I will soak my scales first," Nidhug told him. "Will there be cinnamon rolls?"

"Only three trays, mistress. The cook thought that while you would be hungry this morning, you would not want to feel too full. She's done a nice kettle of porridge, two hams and four dozen boiled eggs for you, as well."

"How well you all care for me," Nidhug said, feeling a bit sentimental. "Aye, I will need to be on my toes this morning, given what I must tell Fflergant and his daughter. Send for the dukes. They must be here tomorrow morning to be told the name of the next king. Now, I must have my soak. My scales are dry from the wind." She hurried off.

When she had soaked for an hour up to her jowls in the warm oil, Nidhug felt refreshed. Arising from the large oval marble tub the dragon let her serving women gently rub the oil into her skin and blot away the excess. Then she repaired to her dining room for her morning meal, and having finished it she prepared to depart for the king's castle. She would walk across the gardens that separated the two castles, giving her time to consider exactly how she would approach the matter of succession. By the time she had reached Fflergant's castle and the throne room, she knew exactly what she must say.

"I called for you almost a full week ago," the old king said by way of greeting.

"And good morrow to you, Your Majesty," the dragon replied. She glanced at the hourglass and caught her breath. He was almost gone.

"Who will follow me?" Fflergant demanded to know. "Cinnia tells me that the dukes have no sons but one. What of grandsons? The dukes must have grandsons."

"They do," the dragon said, "but none are suitable. Several are already wed, and the rest too young to be either king of Belmair, or a husband."

"How young?" the king wanted to know.

"The oldest of them is eleven, Your Majesty," the dragon answered.

"Eleven. In three years he would be mature enough to be a husband," Fflergant said. "And in the meantime there could be a regency to rule for him."

"I will turn him into a toad," Cinnia said darkly. "You will not wed me to a child, Father. It is past time for the tradition of kings only rule Belmair to change. You have no other choice. I must be Belmair's queen in my own right. I will not take a little boy for a husband and then be told what to do by a regent's counsel. I am seventeen, not twelve."

"What other choice have we?" her father asked, desperately looking to the dragon.

"It is not a question of choice for Belmair," the dragon said. "It is my decision who rules. The Great

Dragon of Belmair has always determined its king from the beginnings of time, and I am the Great Dragon, Nidhug XXII. Fflergant of Belmair will be followed by Dillon, son of Kaliq of the Shadows."

*"A Hetarian?"* the old king gasped, and fell back in his throne. A dozen grains of purple sand remained in the top half of the life glass.

Seeing how near to death Fflergant was, the dragon stopped the sands flow.

Cinnia noted Nidhug's action, and looked to her mentor questioningly.

"I am permitted to do such in extreme cases," Nidhug explained softly, and the girl nodded. Then the dragon turned to the old king. "Your Majesty, I know this must seem more than odd, but you must trust me as did your last three predecessors. The son of Kaliq of the Shadows is meant to be Belmair's next king. His mother is a faerie woman called Lara. She was born in the faerie forest, and raised by her Hetarian father, who also has faerie blood. She is a great woman who has always used her powers for the good. Lara's mother is Ilona, queen of the Forest Faeries. Dillon is more than worthy of your daughter. He is fair to look upon, and has lived twenty-two years."

"I will not wed a Hetarian," Cinnia said. "They are a cursed race, Nidhug, and you are mad to even suggest it. He will bring discord to Belmair. Is that not why we sent his ancestors from our world? If you try to force me to this I will find a way to kill him."

"The Sorceress of Belmair should be wed only to a

great sorcerer," Nidhug told the girl in a quiet voice. "It was your ancestors who exiled the dissenters from this world, sending them to the place you called Hetar, and now you scornfully refer to them as Hetarians. But that world already had a people upon it. People much like the Belmairans. They are Terahns, and they called their world Terah. They prefer peace to war. They are artisans and simple folk content to be with themselves. And until recently the two peoples knew little of each other. In Hetar, except for those who call themselves Coastal Kings, none of the Hetarians knew of the Terahns. Dillon's mother changed all that for it is she who is meant to eventually unite the world upon which she lives into one world of peace, unity and prosperity. It is not an easy task, and even she is not aware of her full destiny yet. This union between you and her son is meant to be, Cinnia. You cannot refuse it. If you do then you must be exiled from Belmair."

Cinnia flushed with an anger that threatened to overwhelm her, but then as Nidhug's words sunk in she grew even paler than she normally was. "I would be sent from here?" she whispered, frightened. But then her courage returned, and she stamped her foot. "You give me a choice between marriage to a Hetarian, or exile? Is it not your duty to protect Belmair? Protect its people? Its ruler? Me?"

"Aye," the dragon said, small puffs of smoke coming forth from her carved nostrils. Cinnia's selfish childishness was beginning to annoy her, and she had to struggle with herself not to become angry. "You have been given a choice, sorceress. Marriage or exile. But either way, Dillon of the Shadows will rule next in Belmair."

Cinnia glared defiantly at the Great Dragon. She wanted to tell Nidhug to go to Limbo. She wanted to scream with her frustration, and her outrage. Belmair needed no foreign king. It was she who should be her world's next ruler. Cinnia, the sorceress of Belmair, had been born to be its queen! But then she felt the cold, weak touch of her father's hand on her hand.

"Tradition, Daughter. *Tradition,*" the old king murmured weakly.

Their eyes met. Hers were angry. His were pleading, and for a moment her resistance dissolved. She had no way to defeat her mentor, and accepting exile would serve no purpose, for if Nidhug had chosen him then this Dillon would be king of Belmair. If she left, some other girl would be his queen, and that knowledge was not pleasing to Cinnia. "I will do my duty and marry this man," she finally said.

"You have chosen wisely as I knew you would," the dragon replied. "The dukes have been sent for, and will be here on the morrow to learn of my decision."

"They will be no more pleased with it than I am," Cinnia said sourly.

"Certainly that is true," the dragon agreed, "but they surely know there is no other choice. There are no suitable males to follow Fflergant."

*Ping.*

The dragon turned at the sound. A single grain of purple sand had fallen from the top to the bottom of the life glass. Eleven grains remained. "You must be wed before the day is out, my child," Nidhug said. "Even my magic cannot hold back what must be, and the new king must be in Belmair when the old king breathes his last." She closed her eyes and silently called out to Kaliq, the great Shadow Prince, to come to her.

"I am here, Nidhug," the prince said as he materialized from the umbrages of the dim room. He went immediately to Fflergant. "Ah, yes, I see your problem. He is close. Greetings, King Fflergant of Belmair. I am Kaliq of the Shadows. I am going to stop time just briefly so I may go and fetch your successor." With a gentle wave of his hand Kaliq did exactly that. Even the dragon was caught in his spell. He paused a moment to look closely at Cinnia. She was lovely, and his son deserved no less. Turning, he slipped back into the shadows of the chamber, emerging in his own palace.

"Dillon," he called out. "Come to me now."

"I am here, my lord prince," Dillon said as he appeared in a puff of pale green smoke. "How may I serve you this day?"

"Sit down," the prince said. "We must talk, and there is not much time." When the young man had settled himself, Kaliq said without preamble, "You are not the son of Vartan of the Fiacre. You are my son, although you mother is unaware of this." To the prince's surprise Dillon smiled.

"Thank you," Dillon said. "I have suspected as much for several years now, but I dared not speak until you did. As much as I love my mother and my grandmother, it was unlikely that the powers I possess came just from the faerie side of my heritage. They are far too strong, and grow stronger. But why do you tell me this now, my lord? Something has changed. What is it?"

"The great star we call Belmair is another world, Dillon. And you are to be king of that world. Even now its old king lies dying. It is your fate to take his place and to wed his daughter. Belmair is protected by a Great Dragon. Her name is Nidhug, and she has trained the sorceress of Belmair in some of the same arts as I have tutored you. We will speak more on this later this evening, but for now you must come with me to catch the last breath of the old king, and then marry his daughter immediately. There is not much time left."

Dillon swallowed hard. "Does my mother know of this?" he asked.

"No," Kaliq said. "I lost track of time, my son, and did not realize Fflergant's death was so close. Come!" The prince flung open his great white cape, and Dillon obediently stepped inside of it.

As the cloak swirled around the two men, Dillon said, "You might have given me a bit more warning, my lord father. What if I don't like the girl?"

"She already hates you—" the prince chuckled "—for she would be queen of Belmair in her own right. Beware of her until you have won her over." He tossed the garment open once again.

Dillon found himself in a square chamber that was softly lit. On one wall was a throne in which a frail old man half sat, half reclined. A young girl, frozen in position, stood near him. On the other side of the throne was a very small dragon, equally still.

"I have frozen time briefly," the prince explained. "The girl is called Cinnia. The dragon Nidhug uses her magic to keep her size small while she is in the company of people. When you become friends she will allow you to see her in all her glory. She is quite magnificent, Dillon, and very wise. It was her decision that you be Belmair's next king, for it is her duty to make the choice. Trust her. She will be your ally." He waved his hand gently once again, and the chamber came to life.

*Ping.*

Cinnia gasped.

*Ping. Ping.*

"Cinnia, sorceress of Belmair, I bring you my son, Dillon, sorcerer of the Shadows. Will you have him as your husband?" Prince Kaliq asked.

Cinnia nodded, glancing quickly at the handsome stranger.

"Speak the words," Nidhug said softly.

"I, Cinnia, sorceress of Belmair, accept Dillon of the Shadows for my husband, and for my king," the girl said aloud.

"Fflergant, king of Belmair, will you accept Dillon of the Shadows as your successor and as the new king of Belmair?" Nidhug asked the old man.

"I do!" he cried loudly with the last of his strength.

*Ping! Ping!*

Six grains of purple sand remained in the glass.

"Dillon of the Shadows," Nidhug said, "do you accept the crown of Belmair, and all it entails?"

"I do," Dillon answered.

"Will you have Cinnia, the sorceress of Belmair, as your wife?"

"I will," Dillon replied. He had hardly even looked at the girl.

*Ping. Ping. Ping!*

"Then take the last breath of Fflergant as he breathes it," the dragon replied. "As he, and all the kings of Belmair have taken the last breath of those who preceded them."

Dillon stepped up on the dais containing the throne. The old man's eyes were closed now. Dillon bent down, and opening his mouth took the old king's last breaths into his body as Fflergant breathed them.

*Ping! Ping! PING!*

As the sound echoed throughout the room the old king suddenly faded away, leaving the chair empty. The sand in the glass next to the throne turned silver, and then it, too, disappeared. And then suddenly the top of the life glass was filled so full with a new supply of purple sand that no grains were able to begin dropping right away.

Cinnia began to cry. Dillon went to her and attempted to comfort her, but she pushed him away angrily. "Leave me be. My father is dead, and I am wed to a stranger."

"You are a stranger to me, too," Dillon reminded her.

"But your father is not dead!" Cinnia sobbed.

"Nay, but until today I thought he was," Dillon said.

Startled Cinnia stopped weeping, and looked at him. "What do you mean?" she asked him.

Dillon smiled. "It is a tale for another day, lady. Now we must mourn the good man who was your father. Tell me of your traditions so we may follow them."

"We have none where death is concerned for at death our bodies simply evaporate here on Belmair. Even the life glass of the king has refilled itself with the death of my father. If we go into the Hall of the Kings now we will find a marble bust of Fflergant in the place designated for it. There will be a new empty alcove waiting for you when your reign comes to an end," Cinnia explained. She wiped her eyes. "We do not celebrate death here in Belmair. We celebrate life. My father was a good king. He will be remembered as such, but he is gone. No further mention will be made of him."

Dillon nodded. "Thank you for explaining that to me," he said quietly.

"Nidhug and I will leave you two to become acquainted," Kaliq said. "I will rejoin you for the meal later." Then, taking the arm of the dragon, the Shadow Prince walked from the small throne room.

"I am twenty-two," Dillon said when they were alone.

"I am seventeen," Cinnia responded.

With a wave of his hand he conjured a perfect white rose, and offered it to her.

Cinnia glared at the rose, and it withered and disappeared in a puff of smoke.

Cinnia." Dillon's blue eyes met her green ones, and he smiled slowly into those startled eyes.

She heard her heart thumping in her ears. Her lips parted softly in surprise at her reaction to him. "Are you attempting to seduce me?" she asked him.

"You can only be seduced if you want to be seduced, Cinnia," Dillon told her. "Do you want to be seduced?"

"No!" She snatched her hand back.

"I think you do, however we will not argue the point," Dillon told her. "But I believe I asked you to tell me of Belmair as I am to rule it."

"Does our world seem very blue to you on Hetar?" she asked him.

"It does," he said.

"That is because most of our world is water," she told him. "Belmair consists of four islands, each a different size, floating within a single great sea. Our island is the largest and is called Belmair. The others are Beldane, Belia and Beltran. Each of the other three islands is a duchy ruled by a ducal family. Those families answer to the king on Belmair. Our kings do not necessarily follow a direct line of descent. It is the dragon who decides who will rule us. In this manner no one family has ever gotten too much power to wield over the others. My father's family came from Beltran. My mother was the youngest daughter of the previous king, who came from Beldane originally. She was very beautiful and very frail. That is why there were no more children after my birth. She died shortly after I was born. I had my father, and I had Nidhug," Cinnia told him.

"Tell me who now rules the three duchies?" he asked.

"Let Nidhug tell you," Cinnia said. "We must feast to celebrate our union, and then you must mate with me before the morrow when the dukes arrive to learn who their new king is. Unless we are well and truly mated, your legitimacy can be questioned, and that will not please either Nidhug or your father, will it? I go now to prepare." In a small flash of light Cinnia was gone from the throne room.

Dillon arose from the step where he had been sitting. "My lord father, I know you are there. Please come to me."

The Shadow Prince stepped from a dusky corner of the room. "Nidhug and I are going to take you to see your kingdom now," he told Dillon. "She awaits us on the battlements of the castle. Do not be frightened by her size when you see her true self."

"When are you going to tell mother?" Dillon asked Prince Kaliq.

"When I return to Hetar," came the answer.

"And when will that be?" Dillon inquired, his tone amused.

"In a few days. Tonight we feast, and then you mate with Cinnia. On the morrow the others will arrive. They will be astounded that an outsider had been chosen to rule over them, my son, but they will accept the dragon's judgment. And, too, my presence will give even greater legitimacy to Nidhug's decision. That you come from Hetar will disturb them, aye. But the fact that you are my son will calm any fears they may have. When that has been accomplished I will return to Hetar to seek out your mother and tell her of what has transpired."

"There are some things back at the palace that I will want," Dillon said. "My staff, Verica, for one."

"You will find everything in your chamber here now," Kaliq told him. "The royal quarters are unique. Both you and Cinnia have a set of rooms, and in the middle of them is the Mating Chamber. But come! Nidhug awaits us, and she wants to show you all before the sun sets this day."

Together, Kaliq and Dillon left the throne room, and climbed to the roof of the castle where the Great Dragon, Nidhug, was even now awaiting them.

# 2

WHEN THEY REACHED the roof Dillon caught his breath in amazement when he saw the size of the dragon in her full glory. The afternoon sun set her iridescent blue and green scales to sparkling. Seeing the two men had arrived, she reached out her hand, and they stepped into her palm so she might raise them up to sit upon her back.

"Look carefully," she told them, "and you will find two small pockets upon my back into which you may safely seat yourselves." When they had, she opened her great wings and rose from the castle's battlements to fly.

"Cinnia said Belmair consists of four islands in a vast sea," Dillon remarked.

"She is correct, of course," the dragon answered as she flew. "Your island of Belmair is the largest, and the most perfect of the four. As you can see there is a small range of mountains to the west. Fertile farmlands, woodlands and valleys cover the rest of the island. The coastline is both sandy and rocky with beaches and hills."

Dillon gazed down. Everything was very green, and it reminded him of Terah except there were not great cliffs and fjords. The woodlands below them now were just coming into full leaf, and the few planted fields were hazy with new growth. The meadows housed cattle and sheep, but curiously he saw no sign of life other than around the two castles. "Where are the villages and the people?" he asked Nidhug.

"There are few and they are widely scattered," the dragon answered.

"Is it like this on all the islands?" Dillon wanted to know.

"Aye, it is," was the answer.

"Why?" Dillon asked the dragon.

"I don't know," Nidhug admitted. "For the last few hundred years the young women on all the islands have been disappearing. The men have had no wives to wed, and fewer and fewer children are being born. Some women are returned to us when they are old, and can no longer have children or be of use. They are not able to tell us where they have been, and are horrified to find themselves old. If it continues, Belmair's civilization will die. That is why I trained Cinnia to become a sorceress, but as powerful as she is, she needed a husband who was even more powerful. Your father knew it, and that is why he brought you here to me to be Belmair's new king. Together you and Cinnia can work to solve the mystery of where our young women have gone, and correct the situation so our population can once again thrive." She turned north now over the great sea, and they were soon flying over a mountainous island, the highest peaks of which were still covered with snow. "That is Belia. It is the smallest of the duchies."

"Have you no idea of who is stealing your women?" Dillon inquired. "You have great magic yourself, I am told."

"My magic is fairly limited to protecting and serving Belmair, and its kings," Nidhug replied. "The magic of the Shadow Princes is the greatest of all magicks."

"Did you know all of this?" Dillon asked Kaliq.

The Shadow Prince smiled enigmatically. "Solve this conundrum, and you will be the greatest sorcerer of your time, Dillon, my son."

Dillon laughed softly. "That I might be a bit of dust in a corner when you tell my mother about all of this." He chuckled.

"She will soon have her own problems to solve," the prince replied with a small smile. "And she knows I would never see you harmed."

"You won't be here," Dillon reminded his father.

"My powers extend to Belmair. You have but to call me," Kaliq answered him.

"That is a great comfort to me," Dillon said drily, "but as I recall you have taught me to puzzle out my own problems." Turning away from the Shadow Prince, the younger man looked down to study the sea as they flew.

Prince Kaliq of the Shadows nodded, satisfied. Between them, he and Lara had raised their son well. Dillon would be a great king for Belmair, and the mystery would be solved because Dillon was not a man to give up. Belmair could not be allowed to die, and Kaliq was himself concerned as to who was doing this, and more important, why?

"There is Beldane," Nidhug called to them. "It is an island of mostly fields and glens. The hunting is excellent on Beldane, and the duke has many lodges scattered about his duchy for guests. Autumn, of course, is the best time for it."

Turning east they flew over the next largest island to Belmair, Beltran, a vast hilly and wooded landscape. Below them a small group of sailing boats was setting out from a harbor below a castle.

"Dreng comes early," Kaliq noted.

"I believe he thinks one of his little grandsons will be chosen to be king for he is the only one of the dukes with male progeny. He will be to Belmair by sunset, for when summoned by me the dukes' boats come by magic in just a short time. We cannot have that," Nidhug said. *"Storm brew!"*

Suddenly below them, the thunderclouds began to roll swiftly in. The sea grew frothy as the waves rose, crashing wildly on the shore, and the lightning crashed about the boats. One vessel was struck, and its mast caught fire. The little fleet struggled back to the harbor, and anchored to ride out the weather.

"It won't clear until dawn," Nidhug said in a well-satisfied voice and she chuckled. "Dreng is bold to think he can make my decision for me."

"How will he feel when he learns I am king?" Dillon asked.

"Surprised. Possibly resentful, but he will accept my will for there is no other choice, Your Majesty," the dragon answered. "When your father came to see me last night, I was amazed afterward that I hadn't realized that someone not born of Belmair must be chosen to follow Fflergant if we are to solve our difficulties. And that someone must have even greater powers than Cinnia. Whoever, whatever, is taking Belmair's young females must be stopped."

"Agreed," Dillon responded, "but I am more curious as to why they are being taken. There is something wicked here on Belmair."

Having completed their tour of the islands, the dragon returned them to the royal castle where she once again condensed herself into a smaller size. "Let us now feast," the dragon said. "And afterward your father and I will preside over your mating with Cinnia. How are you getting along? She is a charming girl, isn't she?"

"She is spirited, much like my younger sister Zagiri," Dillon noted. Then he told Nidhug and the prince of his attempts to charm Cinnia, and of how she had rebuffed him.

"A kitten into a viper." Nidhug chuckled. "The naughty girl, but I am quite enchanted that you turned the viper into pink snowflakes, Your Majesty. It is obvious that Prince Kaliq has taught you about women, as well as magic."

"Do not women possess a magic of their own that is to be courted?" Dillon asked her with a smile.

The dragon rolled her beautiful eyes, and her eyelashes fluttered coquettishly. "I am, for the first time, envious of a human female," she said.

Her two companions chuckled. They entered the Great Hall of the castle. It had a high ceiling with beams carved and gilded with both gold and silver, as well as painted in red and blue. The arched windows lining the hall on both sides were recessed into the stone walls. The glass in them was clear with designs showing pastoral scenes in stained glass. Beautifully woven silk and wool tapestries hung on the gray stone walls between the windows. There were three great fireplaces in the hall, one on either side of the chamber, and the third behind the high board. The floors were slabs of gray stone.

The hall was empty but for Cinnia, who waited for them before the high board. She was garbed in a simple loose purple silk gown with a boat neckline and flowing sleeves. A thin chain of gold links decorated with pale amethyst crystals sat upon her hips. Her long black hair was pulled back into a single strand. She looked both fragile and strong at the same time. Kneeling before Dillon, she said, "I bid you welcome home, Your Majesty. The meal is ready at your command."

Dillon raised her up. "Do not kneel to me again, Cinnia. If it is Belmairan tradition that a wife kneel before her husband, it is a tradition that I will not continue.

You are a great sorceress, and you are my wife. I mean to make you queen."

Her green eyes lit up with joy, but then the happiness faded away, and she shook her head at him. "I would be nothing but a consort if Your Majesty desired it, but I would have no authority even over our household. In Belmair, all is the king's."

Dillon turned to the dragon. "Is this a tradition that is written in stone?" he asked.

"Nay, it is not. But it has always been done this way," the dragon answered him.

Dillon considered, then said, "As I am not Belmairan born, but am now nonetheless the undisputed king of Belmair, could I not make this change, and allow others to understand this is my way of honoring Cinnia, the great sorceress of Belmair, who is now my wife? Whose help I will need if I am to govern wisely and well?"

"There will at first be a certain amount of grumbling," the dragon replied, "but I believe that to honor Cinnia as your first official act as Belmair's king would quickly be seen as respecting Belmair and its traditions."

"Then I shall do it," Dillon said. He turned to Cinnia again. "You understand that the final word in all things but the household will be mine?"

"I do, Your Majesty! Thank you!" Her green eyes were shining now.

"And you will call me by my name when we are in private, or in an informal setting?" he asked smiling at her.

She nodded. "I will, Your…Dillon."

"Then it is settled, and now please see that the meal is served. Our guests and I are hungry," Dillon told her with a grin.

Taking her arm, he escorted her up onto the dais and seated her to his left at the high board. The prince sat on his right, and the dragon to Kaliq's right. Cinnia signaled the servants to begin serving the meal, and Dillon watched, amazed at the separate menu of foods brought to the dragon. When the meal had concluded, and Nidhug had consumed the final of her eight sherry-soaked whipped-cream cakes, a minstrel came into the hall and sang for them. A serving woman appeared and whispered something into Cinnia's ear. She nodded.

"It is time for me to go and prepare for our formal mating ritual, my lord," she said rising from her seat. "You will be sent for when I am ready." Then before he might speak she hurried away.

"What preparations will she make?" Dillon asked Nidhug.

"She will be thoroughly bathed so her body is pleasing to you," the dragon replied. "The ritual consists of you coupling with her before witnesses, in this case the prince and me. Once you have been joined none has the right to separate you. This is why I prevented Dreng from arriving tonight. Your father accepted you as his successor. She accepted you for her husband, and as her king. You took Fflergant's last breath. Now the last thing to be done is the joining. Once that is accomplished the deed is done, you will be king of Belmair until the last of the purple sands in your life glass is gone to the bottom. From the looks of the glass, that will be many years hence, Your Majesty."

"If she is to bathe, then I should like to bathe also," Dillon said, but the dragon shook her head.

"Nay, not until afterward. Cinnia's body must be imprinted with your natural scent so it will always recognize you," the dragon explained.

"Belmairans have sensitive skin," the prince explained to his son. "Once her skin has been imprinted by yours, it will always recognize you even if you scent yourself."

"How odd," Dillon murmured low. Then he said to Kaliq, "What other little surprises are in store for me?"

Kaliq shrugged. "I have never lived in Belmair," he replied.

"Is Cinnia a virgin?" Dillon asked the dragon.

If a creature could looked shocked, Nidhug certainly did at the query. "Of course!" she exclaimed. "Why would you think otherwise?"

"It is not a requirement in either Terah or Hetar that a girl be a virgin on her marriage. That she cleave to her husband once she is, is expected," Dillon said. "I ask because a virgin would require more gentleness, more care, than a girl who has experienced passion a time or more. Is she aware of the differences between bodies male and female? Does she have any idea of what to expect?"

"Aye, she knows what is required," Nidhug answered him. "I have taught her myself. Knowledge she has. Experience she is lacking." The dragon chuckled. "Again, I must express my envy for my pupil. Your father's prowess as a lover has extended even here to Belmair. I can but imagine what his son, and the son of a faerie woman, is like."

"For Cinnia's sake," Dillon asked his two companions, "can you render yourselves invisible if you must be within the chamber? I have made love to women in my father's hall surrounded by his brothers and their women. But this will be her first experience, and I think she should be put at her ease as much as possible."

"Are you as fierce with your opponents as you are tender with your wife?" the dragon wondered aloud.

"I am," Dillon surprised her by answering.

The serving woman now returned, and going directly to Dillon said, "Your Majesty, my lady awaits your coming."

Dillon arose and followed the woman out of the hall. He was interested to see that they traveled along a well-lit corridor, at the end of which he saw a large oak door. The serving woman stopped and pointed before turning about and hurrying off back down the hallway. Dillon saw no knob upon the door, so putting out his hand he silently commanded it to open. The door remained shut. *Interesting,* he thought. And then he smiled. "Open for King Dillon, and in future always recognize my hand upon thee, or my footfall as I approach thee."

The door swung open, and Dillon stepped into the chamber. It was a circular room with a stone floor and a glass ceiling that came to a witch's peak. There was but one piece of furniture in the room, an enormous oaken bedstead hung with gold and red tapestried curtains. The pillars of the bed were carved around with grape-vines. The headboard, though half-hidden by goose-down pillows, showed a stag and a doe as they ran through a forest. The wood canopy had a glass top that allowed those in the bed to gaze up through the glass ceiling to the night sky.

"Are you going to take off your garments?" Cinnia asked him.

He had been so intrigued by the simplicity of the chamber and the intricacy of the bed's carvings that he hadn't looked to see if she was in the bed. She was, sitting up, a scrap of silk covering her breasts.

"Have you ever seen a naked man?" he asked her as he began to strip off his clothing. He let it drop to the floor for there was no place where he might lay them.

"Nidhug has shown me pictures," Cinnia said. "But, nay, I have never seen a naked man not in a book. Are Hetarians different from Belmairans?"

"Since we come from the same root stock originally, I do not think so," he said. He was fully naked now, having kicked his soft felt shoes off. He turned so she might look at him. "What do you think? Am I the same as the men in the book?"

"You are bigger," she replied.

"How?" he asked her.

"All over," she said. "You look very strong, my lord."

"I am. I have been trained to be not just one thing,

but many. My grandfather was a great swordsman, and my mother is famed as a warrior, as well."

"We rarely fight here on Belmair," Cinnia told him. "We are a peaceful folk."

"Peace is the better route," he agreed, "but sometimes you must fight to protect what you hold dear else it be taken from you. I prefer the use of magic to solve problems, but I have also been trained to be a warrior by the same Shadow Prince who trained my mother before me. If I must fight, I can."

"Have you ever fought?" she asked, curious.

He nodded. "Once, my oldest sister could not discourage a persistent suitor. I was forced to do battle with him."

"Did you kill him?" she wanted to know.

Dillon nodded. "He refused to be satisfied otherwise. It made me sad to do it, but there was no other way. He threatened to kill Anoush if she would not wed him."

"Did she marry another?" Cinnia inquired.

"She is not ready to wed," Dillon said, and he walked toward the bed, and reaching it, climbed into it. "Now, however, is not the time for stories, Cinnia. We must complete a mating cycle tonight so that the three dukes can accept the dragon's choice more easily." Reaching out, he drew her gently toward him. "You have never known a man, I am told. But have you played lover's games with any young men?"

Cinnia shook her head wordlessly.

"Have you been kissed upon your lips by any other than a family member?" he asked her. But he knew the answer before she even gave it. She was a total innocent for all the books she had read, for all the dragon's teachings. "Then we must begin with the kissing," he said in a firm tone. His lips brushed over hers, and the touch of his mouth caused Cinnia to gasp softly. He pressed his lips harder against hers, and Cinnia tried to push him away. In doing so the silk coverlet that had covered her breasts fell away, and her breasts pressed against him.

*"Ohhhh!"* Cinnia cried out, surprised.

Dillon's head was spinning at the touch of her body against his broad, smooth chest, but her startled cry caused him to ask, "What is it? Are you all right?"

Suddenly Cinnia was no longer in his arms, and a small black-and-white bird fluttered to the top of the headboard.

Dillon didn't know whether to laugh. "We must be joined tonight, Cinnia. You cannot use magic when we make love." He reached his hand out to the bird but it scampered down to the end of the headboard. *Cat! Be that!* Dillon thought, and a large golden feline jumped up quickly from where he had been to snatch the bird from its perch, and hold it gently between its paws. They were quickly themselves again, and she lay naked in his arms.

"That wasn't fair," Cinnia said petulantly.

"I know you are afraid," he said to her, and his hand stroked her silky black hair. "That is all right, my young queen. I mean to take my time and to be gentle with you. My blood runs hot, Cinnia, but I have been taught by the masters of passion how to give pleasure to a woman.

Even a frightened little virgin. You need do nothing but follow my lead tonight. In time I will teach you to give pleasure, as well as receive it. But tonight we have a small duty to perform, and I would have you enjoy it, not be terrified by it."

"There are no witnesses," Cinnia said weakly.

"Show yourselves," Dillon said, and both Kaliq and Nidhug appeared.

*"Oh!"*

"I thought you would be more comfortable if you could not see them," he said.

"Yes, I would," she admitted, and their witnesses disappeared once again.

"Now, where were we?" he pretended to ask himself. "Oh, yes! I was trying to teach you to kiss decently." He swooped down again to take her lips with his.

Indignant, Cinnia wanted to protest the insult, but when his mouth found hers she discovered she wanted nothing more than to prolong the kiss, and they did. One kiss melted into another, and another and another until she was dizzy with the distinct feeling of something pleasurable happening to her. But when she felt his hand upon her breast she stiffened nervously.

"It's all right," he murmured in her ear. "A woman's breasts, while meant to nourish her young, are also meant to be admired, and caressed, Cinnia. And you, my queen, have beautiful little breasts." Bending his head, he kissed a nipple while his supple fingers traced the small globe gently. Then opening his mouth, he took the nipple into it and sucked it.

Cinnia shuddered as the sensation of his tug upon her breast traveled all the way down her torso into her belly and beyond into the sacred place. This couldn't be right, she thought nervously. Something that felt so wonderful…better than anything she had ever experienced…should not feel so incredible. "You must stop, my lord," she managed to say to him, her fingers winding into his thick dark hair and pulling at it.

He lifted his head. "Why?" His blue eyes were dark with his rising desire.

Her breast felt suddenly bereft, Cinnia thought, and the nipple puckered with the sensation of the cool night air. "Because this cannot be right," Cinnia said to him.

Dillon laughed low. "Nay, my young queen, it is very right. It is almost perfect."

"But the joining is, I am told, when our bodies become one," Cinnia protested. "How can they become one when you do naught but kiss and caress me?"

"A proper joining requires that your body be prepared to receive me. If I forced myself upon you with no care for your comfort I should be little better than an animal. Kissing and caressing are but a small part of the preparation, Cinnia. You must trust me for I have loved many women, and never yet had a complaint," he told her.

"I do not want to hear about your other women!" Cinnia said angrily.

"And you shall not. I have mentioned it only to reassure you that I know what I am doing, my queen. But you, my little virgin, seem to have a great many opinions for a girl who has yet to know a man."

"I have done much studying on this subject. *Ohhh!*" He was nibbling her fingertips, and now his lips traveled up her slender arm to her rounded shoulder. Cinnia felt absolutely weak. *"Ohhh!"* His tongue was licking up the side of her neck, and now as he lay her flat, his tongue caressed her throat, his lips pressing a kiss into the hollow of it where he paused to enjoy the sensation of the blood pulsing beneath her skin. Her flesh was smooth, soft and sweet to the taste. *"Ohhh!"* His tongue moved quickly down, sliding between her breasts to lick at her belly. Cinnia shivered. "It is too much," she told him softly.

"It is but a beginning," he murmured as low. He lay his dark head upon her belly, and let his fingers play with her now. The tips trailed over her shapely silken thighs, coaxing them open for him as they pushed between the flesh and twined themselves in the thick black curls at their junction.

Cinnia stiffened defensively.

"It's all right," he soothed her, and he pressed a finger against her slit, which was already showing signs of moisture.

*"Ohhh!"* she exclaimed as the finger slipped past her nether lips.

Dillon sought for her pleasure point, and finding it he began to tease at it.

He was her husband, Cinnia had to keep reminding herself. Whatever he was doing was certainly proper, but oh! The ball of that wicked finger was arousing in her feelings such as she had never imagined existed. She was tingling all over right down to the soles of her feet, and it all seemed to emanate from that finger. *"Ohh! Ohh! Ohhhh!"*

Cinnia gasped as a feeling of sweet release seemed to pour over her. "Oh, that was so nice," she told him. "Is it always like that?"

"You will have to tell me," he said, smiling down into her face.

"Do you think I am ready for the joining yet?" she asked.

"Let us see," he replied, and he carefully pushed a single finger into her sacred place, all the while watching her face as he moved the finger gently back and forth. When she made no protest or complaint, he withdrew the single finger, and then pressed two fingers within her. Her green eyes widened slightly as he moved the twin digits back and forth at a more rapid pace. She was tight, but she was very wet now. "Aye, you are ready," he told her as he again withdrew his fingers, putting them in his mouth to suck upon them. "You taste sweet and salty all at the same time," he told her as he covered her body with his, pushing her legs up as he did.

"The book says it hurts the first time," she told him, her eyes now showing a small bit of fear.

"Only for a moment, my queen," he said as he positioned himself. He had initiated virgins before. Some were eager, but others like Cinnia were hesitant. With virgins like Cinnia there was only one way to handle the matter once she was ready. Pinioning her arms above her head he filled her, tearing through her maiden's shield with a single hard thrust, as she cried out with shock. "There, my queen," he said, brushing away the surprised tears that had appeared upon her cheeks, "the deed is done, and the worst is over." Then releasing her arms he began to ride her with slow, deep thrusts at first that became deeper and quicker as she began to respond to him.

It had hurt, but the pain was as quickly gone as it had come. She concentrated upon the sensation of the manhood now plundering her. He was big. Of that she was certain despite her inexperience. He filled her full with his great length. Cinnia was filled with fierce emotions. Her hands clutched at his shoulders, her fingers digging into his muscled flesh. Then unable to help herself she began to claw at his back, whimpering as she sought for something she couldn't even understand.

Dillon laughed aloud as he felt her nails raking at him. She was feeling passion! He had aroused her to passion! A virgin, well, no more a virgin. He drove harder into her, sensing her desperate need for satisfaction. Hers and his own. Her legs, with some primitive instinct, wrapped about his torso, giving him deeper access. She was tight, and she was so wet and sweet for him.

*"I want!"* Cinnia cried out. *"I want it!"* she sobbed. She could put no name to what it was she wanted, but she suspected that he would know.

"And you shall have it, my queen," he promised her.

His length flashed faster and faster within her. And then he felt her crisis building, building, coming, coming.

Cinnia screamed as pleasure such as she had never known rose up to enfold her. She was drowning in it. She could scarcely draw a breath for it consumed her, raising her up, up, up, and then flinging her down. She vaguely heard the sound of her cries that were mingled with another sound. His cries.

The room was suddenly filled with a golden light. The air crackled loudly with their passion. There was even a thunderclap. Kaliq and Nidhug, revealed by the brightness, looked at each other, startled. And then the dimness came once more, and the sounds of the couple's heavy breathing as they returned to reality. Dillon and Cinnia lay sprawled next to one another. She seemed to be caught in the throes of a half-conscious state, her breathing rapid, but calming slowly.

*Father! What has just happened?* Dillon asked Kaliq in their silent language. *Never before have I had such a reaction to and with a woman.*

*She is magic as you are, my son,* the prince told him. *All the women you have known before were mortal, and while she is mortal technically, she is also a sorceress.*

*Will it be like this all the time with her?* Dillon wanted to know.

*I do not know,* the prince responded honestly. *But now it is time for sleep.* Kaliq waved his hand over the bed, and it disappeared with its occupants. Then he and the dragon exited the chamber, and it folded in upon itself.

"I put them in her bedchamber," Kaliq told Nidhug.

"Let us go and have some wine," the dragon replied. "And perhaps we can decide what happened to cause such a reaction between them. Come, I have a small privy chamber here in the royal castle." She led him to it, and conjuring up two goblets of wine the prince and the dragon sat companionably. "I have seen many joinings between the king and his bride in my lifetime, but never have I seen happen what happened tonight," Nidhug said. "Your experience in the amatory arts is, of course, greater than mine, Kaliq. Have you ever seen such a mating as took place between your son and Cinnia?"

"Nay, I have not," the prince admitted. "It is obvious to me, however, that if they use their powers together they can accomplish much good for Belmair."

The dragon nodded. "I hope," she said, "that they will fall in love."

Kaliq chuckled. "I did not know you were such a romantic, Nidhug," he remarked. "Have you ever been in love?"

"Alas, male dragons are few and far between. Have you any on Hetar?" she answered him. "In my youth, some twelve hundred years ago, I did mate with a handsome specimen, but then he flew off when he learned that I was the Great Dragon of Belmair. I stored the egg from that encounter in a cave on Belia. One day when I feel my time is coming to an end, I will hatch it. It is, sadly, the way of the Great Dragons of Belmair. And then I will live just long enough to raise my offspring, and pass on to it all the knowledge it will need to be the next Great Dragon."

"You have a purpose in life, which is more than many have," Kaliq said. "To have a purpose is important, Nidhug. And in answer to your question, nay, we have no dragons on Hetar."

"How long do you mean to remain here?" the dragon inquired.

"A day or two more to be certain Dillon and Cinnia can manage together. After that I must leave them in your capable hands, old friend. And I shall then have to seek out Dillon's mother, and tell her of what has transpired. Her life has been most circumspect these past few years. This is but the first of the changes that is to come into her life. Lara is not fond of change." Kaliq chuckled.

"Why did you never tell her that you were Dillon's sire?" the dragon asked him.

"Because she was very young, and just coming into her powers when I brought her to Shunnar. Because I knew she could fall in love with me, and it was not at that time her destiny to do so. Lara was born to accomplish several things, certain of which she has already done. But other things lie ahead for her. She yet has enemies, some of whom she is aware. Others of whom she has yet to meet. She was meant to be with Vartan, and to become a part of the Outlands, which she did. And she loved Vartan enough to want to give him a child, for as you know faerie women only give children to those they love. I don't know why, but in a moment of weakness I implanted my seed within her. And when she was ready for a child my seed grew, and she believed it was Vartan's son. It was better that way, Nidhug. If it had been known at the time that Kaliq of the Shadows had given a child to a faerie woman, who knows what Dillon's life would have been like. And Lara would have remained with me and accomplished none of what she needed to do. She would not have left her child to my brothers and me."

"Yet from all you have shared with me previously she did leave her children to follow her destiny," the dragon said.

"Aye, she did. But the children were with the Fiacre, and always safe, living as normal mortal children live. But of course early on Dillon began sensing that he was different, and his fascination with magic was unquenchable. Lara thought his talents came from her, and decided that I must be the one to teach him. He has been with me since he was twelve, and it has been a joy," Kaliq said, his face alight. "I will miss our daily contact, but our magic allows us to be together quickly."

"And you believe that together he and Cinnia can solve the mystery of why our young women have been disappearing over these last hundred years?" Nidhug asked.

"Look what their simple joining created tonight," Kaliq reminded the dragon.

Nidhug nodded. "Do you think it will happen every time they join?" she wondered.

"I frankly admit to not having an answer to that question," Kaliq said.

"Can you give them love?" the dragon asked sentimentally. "A marriage is so much better when there is love."

"I could give them love," Kaliq said quietly, "but it is better if they find that love for themselves. It is there, Nidhug. My son knows how to please a woman, but he has never loved one. And your young mistress is innocent where men are concerned. Tonight they have begun their adventure. In time the love that is buried within each of them will claim them. We have but to wait and be patient."

"My lord Kaliq," the dragon ventured slowly, "do you know the answer to the mystery of Belmair's missing women? I know you know far more than you are ever willing to admit. But that is the nature of your kind."

"I do not know," Kaliq told her. "But I believe by combining their powers my son and his bride can overcome whatever the difficulty is."

"Is it evil?" Nidhug asked him.

"I cannot tell. It cannot, however, be good, but sometimes there are those who cause unintentional wickedness. Dillon and Cinnia will learn the truth," the prince promised the dragon. "Belmair is theirs, and they will not allow it to be destroyed."

The dragon nodded. "I will show you to your bedchamber now," she said. "Then I will return to my own castle. Tomorrow will be a long one, and the dukes will need all the reassurances I can give them that what has transpired is the right thing." She arose and led Kaliq from her privy chamber to another room where a silent servant awaited to help the prince prepare for sleep. "I bid you good-night, my lord," the dragon said, and then she was gone.

Kaliq allowed the servant to bring him water to wash. He ordered a tub for the morning, and requested that he be awakened at sunrise. The servant bowed himself from the chamber, and Kaliq was alone. The last few hours had been amazing. He wondered if he might gain entry to the Dream Plain from Belmair. If he could find Lara, then perhaps they might speak and he could tell her what he had done. But then he decided against it. He owed Lara the courtesy of telling her face-to-face. The prince slept.

In the morning after he had bathed and eaten, he asked the servant assigned to him to take him to the young king. He found his son busy studying a map of Belmair in a light-filled library. "Good morning," he called to Dillon.

"Good morning, my lord," Dillon replied. "I am looking over this new world you have given me to see if there is something wrong somewhere that will give me a starting point to solving the mystery, but it all seems ordinary."

"Where is Cinnia?" Kaliq asked.

"Preparing herself to meet the dukes later," Dillon said.

"Should you not be doing the same?" Kaliq said. "You must honor these men, my son, for you can be certain they were not expecting the king they have been given. You will need to exercise a great deal of diplomacy with them. The people we know as Hetarians were exiled because they wanted to make changes in tradition here, but they were also sent away because they were willing to fight over it. The Belmairans think themselves above that kind of thing."

"Their need to hold to their traditions and not change is similar of the people of Hetar," Dillon noted. "Everything changes, my lord. Nothing remains the same."

"Nay, it doesn't," Kaliq agreed, "and that is precisely where the problem lies here. For over a hundred years the Belmairans have had a problem, but because the problem did not jibe with their traditions, they ignored it. Now it could be too late."

"You cannot know if it is too late until we learn what is causing this problem," Dillon said in logical tones.

Kaliq chuckled. "Precisely, my son," he replied. "Now go and dress yourself properly so you may greet your guests with honor."

"I have no clothing but what I was wearing yesterday when we came," Dillon said.

"You will find your possessions in the king's bedchamber. Come, and I will show you," Kaliq said. "Do you know how to return to the royal apartments?"

Dillon grinned. "I do," he said, and then he proceeded to lead his father to them.

There he found the carved and painted wooden wardrobe filled with beautiful garments. The robes and tunics were decorated with embroidery, bejeweled and ornamented with gold and silver. There were trousers and capes. The fabrics were rich. Silks, soft wools, cottons. Many of the garments were white, for that was the color the princes wore most, and Dillon was considered one of them because of his father. In a painted chest with drawers the young king found accessories of all kinds, and a large box filled with magnificent jewelry. The wardrobe also contained shoes and boots of fine leather in several colors.

Dillon examined it all, and then turning to his father, said with a wry smile, "You have provided me with a fine dower portion, my lord Kaliq."

The prince chuckled. "You are a king now, Dillon. It is fitting you present yourself like one." He clapped his hands, and a servant hurried in to bow before them. "Help His Majesty to prepare himself for his guests," Kaliq told the man. Then he turned to his son again. "I will await you in your day chamber," he said.

When Dillon appeared almost an hour later, he was garbed in flowing white trousers and a long white tunic that was bejeweled and decorated with pure gold threads upon the wide cuffs of his sleeves and six-inch-wide border at the tunic's bottom. The tunic's neckline was a round one. There was a heavy gold chain about his neck, and on eight of his fingers he wore a ring, each with a different colored stone. Diamond. Ruby. Sapphire. Emerald. Amethyst. Topaz. Peridot. And a great black pearl on the middle finger of his left hand. On his feet were red leather slippers decorated with gold.

"Will I honor the dukes, my lord?" he asked Kaliq.

"You will," the prince said, nodding, satisfied, and for the first time realizing what a truly handsome man Dillon had become. Tall and slender with a body well toned by his physical activities. Slightly tanned from the desert sun that Dillon loved so well. His dark hair was cropped short and styled simply. The blue eyes that had once appeared to all as Vartan's were now the bright blue of a Shadow Prince. "You have the natural presence of a king," Kaliq noted. "Your mother would be proud of you."

"Will I ever see her again?" Dillon asked, and for the first time since they had arrived in Belmair yesterday his voice sounded vulnerable. Dillon had always been very close to Lara, who loved him with a love all mothers kept only for their firstborn.

"Of course you will see her. As soon as I tell her what has happened she will want to come, and she will not be satisfied until I have brought her, nor will she be happy until I have given her the magic for reaching Belmair," Kaliq assured the young man.

The door to the day chamber suddenly burst open, and Cinnia appeared. "The dukes are just landing now," she told them. "We need to be in the throne room to greet them." She looked at Dillon, surprised. "You look nice," she said. But she never questioned where his garments had come from for it was obvious to her that magic was involved in his wardrobe. "They will be pleased after the shock has worn off. Perhaps I could look a bit more elegant."

"Allow me," Kaliq said, and with a wave of his

hand turned her red gown into a flowing white silk one, whose bejeweled and gold decoration matched Dillon's garments. On her small feet were identical red leather slippers. About her neck a delicate gold chain. From her ears hung ear bobs with all the same jewels found in Dillon's rings. On her left hand was an elegant but simple red-gold betrothal ring. The prince looked at her a moment, and then with another wave of his hand Cinnia's hair was drawn back into a mass of curls and waves dusted with gold. "That should do it," he said.

Dillon, with foresight, conjured a full-length mirror so Cinnia might see herself.

Surprised she nodded her thanks to him, and then studied first her image, and then the image in the glass of them together. A small satisfied smile touched her lips. "We are quite magnificent," she noted.

"Indeed, my queen, we are," Dillon agreed. "Now come, and let us greet our guests. If we do not hurry, they will be there before we are."

Accompanied by the great Shadow Prince the young king and queen walked quickly through the castle corridors to the small throne room. The smell of death was now gone from the chamber to be replaced by the fresh scent of honeysuckle and woodbine set into several tall-footed vases set about the little room. Dim and bleak the previous day in the presence of death, the area now glowed with bright golden light that poured through windows that yesterday had been darkened and almost invisible.

Dillon took two steps up onto the dais to stand before

his throne. To his right the dragon stood silently, and to his left Kaliq of the Shadows took his place. Cinnia stepped one step up to stand before her smaller throne. From the little balcony that served as an awning above the two thrones, a flourish of trumpets sounded. The double doors to the room were flung open, and the three dukes strode into the room. Seeing the young couple in all their regal garb the trio stopped. Surprise was very evident upon their faces.

Nidhug stepped forward. "Greet your king, Dillon of the Shadows, Tullio of Beldane, Alban of Belia, and Dreng of Beltran!"

The three men bowed almost automatically, but then Dreng burst out.

"A Hetarian, Nidhug? You have chosen a Hetarian for our king? What kind of a jest is this that you tease us with, dragon?"

"There is no jest, Duke Dreng," the dragon answered. "Tradition will not allow Belmair to be ruled by a queen in her own right. There was no man of sufficient birth here for her in Belmair. And what simple man would take the sorceress of Belmair for a wife? But tradition demanded she be wife to the next king."

"Fflergant is dead?" Alban of Belia asked, although he knew the answer to his own question even as he asked it. Still, he had to ask.

"Aye, the old king is dead," the dragon confirmed. "But before he died he accepted Dillon of the Shadows as Belmair's new king, and he accepted him as husband for Cinnia. He saw them take their vows before me. Then the young king had Fflergant's last breath as tradition demanded."

"And the joining?" Tullio of Beldane demanded to know.

"The joining took place last night, and was witnessed by me, and by the king's father, Prince Kaliq of the Shadows," the dragon told the three dukes. "Now give your loyalty to King Dillon, my lords. All that has taken place in the last day is my will. The will of the Great Dragon of Belmair. Will you deny me?"

The three dukes fell to their knees together before Dillon and spoke with one voice. "We pledge our loyalty to our new king, Dillon of the Shadows. May your life be long and your reign a happy one, Your Majesty."

"Rise up, my lord dukes, and welcome to our home," Dillon replied. Reaching out, he drew Cinnia up to stand next to him. "Tradition dictates that only kings can rule Belmair, but Cinnia will be your queen, not simply my consort. While my word will be final, her words will be listened to and considered well, my lord dukes. This is my first act as your king. My second will be to learn what wickedness works itself in Belmair that has stolen your young women away and puts us in danger of extinction. Together my wife and I will combine our magic to correct this problem. We will work together with you, my lord dukes, and soon all will be as it should be."

The three dukes had arisen to their feet as Dillon had spoken. His words had surprised them. They had not expected a foreigner to understand their ways, their centuries-old traditions. And they were not really convinced that he did. He was not, after all, one of them. Publicly elevating Cinnia's opinions to importance was in and of itself suspicious. Dreng of Beltran, who was the boldest of them, finally spoke.

"Your Majesty, may we deal frankly with you without fear of reprisal?"

"You may always voice your opinions to me freely, my lords. I may not always agree with you, but I will certainly never punish any for speaking out. Are not the dukes of Belmair the king's closest advisors? But whatever you do, do not tell me what you think I wish to hear, for none of you can even begin to imagine what I think," Dillon responded. "Honesty does not displease me, but duplicity will."

Dreng of Beltran looked uncomfortable. He struggled to find the right words. No matter what the king said, he did not believe Dillon could be that open-minded.

"You wish to ask me why the Great Dragon chose the son of a Shadow Prince from Hetar to be your king over your oldest grandson, Calleo, do you not?" Dillon asked.

Dreng of Beltran grew red in the face. "Majesty, I mean no disrespect," he said.

"It is a fair question, my lord," Dillon replied. "Calleo is a boy who has lived barely eleven years. He is not old enough to rule, and you, my lord, are not clever enough to rule for him. None of you are for that matter. The problems besetting Belmair require a fresh eye. And, too, your grandson is not old enough for a joining. By your own traditions, his kingship would not be legal without the joining. Such a choice could have caused strife among the Belmairans, and strife is the very thing Belmairans seek to avoid, is it not? I am told that you despise those you call Hetarians. But I am not a Hetarian."

"But you come from the world of Hetar," Duke Alban of Belia said quietly.

"I was born in the Outlands, a place reviled by Hetarians. The man I spent half my life believing was my father was the clan chief of a people known as the Fiacre. He was murdered in a plot conceived by Hetar's rulers. He had displeased them by fighting back when they attempted to invade the Outlands. He had organized the seven tribes inhabiting the region into a single government. Under his leadership, and that of my mother, they had driven Hetar from their lands, and punished them, as well.

"My mother is a faerie woman with some small amount of mortal blood. Her name is Lara. Her parents are Ilona, queen of the Forest Faeries, and John Swiftsword, now deceased, a Hetarian mercenary who earned the rank of Crusader Knight. He was of mixed mortal and faerie blood. My grandfather died in a great battle against the forces of darkness. He was called the greatest swordsman in Hetar's history. While my mother's early years were spent in Hetar, she left it to follow her destiny, which is not yet entirely fulfilled," Dillon explained.

"When I was twelve," he continued, "I was sent to Prince Kaliq to be trained in the magic arts. I have, since an early age, exhibited a strong leaning toward these arts, and my mother believed that only this Shadow Prince could train me properly. The ability for magic is a great gift, my lords, a great responsibility, and an equally great burden for those who have it. I have lived in the world of the Shadow Princes since I was twelve, and only when my fate became clear did my father reveal the truth of my parentage to me. I am of the Shadows. I am faerie. But I am not Hetarian."

"We call the world from which you come Hetar," Duke Alban said.

"How did you know you might send your dissenters to that which appears to be no more than a star?" Dillon queried him.

"We told them," Kaliq said quietly. "When we saw the trouble some were causing here in Belmair we offered to share a portion of our world with them where they might be isolated. The Shadows know all that occurs in the cosmos. It is our calling."

"So you called your rebels Hetarians after the world to which they were sent," Dillon mused aloud. "Did you ever consider there might be other races upon that star?"

Duke Alban shook his head. "The Shadows offered us a solution to our problem, Majesty, and we accepted it," he said. "Whatever else was involved had nothing to do with Belmair."

Dillon nodded as if in agreement with Duke Alban. *You have given me a far greater task than I first realized, my lord father,* he said silently to Kaliq. *I am beginning to see where the Hetarian attitude was born.* He heard Kaliq chuckle so softly that only his ears might hear it.

"My lords," Cinnia spoke. "We have prepared a feast to celebrate your coming. Will you join us? And Duke Dreng, I would ask that you allow me to send a servant to fetch your grandson, Calleo, and permit him to join us."

"I will right gladly," Dreng said.

"I remember being eleven," Dillon noted. "I suspect the lad will be vastly relieved not to have to marry a sorceress this day."

And his companions within the room laughed loudly, the dukes slapping each other on the back. Kaliq caught Nidhug's eye, and the dragon nodded, well pleased by how the morning had gone. Despite Kaliq's assurances, she had been concerned at how the three dukes would take the appointment of a foreigner to their throne. But it had gone well. Dillon had acquitted himself admirably before the trio of Belmair's high aristocracy. He obviously had his father's ability to charm. And Cinnia had behaved beautifully due in part, the dragon suspected, to her husband's public behavior toward her. Dillon had not robbed her of her dignity.

"Thank you," she said quietly to Kaliq.

The prince turned his beautiful bright blue eyes upon Nidhug. "You are wise beyond all others of your race that I have known," he told her. "I will see that my son heeds your advice, my lady dragon." He took her hand up, and kissed the blue-green scales. "Allow me a small indulgence," he said to her, and then he murmured a small spell, and Nidhug's elegant claws were suddenly sheathed in pure gold. "Ah, yes, much better," Kaliq told her. "You have such lovely claws. They are beautifully shaped."

"Oh, how wonderful!" the dragon cried holding out her hands to admire his handiwork. "Thank you, my dear Kaliq." She looked into his eyes as she spoke, and suddenly in an instant Nidhug knew what it would be like to be made love to by this great lord of the Shadows. She drew in a sharp breath as heat suffused her body, which threatened to expand to her normal size. She swallowed back the flame in her throat and for a brief moment she glowed ruby-red. Fortunately no one saw what was happening, and the dragon was saved embarrassment. "Kaliq!" she scolded him, and the Shadow Prince shrugged apologetically.

Then together they entered the Great Hall of the castle where the banquet awaited.

# 3

"MY SON IS *where?*" Lara, Domina of Terah, said.

It was afternoon in the desert palace of Shunnar. The private garden of the prince was hot, and the heady fragrance of damask roses hung heavy in the air. Along a wall decorated by a stand of tall hollyhocks in reds, pinks, yellows, peach and lavender, several small green birds hovered over the blossoms, their tiny wings beating furiously as their long beaks sipped nectar from the flowers. The garden's fountain tinkled soothingly, the sunlight giving the arc of spray from it a rainbow appearance.

"Dillon is now the king of Belmair," Kaliq said quietly.

"Why is my son *king* of a nebulous world of which I know less than nothing?" Lara demanded of him. "I recall my mother mentioning it briefly many years ago.

She said the magic kingdoms call the great sky the Cosmos, and that there were other worlds within it, and the star we call Belmair was one. I could hardly conceive it then. And now you tell me my son is no longer in our world? That he is there?"

"Dillon was needed, and it was his fate to be there," Kaliq said. "The dragon needed him, Lara, my love."

*"The dragon?"* Her voice had risen at least a full octave. *"What dragon?"*

"The Great Dragon of Belmair, Nidhug," Kaliq replied. "You must calm yourself, my love, for all is well. Dillon is exactly where he should be at this time."

"You had no right to steal *my* son and send him to some other world in this Cosmos of yours!" Lara cried. "Why, at least, did you not tell me first? I have always trusted you, Kaliq. Why did you feel it was necessary to do this without speaking to me beforehand? You know how much I love Dillon." Her beautiful green eyes were filling with tears. "Will I ever see him again?" Her voice had begun to quaver just slightly.

Kaliq put his arms about her. She was, he thought sadly to himself, as beautiful, as vulnerable, as compelling as she had ever been despite the fact that her oldest children were grown, and her younger children half-grown. "Of course you will see Dillon again. I will take you to Belmair anytime you want to go, Lara, my love."

For a brief moment she was content to be in his arms, but then she shook him off angrily, stepping back, looking up into his handsome face. "*My son! He is my son!* You have overstepped your bounds, Kaliq. How dare you make a decision like this for Dillon without even consulting me first. *He is my son!*" she repeated.

Kaliq drew a long breath, and then letting it out he said, "*And he is my son, too, Lara*. I cannot fathom that in your faerie arrogance you have believed all these years that his incredible talents and his wondrous powers came just from you. The child of a faerie woman and a mere mortal man could not have gained the wisdom and skills that Dillon showed from his earliest childhood."

She had been standing, and now she sat down heavily upon a marble bench near the fountain. "I was the child of a faerie woman and a mortal man," she said.

"Your father had faerie blood in him, too, Lara. You know that even if he did not," Kaliq reminded her.

"You said you could not give me a child," Lara reminded him weakly.

"I lied," Kaliq told her bluntly. "We Shadow Princes can reproduce whenever we choose to, although we do not do so often anymore. There is no real need for it given our longevity. Now and again one of us will spawn a child. We give our lovers female children as a rule. But I wanted a son."

"Why did you not tell me?" Lara said.

"Because you were very young then, and while I realized that you were in love with me, I could not keep you. Remember, I know much of your destiny, Lara, my love. You were not meant to remain your life long here in Shunnar. Think of what you have accomplished since you left here all those years ago. You have lifted a curse from Terah, set the powers of darkness against itself, begun a peaceful revolution in Hetar. You have rescued a people from certain extinction and fought successfully in two wars. You have birthed five children. None of it would have been possible had you remained in Shunnar. Think of me as selfish if you will, but I wanted my son born of your loins."

"How was it possible?" Lara asked. "I was with Vartan for months before I loved him enough to give him a child. Tell me what magic you worked upon me?"

"You were in love with me," Kaliq began. "I was able therefore to plant my seed within you. The magic involved was that my seed would only bloom when you were ready to give another your love and a child. Vartan, like me, had dark hair and blue eyes. It was a simple thing to have people believe Dillon resembled Vartan because of that. But have you not noticed that recently his eyes became the bright blue of the Shadows?"

"You are not selfish," Lara said angrily. "You are arrogant, Kaliq!"

"No more so than you are, my love," he told her, a small smile touching the corners of his sensuous mouth. "We belonging to the magic kingdoms have a tendency to be so." Reaching out, he took her hand in his, holding it just tightly enough so she could not snatch it back as she immediately attempted to do. "Do not be angry with me, Lara."

"Tell me why I shouldn't be angry at you, Kaliq?" Lara said furiously. "Why did you not tell me this years ago? After Vartan died at least? You are no better than Kol, the Twilight Lord, secreting your seed within me."

"I did not tell you because I wanted you to continue to believe that Dillon was Vartan's son. Dillon needed to believe it, too, because he needed the normalcy that being the son of a mortal man gave him. He needed to know in those early years that he was Fiacre, that he belonged where he was, especially when you were away so often. And as Vartan's son he held the responsibility for his sister Anoush when you were not with them. Oh, Noss and Liam had physical custody of the children, but Dillon felt Anoush was his charge despite that because she was his blood. As it was Dillon showed his talents from an early age, and the Fiacre were uncomfortable with those talents as they were with you and your magic. They tolerated Dillon because he was their martyred leader's son. Would they have done so had they known he was in truth my son?"

Lara sighed. "No," she admitted, "they would not have."

"You have protected Dillon in your way over the years. I have protected him in my way. And do not dare to compare me with Kol! My love for you has always been a pure love. His was not. He would have kept you a prisoner in the Dark Lands had he had the power to do so. I allowed you to go free to live out your destiny."

"I have wounded you," Lara said softly. "I did not think such a thing was possible, Kaliq. You still love me." She freed her hand from his.

"I have never stopped loving you, Lara," the prince

admitted. "Does it please your cold faerie heart to know that, my love?" he taunted her.

The green eyes met his. "Aye, it does," she said cruelly.

The prince laughed aloud. "Faerie witch," he said in a fond tone.

"Does Dillon know the truth of his parentage?" Lara asked.

"I told him before I took him to Belmair," the prince said. "Do you know he told me that he has suspected it these last few years?" Kaliq shook his head. "He is an amazing young man, my love."

Lara nodded. "He is," she agreed.

"Do not be angry with me that you must share him," Kaliq said.

Now it was Lara who laughed. "You are the most devious man I know," she told him. "Charming, but devious, and I think, utterly ruthless. Why did *our* son have to go to this Belmair? As I recall, my mother said it was a peaceful and prosperous place."

"Peaceful, aye. But they have a mystery that unless solved will destroy them," Kaliq said. And then he began to tell Lara the story of Belmair, and its connection with Hetar. How aeons before the divisive among the Belmairans had been exiled to Hetar so that Belmair could retain its peaceful ways. How Hetar had lost that knowledge of its history over the ensuing centuries. "They are much like the Hetarians, except they are peaceful and have no great passion for acquisition. They live according to ages-old traditions and laws. Their kings have always been chosen by the Great Dragon, who is Belmair's protector. They are not always hereditary."

"But why did this dragon choose Dillon?" Lara wanted to know. "Why a young sorcerer from Hetar?"

"Because the daughter of the old king is a sorceress of much skill. She has not Dillon's talents for magic, but she is strong enough to work with him."

"And why would she?" Then suddenly Lara shrieked, and jumped up. "You have mated them, haven't you? Not only have you taken my son from me, you have given him to another woman! Tell me why I should not kill you, Kaliq?" Lara demanded.

"Well," he replied, struggling not to laugh at her, for he knew she would never forgive him for it, "you cannot kill me. And yes, they are married. It is the tradition on Belmair that if an old king has an unmarried daughter, the new king must take her as his wife. They must be joined physically for the succession to be official. And the dragon and I stood witness to the event. Dillon is king of Belmair now, and Cinnia is his queen."

Lara sat back down. "There should be something I can do to punish you," she muttered darkly. Then, "Will he be happy with her? Please tell me he will be happy."

Kaliq took Lara's hand again, and then he told her of what had happened when the joining of Dillon and Cinnia had reached its culmination. "They will love one another eventually," he said. "But first they will need to reach an understanding, for Cinnia is proud of her abilities and has no real idea of how much more powerful Dillon is. When she learns it, her pride will be hurt, and it will take her a while to accept the knowledge."

"Is she a fool then not to realize a Shadow Prince's son is stronger than the piddling magic her dragon taught her?" Lara queried him.

"Cinnia, like all Belmairans, has lived an insular life," Kaliq explained. "She knows little of other worlds. She has no idea that Nidhug's own powers are limited. Cinnia is known as the sorceress of Belmair, Lara. She is considered powerful among her own people. There is little magic in Belmair but for Nidhug and Cinnia's."

"What of its faerie population?" Lara asked.

"The Belmairans do not speak of faeries," Kaliq replied slowly. "I do not think that there are any in Belmair."

"Every world has faeries," Lara said. "They are a part of its creation."

"If they exist there, then they are secret creatures," Kaliq responded, "for I have never heard of any. Perhaps faeries existed in Belmair at one time, but they no longer do. It is not a large world, Lara, and it only consists of four islands in a great sea. There is more water than land mass to Belmair."

"When can I see my…our son? You said you would take me there, Kaliq."

"Let him have a little time to acclimate himself," the prince suggested. Then, changing the subject, he asked her, "Will you tell Magnus the truth of Dillon's blood?"

"Certainly not!" Lara exclaimed, and she laughed. "My poor husband is jealous enough of you as it is. I have finally after all these years managed to allay his fears. I did not even tell him I was coming here when you called to me. I left him sleeping in our bed, and I had best get back soon else he awakens and finds me gone."

"Changes are coming," Kaliq said to her as she arose and prepared to return to her own home.

"I know," Lara told him. "I sense it, but not yet, Kaliq. I have time." Then with a twist of her wrist and hand she left him in a puff of pale mauve smoke.

The Shadow Prince remained seated within his garden. He wondered how Dillon was doing. He had left him almost two days ago now. He almost withstood the urge to use his magic to check on his son. Dillon was a man grown, and he had to find his own way. Still Kaliq could not resist taking a small peek. Reaching into his white robe he drew forth a small crystal globe. "Show me my son," he commanded it. The globe darkened, and then as it lightened Kaliq saw Dillon in a library with Cinnia. They were obviously engaged in a heated exchange. He wished he might hear them, but it was enough to see Dillon. "Cease," he told the crystal, and it instantly cleared.

CINNIA SHIVERED SUDDENLY, and shook off the sensation.

"What is it?" Dillon asked her, seeing her body shake momentarily.

"Nothing. Just briefly I felt as if someone was watching us," Cinnia said. "And then it was gone. My father's death, our marriage. It has all made me very nervous."

"If you sensed someone watching, then someone was," Dillon told her.

At once she was fascinated. "Teach me that kind of magic," she said to him. "Nidhug never has. I just know potions, shape-shifting, simple spells, but nothing like being able to watch others. That is a valuable tool to have."

"We would need a crystal sphere or a reflecting bowl," Dillon said, "and I have neither. My father saw my wardrobe and the like was transferred from my rooms at Shunnar, but I shall have to ask for the rest when I see him again," he told her.

"Oh." Cinnia was disappointed.

He had lied, but he was in no mood to get into another argument with her. She was the most argumentative female he had ever encountered. She questioned his every move, and while Cinnia was a passable sorceress, and there were no other in Belmair according to Nidhug, she was not mature enough in his opinion to be given access to greater knowledge at this time.

"What are you contemplating, my lord?" she asked him. "Your brow has quite furrowed. That is something I have now learned about you so that I know when you think seriously," Cinnia told him.

"I am considering how best to approach the problem of the missing females," he told her. "Magic is obviously involved here, Cinnia. Now the question is just what kind of magic? And why are these females being stolen away and some returned when they are ancient?

And why can they not remember where they have been, and are most distressed to find themselves old?"

Cinnia shrugged. "If the answers to those questions were known I should not need a powerful sorcerer for a husband," she said.

"Who possesses magic in Belmair besides Nidhug and you?" he questioned her.

"Magic has never been an attraction for Belmairans," Cinnia answered him. "Those who count themselves among the scholars are more interested in the history of our land. In the Academy, which is near the castle, they argue the points of our history day and night. The rest of our citizens are farmers, fishermen, artisans and merchants," she told him. "I am useless to you, I fear."

"Nay, you have been a great help to me. At some time, somewhere, here in Belmair, there was magic, Cinnia. I will go and speak to the members of the Academy to learn more about the history of this world in which we live. I shall be back in time for dinner, and tonight I shall expect you to share your bed with me."

"I was quite worn after the joining," she replied. "I am still tired, my lord."

"What is it, Cinnia?" he asked in a gentle voice. "You may speak freely. You are my wife. Did you not enjoy the joining?"

"I did not feel in control of myself," she told him candidly.

"Lovers are never in control of themselves, Cinnia," Dillon said, reaching out across the rectangular table where they were sitting to take her hand in his. Turning the hand up, he kissed the palm, and then the sensitive inside of her wrist.

Cinnia colored. *"There!"* she exclaimed. "It is happening again. You touch me, kiss me and I am not myself. I am confused by it."

"It is the same for me, as well," he told her. "I feel the softness of your skin beneath my lips, breathe the scent of moonflowers that surrounds you, and I am lost, Cinnia. Each of us, the individual, the I becomes *we,* a single unit."

"But I have never felt like this before!" she wailed at him. "I am..." She hesitated, but then she burst out, "Afraid! I don't want to lose myself to you, to any man."

"We do not lose our singleness just because we make love," he told her. "We blend and combine our passions, Cinnia." Then raising her hand up again, he kissed the back of it and pressed it briefly to his cheek. "I must go now," he said, and standing up, he hurried from the library. Finding a servant he asked the way to the Academy.

"I will take you there myself, Your Majesty," the servant said, and he led Dillon outside, over the drawbridge and down a short gravel path to a porticoed building. "There is the Academy," the servant told him, pointing. Then he returned the way he had come, leaving Dillon standing before the building.

After a moment Dillon walked forward, and opening the door to the building he stepped inside. He was in a large foyer, and before him was a desk with an elderly man seated behind it. He stepped forward, and the man seeing him arose and bowed.

"Your Majesty," he said. "Welcome! I am Byrd, the head librarian. How may I serve you?"

"I am seeking the history of magic in Belmair," Dillon said. "Do you have someone well versed in the subject?"

Byrd thought. And he thought. Finally he said, "That would be Prentice. He concerns himself only with the obsolete in our history. He isn't particularly well-thought-of that he would waste his time on the outmoded. Are you sure I couldn't offer you another scholar? One who is more up-to-date in his thinking and his knowledge, Your Majesty."

"Nay, I will need to see Prentice," Dillon replied.

"Very well, I shall send for him," Byrd said.

"Nay, I will go to him," Dillon answered. "Where is he?"

Byrd reached into his black robes and drew forth a miniature life glass attached to a golden chain. He peered closely at it, and finally said, "At this time of day, Your Majesty, in fact at any time of day or night, Prentice can be found in his chambers, which are situated in the lower level of the building. He has no need for light or air it seems. Page!" he called, and a young boy came from the corner bowing before the two men.

"Take His Majesty to Prentice," Byrd told the page.

"Thank you," Dillon said.

"It has been a pleasure to serve Your Majesty. It is rare for the king to take an interest in us and what we do. I am honored, and I will tell the scholars of your visit," Byrd replied, bowing again before returning to his place behind the desk.

Dillon followed the young page from the chamber, and down one, two, and finally a third flight of stairs. The first flight had been marble. The second was stone. The last wood. Down a dimly lit corridor they walked, and finally the page stopped before a wood door with a rounded top. He rapped upon the door several times before it was flung open by a tall, gaunt man with a shock of graying red hair. The page jumped back, frightened, and with a small cry turned and dashed back down the corridor to the stairs.

"Well?" the man in the door demanded. "What do you want?"

"Information," Dillon said, amused. "You are Prentice, I assume."

"If it has to do with our ancient past, come in. If it doesn't then go back from wherever you came," Prentice said bluntly.

Dillon bent to step through the doorway and into the scholar's chambers. He heard the door close behind him. "I want the history of magic in Belmair," he said, turning back around to face the scholar.

"Who are you?" Prentice demanded to know.

"Your king. My name is Dillon, and before you ask, nay, I am not of Belmair. I was born on Hetar. My father is Kaliq of the Shadows, and my mother, Lara, a faerie woman, Domina of Terah. And now, Master Prentice, I should like some answers."

"So old Fflergant is dead," the scholar said. "He was a good king, but dull as mud. You've married the daughter, Cinnia? She's a sorceress, you know."

"I have wed Cinnia. I'm a sorcerer," Dillon replied. "Nidhug believes that by combining our powers we may be able to learn why the women are disappearing from your world before none are left and Belmair ceases to exist."

Prentice nodded. "Of course you are right, Your Majesty. Magic will be involved somehow. Sit down! Sit down! I would make you some tea, but I seem to have broken all my cups." He shrugged. "No matter." He sat down opposite Dillon.

*"Tea, appear. Here."* Dillon said, and at once a tray with two steaming mugs of tea and a plate of biscuits appeared upon the table between them.

Prentice chuckled. "Thank you," he said. "I don't suppose you could conjure up any wood for my hearth. They are supposed to bring it to me, but seldom remember."

Dillon made a small gesture with his hand, and the wood basket was filled to overflowing. Then he pointed a single finger at the little hearth, and a fire sprang up.

"Now that's a fine, practical magic to have," Prentice said as he picked up the mug of tea and reached for a sugar-frosted biscuit.

"Your wood basket will never empty no matter how much wood you use," Dillon told him. "Nor will your fire go out. Consider that a small payment in return for your knowledge."

"I don't suppose you could include the tea trick, too," Prentice said hopefully.

Dillon chuckled. "From now on when you wish tea just tell the mug to fill itself, and it will," he said to the scholar. "Now, tell me of magic here in Belmair."

"It's been centuries since anyone except the dragon has practiced magic," Prentice said. "Once that wasn't so, but somewhere along the line the magic was lost to us."

"Were there any magic folk here in Belmair?" Dillon asked. "Faeries? Pixies? Gnomes? Every world has magic folk of its own."

"I seem to recall hearing of magic folk somewhere in our distant past, but it is not at my fingertips. Still I have the best ancient histories here in my rooms. I could seek out the knowledge that you need, Majesty. It might take a while," he said, a languid hand waving at the shelves of books all about the room. "But I will find what it is you need to know."

"Then do so, my friend," Dillon told the scholar. "The rulers of Belmair have waited for over a hundred years. I can wait a little bit longer to learn what I need to know. Can you tell me about the Hetarian exiles?"

"Ah, now there I am quite conversant," Prentice said eagerly.

"Speak, but condense it for me," Dillon told the scholar.

"The official history taught to all the children is that those cast out of Belmair were dissidents who fought tradition and wished to make changes. Well, that is true, but there is much more to it. The old king was in his last hours. He had twin sons. Each wished to rule in their father's place. But the dragon, in an effort to prevent these brothers from killing each other over the kingship, chose a young man from another of our aristocratic families. One of the twins accepted the dragon's decision and swore his allegiance to the new king. But the other brother would not. Instead he attempted to change the structure of our government. When he could not he attacked the castle with his adherents. There was no other option but to banish them. We do not fight each other here in Belmair. We follow the traditions and customs of our ancestors for they are good customs and traditions. We do not want change."

"And yet you have gotten change," Dillon said. "I am not Belmairan born."

"But the dragon is our tradition, and it is the dragon's decision who will be king," the scholar said. "The dragon chose you. And even I comprehend why someone from another of the worlds in the Cosmos was chosen. There was no one here in Belmair. It was that simple. And you could end up being Belmair's last king if the problem of our lack of children isn't solved soon, and quickly."

"I agree," Dillon said. Finishing the last of the tea in his mug he stood up. "I will leave you to your work, scholar Prentice. I will come now and again without warning. Do not be frightened if I suddenly appear as I am now leaving you." Then Dillon moved into the shadows of the chamber, and was gone.

"Most convenient," Prentice said to himself, and he set to work seeking out the books he would need for his research. Let the others among his kind mock his fascination with the past. With luck, his knowledge, coupled with the sorcerer's skills, would save them all, the scholar thought almost smugly.

DILLON HAD REAPPEARED within his own rooms. He sat down in a chair by his fireplace and began to consider other alternatives available. What if all the young women left in Belmair were gathered into a single place upon each of the world's islands? It would certainly be easy to protect them if they were in one place. But it would also make them vulnerable to capture. Until he knew exactly what he was dealing with, or who, Dillon realized they could do nothing. Why were these women being taken? And why were only some of them being returned rather than all of them? King of Belmair, he thought wryly. His father had certainly not set him to an easy task. But then he had been becoming a little too complacent in his life, and a bit smug in his talents of late, Dillon admitted to himself. Being given this problem to solve would be a test of all he had learned over his years at Shunnar. Was he really as good a sorcerer as he believed himself to be? Well, he decided, he was certainly more powerful than his wife.

Cinnia. She was both a problem and a delight to him. She was intelligent. Of that Dillon had no doubt. But she was also prideful and stubborn. She was known as the sorceress of Belmair, but then Belmairans were not a complex people. Their descendants on Hetar were far more sophisticated. Still, they sprang from the same root stock.

Cinnia, however, was not like the women he had known. She did not seem to be in the least interested in taking pleasures with him. She had accepted the joining, but after that she held him at bay. His mother was a woman of great passion, and his sisters would follow her lead. The oldest of his sisters, Anoush, had already had at least two lovers, but she was not yet quite ready to wed. Cinnia had exhibited great passion in the joining, but since then she had been cold and distant toward him. He didn't understand.

He was handsome. Skilled. Patient. Lustful. What more did a woman want in a lover?

He had been given a serving man, one Ferrex by name. Ferrex was neither old, nor young. He was almost as tall as Dillon; quite dignified with a totally bald pate and dark gray eyes. Now he came silently into the room, waiting patiently for his master to notice him. As Dillon seemed quite deep in thought Ferrex finally murmured, "My lord."

The younger man looked up. "Ah, Ferrex, I have strayed from my schedule, haven't I? Have I missed anything that I should not have?"

"Not to my knowledge, Your Majesty, but I did not hear you come in," Ferrex said.

"More often than not I travel by magic," Dillon explained. "It is more direct. You will not hear me come in unless I call for you. I was at the Academy speaking with Prentice, the scholar on ancient Belmair. I need to know more of your world before I can even begin to solve the problem of the missing women."

"My niece was taken several years ago," Ferrex said. "My sister sent her to pick berries and watercress for the meal. She never returned, and no trace of her was ever found. She was just fifteen."

"Here on Belmair isle?" Dillon asked his servant.

"Nay, on Beldane," Ferrex answered him.

"This is happening on all the four islands?" Dillon queried the man.

"Aye, Your Majesty. None have been spared," Ferrex replied.

"Did you want something?" Dillon said.

"The young queen was wondering if you planned to join her for the evening meal," Ferrex said quietly.

Dillon turned his head, and saw the sun was low on the horizon. "I did not realize how late it was," he admitted. "Aye, go and tell Her Majesty I will join her shortly."

"I will send your page, Your Majesty," Ferrex said. "Then I will return to see you properly garbed for the evening." He bowed himself from the room.

Dillon smiled to himself. With Ferrex in his employ, the king of Belmair would never appear not at his best. And when he had finally bathed and dressed, Dillon had to admit that he looked the part he suddenly found himself playing. He descended to the Great Hall in a fine ruby-colored silk robe with a keyhole neckline and wide sleeves, the turned-back cuffs of which were embroidered in red crystals and tiny black beads.

"I thought you had gone," Cinnia greeted him.

"Where would I go?" he asked her, accepting a goblet of rich red wine.

"Back to Hetar, perhaps?" she said.

"You are an odd creature," he told her. "One moment you are pleasant, the next you are as sour as an old woman, and you refuse to take pleasures with me."

"You Hetarians go on much about taking pleasures all the time," Cinnia answered him. "Why is it so important to you? The night should be for sleeping and restoring one's energies, my lord. Not for adding to your exhaustion."

"Taking pleasures is very relaxing," Dillon said to her, surprised. "And pleasures are not necessarily confined to the nighttime hours. They can be taken at any time and in anyplace. I have made love in a garden beneath the noonday sun, and in a desert oasis with only the stars for light, as well as in my bed."

Cinnia wrinkled her nose. "Have I not said I do not wish to hear about your other women, my lord? It is not a subject that is of interest to me, nor are your exploits. But as I do not wish you to be discontent in Belmair for we need your magic, let us set a time each week for us to take pleasures together. If your lusts need to be released more frequently then you have my permission to take a concubine for your pleasures."

"Nay, Cinnia, only you will serve my lusts, and you will do so when and where I desire it," Dillon told her.

"How dare you order me about!" Cinnia cried out angrily.

*"Dare?"* He laughed briefly. "May I remind you, Cinnia, that I am the king of Belmair. And you are its queen only because I permit you to be. I think perhaps the time has come for me to teach you that lesson so you will not forget it again." Reaching out he yanked her into his arms and kissed her hard. "Soften your lips," he commanded her, and then he kissed her again. This time the kiss was slow and hot.

Her heart was beating wildly, but she wasn't going to let this foreigner they had made her marry control her. Cinnia bit the lips kissing hers.

*"Ouch!"* Dillon yelped, surprised that she would fight back. But then taking her by her arm he dragged her across the hall, sat down upon a chair and yanked her down across his lap, pulling up her silk skirts as he did. His big hand descended to make contact with her bare flesh as he licked the blood from his lips.

Cinnia squealed furiously. "Stop that at once, you brute!" she commanded him.

Dillon began to spank her in earnest. "Did no one ever bother to teach you manners, you vicious little bitch?" he demanded. *Eight. Nine. Ten.*

"I hate you!" Cinnia yelled, and she struggled to escape his grasp.

"Your behavior and attitude haven't exactly warmed my heart, either," he growled at her. His hand continued to smack at her round bottom. *Fourteen. Fifteen. Sixteen.*

"I'll never take pleasures with you again, you beast!" she threatened.

"Oh, yes, you will," Dillon replied. *Twenty!* "I'm going to teach you how to be a woman, Cinnia." He dumped her onto the hall floor, and stood up. *"Anytime. Anyplace."* He quickly pulled her up. *"Here. Now!"*

Cinnia suddenly found herself being drawn down into his lap, and onto his manhood. She gasped with surprise to find herself very wet and ready for him. How could this be? He had been violent with her, and not at all a lover. She moaned low as her burning buttocks made contact with his bare thighs, and she felt him inside her fully sheathed. "The servants!" she cried softly.

"Will learn to be discreet," he said as softly. "Now ride me, my queen, and ride me hard. If you do not give me pleasures, Cinnia, I will move us to the high board, and take you there until you do," he threatened her. "I will lay your naked body upon that polished wood and make you scream for all in the castle to hear. Now, ride me!"

Cinnia began to cry. "I don't know how!" she sobbed.

"Move yourself up and down upon my rod, my queen," he told her, and when she began to comply he encouraged her, "That's it, Cinnia. Now faster, and yet faster!"

She jogged up and down upon his manhood, her pace growing quicker with each passing moment. He held her gently about the waist, encouraging her onward. Her eyes closed and she grew languid as in spite of herself Cinnia began to enjoy the conjunction between them.

His hardness felt so good. He probed her deeply and suddenly something within her responded. "Oh, yes!" she cried low. "Yes!"

Dillon smiled to himself. He had found her magic center. Every woman had one. It was just a matter of finding it. He helped her to help him work it, and very quickly Cinnia was whimpering as the pleasures began to flood her. "That's it, my queen," he murmured in her ear, and he kissed her mouth in a long and lingering kiss. This time she did not bite him. And then he felt the quivers within her beginning to rise up to overwhelm her. He allowed her the moment, and when she fell forward on his shoulder he gently lifted her off of his turgid manhood cradling her against his silk-covered chest. It would quiet itself shortly, and he was not at all ready to give up pleasures. The night was young. "Are you ready to eat now?" he asked her casually.

"You are a horrible man," Cinnia murmured, her eyes still closed.

"When we have finished our meal I will show you some other places a man and a woman may take pleasures together," he purred in her ear.

She wanted to stand up, but she knew that right now she couldn't. How was it possible that he could make her feel this way? But it felt so right nestling against him.

Finally Cinnia thought she might stand up. "I'm ready now," she told him and arose from his lap, wobbling just slightly. She felt his hand beneath her elbow and while she wanted to tell him she was perfectly capable of walking by herself, Cinnia didn't dare because she knew it wasn't true, and worse, so did he.

He seated her at their high board and took his place next to her. And then as if by magic the servants began entering the hall with the steaming bowls and platters with their meal. If any of them had seen or heard what had just transpired between their master and their mistress, they showed no evidence of it. Dillon filled his plate with raw oysters, prawns, ham and meat pie. Cinnia took prawns, capon and an artichoke. There was bread, butter and cheese, which they shared.

"The hall is too big for just the two of us," Dillon noted. "Is there a smaller chamber we might use?"

"My father always ate in the Great Hall," Cinnia said.

"I am not your father," Dillon responded. "The hall is a grand place for entertaining, but you and I need a more intimate place to dine when we are alone."

"It is tradition..." she began.

"Some traditions need to be changed. It is ridiculous for two people to eat in a hall built for great feasts. And it makes extra work for the servants who have to trot the length of this hall simply to bring us a platter or bowl so we may take a bit of food." Dillon looked out over the hall to where the servants stood attentively awaiting an order.

"Who is steward here?" he asked.

A plump, short man stepped forward. "I am, Your Majesty. My name is Britto." He bowed politely. "How may I serve Your Majesty?"

"Is there a smaller chamber where the queen and I may eat when we are alone?" Dillon asked the steward.

Britto's brow furrowed in thought. *Say no.* The steward heard Cinnia's voice in his head, for a quick look in her direction told him she had not spoken aloud. *Say no!* came the command again. "Your Majesty, I regret we have no other accommodation for your meals," Britto said apologetically.

"You are certain, Britto?"

"Yes, Your Majesty, I am certain," the stewart said nervously.

"Then there is nothing else for it but that I make the Great Hall smaller when it is just the two of us," Dillon replied calmly. *"Hall, small,"* he said. And suddenly the chamber walls seemed to move in, and the length of the room shrank by three-quarters.

Britto's eyes grew wide with his surprise, and the waiting servants murmured anxiously as they suddenly found themselves in a considerably smaller space.

"What have you done?" Cinnia demanded to know.

"It's a simple charm," Dillon told her. "When we leave the hall it will return to its original size. But if it is just the two of us, or we have fewer than ten guests, the hall will retain a lesser proportion. Your precious tradition is preserved, Cinnia." He looked down at the steward, who still stood before the high board. "And in future, Britto, you will accept my orders over those of the queen. Do you understand?" Dillon picked up his wine cup and drank deeply.

Britto swallowed hard. "I heard her, Your Majesty.

Plain as day, I did, but she never opened her mouth," the steward said, looking distressed.

Dillon laughed. "I'm surprised all of Belmair didn't hear her she was shouting at you so loud, Britto. Your mistress is a prankster, are you not, my queen?" He caught Cinnia's hand up, and kissed it. "She will not do it again, however, will you, my pet? It really is not kind to frighten our good servants."

"I am sorry I startled you, Britto," Cinnia said, extricating her hand from her husband's. She glared at Dillon. "How did you know?" she murmured at him as the servants now returned to their duties and began clearing the high board of the dishes.

"Speaking silently comes naturally to me," he told her. "That is one of the ways my mother first knew of my talents. Certainly you didn't think I wouldn't hear you?"

"Why did the dragon pick you?" Cinnia responded with her own question.

"Because she needs a sorcerer with true strength, and I am he," Dillon replied. "You simply do not have the skills to overcome whatever magic is at work in Belmair. I do. But I will need your help. The dragon would not have taught you magic if you could not be of help to me. You must stop being angry at me, Cinnia, because I am king. You could not rule by those traditions that you seem to hold so dear. And you will never lose your fear of taking pleasures with me until you stop being afraid of losing yourself to our passion, for there is great passion between us. You are my wife. I want no other woman."

"How can you say that and mean it?" Cinnia said. "Until several days ago I knew nothing of you. But within moments of our meeting we were wed. And after that we were joined, to legitimize your selection by the dragon as this world's king. You know nothing of me." Was he, she wondered, the one she had sometimes felt watching her? A feeling had come upon her at times in the last few years that she was being spied upon. Nay, it could not be Dillon spying. The feeling was not the same and he had not been aware of her existence in years past.

"But I do know you," Dillon continued. "You are beautiful, which is obvious to all who look upon you. You are intelligent, and perhaps a bit too proud. You are kind, for I saw how gently you spoke with your father in the hour before his death. You have manners. And you have magic about you, for 'twas not only I who created that spectacular effect that was the result of our joining, Cinnia."

"It didn't happen before we ate," Cinnia answered him. "And of course I am proud. I was born royal."

"It didn't happen earlier because we were angry with one another. We were not making love. We were making war," Dillon told her. "When I make love to you, my queen, you will experience passion again as you did at the joining. As for pride I recognize it easily. My grandmother has the same prideful bearing that you do. She was born a queen, and she never lets you forget it.

Now, the table is cleared. I believe that we have some unfinished business." He stood, drawing her up with him. "Come!"

"I don't know you," Cinnia said as he led her out of the hall and upstairs to their apartments where their servants were awaiting them.

"What would you like to know?" he asked her. "You can see that I am handsome," he teased her.

"And vain!" she shot back. "You told me you are twenty-two to my seventeen. You have siblings. How many? Are they brothers or sisters? I'll tell you what I do know. You seem kind. And your brow gets wrinkly when you concentrate on something. And I know that your magic is far greater than mine. But you could teach me."

"I have three sisters and a brother," he told her. "Anoush is the oldest. She is your age. Zagiri is thirteen. The twins—Taj is the boy, and his sister Marzina—are nine. My little brother is my stepfather's heir. On Hetar it is believed I am the son of the martyred Fiacre clan chief Vartan. Anoush is his daughter. As for teaching you my magic, Cinnia, eventually I will share some of my knowledge with you, but right now you are not mature enough, and your temper is much to quick to be entrusted with too much power." His hand touched the door to their apartments, and it sprang open for him. "We will bathe first," he said to her. *"Together."* Ferrex and Cinnia's serving woman, Anke, hurried forward. "Prepare the bath," Dillon said. "Anke, take your mistress, and when she has disrobed bring her to the bath chamber."

"Yes, Your Majesty," Anke said. Like Ferrex she was neither old nor young. She was of medium height with a sweet face, slightly plump with pretty brown eyes and brown hair she wore in two thick braids woven about her head.

"Do not dally, Anke," the young king said.

"No, Your Majesty, I won't," Anke answered, and she led her mistress away.

"He wants us to bathe together," Cinnia said to her servant. "Is that not shocking, Anke? I shall not do it. Lock the bedchamber door."

"Nay, mistress, I will not argue with my master in a matter so insignificant," Anke told Cinnia. "Lovers like to bathe together, and it is time you became lovers. He is the king, and he is your husband. That is not likely to change. This is a good way for you to become better acquainted with one another. You have not lain with him since the joining. You will cause gossip if you continue to behave like a skittish doe with her first buck."

"In the hall before the meal..." Cinnia began.

"He took you for a little joggity-jog," Anke said. "I know."

"You know?" The girl's cheeks grew red.

"As soon as the servant entering the hall saw, she withdrew and warned the others not to disturb you," Anke said in matter-of-fact tones. "She heard your cries as he was spanking you, and hurried to aid you, but saw you needed nothing, and did not require any rescue," Anke finished. "He's a fine man, mistress, and should give you great pleasures if you will let him." She quickly drew off Cinnia's silk gown and chemise. Then sitting her mistress down, she brushed her long black hair out and pinned it up. "Come along now," she said, leading Cinnia brisky from her chamber to the bath chamber.

"I'll leave you a night garment on the chair by the fire so it may warm. You may want it later, mistress. Ah, here we are!" Anke flung open the door to the bath chamber. Warm, moist steam billowed out into the small corridor. "I bid you good-night, mistress!"

Gently the serving woman pushed Cinnia through into the room and shut the door behind her quietly.

Cinnia stood silently for a long moment. The door behind her opened again, and turning she saw Dillon step through. *Oh my!* Cinnia thought as she looked at him naked. The joining had been such a tumultuous affair she really had not gotten a good look at him. She saw now that he had a big body, but it was proportioned properly.

Broad chest. Narrow hips. Long, shapely legs. He turned briefly to shut the door behind him. His buttocks were lovely. Nicely rounded, firm, and she had the most incredible urge to fondle them with her hands. Cinnia's cheeks grew warm with her lascivious thoughts; and when he turned back to her he grinned. Her cheeks grew hotter. Could he know what she had been thinking? It was untenable! "Stop that!" she commanded him. "It is not polite to intrude upon others' thoughts, my lord."

He walked across the room and, reaching her, smiled down into her eyes. "I want to hear you call me by name, Cinnia."

"You are the most arrogant man I have ever met, *Dillon,*" she answered.

He grinned again. "I probably am," he agreed. "The result of my exalted pedigree, my queen. Now, let us bathe each other."

The bathing chamber consisted of several small rooms. In the first, two indentations in the shape of shells had been imprinted into the marble floor. A gold spigot, fashioned like an openmouthed fish, sprang from the wall bordering each of these recesses in the floor. Faintly scented lukewarm water poured from them. Next to each shell was a small table upon which rested a large sea sponge and a round, flat dish of thickened soft soap bearing the same fragrance as the water.

She found herself quickly over her shyness regarding their nudity. She stole a quick look at his maleness. She was hardly familiar with the masculine body, but she doubted his manhood would be called insufficient by any standards. And if she was to admit it to herself he had indeed given her pleasure in the joining. It was that that most disturbed her. They were barely acquainted and she had enjoyed it. What did that say about her? Belmairans did not have the easy morals of Hetarians. Cinnia stepped into the shell.

"Now it is your brow that furrows," Dillon said to her, and he directed the spigot head to wet her body.

"Are you invading my thoughts?" she said sharply.

"You asked me not to, and so I am not," Dillon answered her. "I would know what troubles you, Cinnia. Can you put it into easy words, or would you prefer I seek those words for myself, my queen?" He dipped the sponge into the soap, and began to lather it over her shoulders and back.

She was silent a long minute, and then she said, "I liked what happened between us in the joining, Dillon. But what kind of a woman does that make me?"

"A passionate one, for which I am delighted," he told her quietly.

"I reacted like an easy Hetarian woman. They were always different that way than we were. Swift to indulge their senses without a care for anyone or anything else," Cinnia told him unhappily. "I didn't know you, and yet I enjoyed the passions we shared in the joining. Nay, I reveled in it."

"How many brides know the men with whom they are matched?" Dillon asked her. "It is rare in my world that women wed men they know well and love. Women in my world marry for many reasons, but love is rarely among them. Respect and love come afterward. Is it any different here in Belmair? And if a bridegroom is skilled and gentle, should his bride not gain pleasures with him? Why should her wedding night be one of fear and loathing, Cinnia? Why should she not have her passions stoked and brought to sweet fulfillment? Who would ever tell you such a terrible thing?" He swirled the sponge over her adorable buttocks, and squatted down to wash her thighs and shapely legs.

Then he stood again and helped her to rinse the soap from her body.

When Cinnia turned to face him her pretty cheeks were pink. But Dillon tipped her small oval face up to his and tenderly kissed her lips. "No one told me anything," she managed to whisper against his mouth. "Oh, I knew the basics of what must be between a man and a woman. Nidhug was emphatic that I learn such things. But we Belmairans are an old and honored race. Passion such as you engendered in me is unknown to us, Dillon."

"Nay, it isn't," he told her. "It simply isn't considered good manners in Belmair to discuss it, my queen. Enjoy it, aye! But discuss it? Nay! Would you like to do my back now?" Handing her the sponge he turned his back to her.

Taking the sponge from him, Cinnia rinsed it, and then dipping it into the soap she began to wash his broad back and shoulders. He was tall, and so it became necessary for her to stand upon her tiptoes. She laved the sponge across and down his body, and when she had finished she rinsed him as he had her, and Dillon turned about to face her.

# 4

"WHY ARE WE doing this?" Cinnia asked him.

"Because it helps us to know and trust each other better," Dillon said.

"You Hetarians are so carnal," she replied, giving him a wry smile.

He took the soapy sponge from her. "And you have been wed to the most sensual of their races, my queen." He drew her into his embrace with his free hand, and bending his head, found her mouth. The kiss he shared with her was long, and grew more passionate with each moment that passed. Her lips were petal soft beneath his, and she did not resist. Rather, he sensed her shy attempt to share his desire. Finally Dillon released her. His bright blue eyes stared down into her face. "I think," he said slowly as if carefully choosing his words, "that with time I can make you as naughty as a faerie." Enjoying the blush that suffused her pale cheeks, he handed her a second sponge. "Now let us wash each other," he suggested.

She mimicked his motions. His sponge swept down her slender throat. Hers followed down his. He laved across her chest, and then began to bathe each of her breasts, tenderly lifting each small globe as he did. Her nipples puckered, and unable to help himself Dillon bent his head and suckled on one. Cinnia whimpered faintly, trying to concentrate on the broad plain of his chest with her own sponge. He made circles as he moved down her torso and over her belly. Then he knelt and began washing her mons, pushing the sponge between her nether lips, rubbing up and down her well-furred slit. When he had finished he washed both of her legs, lifting them up to bathe her small feet. When he had finished he rinsed her off, saying, "Now it is your turn, Cinnia." And he forced her to her knees before him.

Gathering up all of her courage Cinnia looked the enemy in the eye. She sudsed the thick mat of fur surrounding his manhood. She lifted the beast up, and ran the sponge back and forth along its length. It stirred, and she dropped it nervously, moving quickly to his long muscled legs and his large feet. When she had finished she moved to stand, but Dillon's hands held her down.

"Stay there," he said and turning he rinsed himself off. When he had finished he pivoted back to face her. "Now, my queen, I am going to give you your first lesson in how to pleasure me. Take my manhood into your mouth and suck upon it. Be gentle, and beware of scraping me with your teeth."

She had never heard of such a thing, but then if the truth be known, he had taught her all she now knew of lovemaking. Following his direction, she took him in her hand, and, leaning, forward, her mouth closed over him. The flesh was warm and tasted faintly of the soap she had washed him with. Cinnia felt his hand upon her head as she began to suck upon him. She heard his indrawn hiss of breath and as she did she realized that the softness in her mouth had begun to grow firmer with each tug of her jaws.

"You can take a bit more," he said, his voice almost strained as he pushed himself deeper into her mouth. "Use the fingers of your other hand to tickle my sacs."

She felt the thickening peg of flesh touching the back of her throat and struggled not to gag. Reaching beneath him, she found his seed sacs, cool and slightly hairy to her touch. She teased them with delicate fingers. As his manhood expanded within her mouth and he groaned low, Cinnia suddenly realized that her simple actions were indeed giving him pleasure. She felt a rush of power as she realized he was as vulnerable to passion as she was. Cinnia sucked harder upon him until her jaws were aching, and she could no longer contain him within her mouth.

It was at that point that Dillon growled a command to her to stop, and taking her by the hand led her to the bathing pool. Looking at him as they moved from one chamber into the other, Cinnia was astounded by the length and size of him. She had never really looked at him as she was now looking at him. He was magnificent! Together they stepped down into the perfumed water. Turning her about so that she was facing up the steps, he instructed her to kneel forward upon the steps, using her hands to balance herself. Then coming behind her he sheathed himself deeply and fully within her body.

Cinnia gasped at his entry. His hands fastened themselves about her shapely hips, and he began to pump her, slowly at first with long, majestic strokes of his cock; then with increasing rapidity, with fierce, hard thrusts of his manhood. She whimpered, a sound of desperation, as he moved within her. "Please!" she begged him. *"Please!"*

"Tell me what it is you desire, my queen," he whispered hotly in her ear.

"Give me pleasures, Dillon! *Give me pleasures!*" she cried. And the room filled with golden light, and the air crackled around them.

"Your wish, my queen, is mine to fulfill," he murmured, kissing her ear, and then nipping hard on the lobe. Finding her pleasure center, he used it well, and she was quickly cresting as the feelings of delight swept over her. Withdrawing from her, he sat down upon the steps, cradling her within his arms, kissing her small face as she floated back to reality once again, and he kissed her slowly, murmuring softly against her lips, "*Anytime, anywhere,* Cinnia." He reminded her of his earlier promise.

She opened her eyes at long last. Every inch of her

tingled with excitement. "Do you behave like this all the time?" she asked him softly.

"You are mine," he said simply. "I am going to fall in love with you, Cinnia. Not because you are beautiful or because you are my wife, but because we were meant to be together like this forever. I don't want you resistant to pleasures. Not when the cojoining of our bodies is such a good thing."

"The light was gold and the air crackled again," she said to him.

"Because we were in tune with one another," he told her. "You were not resisting me, my queen." He dumped her gently from his lap into the warm scented water. He was still fully aroused, his manhood engorged with his lust.

Cinnia stared. "You are not satisfied," she said. "And yet I was. Why?"

"I learned long ago how to prolong my desires," Dillon told her. "I will make love to you again several times before we sleep. It pleases me to see you fulfilled, and there is time for me to reach that perfect state. We will relax together in the pool."

The watery enclosure was square, and had a depth of five feet. On one side of it was a pink marble flower from whose center water sprayed forth. The ceiling was glass, and revealed the velvety-black night skies above them ablaze with stars. He noted to her that the sky they watched now was different from that he was used to in Terah, or his father's palace of Shunnar.

"What is the biggest difference?" she queried him.

"I cannot see Belmair," he said with a smile. "What is that bright star?" He pointed to a particularly bright orb almost directly above them now.

"That is Hetar," she told him. "It is magnificent from afar, isn't it?"

He nodded, agreeing. "It is." Then he asked her, "Why do you have no siblings?"

"My mother died shortly after giving birth to me," Cinnia said. "My father chose not to remarry although there were several women of suitable families who would have made him a good queen. But since king's sons here in Belmair do not necessarily follow in their father's footsteps he felt no great urge to sire a son," Cinnia explained. "He wed late in his life, and might not have married at all but he saw my mother once, and fell in love with her. They were wed for over two hundred years before I was born, and I was quite a surprise to them I can assure you." She chuckled with her memories. "When a child was not born to them in the first years of their marriage they assumed they would never have one. Belmairans live a normal life span of several hundred years, but we age incredibly slowly," Cinnia explained to him, for she could see he was somewhat confused.

"But you said you were seventeen," Dillon said.

"I am," she told him. "But I will live several hundred years if illness does not fell me first," Cinnia said. "How long will you live?"

"I don't know," he said. "My father has lived since the beginning of time itself. My mother, being mostly faerie, should live for several hundred years. I suppose I will live at least as long as she does." He swam across the pool to stand beneath the spray of water from the pink marble blossom. Their life spans were similar. He would not be forced like his mother to watch as Cinnia grew older, and he remained the same. It was likely that they would age together. Had the dragon and his father been aware of that? Dillon wondered. He would remember to ask Kaliq when next he saw him. Cinnia was looking at him, and the young king suddenly became aware of his throbbing member. He needed to couple with her again. He swam back to where she was awaiting him.

Cinnia leaned against the marble walls of the pool, enjoying the warm water as it lapped against her. This bathing had been a surprisingly good idea of his. She did feel more comfortable in his presence, and she was learning little bits and pieces about him. Her eyes closed and she listened to the flower fountain as it sprayed into the water. It was a most soothing sound. And then she sensed him. Her eyes flew open and he stood directly before her.

Taking her small face between his big hands, he kissed her slowly, lingeringly. "Now once more, my queen," he told her.

She felt his hand cupping her bottom as he lifted her up.

"Wrap your legs about me, Cinnia," he directed her.

As she did she felt his thick length pressing once again into her body. Cinnia sighed, clinging to him as he moved hungrily within her until she was dizzy with her own lust, and the pleasures being joined with him brought her. But then suddenly he withdrew from her, and she protested. "No, Dillon! No!"

"Come," he said without explanation, and led her from their watery playground into the third chamber of the bath. Here the air was filled with an exotic and elusive perfume. There was a wide marble bench upon which rested a large pile of fluffy towels. Taking one he began to dry her. The towel was warm. When he had almost finished he lay several towels upon the bench, and instructed her to sit down. When she had he dried her feet, kissing and sucking upon the toes as he did so.

Cinnia couldn't help but giggle. "You are a great fool," she told him.

"Lay back," he said in reply, and when she was stretched out upon the wide bench he spread her legs wide, and seating himself he leaned forward to peel open her nether lips with his thumbs, and lick the sweet coral-pink flesh.

Cinnia gasped, shocked. "What are you doing?" she asked, attempted to rise up.

"Stay still!" he told her sharply. "This is but a new pleasure for you, my queen." Then his tongue began to explore her slowly as he licked and probed and tasted her.

Cinnia's senses whirled with the sensations he was engendering. They were delicious, and she suspected, very naughty pleasures he was offering her. He seemed to be in no hurry to end the delightful torture. His tongue licked one side of her flesh, and then the other. He explored carefully, and when the tip of his tongue met what was an incredibly sensitive part of her, Cinnia squealed nervously. Immediately he began to taunt and tease that tiny jewel until she was almost mindless with the delight, and when she was certain he was going to kill her with it, Dillon was mounting her once more, and thrusting deeply into her body. “And again, my queen,” he said.

He rode her hard. Their breathing became ragged and rough as he pushed into her again and again and again. He was a fierce lover now, and Cinnia reveled in the wildness they were sharing. She wrapped herself about him so he might have deeper access to her. Their fingers intertwined restlessly as they climbed and climbed and climbed until they could climb no more. Then together their passions burst. Her cry echoed about the room. His shout as he allowed his juices to finally erupt mingled with her soft cries of pleasure, totally and completely fulfilled. The room was bedazzled and drenched in a quivering golden shimmer, and the sounds of crackling light could be heard. The glow danced about them, tiny darts of lightning shining within it, snapping noisily. And then the chamber grew quiet and dimmed as the light faded away and they collapsed in a tangle of arms and legs upon the wide marble bench. Finally Dillon pulled himself up and stood. Cinnia lay pale, her breathing now quieted, but obviously weak with satisfaction. He bent and, picking her up, carried her from the bath, and into her bedchamber, where, drawing back the coverlet on the bed, he lay her down. Walking to the hearth, he added more wood before returning to the bed and climbing in with her.

"Your sensual nature will be the death of me," Cinnia murmured.

"Not for at least a thousand years," he replied, and he pulled her into his arms. "I'm going to sleep with you tonight. I cannot be certain yet that my lusts are satisfied."

"Mine are," she half groaned. "Your passions are enormous."

He laughed softly. "Are you learning to trust me, my queen?"

"It would seem I have no choice," Cinnia answered him.

"Passion is not so terrible, is it? You seem to enjoy my attentions," he teased her.

"I do," she admitted softly.

"I want you to trust me in other things, too, Cinnia. If you do we can solve this problem besetting Belmair," Dillon told her.

"And you will teach me some serious magic," she said sleepily.

"When you are ready, aye, I will," he promised her.

"Good night, my lord."

"Good night, my queen," he replied. But he lay awake for several minutes listening to the sounds of her breathing, enjoying the voluptuous young body within his embrace. Cinnia was not an easy woman to know, he thought to himself as he had earlier. Though the Belmairans scorned those they had sent into exile many centuries before, they were much like them in their desire for order and conformity. Their need for tradition, sameness. But the king their dragon had chosen was anything but Hetarian or Belmairan in his thoughts and methods. It was going to be an interesting time as they all came to terms with one another.

Several days later the scholar Prentice sent a request to the king that he come to his chambers at the Academy. Gara, who had been assigned as the king's new secretary, set the message aside, for he did not think a missive from an unimportant scholar worthy of his master's immediate attentions. Gara knew of Prentice, for he had been educated at the Academy. The fellow was half-mad it was said. But then Dillon thought to tell Gara that he was awaiting word from Prentice.

"A message came yesterday, Your Majesty," Gara quickly said, "but this Prentice is not a scholar highly thought of by the Academy. I considered it of no account."

"Prentice is doing some very important research for me on ancient Belmair," Dillon told his secretary. "In future all communication from him is to be brought to my attention immediately. I apologize I did not advise you of it sooner," the young king said, soothing the ruffled feelings he saw rising up in Gara. "The administration of a world is quite new to me. I understand that you served the old king's secretariat."

"Indeed, Your Majesty, I did," Gara replied. "And I will serve you personally with every ounce of my skill and loyalty. I shall put Prentice on my list of important personages immediately."

"Thank you," Dillon replied, smiling. "Now I shall go to the scholar and see what it is he had found for me." He left his library. Gara, mollified, carefully scribbled Prentice's name into a small book upon his desk. Out of sight of his secretary Dillon swirled his cloak and directed his magic to the scholar's chambers. Stepping from the shadows, he greeted him. "Good morrow, Prentice. I have just now been informed of your message. Such a delay will not happen again."

"Your Majesty!" Prentice jumped, slightly startled by Dillon's appearance, but he realized he would have to get used to such comings and goings. The king did have the blood of the Shadows in his veins. "No, no, I understand. You have been given Gara for your secretary. A good man, but his name does mean *mastiff,* and he will guard you carefully from what he considers unimportant distractions," Prentice said wryly.

Dillon laughed. "He has added your name to his list of important personages."

The scholar barked a sharp laugh. "How it must have galled him." He chuckled. "I do not believe, Your Majesty, that I have ever been considered a personage of import."

"What have you found?" Dillon asked him.

"I sought out from our archives histories from our furthest known past," the scholar said. "And within I found two small references to the *wicked ones.* Both said virtually the same thing. That the *wicked ones* had been told to depart Belmair. There is nothing else. No explanation of who these *wicked ones* are, or why they were told to leave or if they did."

"Are you certain these two references do not refer to those sent to Hetar?" Dillon questioned the scholar.

"Those histories themselves were written at least two centuries before that event took place, Your Majesty," Prentice replied. "However, there is a locked room hidden somewhere within the archives that is forbidden to us all. Byrd would have the key to that room, for it is passed down from one head librarian to the next. If I could gain access to that room perhaps I might find the answers you are seeking."

"I shall speak with Byrd, and have him give you the key then," Dillon said. Then stepping into the shadows of the scholar's chamber, he directed himself to where the elderly head librarian sat behind his desk. "Good morrow, Byrd," Dillon spoke.

The old man looked up. He had been concentrating upon a book, and his hearing no longer good, he had not observed Dillon's arrival. "Your Majesty!" He stood politely.

"You hold a key to a locked room within your archives," Dillon said. "I should like that key, and then you will take Prentice and me to that room."

"Your Majesty, I will gladly give you the key," the old man said, and he carefully extricated an old-fashioned brass key from the large key ring attached to his rope belt, handing it over to Dillon, "but I cannot take you to the room because I do not know where it is."

"How can you not know where it is?" Dillon asked him. "You have a key. Did not your predecessor tell you where it was when he passed the key on to you?"

"My predecessor did not know where the room was, nor did his predecessor, and so forth back many, many generations, Your Majesty. The key has been passed down to each of us holding this post at the Academy, for it is tradition that the head librarian hold the key to the forbidden room, but no one has ever known where the forbidden chamber is. That, too, is tradition."

"Are you even certain it exists?" Dillon asked Byrd.

"Of course it exists. I have the key to it," the old head librarian replied.

Dillon didn't know whether to laugh or to weep at Byrd's answer. Thanking him, he returned to Prentice's rooms by more conventional means in order to have a few moments alone to think it all through. Entering the scholar's abode, he told him of his conversation with Byrd. Prentice did laugh out loud at the old man's assurances that even though no one knew where the room was that it did exist because he had the key. Dillon joined him in laughter, and they sat down together over two cups of strong tea.

"Come with me into our archives, Your Majesty," Prentice said. "Perhaps two sets of eyes can find the door to this room."

Together the two men went to the archival chamber, but although they searched and searched for several long hours, they could find no evidence at all of a hidden chamber. They finally returned to the scholar's cozy chambers.

"I wonder now myself if this room exists," Prentice said.

"It exists," Dillon said certain. "A head librarian in your distant past filled that room with books he did not want scrutinized by just anyone. He locked the door to that chamber, and the key has been past down ever since. I do not believe this is a myth, Prentice. But somewhere along the line, that room was enchanted and concealed by means of magic. It can only be found by magic. I will need more help than Cinnia or the dragon can give me, for this is special magic that was worked to hide that room. I will call upon my father and ask that he send my uncle, Prince Cirillo of the Forest Faeries to me. Cirillo and I are of an age, and we were raised together in my father's palace of Shunnar where we studied the strongest magic. Together he and I can find this chamber, and then, Prentice, we will unlock its secrets!" Dillon stood, and with a swirl of his cloak he disappeared.

The scholar ran a bony hand through his graying red hair. The young king was quite interesting and intelligent. And his interest in Prentice had already drawn the curiosity of several of the more important scholars at the Academy. *In time,* he thought, *I shall be vindicated, and others will see that my studies of our ancient past are not foolish.* And now he would meet a faerie prince. Prentice wondered if there had ever been faeries in Belmair. Until now he had never considered it.

Dillon returned to his library. "Permit no one to disturb me," he told Gara. Seating himself by the fireplace, he said silently, *Father, I need you.* Several moments later Kaliq appeared from the shadows in the room. Rising to greet his sire, Dillon embraced him, and without any preamble said, "I need Cirillo. Can you bring him to me? Or must I return to Shunnar and meet with him there?"

"I can bring him," Kaliq said, "but whether your grandmother will allow it is another thing. You know he is her heir, and she dotes upon him. Then, too, there is the fact that I doubt your mother had gotten around to telling her yet of your good fortune. Why do you need him?"

"I have set a scholar from the Academy to work attempting to learn if there was once magic in Belmair. He found two small references to *wicked ones* who were told to depart Belmair. It was two centuries before the Hetarian exile, so we are certain it does not refer to that. There is a locked chamber in the Academy archives with forbidden books. The old head librarian possesses a key to it, but no one can find the room. My scholar, his name is Prentice, and we have looked ourselves. It is obvious to me that the room was hidden by faerie magic. Cirillo was also very good at solving puzzles when we were boys together. I will wager he can find that room."

Kaliq nodded. "Aye, faerie magic can be quite convoluted when they wish to hide something. I would be interested to know why they wanted the room with the forbidden books hidden. The answer to that may actually be the answer you seek. I will ask your mother to intercede with Ilona for us."

"You've told her then," Dillon said, "and yet you live, my lord."

The Shadow Prince laughed heartily. "Aye, I've told her. She kept castigating me for deciding your future, and reminding me that you were *her* son. When I told her you were my son, too, she was even angrier at first, but eventually she overcame her ire. Of course it is not something she will tell your stepfather. It seems after all these years he is still jealous and wary of me," Kaliq said, amused.

Dillon laughed, too. "Aye, when I lived with them in Terah, Magnus was never certain when you would suddenly appear from the shadows, and come into their life again." He engaged the Shadow Prince with a look. "You will always love her, won't you, my lord? My mother is your weakness, I fear."

"I will always love her," Kaliq agreed, "but believe me when I tell you she is not my weakness. If she were, you would have been born several years earlier, and lived an entirely different life. Loving her as I do I could still let her go. But we are not discussing your mother, Dillon. I will return to Shunnar immediately and see how we may arrange for Cirillo to join you here in Belmair. How is your sorceress wife?"

"Her powers are small, but eventually I will teach her so she may be stronger," Dillon replied. "Right now I am educating her in the ways of passion. She is reticent, for they do not speak of love in Belmair. She is less reserved with me now than several days ago," he said with a smile.

"Does the chamber glow golden and the air crackle when you possess her as it did in the joining?" Kaliq asked, curious.

Dillon nodded.

Kaliq shook his head. "There is no doubt in my mind that you were meant to be together. I always sensed the woman you wed would be the great love of your life. That is why I encouraged you to pleasures early. I wanted you skilled in passion, and I wanted you to be satisfied when you did marry."

"You were wise, my lord," Dillon told him. "I want no other."

"Will you love her?"

Dillon smiled. "Aye, I will, and Cinnia will love me although she yet bridles against me like a skittish young mare. She is a riddle, but I will solve her!"

"I am pleased," Kaliq said, and then he was gone. He was pleased, the Shadow Prince thought as he reappeared in his own library in his palace of Shunnar. Dillon was strong, as Kaliq was strong. Vartan, a good and loving man, had needed Lara to direct his every step. He had been a magnificent warrior. There was none better in battle. But he had not the skills to plot and to plan. He could have never produced a son like Dillon, the prince considered smiling slightly. He had been in Belmair a week now, and already he was on the trail of the mystery plaguing his new kingdom.

Kaliq poured himself a goblet of cool frine and drank

half of it down. Setting the goblet aside upon a table he spoke in the silent language. *Domina of Terah, heed my call. Come to me from out yon wall.*

After several minutes the marble wall seemed to fade in one spot, and Lara stepped into the chamber. "Greetings, my lord, what mischief are you or have you perpetrated now? You do recall it is the middle of the night in Terah. I cannot remain long lest Magnus wake up and seek me." She was wearing a house robe of peach silk.

"I need you to help me convince your mother to let Cirillo go to Belmair for a short while," Kaliq said candidly. Did she ever look less than beautiful? he wondered.

Lara burst out laughing. "I haven't even told mother yet that you have taken my…our son away from Hetar. Now you wish me to convince her to allow her only son and heir to be whisked away? I do not think she will permit it."

"Dillon needs his aid," Kaliq said.

"What has happened?" Lara demanded to know.

"Nothing yet," Kaliq responded. "There is a hidden chamber in a great library, and while all know it is there, they cannot find any evidence of it. We need to find it, and get into the room. The books there will probably tell us what magic existed in Belmair once and why it is gone. If indeed it is gone."

Lara nodded understanding. "You think it is faerie enchantment, and only a faerie can undo it," she said. "I could go to Belmair and help my son."

"You are faerie, my love, but not entirely. I would

take no chances with this. Besides I suspect your brother will enjoy escaping his mother for a brief time. And he will particularly enjoy a fresh hunting field."

Lara laughed again. "He does enjoy women," she admitted. "He has our mother's sexual appetites. It is certainly not from Thanos, his father, who is surely the most conservative faerie man I have ever met. Very well, I will help you. But first I must tell my mother of Dillon's true parentage."

"We will go together," Kaliq said.

"Not now," Lara told him. "I must away home. In the morning I will tell Magnus that I am going to visit my mother for a day or two. He prefers it to mother visiting us. Whenever she does, Magnus's mother, Persis, learns of the visit and hurries to visit us at the same time. The two are in constant competition over the children although I will say Persis favors Taj to the girls."

"Will you ever give Magnus another child?" Kaliq asked her.

"Why would I? I have given him three, and he has a son to follow him now," Lara responded to the question. "Nay. I have enough children. I shall have to watch four of them grow old, Kaliq. Dillon, of course, will live long. Did I tell you that Hetar is proposing a marriage alliance between Marzina and Egon, Jonah and Vilia's son?"

"Turn it down," Kaliq said. "The Twilight Lord took pleasures with Vilia upon the Dream Plain. While the child is Jonah's seed, for he had already been conceived when Kol took Vilia, Kol's essence bathed the child before its birth."

Lara shuddered at the mention of Kol, the Twilight Lord. "He was certainly busy, wasn't he," she said acerbically.

"The boy will be evil and grow more so as he ages. Your innate goodness has kept Marzina safe, but a child born of her loins and Egon's seed would be a disaster. Of course that is what Kol hoped for when he violated you, and then took pleasures with Vilia. Jonah's wife, like Kol, is a descendant of Usi the Sorcerer, who caused such misery in Terah. A child born of Usi's blood on both sides is certain to be dangerous."

"How long have you know about Vilia's ancestry?" Lara asked him.

"We always knew that Usi had two concubines he had impregnated. We knew that when Usi's brother had no sons it would be Usi's son he made his heir, and so the line of descent has been clear there. We did not know about Vilia until Kol took pleasures with her on the Dream Plain. There was no need for him to use her unless he had a very good reason. He could not create a son with his cousin, but he could influence who that child would be by bathing the unborn creature in his juices. And doing that with just any woman wasn't enough. He needed a child that carried Usi's blood as Vilia's son did through her," Kaliq explained.

Lara nodded. "I will tell Magnus," she said. "We will meet in my mother's forest palace tonight." Then, stepping back into the shimmering tunnel through which she had traveled earlier, she was quickly gone from his sight. She stepped from the tunnel into the small windowless room she used for these journeys, and hurried back to her bedchamber where she was relieved to see her husband sleeping soundly. Lara slipped back into bed.

When the morning came she told her husband, "I think I shall go and visit my mother today, my darling. It has been some time since I last saw her. The children will be at their studies, and Anoush will work in her herbarium as she does most days."

"Must you go?" he grumbled. "I miss you when you are gone. How long will you remain with Ilona?"

"A day, possibly two," Lara said, stroking his rough cheek. "Isn't it better I go and visit with her, than she come here? You know as well as I do that your mother has a spy or two among our servants. The second my mother arrives, yours will be close behind. Then they will quarrel over the children as they always do. I just want to spend some time with Ilona without any fuss."

He chuckled. "Why are you always right?" he asked her.

"Because I am," she teased back.

"Go then with my blessing, Lara, my wife," Magnus Hauk, Dominus of Terah, told her. "Go and enjoy your faerie world with your faerie cakes and wine. And take my love and deepest respect to your mother. Maybe I will call Dillon home to visit with me while you are gone. We haven't seen him in some time, either."

"Dillon contacted me last night on the Dream Plain,"

Lara lied. "He is off on some magic business of Kaliq's, and will be gone several weeks. He didn't want us to worry, Magnus, my love."

"Drat!" the Dominus swore lightly. "Well, perhaps I shall take Taj and visit Uncle Arik at the Temple of the Great Creator. It's time my son began learning some of the responsibilities that will be his one day."

"What a grand idea!" Lara said. "Give your uncle my love." Her conscience was now clear.

They dressed and ate breakfast together. Then Lara sought out her children to tell them she was going to visit their grandmother.

"Your father and Taj are riding to the Temple of the Great Creator and so it will just be you girls," Lara said. "Anoush, I expect you to keep order among your sisters. Zagiri, Marzina, you will listen to your elder sister, remembering she speaks for me. And no, Marzina, you may not ride Dasras in my absence. He is much too big a horse for so little a girl. Do you understand me?"

Marzina looked up at her mother with her beautiful violet eyes. "Yes, Mama," she said meekly. "But can I ride out on his daughter? She doesn't have Dasras's wings, but she goes so swiftly on her four feet. And, yes, I will take a groom with me."

"If Zagiri goes, too," Lara said, "yes, you may ride your own horse."

"Thank you, Mama," Marzina said.

Zagiri rolled her eyes. It was a look that said "she'll disobey you if she thinks she can get away with it." "Give Grandmother my love, Mama," Zagiri said.

"I will bring her all your loves," Lara said, and then kissing each of her three daughters, she hurried off to the small windowless room she used for privacy. Closing the door she looked directly at a wall and said silently, *Open!* A shimmering tunnel of light appeared before her. Again her silent voice commanded, *Golden road I wish to roam. Take me to my mother's home.* Then she stepped into the tunnel and walked quickly through it, exiting into the dayroom of Ilona, queen of the Forest Faeries.

"Good evening, Mother," Lara said. "Kaliq should be joining us shortly."

"Lara! What a lovely surprise!" Ilona said rising to kiss her daughter. She drew Lara down onto a pale lavender silk couch with her.

"If Kaliq is coming it must be important," Ilona noted. *Wine!* A carafe and three crystal goblets appeared on the low brass table before them. "Can you give me a hint?" Ilona smiled, reaching out to stroke Lara's face, an almost mirror image of her own, with her slender fingers.

They looked like sisters separated by a year or two rather than mother and daughter. Their faerie blood allowed them to age very slowly. Ilona was over four hundred years old, but she didn't look a day over twenty-five.

"I am here!" Prince Kaliq suddenly appeared. "Ah, Lara, you arrived before me. Have you told your mother yet?"

"Told me what?" Ilona filled the three goblets with wine.

"Nay," Lara said sweetly. "On reflection, I thought I should leave it to you, my lord." She smiled brightly at him.

"I will tell half," he bargained with her, "and the second part needs my voice. You must tell your mother the beginning."

Lara stuck out her tongue at him. Turning to her mother, she said without any preface, "Kaliq has recently told me that Dillon is his son, and not Vartan's."

"Of course he is," Ilona replied calmly. "All that talent for magic he has did not come from just you, and it certainly didn't come from Vartan who could do nothing more complex than shape-shift into a bird."

Lara looked astounded. *"You knew?"* Was she a fool that she had not guessed it?

"I suspected it although each time I broached the subject yon wily prince either denied it or led me into another topic," Ilona said, amused. "Well, I am glad now that it is all out in the open. What did Magnus said?"

"It is in the open only in the magic world," Lara said. "I have no intention of telling Magnus. Despite my husband's best intentions he is still jealous of Kaliq. I wish to remain with my mortal husband until he is no more. If I told him that Kaliq is Dillon's sire, do you really think he could accept it? Especially as he loves Dillon as his own. You will say nothing to him, Mother. Do you understand?"

"I can't believe he hasn't figured it all out himself," Ilona muttered.

"I didn't," Lara replied. "I believed Kaliq when he lied to me. After all, is not the great Shadow Prince my closest friend? My friend would not lie, but he did, didn't you, Kaliq?" She smiled at him again, but it was a wicked smile. "Now, do tell my mother all the rest of it, my dear *friend,*" Lara said in dulcet tones.

"You are still angry with me," Kaliq said softly.

"Aye, I am," Lara admitted. "If Magnus ever learns the truth he will think that I lied to him because he believes his faerie wife to be indomitable."

"Now, do not quarrel with the man, Lara," her mother said. "Shadow Princes rarely fall in love, but if they do their love is an endless one. Kaliq cannot help himself."

"Thank you, Ilona," the prince responded drily.

"Tell her," Lara taunted him, and she laughed when a tiny flash of irritation appeared in his bright blue eyes.

*"What?"* Ilona repeated.

"My son was needed on Belmair," Kaliq began.

Ilona's green eyes darkened. *"What have you done?"* she demanded to know.

"A powerful sorcerer was needed on Belmair," Kaliq continued. "The old king was dying. The dragon could find no successor to him, and the king's daughter, the sorceress, wanted to be queen in her own right. Belmair is not ready for such change. Their world has found perfection by living in an orderly fashion. Change needs to be introduced slowly to the Belmairans, Ilona. You know I speak the truth. With King Fflergant dying, an heir had to be found. The sorceress needed a husband, and Belmair needed a new king. I spoke with the dragon myself, and she agreed that Dillon was the answer. The sorceress needed a husband she could not intimidate although if the truth be known the dragon could teach her little, and Cinnia, for that is her name, can only do simple sorcery. But she is beautiful and clever, and Dillon is already half in love.

"Belmair, however, has a problem that has plagued them for over a hundred years, but being the people they are, they have avoided the issue because it was distressing. Now their world stands in danger of extinction unless the answer to the mystery can be found. For a little over a century young women of marriageable age have been disappearing from Belmair. Sometimes one of them will return, but when they do they are old, and have no idea where they have been or what has happened to them. Dillon is now attempting to learn what magic exists on Belmair for other than the dragon, and now Cinnia, the Belmairans have no remembrance of magic in their world."

"But of course it is magic!" Ilona said impatiently. "So you have wed my darling grandson to a Belmairan princess, and made him a king. Is it totally legal by their laws? And have the Belmairans accepted him?"

"Everything was done according to their traditions," Kaliq assured her. "And the three dukes have approved the dragon's choice and pledged their loyalty to Dillon."

"Well," Ilona allowed, "that is something at least.

And the girl. Cinnia? Has she received him as her bridegroom and her king?"

"Before everything could be legal a joining had to take place. Both the dragon and I bore witness to it. Cinnia seems content, Ilona. And my son has had enough women in his lifetime to be ready to settle down now with one," Kaliq told Ilona.

"If she's mortal she will die, and he will know others," Ilona said drily.

"Belmairans live several hundred years," Kaliq informed her. "It is something in the water, I believe."

"Tell her the rest," Lara said.

"What rest? There is more?" Ilona sounded outraged.

"Your mother knows the rest." He turned to the faerie queen. "It is the true history of Hetar to which she refers," Kaliq explained.

"Oh, of course I know that," Ilona said. "It is, after all, a part of the history of the Forest Faeries, for we, like the Shadow Princes and the Terahns, are native to the world of Hetar. We were already long here when they came."

"Why did you never tell me?" Lara asked her mother.

"There was no occasion to tell you. Until now it should not have mattered to you. Belmair is that great star in the evening sky, and nothing more," Ilona explained.

"Until now," Lara said softly.

Ilona nodded. "Aye," she agreed, "until now."

"I need Cirillo," Kaliq said.

*"What?"* Ilona cried. "You are not satisfied with

removing my favorite grandson from our world? You would take my only son and heir, as well?"

"Dillon believes there is faerie magic involved in Belmair's difficulties," Kaliq explained. "Only a faerie prince can undo faerie magic, Ilona. You know that is truth."

The queen of Hetar's Forest Faeries glared at the Shadow Prince. "Indeed it may be truth, but I cannot put my only son at risk even for you, Kaliq. And you are cruel to even ask it of me."

"There is little risk, Ilona," Kaliq assured her. "A door to a room of forbidden books has been hidden within Belmair's Academy library. We know that all the books and histories referring to magic in Belmair are within that room. Only Cirillo can find that door, and we need to find it if we are to learn the kinds of magic that once existed in Belmair. Only then can Dillon begin to solve the puzzle of the missing women, and why whoever is taking them needs them."

"Thanos will have a fit," Ilona said. "He dotes on his son. Would you go with him? Remain by his side and protect him?" she asked.

"Aye, I will," the Shadow Prince promised her. "I will guide my son and yours as I have always done, Ilona."

"Is there another way?" Lara, who had been silent until now, asked him. "I do not want my younger brother in any danger, Kaliq. Could I not find the door for Dillon?"

Kaliq shook his head. "Your blood is not one-hundred-percent faerie, my love. And even if it were you could not undo this magic. Only a faerie prince can overrule a spell created by other faeries."

"You cannot even be certain it is faerie magic," Lara replied.

"If it isn't then Cirillo will be gone but a few hours," Kaliq said. "But you yourself know that all worlds have faeries living within them. Dillon believes it is faerie magic, and I must concur with him that it probably is. We need Cirillo."

"For what do you need me?" Prince Cirillo of the Forest Faeries had just entered the room. "Mama." He kissed Ilona's cheek. "Big sister." He kissed Lara's cheek. "I shall not kiss you, my lord, never fear," he told Kaliq with a grin. He was a tall, slender, handsome faerie man with silvery-blond hair and crystal-green eyes. He was garbed in beautiful ice-blue silk garments.

"I suppose you are in the mood for an adventure now that you have discarded your latest little mortal lover," his mother said drily.

An interested look came into the faerie prince's eyes. "*An adventure?* Aye! I should enjoy a good adventure! It's dull as muffins around here these days."

Lara laughed and shook her head.

"Clarify it to him," Ilona said, her voice tinged with irritation.

The Shadow Prince took his time, and explained to Cirillo all that had happened to Dillon, and the reason his assistance was necessary. When he had finished he asked the young man, "Are you ready to come with me now?"

"Indeed, my lord, I am! It's been over a year since I last saw Dillon. So he's your get, my lord? Well, I suppose I knew it all along. His powers are so extraordinary. No mortal could sustain them." The young faerie prince chuckled. "And you've given him a kingship and a wife. You quite dote on the lad, don't you, my lord? Is she pretty?"

"She is beautiful as you will shortly see, Cirillo."

"Blond? Brunette? Redhead?" Cirillo asked.

"Her hair is as black as a raven's wing," Kaliq answered.

"Then she'll be fair," Cirillo said.

"Her skin is like moonlight," Kaliq told him.

"Eyes? Let me guess? Violet? No. Blue? Perhaps. No. Ah, green! Am I right? Green?" His look was both boyish and eager.

Kaliq nodded. "As green as springtime," he responded.

"There is faerie then somewhere in her blood," Cirillo remarked. "If her eyes are green then a faerie once mated with one of her ancestors. And a sorceress to boot."

"Her sorcery is limited, but on Belmair it is considered unique," Kaliq said.

"How long will it take us to get there?" Cirillo wanted to know.

A stricken look touched Ilona's beautiful face. "You will be careful, Cirillo," she said to him, her hand touching his silken sleeve. "And you must come quickly back, for your father will give me no peace until you are safely again within our forest kingdom."

"I'm being asked to find a door, Mama, not fight Belmair's dragon," Cirillo said patiently to his mother. He patted the hand clutching his sleeve.

"You are sometimes reckless, Cirillo," Ilona said. "I would simply beg you remember that you are heir to our forest kingdom."

"I will remember," he promised her. Then he turned to Kaliq. "Can we go now, my lord?" And he stepped next to the Shadow Prince.

"We can," Kaliq said, enfolding them both in his cloak, and before either Ilona or Lara could say another word the two men were gone.

To Lara's amazement her mother gave a little sob. "Mother!"

"He is my baby," Ilona said, and she wiped a single tear away. "I am allowed a tear now and again, Lara. The last time I wept one was the day I left you."

"He will be all right," Lara comforted her mother. "And he will be with both Kaliq and Dillon. He'll return in a day or two with all sorts of gossip about Belmair, and you will enjoy listening to him spin his tales of adventure."

"Do not speak to me as if I am some old woman," Ilona snapped, her composure restored. Then, "Are you going home now?"

"Nay, I think I shall remain with you for a few days, Mother, if you would not mind my company," Lara told her. "Magnus has taken Taj to visit his uncle at the Temple of the Great Creator, and Anoush is watching her sisters."

"Well," Ilona allowed, "I suppose it would be nice to have your company. It has been some time since we have had a good visit. Every time I go to Terah that wretched old cat, Persis, invades your castle, and we have no time together. Yes. Remain if you choose. I do not object," the queen of the Forest Faeries said. "What gossip do you have?"

"Hetar wants Marzina for Egon, but Kaliq says no," Lara replied.

"He is right," Ilona answered. "I hear the boy is a little tyrant. Have you heard that a civil war has broken out in the Dark Lands between the adherents of your twin sons?"

"I don't want to know," Lara said in a hard voice. "They are Kol's, not mine."

"You birthed them," Ilona reminded her daughter. "Everything is going quite nicely, my daughter. Kol remains imprisoned where none can reach him, and his brats have begun a war to further disrupt the Dark Lands. No one knows where they are, of course, but each of them has his adherents. They quarrel for supremacy. Eventually, of course, when they reach maturity in a few more years they will come into the open, and then, Lara, the real fun will begin. One of them will have to be killed, and since neither of them under their own laws can destroy the other it will be both fascinating and exciting to learn which one will survive.

It could take years before the Dark Lands are again in a position to threaten the rest of Hetar. You did a great service, my daughter. Because of you the light is stronger than the dark," Ilona concluded.

"It is a part of my life I can never forget, Mother," Lara told her parent, "but I do not wish to remember, either. Please do not remind me of it."

"Then we will speak on your half brother, Mikhail. He has been elected to the High Council as a representative for the Crusader Knights," Ilona said. "And he is, it seems, quite respected. Your wretched stepmother, of course, is not satisfied. She wanted him to follow in your father's footsteps. Her other four roughnecks are all in training, for as the sons of John Swiftsword they are entitled to places within the ranks of the Crusader Knights. Mikhail holds a position among them, but prefers to serve within the political venue as opposed to the military. Of course none of your stepmother's brats will ever be the swordsman your father was," Ilona said smugly.

"Hopefully the Crusader Knights will never be needed again," Lara told her mother. "The women of Hetar are slowly but most surely gaining equal power with the men. But it is a waiting game, I fear. In the meantime it is good that young men like Mikhail are willing to serve on the council. We speak now and again, and he is a forward-thinking man. I will forever be grateful to my father for telling him of me when Susanna would not. When he came to me on the battlefield after we had defeated Kol's army of darkness to tell me that John Swiftsword was dead, and that he had been proud of me…" Lara own eyes grew teary with the memory. "I promised myself then that I would stay in contact with him no matter my stepmother, and I have."

"He is a fortunate mortal to have you as his half sister. Did you tell him of your father's faerie blood?" Ilona asked.

"Aye," Lara said, "and he laughed when I did. He said it would be our secret, and he would not reveal it to his brothers or his mother. Mikhail is a good man."

"How long do you think Kaliq will keep Cirillo away?" Ilona said, changing the subject. "I imagine if it is not too long Thanos need not know until after the fact."

Lara laughed. "I think you are safe keeping Cirillo's whereabouts from his father. As long as Thanos is involved in his arboretum you will be safe from his curiosity, Mother. The trees are his passion, aren't they? So let us, you and I, enjoy ourselves these next few days while our men are about other things."

Ilona smiled. "I never thought to have a friend in my daughter, Lara, but I can see that I do. Aye! We will drink wine and eat sweetmeats and do the outrageous things that women love to do. I have these two marvelous mortal masseurs I have enchanted. Shall I call upon them?" And the queen of the Forest Faeries smiled wickedly.

# 5

CIRILLO OF THE Forest Faeries was enchanted by the beauty of Belmair. "Oh, yes," he said. "There be faeries here. It is too lovely a world for our race not to inhabit." Then he embraced Dillon. "Hello, Nephew! It is good to see you again."

"Uncle," Dillon welcomed Cirillo with a grin. "My lord father," he greeted Kaliq.

Cinnia stared openmouthed at Cirillo. Never in all her life had she ever seen such a beautiful creature. Unable to help herself she reached out to touch his pale gold hair, for she had not seen its like before. It looked like spun silk, or perhaps spider's silk or milkweed floss. It felt like… She gasped as his hand grasped hers. Her eyes met two crystal-green eyes. Cinnia swallowed hard, and a deep blush suffused her pale skin.

"You will be my new *niece,*" Cirillo purred seductively, and he placed a warm lingering kiss upon Cinnia's small hand.

"Is it not possible for you to meet a woman without trying to seduce her, Cirillo?" Dillon said, his tone just faintly tinged with irritation.

Cirillo sighed. "I suppose since she is your wife you will be jealous if I do," he said, his tone sorrowful. He smiled at Cinnia as she snatched her hand away from him. "I am very sorry, my beautiful one, but I cannot oblige the longing I see in your eyes. You are, alas, now family."

"What you see in my eyes, my lord, is shock that you would be so forward with a woman you have not even yet met," Cinnia said outraged, and frankly embarrassed by her own girlish and gauche actions.

"Indeed, *Uncle,*" Dillon teased Cirillo. "But let us have do with the formalities. This is Cinnia, my bride and my queen. Cinnia, this is my uncle, Cirillo, prince of the Forest Faeries, who has come to lend us his aid."

"My lord," Cinnia said, dropping him a curtsey as Cirillo bowed politely.

"I think Nidhug should join us," Kaliq said.

"I'll go and fetch her myself," Cinnia said, and hurried away from the hall.

"You did not exaggerate, my lord Kaliq," Cirillo said. "She is a great beauty."

"And she is my wife," Dillon reminded the faerie prince once again.

"It will be difficult," Cirillo admitted, "keeping my

hands off of her, but I will. It would never do for us to quarrel."

"The dragon is a female," Dillon said drily to his uncle. "Charm her."

"Does she have a weakness?" Cirillo asked seriously.

"She is a serious gourmand," Dillon replied, half laughing.

"I have promised your grandmother that I would return Cirillo as quickly as possible," Kaliq said. "And unscathed. Once Nidhug joins us we will go to the Academy to seek the hidden room and its forbidden books within its library."

His two companions agreed, and wine being served they descended in to small talk until Cinnia returned with the dragon. Coming into the hall, they made their way to where the three men sat. Looking at the faerie prince, Nidhug murmured something low to Cinnia, and then the two laughed.

Dillon came forward to welcome the dragon into the hall. "Nidhug, I greet you," he said, holding his two hands out to accept her elegant paws into them.

"My lord king," the dragon said, nodding in return. Then her shimmering gaze turned itself to Kaliq and Cirillo. "Kaliq of the Shadows, I greet you. And this beautiful fellow will be Prince Cirillo." Her voice had gone a trifle more seductive as she spoke.

"I greet you, Nidhug," Kaliq said.

"Madam, I greet you," Cirillo said. "No one told me a dragon would be so…so beautiful. I have never seen your like before."

"Of course you haven't, my dear boy." Nidhug simpered, her heavy, thick purple eyelashes fluttering just slightly. "There are no dragons in Hetar."

Cirillo was delighted by her response. The dragon knew how to flirt. He held out his hand to her, and upon the open palm was a small silver plate covered with candies.

*"Ohhh,"* the dragon said delightedly. "Truffles! I adore truffles. How did you know, my dear boy?" She reached out with her paw, and Cirillo saw her gold claws had painted red tips. Nidhug used those elegant claws to impale several truffles, and then she popped them into her mouth. An expression of utter bliss bloomed within her eyes. "Delicious!" she pronounced. "The best I have ever eaten, dear boy. Faerie made, I have to assume, are they not?"

He nodded.

"Put them away for now," Nidhug said. "But I shall want them later. Can you arrange that for me?" The eyelashes fluttered again.

The flat silver plate disappeared from Cirillo's hand. "I can arrange anything you desire, madam," he told her.

"Nidhug," the dragon practically purred at him. "Do call me Nidhug."

"Are we all ready to visit the Academy now?" Dillon asked impatiently. "I think we should use our magic to get there." Taking Cinnia's hand in his, they disappeared. The dragon followed immediately.

Kaliq looked at Cirillo. "I recognize that look," he said.

"Have you ever?" Cirillo asked.

Kaliq shook his head. "Never," he said.

"I am tempted," Cirillo admitted.

Shaking his head, Kaliq flung his robe about them and they quickly reappeared in the main foyer of the Academy, where Dillon was now taking the key to the chamber of forbidden books from Byrd. The head librarian looked askance at Kaliq and Cirillo, who were strangers to him. He frowned when Prentice joined the group.

Following Dillon and Cinnia, they entered the beautiful library. It was a large round white marble chamber filled with rows and rows of tall oak bookcases holding the manuscripts and volumes of the history, fiction and poetry of Belmair. Its roof was domed and pervious, allowing the light to pour into the chamber.

"Where do we begin?" Dillon asked Cirillo. "Prentice, stay near."

The faerie prince began to slowly encircle the room facing the smooth walls as he did so. He stopped once. Shook his head and moved on. He stopped a second time, and when he did he was smiling. "It's here, Dillon."

"How do you know?" Dillon asked him. "I don't see anything."

"That's because you aren't all faerie," Cirillo said. *"Door appear. Here!"*

And before their surprised eyes a small paneled oak door with a rounded top became visible.

"Give me the key," Cirillo said, and receiving it he put it into the lock and turned it carefully. The door opened easily. The faerie prince held up a warning hand. "Wait. I need to know exactly how the door is enchanted." He pulled the portal closed and turned the lock. The access immediately disappeared again. "Dillon, you say the spell, and let us see what happens."

Dillon took Cirillo's place and said, *"Door appear. Here!"* Nothing happened, and the doorway remained invisible to them.

Cirillo shook his golden head. "Whoever fashioned this spell didn't want just anyone gaining access to this chamber, for only a faerie prince can open it."

"Can you imbricate the spell?" Dillon wanted to know.

"I don't know," Cirillo answered honestly. "I must attempt another small trial. *Door appear. Here!*" The door revealed itself once again. Cirillo turned the key, and flung open the entry. Turning to Prentice, he asked, "Are you the king's scholar in this?"

"I am," the scholar said, bowing.

"Are you brave enough to enter this chamber, and allow me to close the door again? I want to know if you can exit the room from your side," Cirillo told him. "If after a few moments you have not come out, then I will reveal the door once more on this side, and open it up for you."

"I will go with him," Dillon said before Prentice

could answer. Taking the scholar by the arm, the two men stepped across the threshold into the small chamber.

Cirillo immediately closed the door, turned the lock and once more the portal was invisible to their eyes. After a few moments both Dillon and Prentice stepped through what appeared to be solid wall, but the door was not visible to them at all.

"We were able to open it from our side," Dillon said.

"It's an amazing piece of magic, isn't it, my lord Kaliq?" Cirillo said.

"It is indeed," the Shadow Prince agreed.

"Can you undo it?" Dillon asked his faerie uncle.

"I won't know until I try," Cirillo said. "I must think on it. In the meantime I will open the door for your scholar so he may begin his studies of the books inside."

"My lord," Prentice spoke. "With Your Majesty's permission I should prefer to remove a few books for study in my own quarters. They will be safe there, and so will I. I am not comfortable in that chamber," he said nervously.

"You will need time to look about the volumes here," Dillon said. "I do not want you to have to hurry yourself because you are afraid. Will you feel safe if my faerie uncle remains with you? After all he is the only one among us who can control the portal."

Prentice nodded. "Forgive me, Your Majesty. I have never before been this close to powerful magic. It is both wonderful and frightening."

Dillon smiled at the scholar. "Aye, it is," he agreed,

"but my faerie uncle will keep you safe. And he will see the books you wish to peruse further transported to your chambers when you have had the time to select them."

"Thank you, Your Majesty!" the scholar said.

"I will remain, as well," the dragon said. "My magic is small, but in the event of danger even a little extra magic helps."

"I welcome your company," Cirillo replied with a smile.

The Shadow Prince raised an eyebrow, but said nothing.

"I will tell Byrd he may close the Academy doors when he chooses. That you will keep the key, Uncle," Dillon said. Then he, Kaliq and Cinnia departed. As they walked back through the gardens toward the castle Dillon told his father, "He wants to seduce Nidhug. Is there no female safe with him, my lord?"

Cinnia gasped. "What do you mean he wants to seduce Nidhug? He is faerie. She is a dragon. It is not possible."

"He will shape-shift himself into a male dragon," Kaliq explained to her. "Or he may turn her into a woman for a brief time. He is a faerie, Cinnia, and faerie lusts can be far greater than mortal lusts. Do not fear for Nidhug. She is more than well aware of his interests. If she does not desire him, she will discourage him in most dragonlike fashion."

"Oh, my," Cinnia said softly.

"Your husband is half-faerie," Kaliq murmured.

Cinnia's pale cheeks grew pink again, but she said nothing.

"Do not tease her, my lord," Dillon said with a small smile. Then he gave a small chuckle. "Trust my faerie uncle in a world lacking in young women to find a female to fuck. Cirillo is truly a wonder in many ways but his instincts for women is unfailing."

"Ilona will have a difficult time finding a queen for him when the time comes," Kaliq noted.

"If faeries are lustful then why would Cirillo's wife care?" Cinnia asked.

"Faeries are faithful to their mates for they mate for life," Kaliq explained. "They do not wed young as you and Dillon have. And not all faeries wed. Most enjoy the freedom to take lovers, and sometimes if they love the lover they have they will give that mortal a child. Dillon's mother came from his grandmother's love for a Hetarian man."

"Are you certain, my lord Kaliq, that Nidhug will be safe with Prince Cirillo?" Cinnia continued to fret. "I do not know if she has ever had a lover."

"You may rest easy on that account," Kaliq assured the girl. "She tells me that she has an egg with her successor secreted in a cave somewhere. She has entertained a dragon lover now and again although dragons are few on Belmair."

"Dragons can create their own successors without the aid of another," Cinnia surprised Kaliq by saying. "This Nidhug told me once when I asked where the next dragon would come from, and she wished to reassure me."

The Shadow Prince smiled. "Nidhug did not lie," he replied. "But I believe from what she disclosed to me once that her egg was the result of a love affair with a male of her species. Cirillo will not harm your dragon, Cinnia, and if she refused his overtures he will cease them. His charms are such that he need force no female to his will."

"But what if he puts a spell upon her in order to force her to his will?" Cinnia worried. Her lovely face was truly distressed.

"He would never do such a thing," Dillon responded this time. "His ego would never allow it. My faerie uncle takes great pride in his own personal allure. From the time we were boys together at Shunnar females of all ages were attracted to him."

"It is apparent that Cinnia knows little or nothing about faeries," Kaliq observed thoughtfully. "There is faerie magic at work in Belmair, yet no one realizes it. Why, I wonder, has the knowledge of faeries been expunged from Belmair's history?"

"It is to be hoped that Prentice can learn that from the books he takes from the Academy's hidden library chamber," Dillon said. "Did you note that there were at least a thousand books in that room?"

Kaliq nodded. "It will take time to sort them all out," he said.

But Prince Cirillo was already doing just that. Shortly after the others had left the faerie man noticed something that neither the dragon nor the mortal with him could see. It was an eye hidden in the intricate decoration of the ceiling above them. His acute faerie senses had alerted him to the fact that they were being watched. Surreptitiously gazing about as he appeared to examine a book he had spotted the open eye before it realized he had discovered it, for having seen it he quickly looked away.

*Oh, yes,* he thought. *Faerie magic.* And he would have to outwit it quickly.

Using a thought spell he spoke silently. *Bring the faerie books to me. That Prentice may both learn and see. And keep him safe from those who spy. Especially all faerie eyes.*

"Gracious!" the scholar exclaimed as books began flying from the shelves and stacking themselves up on the table before him.

"It would seem you have what you need," Cirillo said briskly. With a wave of his hand he transported both Prentice and the books back to his own chambers. *"Quickly!"* he said to the dragon, and grabbing her paw he pulled her swiftly from the hidden room whose walls had suddenly begun to close in on them. There was a high-pitched shriek as they dashed through the open door before it slammed shut behind them and disappeared from their view.

"What just happened?" Nidhug asked Cirillo.

"Whoever enchanted the hidden room to keep it from the Belmairans set an eye amid the ceiling decoration to spy should anyone manage to get into the room," Cirillo explained. "And they set a spell to close the chamber up should anyone linger too long within it." He looked at the marble wall before him. *"Door appear. Here!"* he said aloud. But nothing happened. And suddenly the key in his hand disappeared.

*"The key!"* Nidhug cried.

"There is no longer a need for it as that small chamber no longer exists," Cirillo explained to her.

"Where is Prentice, and the books that came from the shelves?"

"Safe in his own chambers, and enchanted so no others of my kind can harm him. I am a faerie prince. No other faerie can undo my spell," Cirillo said.

"Oh, dear," the dragon fretted. "I wonder if Prentice has what he needs."

"He has every book in that library that held any reference to faeries," Cirillo said. "Whether it will be enough only time will tell us." He smiled up at Nidhug. "And now, my dear Nidhug, would you like to go somewhere private so we may get to know one another better? I will admit I have not seen many dragons, but you are surely the most beautiful one I have ever laid my faerie eyes upon."

The dragon fluttered her gold tipped purple eyelashes at him coquettishly. "Have you the power to shape-shift yourself into one of my kind?" she asked him.

Cirillo smiled again. "I do. And after we have tasted passion as your species, will you allow me to change you briefly into a mortal so we may taste it again? I much enjoy mortals as lovers," he admitted.

"Let me see what sort of a dragon you can be," Nidhug said. "And yes, you may change me afterward into a mortal for a time. I have always wondered what it would be like to have a mortal body. They seem so frail. *Ohhh, my!*"

Before Belmair's Great Dragon there suddenly stood another dragon. He stood just slightly taller than Nidhug, and he was absolutely gorgeous. His scales were a pale ice-blue edged in gold. The crest upon his head was both silver and gold, and enclosed with a bejeweled crown. His delicate wings were a mixture of both gold and silver, giving them a giltlike appearance. The claws on his paws and feet were silver tipped in gold. "Do I please you, my dear Nidhug?" Cirillo's seductive voice asked her.

"You do indeed," the dragon female replied. "Follow me." And she rose up, the ceiling of the Academy library dissolving before her as they soared together into the sky above them, which was now brilliant with the coming sunset. Shaded against the reds, the oranges and golds of the sky the two dragons flew together over the darkening sea to the mountains of Belia, and into a cave that Nidhug favored. The cave was high and dry, and lit by flickering scented torches.

Cirillo found it fascinating that there was no love play involved in their mating. Once deep within the chamber of the cave Nidhug lifted her dragon's tail, and he observed her wet and throbbing sex, which glowed a bright scarlet. Strangely excited by the sight he felt his dragon male organ swell with the strongest lust he had ever experienced. With a roar he thrust it into her, his paws reaching around to hold her steady as he pounded within her until she began to bellow her pleasure, and they both were breathing fire that scorched the walls of the cave. He actually felt the walls of her sheath enclosing him, squeezing him hard, and then dissolving into shudders of pleasure. Knowing he had more than satisfied her he released his lustful juices into her, realizing as he did that he, too, had been gratified by their mating.

"You are a magnificent lover," Nidhug praised him when they had recovered from their passions and lay quietly upon the cave's floor. "Quite the best I have ever known."

"Let us see if you appreciate me in my faerie form when I make you briefly mortal," he told her.

"I must rest first," Nidhug said. "Your exertions have quite exhausted me, my dear Cirillo. When I am ready we will return to my castle, and it is there we shall enjoy each other again. This time I shall play the mortal to your faerie prince." She simpered, and then she closed her eyes, and began to snore lightly.

Cirillo followed suit, for if the truth be told he was tired himself. It amazed him to learn that his lustful nature could be transferred into the body of a male dragon without losing a bit of his energy. When he awoke he found himself alone. "Nidhug?" he called.

A moment later she appeared cradling a large sea-green egg in her arms. "This is my heir, Nidhug XXIII. Will you give it your faerie blessing, Cirillo of the Forest Faeries?"

"Of course!" he said, touched by the maternal look in her eye. "Blessings upon you, Nidhug XXIII. May you faithfully serve Belmair as your honorable ancestors before you have done. Know that you will always have the friendship of my people." Reaching out, Cirillo touched the egg gently with his dragon's paw, and it glowed golden in response.

"Thank you," his female companion said. "I will restore the egg to its nest now. Then we will return to my castle. I am eager to see what kind of a female you will make of me, my dear Cirillo." She disappeared back into the dimness of the cave, and when she returned the egg was no longer in her possession.

"You have honored me in revealing your offspring to me," Cirillo told her.

Nidhug dipped her head slightly in acknowledgment of the compliment. "Belmair is changing," she said. "My offspring will need all the good fortune it can obtain when the day comes for it to take my place. I am not old by dragon standards at all, and so it will be some time before I decide to birth my hatchling, and then it will take at least another thousand years to train it properly."

"You did not say if it is a female or a male," Cirillo said.

"I do not know," Nidhug told him. "It will make that decision itself in the moment before it bursts through its shell. Come now, my prince. I am eager to enjoy another lustful bout of passion with you." Moving to the cave's entry, she unfurled her wings, and rose up into the midnight-black sky. He followed, and together beneath the light of Belmair's twin moons they returned to the dragon's castle.

Tavey awaited them. His eyes were curious of his mistress's companion, but they widened when the pale blue dragon morphed into an extraordinarily handsome faerie prince. "Mistress," he managed to say. "The supper is waiting."

"This is Tavey," Nidhug introduced her serving man. "And this gentleman is the king's uncle, Prince Cirillo of the Forest Faeries. He is my guest. See that a place is set for him at my table."

"At once, mistress," Tavey bowed.

"Tavey has been with me forever," Nidhug said as she led Cirillo to her dining chamber. "Nothing surprises him." Seating herself at the head of the table she indicated that he was to sit on her right. He looked astounded as the food was brought in, and Nidhug swallowed down two barrels of raw oysters, three dozen broiled salmon, two dozen baked chickens, a whole side of roasted beef, a roasted wild boar and three sides of venison followed by a platter containing forty-eight artichokes that had been steamed in white wine and were served with a mustard sauce for dipping, an enormous bowl of salad greens and a wheel of cheese, as well as several loaves of bread.

The faerie prince enjoyed such foods, but certainly in moderation. He managed a dozen of the cold raw oysters, some boar and venison, an artichoke and some salad. The wine served was a dark red, heady and rich.

His goblet was never allowed to empty. They carried on a conversation as they ate. "How long have you guarded Belmair?" he asked her out of curiosity. "Being the twenty-second of your name I assume there were many dragons before you."

"Only one," Nidhug admitted. "My father was here at Belmair's creation. I was hatched shortly after. He watched over it as its mortal population developed and grew. But he did not like mortals. He retired to his sanctum on Belia a thousand years later, leaving me to care for Belmair's fate. As I was a female he advised me to put a number after my name. It would make me, make the lineage from which I sprang, seem more impressive, he said. And so I chose twenty-two. I think it is a grand number, don't you, Cirillo? I picked Tavey and some others from among the Belmairans to serve me. Then I gifted them with lives as long as my own for I do not like change at all. When I die they will age in that instant, and die, too. Until then they remain exactly as they were when I took them into my service," she told him. "Ah, here is dessert! I'm afraid I have a terrible sweet tooth," Nidhug admitted as the servants brought in several sponge cakes filled with fresh whipped cream and soaked in wine, a platter of brightly colored jellies, another filled with fruit tarts, and a bowl of grapes and melon slices.

As he ate a cherry tart, Cirillo watched, delighted, as Nidhug gobbled down the cakes, the jellies and the remainder of the tarts. Her appetite was a wonder.

"Shall I have Tavey bring the bowl of fruit to my

bedchamber along with some wine and restoratives?" she asked him slyly.

He nodded.

"What kind of a woman will you make me?" she asked.

"Based upon your appetite I shall make you a woman of generous proportions. Faerie women are too slender for me. I prefer a nice mortal lass with some meat on her bones," Cirillo said candidly. He arose. "Are you ready, my dear Nidhug?"

"Tavey," the dragon called to her servant. "Bring the fruit and some wine to my bedchamber. And when you have departed it know that I do not wish to be disturbed until tomorrow afternoon."

"Of course, mistress," Tavey replied with a bow, picking up the bowl of fruit and hurrying off.

When they reached the dragon's bedchamber they found the fruit, and a decanter of wine awaiting them. The great four-poster bed had been turned down. Cirillo shut the door firmly behind them and turned the key in the lock for extra privacy. He turned to face Nidhug. "Are you ready?" he repeated, and when she nodded he said, *"Dragon before me, disappear! Mortal woman now appear!"*

And as he watched the dragon scales melted away, and a beautiful woman took shape before him. She was big boned with large breasts, full hips and well-fleshed thighs. Her belly was slightly rounded but not ponderous. Her hair was a deep auburn red, and her eyes were purple. Looking into those eyes he saw the dragon looking back at him. Cirillo smiled, well pleased. "You are as perfect as a mortal as you are as a dragon."

"Let me see!" Nidhug turned about to face the large mirror that stood on the floor of the chamber. "Oh," she said, and it was obvious she was pleased with what she saw. "I am quite a pretty woman, aren't I? Oh, look at my nipples! They are the size and color of pale pink cherries. They look quite good enough to eat!"

"And so I shall eventually," Cirillo promised her, smiling.

"I'm naked," Nidhug observed. "I like the nice warm gold tone you have given my flesh." She touched herself. "It is so soft. No wonder mortals are so easily wounded. Their skin is practically permeable. Still, it is pretty." She turned her eyes upon him. "Why, my dear Cirillo, are you still clothed?" With a snap of her fingers she undressed him, and they both laughed. "I must say," Nidhug complimented him, "that your manhood seems quite delightfully large. I think I shall enjoy it every bit as much as I did your dragon's spear earlier in the cave. I thought I should be burst asunder when you put yourself into me. It was quite delicious." She smiled into his green eyes, for he had made certain she would be of a height to do so. "Shall we get started again? What shall we do first, my dear Cirillo? You must lead the way for I only know the basics of mortal couplings."

"Turn about, and gaze at yourself in the mirror," he said, coming to stand behind her. He gathered up her very full breasts in his hands and fondled them, squeezing them, pinching the nipples and pulling upon them.

"Take your hands and draw your nether lips apart for me," Cirillo said. "Ah, how lovely you are, my dear Nidhug."

"Are we going to couple or not?" she demanded to know.

"Mortals take time for love play, and you will find if you relax that such play is well suited to mortal bodies." Holding one of her large breasts in his hand he reach down with the other hand to find her female center, tweaking it strongly.

"Oh, my!" Nidhug exclaimed.

"You see," the prince said.

"Do it again!" she said eagerly, and he complied until she was wet and squirming; her full fleshy buttocks rubbing against his groin.

"Oh, my!" Nidhug said again as she felt the thick length rubbing between the cheeks of her ass. "But that is not where it goes?" she asked curiously.

"Sometimes, but most of the time not," he said as he turned her about, and his mouth found hers.

Nidhug, being a dragon, had never before experienced the touch of another's lips upon her. It was the most exciting thing she had ever known. The full lips he had given her kissed him back. Her mouth opened of itself it seemed, and she felt his tongue caressing her tongue with such fiery intensity that a moan escaped her throat. Her breasts were crushed against his chest. Her thighs pressed against his thighs. His manhood throbbed against her leg, and she felt a companion throbbing deep past her nether lips. She moaned again and he slowly backed her up against the bed, pushing her down, lifting her legs up holding them firmly, and then thrusting hard into her as he stood before her. Nidhug gasped with the instant pleasure that swept over the mortal body she now wore as again and again and again he fucked her until she was screaming with her delight, and reaching a peak, fell away into a dark, soft place. When she came to consciousness again they were both in the bed, side by side. "That was quite marvelous," she told him. "You more than outdo your reputation."

"My dear Nidhug," Cirillo told her. "We have only just begun our evening of sport. It is at least five hours until the dawn, and I intend to have you in every way that a faerie man may have a dragon who wears the form of a mortal woman by the time the sun rises over Belmair."

Nidhug shivered with anticipation. "Let us not waste a minute," she told him. "I quite like the way in which this mortal female's body enjoys passion."

And they did not waste a moment of their time together in the hours that followed. But while they sported with each other, the scholar, Prentice, began his careful search through the great pile of books upon the long oak table in his first chamber. At first he was concerned, for when he had taken a volume down from the stack to peruse, the other books disappeared. But when he would reach out his hand the books would appear again, and he realized that Prince Cirillo had put a small spell upon the books in order to keep them hidden should anyone enter Prentice's rooms. If a visitor came calling it would appear as if the scholar had only one book before him that he was studying. The wealth of information was enormous, and Prentice immediately began making notes. By the time the young king came to visit him the following afternoon the scholar knew one thing for certain. A race of faeries had once existed in Belmair. But where they had gone, and what had happened to them he had yet to discover.

Dillon sent for his wife, Kaliq and Cirillo. They arrived at the scholar's rooms posthaste. "Here is what he has found so far," the young king said, indicating the wealth of notes spread out upon Prentice's oak table.

At the other end of the table the scholar was reading intently. He looked up at the sound of Dillon's voice to the others. "There are faeries!" he said excitedly.

"What kind?" Cirillo asked him.

Prentice looked puzzled. "Faeries," he repeated.

"We are not all alike," Cirillo explained patiently, realizing how truly ignorant of his race this mortal was. "Some of us favor the forest as my family, some the meadows, some water, others the hills and mountains. Some are as I am. Others are small, and there are those who are smaller yet, and can live in places like seashells and flowers. Like you mortals some are fair, others dark. Now tell me, if you know, just what kind of faeries have you discovered here in Belmair?"

"All I can tell you, my lord prince," the scholar said politely, "is that faeries did once exist here in Belmair. I was not aware that they were of different species, shapes and sizes, however. I am grateful to you for this information. I have looked at books with a later date than the earlier ones in hopes of saving us time. Now I realize that I must begin with the oldest of the books." He sighed, disappointed.

"Do not be discouraged, Master Prentice," Cinnia said to him, patting his hand. "This is a great task you have undertaken, and I would trust no one else but you to do it."

He gave her a wan smile. "The other scholars think little of me, I fear," he told her. "They cannot seem to understand the importance of knowing all the history of our world. They think it unimportant, but I believe that we learn from our history, and if we do not then we will only make the same mistakes again."

"Sometimes we do anyway," Cinnia said, "but I agree with you nonetheless."

"A wise observation for one so young," Kaliq remarked.

Cinnia favored him with an amused smile. "Thank you, my lord," she said. Then she turned back to the scholar. "Let me stay with you, Prentice. If two of us are reading we will make the work go faster, and hopefully find what we are looking for quicker."

Prentice looked somewhat distressed. "But you are my queen," he said. "Surely such humble pursuits are not for you."

"I think that the scholar is uncomfortable having a woman in his chambers with him. There are no women scholars here in the Academy that I have seen," Dillon said.

"Oh, no, Your Majesty, there are no women scholars!" Prentice burst out. "But I for one do not understand why. If the queen would like to join me then I will put aside my own foolishness, and welcome her. There are a great many books to search through."

"I will gladly remain," Cinnia said, and she drew a chair up to the table. "Where are the other books?" she asked.

Prentice chuckled. "A spell has been cast over them to keep them hidden until needed." He chortled. "'Tis really most ingenious." He reached his hand out, and the stack of books was revealed. Selecting one he handed it to Cinnia. "Here is one of the earliest texts," the scholar said to her. "See if you can find anything of interest in it." He instructed her as he took a second book from the pile. When he withdrew his hand the other volumes disappeared from their sight, leaving the rectangular oak table apparently empty but for the two books selected. Prentice chortled again. "So clever, so clever!" he said, delighted by this simple magic.

"We will leave you then to your pursuits," Dillon said, and with a snap of his fingers he transported himself, Kaliq and Cirillo back to the Great Hall of his castle. Seeing the trio the servants rushed forward to bring goblets of wine. They settled themselves before the fire and began to talk. "What sort of faeries do you think existed here at one time?" Dillon asked, looking to his uncle.

"They still exist," Cirillo replied. "If they did not the watch eye in the hidden room would not have awakened, observed us and folded the chamber in on itself, which in effect has destroyed it and its contents. Whatever else was in that room is now gone. I find this whole situation interesting. According to the scholar it was the Belmairans who set up a room with what they had decided was forbidden reading matter. Why, I wonder? But it was faerie magic that hid that room away from even the scholars of the Academy. Again, why? Nidhug does not know. But whoever secreted that room wanted it to remain hidden, and when my faerie magic opened it up to prying eyes it acted to protect itself from discovery. That is why I placed an enchantment upon Prentice's rooms and upon the books themselves. I was fortunate to retrieve the volumes that I did. I hope that one of them will give us the answers we seek. Or at least a start."

"Will they be in all of Belmair, in all the dutchies, do you think?" Dillon wondered aloud.

"How many duchies are there?" Cirillo asked Dillon.

"Belmair is made up of four land masses. Belmair, the largest; Beldane, Belia and Beltran," Dillon explained. "Each duchy is separated from the others by a great sea that surrounds it. This world is mostly water."

"Interesting," Cirillo said. "Yet your castle and Nidhug's sit nowhere near the sea. Why is that, I wonder?"

"I haven't been here long enough to ask such questions," Dillon reminded his uncle. "I am far too busy trying to learn about this world, and about the wife I have been given. Cinnia is not an easy girl."

"Ah, but is she passionate?" his uncle wanted to know. "If a woman is passionate it is easy to forgive her faults."

"The passion is there," Dillon said. "She needs tutoring in how to use it."

"If we could only introduce her to a banquet at Shunnar." Cirillo chuckled.

Kaliq laughed. "I do not believe Cinnia is ready for such an experience," he said.

"Remember, Uncle, it is my wife to whom you refer," Dillon warned. "The women we pass around at the banquets at Shunnar are familiar with us, and with our ways. The women of Belmair are more reserved than those who live in Hetar. That was part of the reason for the exile of those sent away all those aeons ago. They wanted change, they were freer with their affections."

"But the Hetarians are so bound by tradition," Cirillo said. "Are they really any different from these Belmairans?"

"Aye, they are," Dillon answered his uncle. "Those we call Hetarians carried their traditions and customs with them, even if they slightly altered and changed them. The point is they kept their heritage as it suited them to do so. They set up their world of Hetar with all the changes they had wanted to institute here in Belmair. Their history, their legends and mythologies they lost as they created new ones until, for them, Belmair was only a great star in the sky. Everything else was lost."

"I am glad I am faerie," Cirillo said. "These mortals are too complex for me."

"There is much to commend both of these worlds," Dillon replied, "but I am beginning to prefer the peace and order of Belmair to all the war and dissent of Hetar."

"Yet that peace and order has a price, my son," Kaliq pointed out. "Because they eschew trouble and will not or cannot make orderly changes, Belmair's world will die if an answer cannot be found to why all the young women have been disappearing for the last hundred years. And you are the king who will have to make the changes that keep this world alive, if it is to flourish once again."

Cirillo suddenly yawned. "This conversation becomes tiresome," he said, and he peered into his silver goblet, which now appeared empty. He wiggled a finger over it, and it slowly filled with sweet red wine again.

"You did not return to the castle last night," Dillon teased his uncle.

"I am sojourning with the dragon, if you do not mind," Cirillo said in a casual tone. "She is a charming hostess, and I am seriously considering stealing her cook and taking her back to Hetar with me."

"Did you take a dragon's form?" Kaliq asked, a small smile playing at the corners of his sensuous mouth; the rest of his question remained unasked, for it did not require an answer.

"Aye, at first I did. We flew across the sea to the

mountains. It was quite an experience. And afterward she showed me her egg. I gave it a faerie blessing, and the wee creature within the egg glowed golden at me when I did." He smiled at the memory.

"And when you had returned?" Kaliq probed further.

"I gave her female form. She had never tasted the passions of a mortal female before, and she told me she quite liked it," Cirillo said. He turned to Dillon. "You say Belmairan females are more reserved, but its dragon female is not."

"I enjoy the knowledge that Cinnia has never known another," Dillon said softly. "She is mine, and mine alone."

"You have begun to think like a Belmairan male, my son," Kaliq said. "It is good that you understand them, but do not become like them," he warned. "Cinnia is not like other Belmairan women. With your aid she will help the other women of her world to move forward in such a way as is pleasing to the men of Belmair." Then he turned to Cirillo. "Do you think Nidhug would mind if I joined you for a short while tonight?"

"You would have to ask her, my lord," Cirillo said, "but I certainly do not mind."

"Try not to corrupt Belmair's guardian," Dillon said drily, but he was smiling. It was as if they were boys again back at Shunnar, and Kaliq was leading them on some new sexual adventure that would expand their horizons along with their experience.

His two companions laughed. Cinnia had not returned by the time the evening meal was served. The three men ate together at the high board in the small dining chamber that Dillon had arranged to get set up. Afterward Cirillo and Kaliq attempted to make conversation, but they were eager to join the dragon. Finally when he held them with him as long as he could, Dillon burst out laughing, and sent them on their way. Cirillo and Kaliq disappeared in a flash, leaving their host still chuckling. With a snap of his fingers Dillon magicked himself to the scholar's chambers where Prentice and his wife were deep in study.

"Cinnia, it is time for you to come home," he said. "Have you discovered anything during these past hours?"

"I am not certain," she answered him, straightening up, for she had been hunching over her book. "Perhaps. Is it time for dinner yet?"

"Past," he told her. "Prentice, you need food if you are to keep up your strength," Dillon told the scholar, and with another snap of his fingers a steaming plate of food and a goblet of wine appeared before Prentice.

"Oh, my," the scholar said, sniffing appreciatively. "Thank you, Your Majesty. I do not believe I have ever been treated to such a fine meal." He took a sip from the cup. "And certainly I have never tasted such a fine vintage as this would appear to be."

"Cinnia will come back on the morrow if it pleases her," Dillon said, and then he and his wife were gone from the scholar's room. They reappeared a moment later in the little hall. "Sit down," Dillon instructed his wife, and with a wave of his hand her supper appeared before her. Taking a decanter of wine from the sideboard, Dillon filled an empty cup, bringing it to her. "Now eat, my queen, and afterward you will tell me what little bit you have discovered this afternoon."

Cinnia began to eat. "That was so kind of you to give Prentice his supper," she said as she buttered a bit of the cottage loaf before her. "I don't think he eats a great deal, and certainly the quality of what he eats is poor, for he seems to consider his personal care a very mundane matter," she noted, popping the bread into her mouth.

"I agree," Dillon said. "The man is too thin, and he will need all his energies to search through so many books. We were fortunate to get as many out as we did."

"The chamber is gone then?" Cinnia asked as she spooned hot stew into her mouth. "Your uncle is certain of this?"

"If Cirillo says it is so, then it is so," Dillon replied. He sat by the hearth as she ate, for the evening was cool and damp, indicating rain ahead.

Suddenly Cinnia's green eyes grew wide, and she stared across the chamber. "Dillon!" she pointed, the spoon dropping from her fingers.

He looked to where she indicated, and saw a small crystal sphere floating to him. Dillon held out his hand, and the round object settled itself in his hand. He looked into it and smiled. "Good evening, Grandmother," he said, fighting back his laughter. He beckoned to Cinnia with his other hand, and she came quickly from her place to sit next to him and look into the ball.

"Do not good evening me, Dillon. Where is Cirillo? He was to be gone a day, and now two have passed. Is he all right? I must speak to him at once!"

"Cirillo is fine, Grandmother. He and Kaliq are enjoying an entertainment at the dragon's castle this evening. I did not go, for I wanted to wait for my wife, who has been with an esteemed scholar from this world seeking the cause for our problem. This is Cinnia, Grandmother. Cinnia, my grandmother, Ilona, queen of the Forest Faeries."

"You are a pretty thing," Ilona said. "Is my grandson telling the truth?" She sent a hard glare in Cinnia's direction.

"My husband would never lie to you, Queen Ilona," Cinnia said. "You know that is so. My husband is noble and loyal."

"You may call me *Grandmother,*" Ilona said. "Aye, you are *very* pretty."

"Cirillo is perfectly safe here, Grandmother," Dillon assured Ilona. "But he may have to remain with us for a time, for while I am a fine sorcerer, and my father's magic is beyond everyone else's, faerie magic more often than not requires faerie magic to undo it. Without Cirillo's aid we would have lost certain valuable books today that may help us. It was my uncle who saved those books. He is certain there are faeries here in Belmair. I can ask him to reach out to you tomorrow, Grandmother. May I keep the crystal sphere?"

"Of course!" she said impatiently. "That is why I sent it. And it was not easy I can tell you. Something actually attempted to block me from reaching you. If you have faeries in Belmair they are bad faeries, Dillon. Be careful. Oh! Your mother sends her love. She'll visit soon." Then Ilona was gone from the crystal.

"Gracious!" Cinnia said. "What a forceful woman your grandmother is."

He laughed now. "Aye, she is very forceful. My uncle is her only son. He will inherit her kingdom one day. He has never left Hetar before, and she is naturally worried for she dotes on him, but then so does my mother."

"She is very beautiful, and seemingly ageless," Cinnia said a trifle enviously. "Does your mother look like her?"

"They are more often than not mistaken for sisters by those who do not know them," Dillon told the girl. "My mother is almost full faerie in her blood. You will like her, and someday when Belmair is safe again I will take you to Terah to meet the rest of my family. They will love you, Cinnia, as I am learning to do."

"You said that your uncle and your father were being entertained by Nidhug? Why did you not join them? I hope you have not offended the dragon," Cinnia said.

Dillon began to laugh, and he laughed until the tears rolled down his cheeks. Finally he regained a mastery of himself as she looked oddly at him. "Nidhug would have been more offended if I had joined the others," he assured Cinnia.

"Why?" Cinnia pursued the matter.

"Because Nidhug, Cirillo and Kaliq are at this very moment in your dragon's bed. Cirillo has temporarily given her the form of a voluptuous mortal woman, and she is enjoying the very vigorous and passionate attentions of my father and my uncle. She is, my uncle says, a most lusty female," Dillon explained.

Cinnia's eyes closed briefly, then opened again. "I have never thought of Nidhug in that manner," she said. "She is the guardian of Belmair, not a lusty female."

"She is both," Dillon said. "Late yesterday, my uncle took on the form of a male dragon, and together they flew across the sea to her favorite den where they made dragon love before returning here to make love as two mortals."

"Oh, my!" Cinnia said, her pale skin coloring.

Dillon put an arm about Cinnia and nuzzled her soft black hair. "It seems to me a rather delightful way to spend an evening," he murmured. "Shall we retire to our bed, my queen?" he asked her, his eyes locking onto hers.

"Yes," Cinnia said without hesitation. "Why should Nidhug have all the fun?"

# 6

NIDHUG WRITHED IN the throes of ecstasy that her mortal body was enjoying, a large cock in her female channel, and another one between her lips. Mortals, she decided, really knew how to have fun. *Harder! Suck harder!* She heard Cirillo's silent command even as her body began to spasm with the ultimate pleasure Kaliq was giving her. But she obeyed his directive, and a moment later his juices slid down her throat in static bursts of lust fulfilled. With a single groan the trio of lovers lay panting as the wildness slowly receded.

"Dragons," Nidhug observed, "can only entertain one lover at a time. I must say this mortal capacity for multiple lovers, while at the same time quite fascinating, is also very exhausting."

"Actually," Cirillo said, "you could take three lovers at the same time, for you have a third orifice a hard cock may explore." Rolling her over he demonstrated with a finger exactly what and where he meant.

Nidhug squealed and squirmed away from the faerie. "I do not think so!" she exclaimed indignantly. "I have my limits, my dear Cirillo."

With an amused smile Kaliq arose from the bed. "I shall leave you two now," he said. He kissed Nidhug's ripe lips, and then her hand. "Thank you, my dear. Cirillo has given you a delicious and seductive female form, and I very much enjoyed sharing it with the both of you."

The dragon eyed the Shadow Prince. He was an elegant male with a beautiful body, and she had enjoyed his attentions. For all Cirillo's charm and youth, it was the Shadow Prince's expertise that had given her the most incredible pleasure she had ever known in any sexual encounter. "I have enjoyed your company, too, my lord," she told him as he quickly dressed himself.

Kaliq turned, and gave her a warm smile. "Good night, my dear Nidhug," he said, and then with a flourish of his long cloak he was gone.

Sensing he might have lost the advantage, Cirillo leaned over and began fondling his lover's large breast. "Mortal or dragon," he murmured softly in her ear, "you are every bit the perfect lover, my dear Nidhug."

"I shall miss you when you are gone," the dragon replied, "and envy my darling Cinnia her nights with the king. Will you stay with me until your departure?" she asked, skillfully soothing his faerie ego. "And before you leave me I should like to see that wonderfully handsome ice-blue dragon once again."

"Now that you have experienced both mortal form, and your own," Cirillo queried her mischievously, "which do you prefer?"

"I am of the dragon race no matter the shape that houses my essence," Nidhug told him. "Should I have to choose I should choose being what I was born to be. A dragon. This mortal body is too frail, and I feel weak and helpless in it although I must admit that I enjoy pleasures far more as a mortal than as a dragon. Still there is a certain advantage to being able to breathe fire," Nidhug told her faerie lover with a smile.

Cirillo laughed. "I understand," he said. "And in either form you are a marvelous partner, my dear Nidhug," he repeated. "I hope that your mistress gives my nephew as much delight as you give me," he told her as he stole a kiss from her ruby lips.

Had he had the opportunity at that moment, Dillon would have told his uncle that he was more than content with his young wife. With each sensual encounter they had Cinnia grew less shy with him. This night she lay naked in his arms almost purring as he kissed his way about her body. There was no inch of her flesh he did not kiss, and having done so he now began anew, this time using his tongue to pay his homage. Cinnia stretched and sighed.

"Does this please you?" he inquired softly, his tongue teasing at her navel.

"It tickles," she answered him.

"But does it please you?" he asked again.

"I did not say it didn't," she replied.

He laughed softly. "You are bedeviling me, Cinnia."

"Am I?" She squirmed slightly beneath his tongue.

"Aye, you are," he said. "I see I shall have to retaliate, my queen." He quickly slid between her legs, pushing them up, his dark head moving from one side of her thighs to the other as he taunted her with his wicked tongue.

Cinnia felt him spread her nether lips open with strong thumbs, and caught her breath. This was a form of lovemaking that Cinnia loved almost as much as when he put himself inside of her. His tongue slowly licked at her, and she began to tingle from the soles of her feet to the top of her head. *"Oh, yes!"* she told him. Why was he waiting? But then the very tip of his tongue touched that sensitive little nub.

Her sharp intake of breath told him he had found her pleasure jewel. He encircled it several times with just the point of his tongue. Then taking it between his lips he sucked hard on it, and she began to whimper.

*"Oh, yes! Yes!"* she half moaned, encouraging him.

She was salty, yet she was sweet like honey. The scent of her filled his nostrils and roused his passions. When she shuddered with her first release Dillon did not wait. Pulling himself up he sheathed his manhood within her, reveling in her cry as she wrapped her body about his, clutching at him frantically.

*"Please! Please!"* she cried to him. Her nails dug into his shoulders.

His mouth found hers as their fingers intertwined. Their tongues frantically dueled with one another as they found their rhythm. Their loins moved in measured cadence; long, slow strokes that made them desperate for more. Quick hard thrusts that eventually brought them to a climactic and fiery explosion of pleasure again and again and yet again until they finally fell away from each other, burning, wet with their exertions and thoroughly sated.

When he was finally able to speak Dillon said to her, "Sorceress, what is it you have done to me? I possess you, and it is not enough."

"Have you fallen in love with me?" Cinnia asked him boldly, propping herself up upon an elbow so she might look down into his handsome face.

He thought a moment, and then said, "Aye, I think that I have, my queen." His hand reached up to gently stroke her lovely face.

"I have never been certain that love really existed," Cinnia said. "Whatever there was between my father and my mother, if it was love, is unknown to me, for she died shortly after I was born. And yet, Dillon, while we have known each other but a short time, you say you love me." She looked deep into his bright blue eyes. "And I believe that what I feel for you is love, too. Have we bewitched each other, Majesty?"

He smiled up at her. "Perhaps, Cinnia, it was something that was just meant to be," he suggested. "I don't want to question it. Do you?"

"What if it is only lust we feel?" she asked.

"I am a man who has known enough women to know that what I feel for you, my queen, is not lust. You, however, must believe in the calling of your heart, Cinnia," he told her. "Only you can be certain whether what you feel for me is love or lust. But I shall believe that you love me for it pleases me to do so." He drew her down so that her dark head rested upon his shoulder.

"Will you give me a child?" she asked softly.

"One day," he told her. "But not yet. First we must learn the mystery that plagues Belmair, and then we must attempt to solve it."

"How?" she said.

"Tomorrow we will think on it, my queen. For now we will sleep," he replied, and safe within his embrace Cinnia slept until the morning.

Prentice, the scholar, however, had slept but four hours. He was awakened several hours before the dawn in the darkest hours of the night. There was someone, he sensed, in his chambers. He could hear the rustling of papers, and arising swiftly from his cot, he called out, "Who is there? What do you want?" Fumbling for a lamp, he shook it, awakening the glow worms who powered it. They blazed brightly, illuminating the scholar's chamber, and Prentice's eyes peered myopically as he carried the lamp toward his table, which was half enveloped in dusk. A movement caught his eye. He saw… He could not quite make it out, but there was something there. "Show yourself!" he called again in what he hoped passed for a commanding voice.

*"Where are my books?"*

"Who are you? Let me see you," Prentice said, half relieved he was not imagining things and there actually was someone or something there.

*"Where are my books? Give me my books!"* the disembodied voice said again.

"Any books in my chambers belong to the Academy. As I am an Academy scholar I am entitled to peruse them," Prentice said. "Who are you that you invade my private chambers, and will not reveal yourself to me?" Where was his courage coming from? the scholar wondered even as he spoke.

*"I will have my books!"* the voice insisted.

Prentice had now located the voice. It was coming from beneath his table. Stepping back a few paces he reached for his broom, which was in a corner.

*"I can destroy you, bold scholar,"* the voice told him.

"My master the king, and his father, the great Shadow Prince Kaliq, will then seek you out and punish you," Prentice said. Then he swooped his broom hard beneath the table. "Get out from underneath there!" he said. "Show yourself to me!"

There was a shriek, and the scholar briefly saw his visitor before it disappeared in a puff of angry dark blue smoke. Prentice wanted to disbelieve what he had just seen, but he could not. Instead he found his cup, commanded it to fill itself and then sat down with his tea to calm his rattled nerves. After a few minutes he decided that as unnerving as the encounter had been, it had also been very exciting. With this quest to learn about Belmair's past magic, his life had suddenly become almost adventurous. He felt the skin of his gaunt face stretching into a smile, and a little chuckle escaped him. Relaxed now he dozed briefly in his chair. When he awoke again and glanced at the clock upon the wall he saw that it must certainly be dawn, or near it. Standing up, he shook out his robes and ran his fingers through his tousled hair. Then he ventured forth from his chambers.

He climbed the three flights of stairs, one wooden, one stone, one marble, to the grand foyer of the Academy. It was virtually empty of course, for the hour was early. At the great bronze doors he waited patiently until the doorkeeper, sleeping in his chair opened his eyes, and jumped up.

"Why 'tis Master Prentice, isn't it?" the doorkeeper said. "Haven't seen you in several years. Are you actually going out?"

"I must see the king at once!" Prentice said, and the doorkeeper immediately unlocked the door, pulling one aside to let Prentice through. At first the bright light of the new day hurt his eyes for he had not ventured from his chambers in some time. What was that lovely smell? he wondered. And then he chuckled at himself for a fool. It was air, fresh with dew and the scent of early-summer flowers. The scholar hurried through the park and gardens of the royal enclosure, reaching the drawbridge to the royal castle, which was down. It was always down, for Belmair was a peaceful world. Swans and their recently hatched young swam in the broad moat among pale yellow water lilies and delicate lavender water hyacinths.

The guard on the other side of the drawbridge greeted him. "Good morrow, scholar. What business have you here?"

"I am Master Prentice, and I must see the king. I was told to come whenever I had found anything of note in the studies I have been commissioned to undertake at His Majesty's request."

"You're an early bird, aren't you?" The guard chortled. "Eager to make an impression on the young king, are you? Well, go along into the Great Hall. The castle steward will arrange for your audience. His name is Britto, and he's a good enough fellow if not perhaps just a little filled with self-importance. Do you know where it is?"

"Thank you," Prentice said to the guard, "aye, I think I can find it. I was in the castle about ten years ago. Nothing has changed, has it?"

"Nay, 'tis as it ever was," the guard said as he waved the scholar past him.

Prentice hurried along, reaching the Great Hall shortly thereafter. "I am seeking Master Britto," he called out, and immediately a short, plump man in dark maroon robes stepped forward, looking the scholar over as if deciding if the tall, gaunt fellow with the shock of graying red hair was worthy of his time.

"I am Britto," the castle steward said.

"I am Master Prentice, the king's personal scholar.

I should like to speak with His Majesty, please, for I have news of great import for him," the scholar said.

"I will bear whatever news you carry to His Majesty," Britto answered loftily.

"I would not offend you, sir," Prentice began, "but I have been personally commissioned by the king to look into a certain matter. I was told when I had anything of interest to report that I was to come to His Majesty directly. I know that being a man of great significance here within the castle hierarchy you will understand my position. I must bring my news first to the king himself," Prentice said politely.

The scholar's tone, his manners and his obvious respect for the castle steward softened Britto's attitude. "You're in luck," he said. "His Majesty rises early. He will be in the little hall having his breakfast now. I'll take you to him."

"Thank you," Prentice replied, and then hurried after the plump man, who was surprisingly quick for a fellow with such short legs. It wasn't far, and the scholar directly found himself being ushered into another chamber where the young king sat alone at his breakfast, one servant only standing behind him.

"My lord, the scholar Prentice," Britto announced their visitor.

Dillon looked up, and beckoning Prentice forward, said, "Have you eaten yet? Britto, have a plate of food brought for our guest. Sit, Prentice," he ordered, gesturing to the chair to his left. "It must be news of some import that brings you out of your lair and into the early-morning sunshine," the young king teased.

For the second time that morning Prentice smiled. "Indeed, Your Majesty," he said, climbing up onto the dais and seating himself in the appointed chair, "it is. Although of what use it will be to us I do not know." His rheumy gray eyes lit up at the sight of the food being set before him. Eggs! He couldn't remember the last time he had seen, let alone eaten an egg. And they were surrounded by a creamy sauce. And a generous rasher of crisp, fatty bacon. The scholar's mouth watered as a separate plate of sweet smelling scones, warm from the oven, along with a little tub of butter and a dish of lingonberry jam was set before him. His hand trembled as he reached for the fork, but then he drew his hand away, and looked to the king. "You will want to know my news immediately, Your Majesty," he said dutifully.

But Dillon had seen the look in the scholar's eyes when the food had been brought. "No, no," he said to Prentice. "Eat your fill first, man. Food is always better hot. Belmair has waited a long time to learn what you have found out so far, and whatever else there is, it can wait a bit longer. Do they not feed you in the Academy?"

"I am not considered among the important at the Academy," Prentice said as he popped a forkful of eggs into his mouth. "They do remember to bring me food at least once daily. Bread. Cheese. Cold meat. A bit of beer." The look in his eyes was blissful as he munched upon the bacon and continued to eat his eggs.

"I've enchanted your tea mugs," Dillon said with a

smile. “I shall have to put a wee spell on your dinner plate. Then all you need do is ask it politely to fill itself with whatever you desire to eat when you are hungry. My mother has always believed a man’s stomach must be full and content if he is to do his best work.”

“It would be a great kindness, Your Majesty,” the scholar said. He quickly finished his eggs and bacon and a scone and a half, washing it down with the fresh sweet cider that filled his cup. Then with a sigh he pushed the plate away. “I was awakened in the middle of the night by the knowledge that someone was in my chambers,” Prentice began.

“Wait,” Dillon said. “I think my father and my uncle should hear this.” He called to them in their silent magical language.

Almost immediately Kaliq appeared before the high board causing the scholar to jump in his chair. “Good morning,” Kaliq said calmly, and joined them at the high board. Immediately a servant placed a plate of food before him. The Shadow Prince nodded his thanks and began to eat.

“I’ve called Cirillo,” Dillon said irritably. “Where in the name of the Great Creator is he? Grandmother will kill me, or make a good attempt at it, if any harm should come to him.” He lowered his voice. “He isn’t still with *her,* is he?”

“They are both inexhaustible,” Kaliq murmured. “You should see the female form he has given her. Breasts like melons, and a sheath that stays as tight as a virgin's and grips you like a vise. Ah, it was quite delightful!"

His words had barely died when Cirillo appeared as Kaliq had, in a small puff of smoke. "Good morning!" he said cheerfully. He had the look of a large cat that had just devoured a plump capon, and a dish of stewed mice in cream.

"Join us," Dillon said. "The scholar has had an interesting night. Possibly in its own way as interesting as yours." He chuckled.

Cirillo laughed, and came up to sit down at the high board.

Dillon turned to the scholar, who had been busying himself polishing off the rest of the scones and jam. "Continue on, Master Prentice. Begin at the beginning."

"I was awakened in the middle of the night by the certainty that someone was in my chambers," the scholar said. "I demanded the intruder show himself to me but instead it cried out to me, *'Where are my books?'* I continued to insist that my unwelcome visitor reveal himself to me, but he eluded me, and continued to demand I give him *his books.* I said that any books in the Academy belonged to the Academy and as a scholar I was entitled to have and read them. But the voice continued in an agitated manner to demand the books."

"Further proof, if further proof was needed, that there is magic at work here," Kaliq said. "Continue on with your tale, scholar, for surely there is more to this."

"Indeed, my lord, there is," Prentice answered. "I had

finally located from where the voice was coming. It was under the table itself, and so I fetched my broom. When the voice threatened me with bodily harm I swiped my broom back and forth beneath the table several times. There was a shriek! I caught a glimpse of…of…I can't believe I really saw what I saw, Your Majesty, my lords," the scholar said helplessly.

"What do you think you saw?" Kaliq asked him.

"It was an eye, my lord. A black pupil in a gold iris. And it had yellow legs with red boots that came to its knees. Am I mad that I saw such a thing?" Prentice asked them.

"It was the guardian eye from the forbidden chamber!" Cirillo said excitedly.

"It had to have reported what happened to its masters, and they sent it to find the volumes you took from that little room," Dillon said.

"But who are *they?*" Prentice said.

"I may know."

They turned to find Cinnia had entered the little hall. She joined them at the high board, seating herself next to Dillon. "In my own readings," she began, "I came across several references to the Yafir. From what I can gather they are a clan of magical beings who can bring great blessings upon those they favor, or great destruction upon those who displease them. My lord Kaliq, do you know of such beings?"

He nodded. "I do," he said. "First, scholar, tell me what happened to the guardian eye?"

"It ran across my chamber as fast as it could, and

then disappeared in a puff of smoke," Prentice said. "It was a sight such as I have never seen, nor hope to again."

"Who are these Yafir?" Cinnia wanted to know. "Are they indeed magic?"

"They are indeed magical," Kaliq spoke. "And they are a race of faeries. We—the magical community—believed them extinct centuries ago. They are a very volatile species. They could be the kindest of the kind, bringing prosperity and blessings upon those they loved. Set a bowl of fresh milk, fresh bread and berries out for them in the evening, and if they accepted your offering good fortune would smile upon you. But gain their enmity, and they would visit all manner of bad luck upon you."

"From what I have found in my readings," Cinnia said, "they lived here in Belmair at one time. Could they be those referred to in later writings as the *wicked ones?* And what happened to them?"

"I recall reading about them in mother's library," Cirillo said. "At one time they inhabited many worlds, but for one reason or another they left those worlds."

"They left," Kaliq said quietly, "either because they were driven out, or because they became dissatisfied with the worlds in which they lived. It's been centuries since they have been heard of in any world. Belmair would appeal to them because it is a small, orderly world whose people are peaceful, and who wish no strong contact or ties with other worlds. The history that mentions the *wicked ones* being asked to leave says nothing further. Is it possible that the Yafir did not go, but rather secreted themselves from the eyes of the Belmairans, causing them to believe that they did depart?"

"But how are we to find out?" Dillon wanted to know.

"Have you not been taught *finding* spells?" Kaliq said.

"I think we must first learn why Belmair wanted these Yafir to leave our world," Cinnia said quietly. "The answer has to be somewhere within the books Prentice has."

"But if it isn't?" Dillon asked.

"It has to be," Cinnia insisted. "It is a part of our history. Perhaps we are looking in the wrong place for these answers."

"Explain," the Shadow Prince said sharply.

"We are seeking answers to why the Yafir and the Belmairans disagreed in the magic books. What if those answers are not in the magic books, but rather in our ancient histories? The situation is, after all, history, not necessarily magic. And how can you find answers if you don't know the questions? Until today, we didn't," Cinnia said.

Kaliq suddenly looked at the girl with new respect. "You are right!" he said.

And Dillon laughed. "We have looked at this situation through the eyes of magic and complicated it. Cinnia's commonsense approach has simplified it for us."

"You do not have the answers yet," Cinnia told them. "I have only posed a what-if to you." She turned to the scholar. “If I show you the books in which I found my reference to the Yafir, do you think you can pinpoint the historical era? Only then can we begin to seek the answers we need.”

“Show me the book in which you read about the Yafir,” Prentice said. “I will date it for you, and then find the volumes we are going to need.”

“Come with me, then, back to the Academy,” Cinnia said.

“Let me transport you. It’s quicker, and we do not want to attract interest among the other scholars, or anyone who might be watching,” Dillon said to his wife.

“Aye, ’tis better. Stand next to me, Prentice, and take my hand,” Cinnia said, and no sooner than he had they found themselves standing again in the midst of the scholar’s cluttered chamber. Cinnia went immediately to where she remembered the stack of books being, and when she reached out her hand the pile appeared. She lifted a small volume from the top. “Here is the book where the Yafir are mentioned.” She opened it carefully, for the pages were thin and delicate, and handed it to Prentice.

Drawing his spectacles from his robe he began to carefully look over the small book. Finally he nodded. “The book is written by the well-known Belmairan scholar, Calleo, who lived in the time of King Napier the IX, who reigned over Belmair nearly forty centuries ago.”

“Then we must look into the history of Napier IX’s reign,” Cinnia said.

"It was a long reign as I recall it," Prentice said. "Over ten centuries, my lady. We will have to look through my library for books concerning that reign. I will have most of them here in my rooms, for such ancient history is not thought useful by those here today."

For the next several days Cinnia spent her time with the scholar poring through shelves and shelves of books, seeking the histories that concerned the reign of Napier IX. Prentice was not an orderly man. Their search would have been easier had he kept the books according to eras or reigns, but he did not. They were scattered here and there upon the shelves, floors and tables. Cinnia cleared one end of the great rectangular table in the scholar's front chamber. And it was here that they began to pile the books covering the reign of Napier IX. When they had close to one hundred books Cinnia deemed she and the scholar should begin reading.

For the next several weeks they devoted their waking hours to reading through the histories. Most nights in the dim chamber she would lose track of the time, and Dillon would grow tired of waiting for her to appear for the evening meal. He would then bring her home by the use of his magic, setting her down into her seat at the high board where for a moment of two she would look startled, before commencing to eat.

One evening, as Cinnia adjusted to finding herself at her dinner table and not at the scholar's table, she apologized to her husband. "I am so intrigued by this mystery, I must solve it," she told him. They were alone,

Kaliq and Cirillo having returned to Hetar until they would be needed again.

"We will solve it, my queen," Dillon promised her.

"What do you do while I am with Prentice all day?" she asked him, curious.

"I have the affairs of our world to administer, for unlike Hetar and Terah you have no counsel to advise your king. Perhaps in the future we will change that," he said. "And I must build my stores of medicines, tinctures, potions and spells. When my father transported my possessions from Shunnar much of what I had was left behind in my little apothecary, for he forgot that room was mine," Dillon told her. "Britto found me a fine apartment in one of the castle towers. It has two rooms—one with a small hearth and a window, and the other an interior space where I can dry the plants Ferrex and I have been gathering these fine summer days while you have been reading in Prentice's dusty rooms." He smiled at her. "I have been able to duplicate some rather lovely lotions that are used to inspire lovers. They must age until winter, however."

"You have occupied your time well," Cinnia said with a smile. "I have read and read and read about the reign of Napier IX, but so far it is just different versions of the same tale. And there is no mention at all of the Yafir. I am fast becoming discouraged. Have you seen Nidhug at all?"

"It seems she enjoyed my uncle's company more than she realized she had, and now she misses it," Dillon responded. "It is usual for the women who become his lover to fall in love with him, but I think our dragon has, too."

"Poor Nidhug," Cinnia said softly.

"Don't feel sorry for her," Dillon told his young wife. "I think she is enjoying the pain of their separation. And he'll be back. He admitted to me before he returned home that he grew quite fond of Nidhug. I do not think I have ever heard Cirillo admit to loving any creature, even his mother. He is quite typical of his race. Highly sexed and selfish. But charming. Now eat your supper, my queen. You look tired."

"I am," Cinnia admitted. "And I am discouraged, but I know I am right. If we can learn what caused the breach between Belmair and the Yafir I am certain we can heal it. But then I wonder if the Yafir are the ones responsible for the disappearance of our women, and I wonder why they are taking them," she said.

Almost ten days later Cinnia found part of her answer, a first reference to the dispute between the Yafir and the Belmairans. It was referred to in the history she was reading as the *Great Controversy.* But there was no explanation of the quarrel other than by name, and that the *wicked ones* had been requested to leave Belmair. Knowing now what she was seeking, she found several more references to the *Great Controversy,* but before she could declare some small piece of the puzzle solved she needed to be able to ascertain that the Yafir were the *wicked ones.* Finally in a yellowed scroll she discovered what was probably one of the first references written about this imbroglio.

By royal decree of His Majesty, King Napier the IX, on this first day of summer, the *wicked ones,* formally known as the Yafir people, have been banished from Belmair, said banishment to be carried out by summer's end.

"Prentice!" Cinnia called to the scholar, and when he came to stand by her side she showed him the words in the old scroll.

"My lady," he said to her, "you deserve the rank of scholar, as well as queen. When we have solved all of this conundrum I shall recommend you to Byrd myself."

"No woman has even attained the rank of scholar in Belmair," Cinnia reminded him. "Such an idea would truly shock the members of the Academy."

"Then it is time they changed their thinking!" Prentice said.

"Be careful," she teased him. "If they hear such heresy they will send you to Hetar for certain." The scholar chuckled.

"Perhaps I would enjoy traveling," he teased back.

*"King of Belmair, heed my call. Come to me from out yon wall,"* Cinnia spoke the simple spell her husband had taught her.

The young king stepped into the chamber. "What is it, my queen?" he asked her.

"I shall never get used to this," Prentice murmured.

"Look!" And Cinnia showed him the reference she had found.

He read it carefully. "This is wonderful, my darling!"

he exclaimed. "We can now be certain that the Yafir and the *wicked ones* are one in the same. I suspect they were not called wicked when they first arrived on Belmair. Is there any reference to what caused them to be exiled?"

"None so far, and I suspect there will be none. Whatever caused Belmair to order the Yafir from our world would not have been important enough to the Belmairans to describe because we are a sensible folk. If we had been banished from some land we would have accepted the directive and gone. It wouldn't matter to us why. The fact that we were not wanted would have been more than enough for us. That is the reason there is no mention of what caused the Yafir to be banished. The decision was made by the king to do it, and that was all there was to it. It would never have occurred to our people that the Yafir would not obey the king's command. And can we be certain they did not? Could this disappearance of our women be due to some other magical beings?" Cinnia asked. "Why would the Yafir remain in Belmair if they were unwelcome? Certainly no one has seen them since that time. And if they are still here, where are they?"

"All excellent questions, my queen," Dillon told her. "Thanks to you we have found the first thread. Now we must follow it until we are able to unravel the entire mystery that has taken hold in Belmair. I believe it is now time to ask my uncle and my father to return from Hetar." He took Cinnia by the hand, and bidding the scholar farewell, returned them to the castle.

Cinnia was laughing as they reappeared. "Our magical means of transport unnerves poor Prentice," she said, "but it is so convenient. I want Nidhug to know what I have found. You contact the Shadow Prince and your uncle. I will call the dragon."

"A fair division of labor," Dillon agreed.

Nidhug was delighted by what Cinnia had found, and praised her. "You are such a clever girl," she said. And then, "Cirillo is returning?"

Cinnia shook her head. "You are a shameless dragon," she scolded. "Here I have been doing all this work, and all you can think about is that handsome faerie."

"So you admit that he is handsome," Nidhug said. "But, my little queen, while you have spent your days lazily reading I have watched over Belmair, making certain that the summer days were perfect and sunny, that the rains came only at night, that the fields were free of pests who would destroy the crops, that the crops were bountiful so each of the duchies will have a good harvest, and finally I have seen that the seas were rich with fish, and the beasts of the field flourished. I do not spend my time in idleness even when I nap for a few years or more. Everything is always as it should be in Belmair thanks to me, for it is my duty to protect this little world of ours."

"It is your nights I was thinking of," Cinnia teased the dragon. "Does he make love to you as a dragon? How can that be?"

"He transforms himself into a male dragon sometimes," Nidhug said. "And other times he transforms me into a mortal woman."

"Oh, my!" Cinnia said.

Nidhug chuckled. "Ah, I see the questions in your eyes, little queen. I will say only that while dragon pleasures and mortal pleasures are delicious, mortal bodies seem to be able to gain more delights. I think your fragile and sensitive skins may have something to do with it, as well as your breasts. Cirillo has given my mortal form fine, big breasts. The Shadow Prince said they were as big as melons and just as sweet."

Cinnia gasped, and then she begged, "No more, dear Nidhug!"

"You don't have very big breasts, do you?" the dragon suddenly noted, peering closely at the young woman.

"I will send for you when our guests arrive," Cinnia said, and then she fled the dragon's castle, not by means of magic, but by her own feet. She needed to walk through the summer gardens that separated the two castles so that her flushed cheeks would cool and pale. She tried to imagine Nidhug with a mortal body, but she could not. All she could see was a dragon with huge melonlike breasts. It was not an attractive picture, but the more she considered it the funnier it became. By the time she was halfway across her own part of the gardens she was laughing so hard she had to sit down.

It was there Dillon found her wiping away the tears of her hilarity. "Are you all right?" he wanted to know, for he was not certain she wasn't weeping at first.

"I am fine," Cinnia told him. And then she related her visit with Nidhug.

"I can only hope our lustful magical natures will not corrupt you," Dillon said to her with a chuckle. "I realize that your Belmairan nature is more conservative than those found in the world of Hetar. My uncle seems to have found a perfect match in Nidhug. As for my father, he has always appreciated beautiful creatures although I have never before known him to sample the charms of a dragon."

"Does he not love your mother?" Cinnia asked.

"Aye, although he conceals his love behind the masque of friendship," Dillon explained. "My mother was born of Ilona, queen of the Forest Faeries, and the Hetarian, John Swiftsword, because such a child of those two people was needed to fulfill a specific destiny. Kaliq has been part of her life from the beginning although she never met him until she left Hetar and fled the Forest Lords. He has struggled with his own love for her to keep her on the path she must travel. He has seen her go to other men, and known it was part of her fate. But even he has admitted to me that he does not know her end. It is, he says, behind a veil that even he cannot pierce."

"When will I meet her?" Cinnia asked him. "We have been wed now several months. I would have thought she would have come before now."

"I think she wanted you to get used to having me for a husband before she made her appearance. Although she has worked hard not to play favorites, my siblings tell me, and I know it for truth, that I have always been her favorite," Dillon said. "We seemed to have this link right from the moment of my birth. I think it was Kaliq's way of keeping her close while not intruding upon her life as she must live it. When I first went to live at Shunnar it was months before she visited me. She told me when she finally came that she wanted me to get used to living there, to living away from her, to come to love the wonders of the desert kingdom as she once had. And of course she was right, and I did."

"There is so much about you that I do not know," Cinnia said. "I wonder if I ever will, Dillon." She reached out to take his hand, and turning her face to him, she kissed him sweetly. "But I have come to love you."

He drew her into his embrace, his mouth kissing her slowly, his hunger for her blazing up and catching her in a scorching hold. His hand reached up to fondle her breasts, and he whispered against her lips, "So perfect, Cinnia. Your breasts are so perfect!" He could feel himself growing hard quickly. His manhood beneath his robe began to throb. Dillon stood, drawing Cinnia up with him. His hands about her buttocks, he drew her against him so she might know that his desire was hot. Then he whispered against her ripe mouth, "Remember, Cinnia, *anytime, anywhere.*"

She almost swooned with the heated words, and then she followed his directions, straddling the marble bench upon which they had been sitting; leaning low and forward as she braced herself with her hands, her buttocks elevated. Her heart beat wildly with her excitement as she felt him behind her. Slowly, oh so slowly, he raised her skirts up, up, up until they rested in the curve of the small of her back. The palms of his hands smoothed over the plump cheeks of her bottom. He squeezed the soft flesh. She felt his fingers slipping beneath her, finding her pleasure jewel and teasing at it. She could feel her own wetness, and whimpered with her need.

And then the fingers were withdrawn. She felt his belly starting to press against her as his manhood began to enter her in a single smooth motion that had her gasping. Once sheathed he remained still, and she felt every inch of him, thick and throbbing within her fevered body. About them the birds sang, and the air was heavy with the fragrance of summer flowers. When she could bear it no longer she cried out softly, "Please, Dillon! Please! I can bear no more!"

His hands tightened just imperceptibly about her hips. "Tell me what you feel, Cinnia, my queen. And tell me what you want."

"I feel you, and you are so hard and so deep. You pulse with your need for me, but you will not satisfy your desires. Why?" she asked of him.

"Because just the sensation of being joined with you gives me pleasure," he said. "And the thoughts of greater pleasure to come make my lusts burgeon. You must learn to enjoy every bit of our intimacy, my queen, not just race to fulfill your needs. When those needs are satisfied so quickly you have lost much of that which you might have gained simply by exercising a little patience." Leaning forward he placed a hot kiss on the small of her back.

Cinnia shuddered, and felt her release. "Oh!" she cried, distressed. "I have lost it!"

He laughed softly. "Nay, my queen, we have only just begun to exercise our passions for each other." He thrust gently within her with several long, smooth strokes.

"Oh!" Her voice was suddenly joyful. "It is still there!"

"Aye, it is. Now let us begin your lesson in patience, my queen," Dillon said as he began to move himself within Cinnia's ripe, young body. When she began to evince signs of pleasure he drew back, remaining still within her silken sheath. Reaching out and forward with one hand he found one of her breasts and eased it from the neckline of her gown. He fondled the tender flesh, pulling and then pinching the nipple until she was trembling with her excitement. Then knowing his own patience was slowly waning Dillon sought for and found her pleasure center and began to use it. His manhood moved back and forth, thrusting hard and fast until Cinnia was sobbing with her desperate need to find release, but he wanted her to have as much pleasure as he could give her. And then she cried out, and her body shook as they reached perfection together in an explosion of passion that would leave them both weak for several minutes to come.

Gazing down on them from a window overlooking the gardens, Kaliq of the Shadows smiled to himself. He had taught his son well. The girl was lost in a swirl of ecstasy such as she would have never known with another man. And Dillon had the perfect partner and the perfect wife in Cinnia. "They are an excellent match," he told his companion.

"Agreed," Nidhug said. "I was not certain you just wished a kingdom for your son, Kaliq, when you first came to me. I ask your pardon for doubting you, great prince. Dillon is very much the equal to my own darling Cinnia. And they have already begun to decipher the mystery, but I will leave it to them to tell you what they have discovered."

"Then they have actually found something of worth," Kaliq replied.

The dragon nodded. Then she turned back to the window. "Oh, how sweet he is. He has taken her in his arms, and is comforting her. He did ride her hard, and in the gardens, too, the naughty boy," she tittered.

"Let them have their moments together," Kaliq said. "Cirillo is as always late. He is either arguing with his mother about coming, or some pretty creature has caught his fancy and is keeping him from us."

A small puff of dark smoke tinged with scarlet came from the dragon's nostrils, but she said nothing in response.

Kaliq, however, had seen it. *Why, Nidhug is jealous,* he thought, surprised. Then he wondered if the dragon actually cared for the faerie prince. He hoped not for she would be doomed to disappointment. "You do remember that faeries have hard hearts," he murmured. "They rarely, if ever, give them to another."

The dragon sighed. "I know," she replied. "But he is such an incredible lover in whatever form he takes. I cannot help myself. It has been at least a thousand years since I took a lover I actually liked. He amuses me with his irreverent faerie ways, and he is so young, Kaliq. His energy is as boundless as his charm. I know better than to fall in love with him even though I will admit that I am a little in love with him. But just a little, Kaliq. Enough to make the whole experience a tiny bit more piquant," Nidhug said.

"Take care, my dear," he advised her. "Your magic is nowhere near as strong as his is. And it is a kinder magic that you possess that fills this world with beauty and peace. Cirillo is like most of his race. Beautiful, charming and totally selfish, with an inborn ability to cause trouble even without meaning to do so."

At that very moment the subject of their conversation appeared. "Hallo," Cirillo said brightly. "Have I missed anything?"

"Only Dillon and Cinnia in delightful and energetic conjunction in the gardens below," the Shadow Prince said.

Cirillo flew to the windows. "Where are they?" he asked. "There is no one down there at all. Just flowers, birds and butterflies."

"Ah, then," Nidhug said, "they are probably on their way into the castle now. Britto!" she called to the castle's steward, and he hurried into the chamber from the corridor where he had been awaiting their summons.

"Yes, my lady dragon? How may I serve you?" the steward asked.

"Tell the king and queen that we are here awaiting them," Nidhug said.

"At once!" Britto replied, and bustled away.

"You have not greeted me," Cirillo pouted to Nidhug.

"You did not greet me, and you should have," the dragon said. "This is my world, Cirillo of the Forest Faeries, not yours. Where are your manners?"

"I said hallo," Cirillo replied.

"Hallo?" The dragon looked sharply at the faerie. "*Hallo?* There are two of us in the chamber, my dear boy. And I do not answer to a general hallo. However if you would like to greet me nicely now, I will forgive you."

Kaliq looked amused. Perhaps he need not worry about the dragon's liaison with the young faerie prince.

Cirillo offered Nidhug his best and most courtly bow. Reaching for a scarlet tipped paw he kissed the sea-blue and spring-green scales. "I greet you, Nidhug of Belmair," he said. *And I am going to fuck the scales off of you tonight*, he told her in the silent, magical language.

"I greet you, Cirillo of the Forest Faeries," Nidhug answered him. *And I will suck your faerie cock so hard it will break off* was her silent reply as she retrieved her paw.

Kaliq, who had heard both exchanges, struggled to keep a straight face. Aye, he thought, Dillon and Cinnia were a perfect match. Now he was beginning to seriously wonder if Nidhug and Cirillo were not a match, too. He wondered if the young faerie had mentioned the dragon to his mother. The Shadow Prince actually shivered thinking of what Ilona, the beautiful and powerful queen of the Forest Faeries, would think if she knew her son was involved with a female dragon.

Dillon and Cinnia entered the chamber, now filled with late-afternoon light.

"Welcome back to Belmair!" they greeted Kaliq and Cirillo with one voice. They laughed, turning their faces to one another and smiling.

*Ah, they have fallen in love,* Kaliq thought to himself, and he was glad. He wanted his only child happy, and it would appear that he was.

*It is good, my friend,* he heard the dragon say.

Turning to look at Nidhug, the Shadow Prince smiled at her and nodded. Then he said in a brisk voice, "Tell us, my children, what you have discovered."

# 7

"I HAVE FOUND evidence that the Yafir are indeed also known as the *wicked ones,* my lord," Cinnia began. "They were banished several thousand years ago from Belmair, but whether they went or not is the question."

"Why were they exiled?" Kaliq wanted to know.

"No reason was given, but as I have explained to Dillon the reason would not have been important for our historians. The king declared it so, and therefore that would be all the explanation needed, for the king's word is law in Belmair," Cinnia explained.

"So all we know is that the Yafir existed, were here in Belmair and were banished because the king wanted it." The Shadow Prince was intrigued. "And there is no proof that they either remained or departed?"

"None that we can find," Cinnia said.

"Exactly when did young women begin to disappear?" Kaliq asked her.

"About a thousand years ago, but it was not particularly noticeable until about three hundred years ago when they began disappearing in greater numbers, and now in the last hundred years it has escalated to the point where there aren't enough females born to serve as mothers to the next generation, which means our population is shrinking. At first the girls taken were sixteen and older. Now they disappear as young as twelve."

"You need to learn if the Yafir are still here," Cirillo said.

"You are faerie, Uncle," Dillon remarked. "Could you not ferret them out so we might speak with them? Perhaps if we could learn why they are stealing these females we might be able to stop the practice."

"I could try to find them," Cirillo agreed. "The question is where to begin."

"Can they be called forth?" Kaliq considered slowly. "Let me think a minute to see if I can remember the hierarchy of the Yafir so we may call their leader to us."

"Without a name?" Cirillo said. "We need the power of name magic to reach out to them. You know that, Kaliq. Without a name the quest is hopeless."

"I may have a way," the great Shadow Prince said. "I must leave you briefly, but I will be back by sunset," he promised, and hurried from the chamber. He sought out a deep shadow, and stepping into it stepped back out in his own palace of Shunnar. He was in his private chamber. Going to a cabinet, he took out a beautiful carved *spell. Come to me from where you abide. From my voice you cannot hide."*

"What prince of faeries calls my name?" a disembodied voice asked.

"Show yourself," Cirillo said.

"You did not request that I show myself. You only asked for my presence," the voice told him smugly.

"Are you so ugly then that you hide yourself from us?" Cirillo demanded to know.

"You have my name, now give me yours," the voice insisted.

"I am Cirillo, the son of Ilona, queen of the Forest aeries, and her heir. These others are Kaliq, the great hadow Lord, Dillon his son, the new king of Belmair, d…"

'I know the girl," the voice told them. "Cinnia, ghter of Fflergant. He is dead then? And how did a rian gain the throne of Belmair. Is it legal?"

lo more answers to your questions until you reveal elf, Ahura Mazda," Cirillo said firmly.

Yafir high lord uncloaked himself. He was tall nder, with eyes the color of an aquamarine and t was silvery-white. He was handsome in a cold ery well, Cirillo of the Forest Faeries, you see was garbed all in different shades of blue with nkle of gold here and there.

ant is gone, and Dillon of Shunnar rules in w. Cinnia is his queen," Cirillo told the Yafir.

you want of me?" Ahura Mazda asked.

ought you here," Cirillo said. "Now let the



metal bowl and set it upon a pale wood table. Reaching for an earthenware pitcher that was filled with water, Kaliq poured it slowly and carefully into the metal bowl. He waited for the surface of the water to calm and clear. When it had he looked down into it, and said, "Satordi, lord of the Munin, come to me."

The water in the basin darkened, and then the surface became as luminous as a mirror. It reflected a long gray face that looked up at the Shadow Prince. "Greetings, Kaliq of the Shadows," Satordi said. "It has been some time since you have called upon the Munin for aid. How may I serve you?"

"I need the name of a Yafir high lord who hides himself in Belmair," Kaliq said.

"An interesting request," Satordi remarked. "Were the Yafir not sent from Belmair aeons ago? Those are memories that I know are kept by my brothers and me."

"Exiled, aye, but whether they went is another thing entirely. Do you retain memories past the time of their exile?" Kaliq inquired.

The Munin lord thought long and carefully. "We have no real record of them after Belmair," he noted. He grew silent again, probing the collective memory banks of his race. "An occasional snippet of passion, a bit of revelry, but nothing to indicate where they are or why we do not have their discarded memories, my lord Kaliq."

"You, or one of your brothers, will have among the memories you keep the name of the high lord of the Yafir from that time. If he was not an ancient then it is probable that he still holds that office, for the Yafir like most of the faerie races live very long lives. Find that name for me, Satordi. Find it quickly!"

"I shall return to you within the hour," the Munin lord said, and his visage vanished from the surface of the water in the basin.

Kaliq sat down in a large, comfortable chair, leaning back to rest his dark head, easing the ache in the back of his neck. He closed his eyes and willed himself to relax. He knew instinctively without being told that the Yafir had not left Belmair. But until he had a name to call forth it would be difficult to learn much more than that. The scent of Damask roses drifted in from his gardens on the warm air. It surrounded him, teasing at his nostrils and lulling him into a light sleep. He sat up fully awake when he realized that the Munin lord had returned. He walked over to the table and gazed down into the carved metal basin as Satordi's face appeared to him.

"The name you seek is Ahura Mazda," the Munin lord told him. "He had only been high lord of the Yafir for fifty years when they were told to leave Belmair. He is likely to still be their leader for the memories we retain of him are of a young and vibrant man, stubborn, proud and oft times difficult. Is there anything else?"

"Nay, there is not," Kaliq replied. "I thank you and your brothers, Satordi."

"To serve you, great Shadow Prince, is our pleasure," the Munin lord responded, and then he faded away in the waters of the reflecting bowl.

Kaliq moved away from the table and back into the



shadows of the chamber. He stepped out again into the room where Dillon, Cinnia, Cirillo and the dragon had been.

They were awaiting him.

"You went to the Munin," Dillon said.

Kaliq smiled. "Aye, and I have the name we seek. It is Ahura Mazda. Now, Cirillo, it is up to you to fashion a spell that will bring this Yafir to us."

"You and Dillon must create reinforcing spells f
my magic," the faerie prince said. "The Yafir are fa
resistant to the magic of others. They will try to
my spell with their own so we will all have to w
gether."

"And Cinnia and I can help," Nidhug said

"My dear dragon," Cirillo told her, "thi
and strong magic we must use. Your mag
tent enough, I fear. Let us handle this ta

"It is not beyond my magic," Nidhug
you into a warty toad, if even briefly,
a weak female, oh prince of the For

"I will be grateful to have you an
magic to protect ours," Dillon sa
are going to need all the help w

"Agreed," Kaliq replied. "
spell now, Cirillo. This Yafi
cause you are both of the f

With a little shrug and
Cinnia and the dragon t
*Mazda, heed me well.*

young king, who is my nephew, and his queen ask the questions of you that they must." He turned to Dillon and Cinnia with a small nod.

"Let me welcome you to our castle, high lord of the Yafir," Dillon began. "May I offer you in hospitality a goblet of wine?"

Ahura Mazda nodded, an amused smile upon his lips. "I will accept your hospitality, king of Belmair," he said. "How is it that you are related to Prince Cirillo?"

"He is my mother's younger brother," Dillon answered.

"And your father?" the Yafir asked.

"Kaliq of the Shadows who stands in this chamber with you," Dillon said.

Ahura Mazda's pale, almost invisible eyebrow was raised in surprise. But recovering, he remarked, "Then you are magic."

"I am magic," Dillon agreed, and handed the Yafir a goblet of wine that appeared suddenly in his hand, creating one for himself, as well, and sipping at it.

The Yafir nodded. "Of course."

"Let us sit, and you will tell me why you did not leave Belmair when you were banished all those centuries ago by Napier IX." He led his guest to a settee where Cinnia and the two men sat down. Kaliq, Cirillo and Nidhug remained standing, at the ready.

"How do you know the Yafir were exiled?" he asked, curious. "Was not the hidden chamber closed and destroyed shortly after you entered it?"

"The guardian was not able to prevent us from obtaining some of the books," Cinnia said. "And those combined with some of Belmair's most ancient texts helped us to learn of you, and that you were ordered away." Cinnia paused and then she asked him, "Why did the king turn on you, my lord? And when he had, why did you not leave?"

"Ah, you Belmairans," Ahura Mazda said, his tone tinged with scorn. "You are so tractable. We did not depart Belmair because we did not want to leave it. For centuries we have been driven from one world to another, called the troublemakers of the faerie races. All we wished was to share this world with you, but that fusty Napier IX insisted that we must leave Belmair. He accused us of everything he could think of, and then said we were no longer welcome here, and must go. Go where? There was nowhere left for us to go. So we did not. We hid ourselves away in this world, indeed beneath your very noses. Only magic could bring us into the light."

"You are welcome to remain," Dillon said. "We ask only one thing of you."

"And what is that?" Ahura Mazda wanted to know.

"Stop stealing the young women of this world, high lord of the Yafir," Dillon responded. "Their families weep for their loss, and those you have returned come back old, and have no knowledge of what has happened to them since you stole them away. Their pain at those lost years is so great that most died within days of their return."

"We need your women," Ahura Mazda said. "Do

not be selfish like Napier IX was when he ruled, oh king of Belmair."

"Why do you need the young women of Belmair?" Kaliq of the Shadows now asked, interjecting himself into the conversation.

"Because most of our Yafir women are dead," Ahura Mazda said. "We cannot survive as a faerie race without children. In return for our faerie blessings we asked that Belmair give us one hundred young women of child-bearing age each year. It was not many, and Belmair had plenty of young women to spare. But Napier IX said no. He said he would not deliver Belmair's pure and innocent maidens into the hands of the Yafir to be despoiled and ravaged. The old fool! Our men wanted wives. They wanted women to bear our children. They were eager and ready to love them. But Belmair's king said no. And then he told us to leave your world. Instead we took the women we wanted when we wanted, and we hid ourselves away from your general population."

"So you have stolen these maidens for wives," Cinnia said quietly. "But if you rebuilt your population why was it necessary to keep stealing women?"

"Your mortal women birthed more sons than daughters," Ahura Mazda said. "We had no choice but to keep stealing women for our men," he explained.

"Why did you not apply to the other faerie races throughout the Cosmos for wives?" Cirillo asked the high lord.

Ahura Mazda laughed a bitter laugh. "Would your queen have sent me a dozen faerie women as brides had

I asked her?" he said. "Would any other of the faerie kings or queens? You all know the answer to that. The Yafir are scorned, and always have been."

"You cannot keep taking our women," Dillon said. "There are not enough now to marry the Belmairan men who want wives themselves. You will destroy us if you keep taking our women, Ahura Mazda."

"Then we shall take your world for our own," the high lord said. "And never again shall we be driven away. Belmair shall be ours. We can wait." And then he surprised them further by disappearing in a puff of scarlet smoke.

"I can force him back," Cirillo said.

"Do not bother," Kaliq replied. "We have learned what we need to know. Now we must take steps to prevent the further chaos that Ahura Mazda wishes to stir up."

"And how are we to do that?" Cinnia wanted to know.

"Well," Kaliq said, "the first thing we must do is figure out how the Yafir steal your females. We should learn where they have hidden themselves. And we must create a protection spell for all of Belmair's remaining young women."

"Now that the Yafir knows we are aware of them," Dillon said, "will they not be more dangerous? Ahura Mazda appears to me to be ruthless and determined."

"We can destroy him and his kind," Cirillo said coldly. "The Yafir have ever been difficult. They are the most mercurial and untrustworthy of the faerie races."

"I felt rather sorry for him," Dillon told his uncle. "If Napier IX had simply cooperated with the Yafir none of this would have happened. I don't want them destroyed. I want to see if we can heal this breach and live in peace with them."

"Hah!" Cirillo replied. "Thus speaks that tiny bit of mortal blood within you, Nephew. One must deal with one's enemies decisively or suffer at their hands."

"I think you are too quick to judge, Uncle," Dillon said. "I will grant you that they are the most mercurial among the faerie races, but what makes them untrustworthy?"

Cirillo shrugged. "I don't know, but they are. Everyone among our kind says it."

Dillon laughed. "And everyone said I was the son of Vartan."

Kaliq chuckled. "Belmair is Dillon's domain now," he said in a quiet voice. "He must decide what he will do about the Yafir, Cirillo. And it is our duty to help him. If he is wrong we will know soon enough, and can rethink this problem. For now we need a strong protection spell for the young women of Belmair."

"I will send out messengers to all the duchies seeking information as to how the women are stolen," Dillon said. "I do not know how much help that will be to us, but perhaps it will give us a better idea of how to protect them while we devise a spell."

"I will take your message to each of the dukes myself," Nidhug said. "If I carry the king's word it will be taken more seriously, especially as I shall go in my full size. I am always extremely impressive full-sized."

"I need to return home to work in my own apothecary if I am to create a perfect spell. And perhaps my mother can make a suggestion or two if I ask her," Cirillo said.

"If she learns what you are doing," Dillon teased his young uncle, "she will make suggestions whether you ask her or not."

"Be careful, Nephew, that I do not tell my sister that you need her," Cirillo taunted Dillon back. "Lara has not visited you yet, has she? I'm sure she is dying to come, and just waiting for the right moment." And then he was gone in a puff of purple smoke.

"If Cirillo doesn't need my help," the young king said, grinning at his uncle's departure, "perhaps I shall go with Nidhug. If both the king and Belmair's guardian arrive in each duchy to tell its dukes what has happened then the matter will be taken most seriously. What think you, Cinnia?"

"I think it is an excellent idea," Cinnia agreed. "You will also by going do honor to Dukes Tullio, Alban and Dreng. They will not forget such a courtesy. Yes, go, my husband. We will not allow the Yafir to destroy us so they may have Belmair for themselves. I am, like you, willing to share our world, but I will not be driven from it."

"Well spoken, Cinnia," Kaliq told her. "And now, my children, I will leave you, too, for you do not need my services quite yet. I will return with Cirillo when he has successfully formulated his protection spell. Shall I bring Lara with me then, Dillon?"

"Aye, I think it is time that she and Cinnia met," Dillon responded.

"Keep safe," the great Shadow Lord said, and then he disappeared.

"I will meet you on the same castle rooftop as before," Nidhug said. "At dawn, Your Majesty. Where would you travel to first?"

"Beltran, I think, Nidhug," Dillon said. "Duke Dreng considers himself the premier duke of this realm, Tullio and Alban do not seem to disagree. So let us visit Beltran first. Then we will go on to whichever of the duchies is closest to it."

"I will see you on the morrow, Your Majesty. Dress warmly for I shall fly high, and it will be cold aloft," the dragon told him. Then with a small bow she departed.

"It is night already," Dillon noted, gazing out the windows of the chamber where they had all been meeting.

"Are you hungry, my lord?" Cinnia asked. "It is past the dinner hour."

"Have the servants bring something to our chambers," he said. "We will sup before the fire, my queen."

They went to their apartment, and Cinnia gave instructions to her servant, Anke. When the meal came Ferrex served it on a small table that had been set before the blazing hearth. There was a platter of large, meaty prawns that had been steamed in white wine; a fat capon roasted golden, stuffed with bread, sage and onions; a plate of artichokes with a little brown crock of sauce made from ground mustard seed, dill and heavy clotted cream; as well as fresh baked bread, sweet butter and a dish containing slices of several varieties of cheese. A bowl of silky custard with stewed apricots had been brought as a sweet, along with a small plate of delicate sugar wafers.

"I like your father," Cinnia told him as they ate. She took a decanter of wine and poured some into his goblet. "Is your mother as nice? I don't remember my mother."

"Would you be jealous if I told you that I adore my mother?" Dillon asked her. "She has been my best friend my whole life. Is she nice? Sometimes," he told Cinnia with a smile. "But she can also be intimidating. When you meet her remember that you are the daughter of one king, the wife of another, and the queen of Belmair. You are every bit her equal socially, Cinnia, and she will respect you for knowing that. But you are not her equal in any other way. You will recognize Lara's uniqueness as everyone does, but do not be afraid. You say you love me. If she sees it, and believes you, she will love you in return."

"You say she is beautiful," Cinnia remarked. "Is she like me?"

"Nay, she is your opposite except that she has green faerie eyes as you do. She is slender and very, very fair. Her hair is like thistledown, all golden gilt. My grandmother, Cirillo's mother, and my mother look like sisters as faerie blood ages very slowly. My stepfather adores Lara. Be warned that it is unlikely my mother has told

Magnus Hauk of my true parentage. He is jealous, I fear, although he has no need to be."

"How will we protect the maidens of Belmair until Cirillo can make his spell?" Cinnia wanted to know. She wondered now if Ahura or another Yafir had been the source of her occasional feelings that someone was watching her. And would the spell protect her from them, as well?

"I think we may have to gather all the women together in one place where we can keep them hidden from the Yafir. The Yafir obviously roam Belmair at will, and take these girls unawares. But if we gather them all up, and secret them where we can guard them we may be able to put a stop to these kidnappings temporarily while Cirillo seeks his protection spell," Dillon said. "This is something I shall discuss with each of the dukes."

"The maidens would be safe in the ducal homes, I'm certain," Cinnia said.

"Perhaps, but if I were a Yafir that is probably the first place where I would seek out the missing females," Dillon noted. "No. It must be someplace no one, not even a Yafir, would consider. Nidhug may have a good idea," he told her.

Cinnia yawned. "If you are starting at dawn, we had best get to bed," she said. "Anke, Ferrex, good night. We will attend to ourselves."

He followed her into her bedchamber. "What if I am not of a mind to attend to myself?" he said, coming up behind her, his arm going about her waist, drawing her back against him. "Will you *attend* to me?" he murmured in her ear.

Cinnia turned to face him, for his grip on her middle was a light one. Her fingers undid the frog closures at the neckline of his dark brocade robe. Leaning forward she kissed the faint hollow in his neck, and her lips moved slowly across the bared flesh, kissing it, licking him. "A good wife always, and gladly *attends* to her husband, my lord," Cinnia purred. Reaching behind him, she began to pull the garment over his head.

Beneath it he wore only a pair of silk drawers. Dropping the robe upon the floor she smoothed her hands over his broad chest. Then slipping to her knees she kissed his belly, and untied the drawstring of his drawers, letting them drop to his ankles.

Dillon kicked the garment away from him, and drew his breath in sharply as his wife took him into her mouth and began sucking upon his cock. Closing his eyes, he let the enjoyment take hold of him. Her tongue swirled about the head of his member as she held the flesh back from it. Her teeth nibbled delicately upon that most sensitive bit of him, and he groaned. Her hand slipped beneath him as she sucked strongly, playing with his sacs, squeezing them lightly. Dillon felt himself grow harder and harder as she teased him sweetly. Finally he dug his fingers into her dark hair, gripping tightly, and said in a tight voice, "Enough!"

Releasing him, she gave him one hot lick from the root to the tip of him. "But you taste so good, my lord," she protested.

He pulled her to her feet, and then pushed her back upon the bed. "You are a very greedy wench," he told her as he fell to lie half-atop her. He took her face in his hands, and kissed her mouth hard. Then half gripping her slender neck, he caressed it, rubbing himself against her. He shifted himself so that he might enjoy her breasts. Kissing them, he then suckled, bit and pulled at the nipples. Then his head moved lower and lower, trailing hot kisses along her torso, her belly.

"Taste me!" she begged him, and gasped at the touch of his tongue on her pleasure jewel. "Oh, yes! Yes! Yes!" she cried softly.

She filled his senses, the fragrance of her lust setting his blood aboil. He sucked hard on the tiny nub of flesh, and Cinnia screamed in delight. He was throbbing, aching with his need, and he waited no more. Driving himself into her in a single smooth thrust, he began to use her fiercely.

"Yes! Yes!" Cinnia urged him onward. "Ride me harder! Harder! Yes! Yes! Harder, my darling Dillon!"

He drove her frenziedly, his cock flashing back and forth, forth and back within her burning wet sheath. "You are mine! I adore you!" he growled in her ear as his loins punished hers. "I could fuck you forever, my queen! *Forever!*"

She clutched at him, her nails raking at his back. Her legs wrapped about him and he pushed deeper and deeper until Cinnia's head was spinning, and she was moaning as pleasures overcame them both in a final tumultuous burst of their mingled juices. Golden light exploded around them, and the air crackled with fire as she screamed her satisfaction, and he roared with his delight. And afterward they fell into a contented sleep, the fingers of their hands intertwined in a sweet embrace.

Dillon awoke in the predawn. Cinnia was sleeping soundly on her stomach, one arm flung out to the side. Looking at her he smiled, and thought that if a year ago he had been told that he would be a king, with a beautiful, passionate sorceress for his queen, he would have laughed. He hadn't known then what he wanted to do with his talents. He had always assumed he would use them for good in Terah or Hetar. Rising, he slipped from her bedchamber into his own.

Ferrex, sleeping on the trundle at the foot of the bed, was immediately up. "Majesty!" he greeted his lord.

"I would bathe, and while I do set out some garments that are both warm and worthy of a visit to the dukes. Tell the queen when she awakes that I will probably be gone overnight. I shall have to accept the hospitality of the ducal trio, and I would not have Nidhug fly home in the dark of the moons so we shall remain with the last duke I visit," he explained to his servant.

"Very good, Your Majesty," Ferrex answered as Dillon passed him, moving into the bath. He then began to carefully lay out garments according to his master's instructions.

Silk drawers. A short silk chemise. A silk shirt. A short white-and-gold brocade tunic that came to the midthigh. White trousers embroidered with gold cuffs just below the knee. A dark green cloak lined in fur.

Dark green leather boots. From the chest containing the king's jewelry he drew out a heavy gold chain from which hung a large purple amethyst cut in the shape of a star with a tail of tiny diamonds.

"I have not seen that before," Dillon said, returning from the bath, a towel about his loins, his hair damp.

"There has been no occasion for you to wear it until now, Your Majesty. This is Belmair's sacred symbol," Ferrex explained. "You have seen the pendant the dragon wears with this very marking, and the queen has a golden wand with this same symbol. You will honor the dukes by wearing it, and they will better understand the seriousness of your visit. That it is not simply a social call, but a matter of Belmair's national well-being that causes their king to come to them wearing the sacred emblem."

"I think, Ferrex, that you are wasted as my servant," Dillon noted. "I hope you will always offer me your wisdom and your advice."

"Your Majesty flatters me," Ferrex said with a small smile.

"Nay, Ferrex, Your Majesty speaks the truth. I mean what I have said to you," Dillon replied.

"I am honored that you would have such faith in me, Your Majesty," the serving man said. "Now let us dress you, for the dragon is always punctual." And Ferrex quickly helped his master into his clothing and his boots. When he had finished he said, "You cannot don a crown, of course, Your Majesty, but wear this." He handed Dillon a thin band of gold that went about the forehead.

Brushing his dark hair, Dillon fit the gold band about his forehead. Then, holding out his hand, he watched as Ferrex pushed the royal ring seal onto the middle finger of his right hand. "Am I ready?" he asked, noting that the sky was beginning to show color upon the edges of the horizon.

"You are, Your Majesty," Ferrex said, handing Dillon his cloak. "Travel safely."

With a quick smile Dillon left the royal apartments, taking the stairs to the roof of the castle from where he would depart. A guardsman greeted him politely as he stepped out onto the flat surface of the battlements. "The dragon isn't here?" he said, surprised after Ferrex's warning.

"She comes now, Your Majesty," the guardsman said, pointing aloft.

And there in the skies between the two castles, Nidhug, the great guardian dragon of Belmair, soared in all her glory. He marveled at her size, and that she could reduce it to something more manageable in order to deal with the Belmairans. He felt like a pixie when she set down upon the castle's roof. The guardsman hurried to place the long ladder kept for this purpose against Nidhug. Without a word Dillon climbed up the ladder, settling himself in the small but comfortable pocket on Nidhug's back.

The guardsman removed the ladder, and the dragon rose slowly into the morning skies, the rising sun touching her gold lace wings so that they reflected themselves onto the earth below. It was one of the most beautiful things he had ever seen, Dillon thought from the safety of his dragon's nest.

"Good morning, Nidhug!" he called to her.

"Good morrow, Your Majesty," she answered. "We shall shortly be out over the sea, and you might wish to contemplate just what you will say to the dukes. I am certain you had no time last night to consider it, for it was late when our meeting broke up."

"Can you tell me about Dreng?" Dillon asked Nidhug.

"A good man, not overly intelligent, but ambitious. As you know he was disappointed when you were chosen to be Belmair's king. It put an end to his ambitions in that direction. But he is a loyal man," the dragon said as she flew.

"And the others?" Dillon inquired.

"Tullio of Beldane is an intellectual. He is apt to examine an issue a bit too closely and a bit too long, but he always comes to the right decision. Alban of Belia is a good fellow. Intelligent, and with a fine sense of humor. You will probably like him the best of the three on closer acquaintance," Nidhug informed Dillon. "Now settle yourself down, my lord. We have a ways to go."

Dillon took the dragon's advice. He closed his eyes and contemplated how he would approach Belmair's dukes. Each would require a different approach if he was to gain their trust and cooperation quickly. Now that the Yafir knew that the king of Belmair was aware of their existence, who knew what mischief they would create. He wanted to make peace with them. He wanted to trust them. But had too many centuries passed for the breach between them to be healed? Only time would tell him the answer. He knew that he could destroy the Yafir if he had to, but the destruction of an entire faerie race would weigh heavily upon his conscience. He smiled to himself. Another tiny bit of his mortal blood showing, Dillon thought. Faeries did not have such troublesome traits as a conscience. He was not certain it was an integral part of his Shadow blood, either. He hoped there was a way to pacify the Yafir, but he also knew that sometimes no matter how hard one tried, peace could not be gained by any other method than force. He wondered if a time would ever come when that rule no longer held.

He was surprised when he heard Nidhug announce, "There is Beltran on the horizon now, Majesty."

Looking in the direction in which they traveled he watched as the faint smudged line ahead of them grew larger and more distinct as they moved steadily toward it. Eventually he could see that the land rolled gently, and was heavily forested. And on the highest hill in the exact center of Beltran was a large building in the shape of a quadrangle, which, as Nidhug was making directly for it, Dillon assumed was the home of Duke Dreng, lord of Beltran. As they grew closer and began their descent he could see what appeared to be tiny figures, who grew larger with each passing minute, running about the courtyard of the building, pointing up.

As they landed Nidhug called out, "Fetch a ladder, for King Dillon is with me!"

Hearing this there was a great rush for the requested ladder, but Dillon noted that one servant separated himself from the others, and dashed madly into the building. The young king smiled, amused. He wondered if Dreng could reach the courtyard before he had climbed down from Nidhug's back. The ladder was brought, and Dillon pushed himself from the small passenger pouch on the dragon's back and climbed slowly down its rungs. Reaching the bottom, he turned to find a red-faced Duke Dreng awaiting him.

"Welcome to Beltran, Your Majesty!" the duke greeted Dillon, holding out his big, rough hand. "We were not expecting you. No messenger was received in advance of your arrival." Dreng sounded slightly out of breath as if he had been running. He was a stocky man with a balding head on top although the rest of his hair was shoulder length.

"The matter that brings me to Beltran, and will also take me to Beldane and Belia, is of such importance, my lord, that I wasted no time in coming. This is not an official or a state visit. Belmair is in grave danger, and I will want the aid of my dukes in solving the problems that lie ahead of us," Dillon said gravely as he shook the duke's hand.

Dreng's look was immediately concerned. "Come in, come in then, Your Majesty!" he said. "Whatever help I may render is yours." The duke led Dillon into his home.

A pretty woman came forward, and Dreng introduced her. "This is Amata, my wife. My dear, the king."

Amata curtseyed deeply. "You are most welcome to Beltran, Your Majesty," she said, smiling. "Your presence honors us."

Raising Amata up Dillon kissed her on both of her cheeks. "Your hospitality honors me," he replied in return.

"I have ordered that the Great Dragon be fed and offered a place to rest after your long journey," Amata said.

"Thank you," Dillon replied with a smile.

"My dear, the king and I have important business to discuss," Dreng said. "We will be in my library, and should not be disturbed." Without a further word he led Dillon down a wide hall with windows on one side, and into a comfortable library. "Sit down, Your Majesty. Let me get us some wine." He quickly poured two goblets, and then joined the king by the hearth.

"I will not waste your time," Dillon began. "Do you recall a legend about a faerie race called the Yafir, and their banishment from Belmair aeons ago?"

"Hmm," Dreng said. "A faerie race? It was not taught in our history of Belmair when I was a lad. And they were banished from Belmair? For what reason? Is it of import to us, Majesty? Why?"

"How many young women have been stolen from Beltran this year?"

The duke considered a long moment, and then he said, "I should have to consult with the Committee for

Missing Maidens, Majesty, but I can tell you that one of my granddaughters, Namia, is among them. She was only fourteen, and as fair a maid as you could imagine. Why do you ask?"

"Do you know how many marriages have been celebrated in Beltran this year?" Dillon pursued the issue further.

"Again, Majesty, I should have to consult with the Keeper of Marriage Records," the duke said. "But there have surely been few as our young women keep disappearing."

"King Napier IX of Belmair banished the Yafir because they dared to ask for one hundred marriageable maidens each new year. The Yafir are a small group, and they had few women. Their women were dying off or past their childbearing years. If they were to survive they needed brides for their men. But King Napier IX refused them, and told them they must leave Belmair. For him, and for the citizens of Belmair, that was the end of it," Dillon explained to his host.

"King Napier IX was right to refuse to give our women to a faerie race," Dreng said, completely forgetting the new king's bloodline.

Dillon smiled sardonically. To remind this duke of just who his king was would only embarrass him, and possibly even make an enemy of him. He was trying to bring peace to Belmair, not open hostilities on another front. Pushing his own anger at the duke's stupidity aside, he said, "Perhaps the Yafir should have applied to other faerie races for wives, but they did not. Nor did they depart Belmair. They took the women they needed for wives from among the Belmairans, and are here among us to this day," Dillon informed Dreng. "It is the Yafir who have been stealing Belmair's maidens."

Dreng's square jaw dropped open at this revelation. "*They did not leave?* But they were commanded to leave by a Belmairan king. Are you certain, Majesty? Forgive me, for I do not mean to question your word, but how can you know this is so?"

"My uncle made a summoning spell and brought their leader, Ahura Mazda, to my castle where we spoke. He admits to stealing Belmair's women over the centuries that have past. He has said he intends to keep on doing it. When I asked why it was necessary to continue kidnapping our women, he explained that while excellent breeders, Belmairan women produce more sons than daughters. And so a constant new supply of women is necessary at all times," Dillon said. "When I explained to Ahura Mazda that this practice had practically decimated our own female population, that we didn't have enough women for Belmairan men to wed, that fewer children were being born and our own population was being decimated, this Yafir laughed. He said in that case, Belmair would one day belong to the Yafir."

"The fellow is too bold by far," Dreng huffed. "You must tell him to take his people and leave Belmair. The women he has stolen may go with them for they have been contaminated by their Yafir husbands and lovers. They can never again be a part of our world, or our society."

"It is not that simple, my lord," Dillon said. Nidhug was right. Dreng wasn't particularly intelligent. He swallowed the urge to turn the duke into a bug and stomp upon him. "Their numbers could in this age be equal to ours, or even surpass ours. They have lived with us, whether you were aware of them or not, for centuries too many to number. Other than stealing Belmair's women they have been good neighbors. We must find a way to solve this problem peacefully, and to protect the women we have left while we are doing it. My uncle is now working upon a protection spell to keep our females safe from the Yafir. As soon as it is perfected we will use it. It may require gathering all the women in each of the duchies together in one place in each province.

"I came to you today, and will go on to Beldane and Belia, to inform you and your fellow dukes of this situation, and so that you be prepared to act when you are required to do so. There is still much we do not know. We do not know how the Yafir lure the women away. We do not know where they make their own homes. And the danger is greater now than ever before, for the Yafir know that we are aware of them and what they have been doing. You need magic to fight magic, Dreng. The Yafir are magic, but then so am I, and my fair queen has been taught certain magic, too, by the dragon," Dillon said. "We will solve this problem to everyone's satisfaction, I promise you."

Duke Dreng shook his head. He resembled a confused bear at this moment.

"What will you do, Majesty, to save Belmair?" he asked.

"I am not entirely certain yet," Dillon answered him candidly. "But know this, I will not allow Belmair to fall into the hands of the Yafir."

Dreng nodded. "What are we to do in the meantime, Majesty?"

"You must advise every household in Beltran to watch their young women closely," Dillon told him. "Never let them be alone."

There was a soft rap upon the library door.

"Enter!" the duke said, and the door opened to reveal the lady Amata.

"Will you come into the hall, Majesty, and take the midday meal with us?" she invited him with a sweet smile.

She was, Dillon ascertained, a second wife, for she was much younger than the duke. "Thank you, my lady," he replied. "I will admit to hunger having left Belmair at sunrise. I did not think to eat beforehand." Nay, his last meal had been with Cinnia the previous night when they had made such incredible love. He missed her already, and thought he could still smell the elusive and seductive fragrance she wore deep within his nostrils. He almost sighed aloud.

"Will you stay the night?" Dreng asked his guest when they were seated at the duke's high board and being offered bowls, platters and plates of food.

"Thank you, but nay. Nidhug and I must reach Belia today. I will spend the night there, and then tomorrow visit Beldane before returning home. I do not like leaving Cinnia, and have never since our marriage been away from her."

"Have you come to love her then?" the lady Amata asked softly, ignoring her husband's fierce look.

Dillon smiled warmly at the young woman, who obviously loved her big, bluff lord. "Aye," he admitted. "I love my queen. I have known enough women in my lifetime to realize what a treasure I have in her."

The lady Amata smiled back at her king. "I am so glad," she said. "A life without someone to love is a great tragedy."

"Woman, you talk too much," Dreng scolded her.

"Nay, she is right," Dillon replied. "You are fortunate in your own wife, my lord duke. Forbid not her words. They are wise."

Dreng looked exceedingly pleased at the young king's pronouncement.

The meal was simple, but well cooked and seasoned. The wine was rich and flavorful. When it was concluded Dillon arose, saying to his host and hostess, "I must leave you now, my lord duke. My lady Amata. I thank you for your hospitality. Share what I have told you, Dreng, with you wife and your counselors. I will send you word as we progress. Nidhug will bring it herself."

"Thank you, Majesty, for coming to Beltran with this news yourself. I see now that the dragon was sagacious when she chose you to follow Fflergant as our king." Duke Dreng bowed low as his wife curtseyed to Dillon.

He took up the lady's hand and kissed it, smiling at her blush. Then escorted by the duke he returned to the courtyard. The ladder was brought, set against Nidhug and Dillon quickly climbed up, settling into the small pouch that had been provided for him. "Farewell, my lord duke," he said, bidding Dreng goodbye as Nidhug, unfurling her lacy golden wings, rose up, up, up, into the afternoon sunshine.

Within minutes the dragon was out over the blue sea again. "Well," she said, "I hope the meal you were fed was better than mine. First those fools offered me hay and oats. When I told them I did not eat such fodder, for I was not a horse or cow, they brought me live creatures, all squawking and howling." She shook her head. "I told them to take the poor creatures away, and bring me food from their kitchens. You should see the slops I was served. It was fit only for the pigs. I can only hope that Alban keeps a better table," she grumbled.

"Reduce your size then when we arrive, and come into his hall with me," Dillon suggested. "You will sit at the high board, and eat what I eat."

"How did Dreng take your news?" Nidhug wanted to know.

"Surprised, of course, but very Belmairan. He thought the Yafir were only legend, for he hadn't been taught of them when he was a boy," Dillon said. "He is, of course, astounded that the Yafir might easily take Belmair from us. But understanding, he stands ready to cooperate when we know what we can do to protect the women. His wife is a pretty girl. Not his first, I am assuming."

"Nay, his first wife, the lady Lygia, died several years ago. I had heard he had remarried," Nidhug said.

"Sweet and soft-spoken," Dillon said with a small chuckle, "but I suspect she gets her way with him easily. A man should have a loving woman like that to care for him."

"You are a romantic fellow, my king," the dragon noted. "But given your heritage I should not be surprised." She grew silent as they flew on toward Belia.

In his place Dillon found himself dozing. The meal and the wine were taking their toll on him. He was therefore surprised when Nidhug's voice pierced his slumber.

"There is Belia below, Majesty," she told him.

"So soon?" he answered her. "Where is Alban's home?"

"Because his duchy is so mountainous, the duke's home is set on a promontory that sticks out into the sea itself. *There!* Straight ahead of us."

Looking where the dragon had indicated, Dillon saw two tall stone towers that were connected by some kind of structure he couldn't quite make out. The men-at-arms on the top of the towers began shouting as Nidhug made her approach. As the towers' heights were not big enough for her, the dragon landed on the lawn before the building.

Immediately servants came running from one of the towers. "Step into my paw," Nidhug said, and when Dillon had she lowered him carefully to the ground. "Behold, King Dillon of Belmair!" she announced loudly to the servants. "Where is Duke Alban?"

An obviously senior servant stepped forward and bowed low to Dillon. "Majesty, we were not expecting you. My master is hunting in the hills. He should be home soon. Come in! Come into the house. The fire is warm, and our wine is sweet."

"The dragon comes, too," Dillon told them, and watched delightedly as Nidhug reduced herself to a more manageable size. Together they followed the servant into Duke Alban's hall. A tall, stately woman came forward to greet them. "Your Majesty," she said. "I am the lady Ragnild, Duke Alban's wife. You are most welcome to Belia. My husband will be back by nightfall. If you had but sent ahead he would have been here to greet you himself." She curtseyed deeply.

Dillon kissed her on both cheeks as he raised her up. "There was no time to send ahead. I have tidings of great importance for your husband. The evening is time enough. I must beg hospitality for myself and the dragon for the night."

"Of course!" the lady Ragnild replied, surprised. She eyed Nidhug nervously.

"Do not fear me," Nidhug said in her most dulcet tones. "Like you, I am female."

"Oh," Ragnild replied surprised. "What will you eat for your supper, dragon?"

"My name is Nidhug," the dragon replied. "And I can only hope you keep a good table, for I do enjoy my food. Especially sweets. My cook has been with me for centuries, and is particularly skilled at cream cakes soaked in wine."

"I see," Ragnild replied nervously.

A servant brought goblets of wine, and they sat comfortably by a large hearth while the lady Ragnild instructed her servants as to the additions to the supper menu. Just as the sun was setting over the sea outside the baying of dogs could be heard. Shortly afterward Duke Alban entered his hall, and seeing the king hurried to kneel before him.

"Rise, Alban of Belia," Dillon said. "We have serious matters to discuss."

# 8

"I HAVE ALREADY visited Duke Dreng on Beltran," Dillon began. "And tomorrow I will go to Duke Tullio of Beldane. The fate of Belmair as you know it hangs in the balance tonight, my lord. There is an enemy in our midst who seeks to take our world."

"I do not understand, Majesty," Duke Alban said. "What enemy?"

"The Yafir," Dillon replied.

"Ahh. I thought them a fanciful legend! But then, were they not banished centuries ago from Belmair?" Alban responded. "The king then was Napier, the VIII or the IX. I can never remember."

"So you've heard of the Yafir," Dillon said. "Dreng was quite surprised to learn about them."

"When brains were being passed around at the dawn of creation," Alban answered the young king, "Dreng's family was somehow forgotten. The dukes of Beltran have never been noted for their intellect, Majesty."

Dillon had to chuckle at this observation. "His heart is good nonetheless."

"I suppose I should not fault him as he is married to my youngest sister," Alban replied. "Although what an intelligent girl like Amata sees in him I'll never know."

"Your sister is charming and wise," Dillon told Duke Alban. "I very much enjoyed her hospitality, and it is obvious that she loves her husband."

Alban nodded, agreeing with a small smile. "I have taken us from the reason for your unannounced visit, Majesty," he said. "Forgive me. You spoke of the Yafir."

"The Yafir felt they had no other place of refuge but Belmair. They did not leave this world. They remained. Hidden from Belmairan eyes," Dillon explained. "Do you know the reason they were banished?" And when Alban shook his head Dillon continued. "Their women, few in number, were dying away. They needed wives. They asked Napier IX for one hundred marriageable women a year. He refused, and exiled them for their temerity. They have been stealing Belmairan woman for wives ever since."

"How are we to stop this theft?" Duke Alban asked, immediately grasping the situation. "Can a mortal race war with a faerie race and win?"

"It is unlikely," Dillon said candidly. "But I am Belmair's king, and I am not mortal. I am both Shadow and faerie. With my sorcerer's skills, with my allies, I believe I can bring the Yafir to an agreement, and thereby avoid a war. It will not be easy, but I believe it can be done. The faerie races prefer revenge to war, and the Yafir have certainly had their revenge upon Belmair over the years. They have almost brought us to the extinction that once threatened them. It will require serious negotiation, but in the meantime the young women must be protected, for the Yafir will delight in snatching them while we parlay simply to show us that they will not stop until it pleases them."

Dillon then went on to explain to Duke Alban how his uncle, the faerie prince Cirillo, had returned to his own world in order to create a spell strong enough to keep Belmair's women safe. When the spell was ready Cirillo would return to Belmair, and they would weave the spell about the women so the Yafir could not take them. "It is then," Dillon told the duke, "that the Yafir will be ready to come to terms with us. In the meantime, though, the women must be protected."

"Belia is the least populous of the three duchies," Alban said. "Our landscape is not particularly hospitable. While we have a few villages in the high hills, most of my people reside along our coastline. But I will send riders out tomorrow to every village to tell them the women must never be left alone. Hopefully we can protect them from harm until your uncle fashions a strong spell that will repel the Yafir." He turned to Nidhug, who was savoring a large goblet of wine, and smiled. "You honor my house, my lady dragon. Have you visited your cave of late?"

"Some months back, my good duke," Nidhug said.

"My egg thrives, and was given a faerie blessing by the king's uncle. But it is not yet time for me to hatch it."

"I would have you know that we keep a watch on your den," Alban said.

"And I thank you for your courtesy," Nidhug replied. "The cave is well protected by certain enchantments so that the egg remains safe. But to know that you and your people watch over it for me, as well, pleases me."

The lady Ragnild came to invite them to the high board. Dillon viewed Nidhug with amusement as she watched the servers coming into the hall. As they reached midhall the line split into two. One serving the king, and his hosts; the other devoting themselves to the dragon's needs. There were several varieties of roasted meats. Two dozen chickens, six sheep, a whole boar, a side of beef. A huge, round loaf of bread was carried to the table by six serving men. A great tub of sweet butter, and two wheels of cheese, one soft and runny, the other hard and golden in color were offered, and the dragon's goblet was never allowed to empty.

Dillon could see that Nidhug was pleased. She ate with great relish, and she ate everything that they brought her. And when after the remnants of her meal were cleared away and six cakes were placed before her, the dragon almost wept with her delight. Four of the cakes were sponge that had been soaked in sweet wine, filled with jam and covered with whipped cream. Another was covered in an orange-flavored icing, and the last was a large, plain cake filled with apples and cinnamon with a topping of sugared crumbs. Nidhug sighed, and proceeded to devour them all.

When she had washed the last crumb down with her wine, the dragon turned to the lady Ragnild. "Lady, you keep a fine kitchen, and I thank you for an excellent supper. Now show me to my bed, for I must rest. My day has been long. Tomorrow will be as long, I fear, and I cannot be certain of a good meal again until I reach home."

Standing, Lady Ragnild looked relieved and curtseyed to the dragon. "I am so glad I could provide you with a tasty supper," she said. Then she led the dragon to the bedchamber that had been set aside for her in the north tower.

"Let me show you my house," Alban said to Dillon.

"I will admit to being curious as to what connects your towers," the king said.

"Come," the duke invited Dillon with a smile. He led him from his Great Hall to show him the structure connecting the halves of his home. It was a wide corridor, stone on one side, great windows that went from floor to ceiling on the other side. Upon the wall hung portraits that the duke explained were his ancestors. "There is the source of our troubles, my revered ancestor, Napier IX. The dragon preceding this Nidhug chose him to be king. There have been few kings of Belmair from Belia. He was unwed, and he was, according to family legend, obdurate, short-sighted and difficult. The king preceding him had no unwed daughter, and my ancestor never married. That is how I knew who he was, and his history. The stories that I had heard say that the Yafir lived in peace with us for the most part, and always repaid a kindness with a kindness. Now that you tell me the whole story I ask myself why we could not have given the Yafir one hundred marriageable women each year until their population had been rebuilt."

"Your thoughts take a different direction than Dreng's. He agreed with your ancestor," Dillon said.

"Dreng's mind is small and narrow," Alban replied. "I do not say that in meanness, Majesty. It is simply the way he and his people are fashioned. While it is rare that there is any change in Belmair, it is rarer still that change of any kind comes to Beltran. I, while as cautious as any Belmairan, am always ready to look at something new, to try something different. I may not change my ways, but I do try. When word came that Fflergant was breathing his last I hurried like the others to the royal castle, wondering if Dreng's young grandson would be the dragon's choice for I could see no other. Imagine my surprise to find you, our new king. A Hetarian! But the dragon had chosen you, and I would never deny Nidhug's decision in the matter of who will rule over Belmair. You will bring change to us, Majesty," Alban said. "But I suspect that you will bring it slowly and carefully so that we are not too discommoded." He smiled. "My oath to you was true, Majesty."

"I know that," Dillon told him. "And while the world I came from is known as Hetar, Alban of Belia, remember I am not Hetarian. I am faerie and I am Shadow.

With these two strengths I can hopefully prevail over the Yafir, and keep Belmair safe."

"Aye," Alban answered him. "I believe that you can, Majesty."

They returned to the hall to speak on other matters, and then the lady Ragnild led the king to a guest chamber high in the north tower. Alone, Dillon looked out over the sea below. The skies above him were filled with stars, and searching carefully he found Hetar twinkling silvery-blue. He had been here on Belmair for several months now, and he realized that while he had good memories of his previous years, he felt more at home here than anywhere else. How odd, he thought, that he should have been born to this destiny. He had always thought he would move between Shunnar and Terah, continuing to learn from Kaliq and from his mother. He had assumed that while his little brother, Taj, was Magnus Hauk's heir, that he would be his mother's right hand.

It had been months since he had seen Lara. Hopefully he would see her soon and introduce her to his bride. He had always been close to his mother, but oddly he found that he didn't miss her. Was it the great distance separating them that made him feel that way? Or was it that he had found purpose as king of Belmair, and a love of his own in Cinnia? Whatever it was, Dillon knew that he was truly happy. And he also knew that such happiness was a rare commodity. Leaving the window, he climbed into bed and slept soundly until he was awakened early the following morning by a man servant sent by the lady Ragnild.

After a hearty breakfast he and Nidhug thanked their host and hostess, bidding them farewell. Out on the green lawn before the two towers the dragon regained her full size. She lifted Dillon up to the safety of the pouch, where he settled in. Her lacy golden wings unfolded slowly, catching the rays of the rising sun. Then the Great Dragon of Belmair soared into the blue morning skies and out over the sea, turning toward Beldane.

They flew for the next several hours, and Dillon told the dragon of his talk with Duke Alban. "I quite liked the man. He is so different from Dreng."

"I knew you would make a friend of him," Nidhug said. "His mind is more open than most Belmairans. Now you will deal last with Tullio of Beldane. Be patient with him. His eagerness to look at every side of an issue can be irritating."

They reached Beldane, and Dillon was charmed by the lovely meadows and glens of the land below him. The duke's gracious manor house was set upon a small hill. Below, his vineyards stretched out, and from above, the workers harvesting the grapes could be easily seen as they went about the business of clipping the bunches of grapes, and setting them gently in willow baskets. Seeing the dragon as she descended, they cried out, pointing skyward. One ran from the vineyards toward the manor house.

Nidhug landed on a gravel path before the house, disembarking the king. Folding her wings, she shrank herself down. She was taking no chances with being fed slops this day. Duke Tullio hurried from the house, a lady by his side. He was a very tall, slender man with thoughtful gray eyes. He bowed low.

"Your Majesty! This is most unexpected, but you and Belmair's dragon are more than welcome to Beldane and to my home. This is my sister, the lady Margisia, who serves as my hostess as I am widowed." He drew the lady forward, and she curtseyed.

Dillon greeted them both, and then he said, "We must speak on matters most serious affecting Belmair, my lord duke. Take me to your privy chamber, and I will begin my discourse. Nidhug will join us."

"Will you honor us at the midday meal, Your Majesty?" the lady Margisia asked.

"We will!" Dillon said enthusiastically.

"I have a particular fondness for sweets," Nidhug said to the lady Margisia.

She appeared somewhat startled to have the dragon address her so directly. She gulped as discreetly as she could, and replied, "I will tell our pastry chef."

"I am one of those irritating creatures who can eat all and everything they desire, and never lose my figure," Nidhug noted. "I shall look forward to our meal."

Duke Tullio led them to his book-filled library, and offering them refreshment, he looked to Dillon. The young king carefully explained the serious problem that Belmair was facing from the Yafir. Tullio listened closely and when Dillon had finished, he said, "You are absolutely certain this creature you summoned was Yafir?"

Dillon nodded.

"Hmm," Tullio said. "But how can you be certain that they did not leave Belmair when they were ordered to go?"

"Because Ahura Mazda said they did not. He had no reason to lie, and he has admitted to stealing the women over the centuries that have passed," Dillon replied.

"Perhaps he has just said that to you because he wanted to frighten you," Tullio responded. "You say he has no reason to lie to you, but how can you know that?"

"I am sure that this Yafir is quite capable of lying," Dillon said. "But knowing the nature of faeries like him, he is less apt to lie when he feels he has the upper hand. Indeed he will brag in a case like that which, of course, he did."

"But—" Tullio began.

*"Enough!"* Nidhug said. "We know what has happened to the young women of Belmair, yet you attempt to argue the point to what end, I cannot imagine. The king has told you what we have discovered. He has told you what we propose to do. All that is required in this matter is your cooperation, my lord. Send to your villages and farms that their young women cannot be left alone. Prepare a place where you may gather them all together when Prince Cirillo's spell is completed. Do you understand?"

"But what if this faerie creating the spell is actually

helping these Yafir?" Tullio wanted to know. "Have you considered that?"

"*This faerie* is my uncle," Dillon said. "Like me, he was schooled by Kaliq of the Shadows. He is totally trustworthy. If you do not trust him, my lord, then you cannot possibly trust me."

"Nay, my lord! You are the king. The dragon's choice! I trust you without question," Duke Tullio protested.

"Then you must trust my uncle, as well, my lord, for I would trust him with my life," Dillon told the duke.

"I will follow your instructions to the letter, Majesty," Duke Tullio responded.

"I would think so," Nidhug said irritably. She was hungry now, and knew that she had a long flight ahead of her if they were to be home tonight.

"I thank you," Dillon said.

They repaired to the Great Hall of the manor house, and were offered a midday meal. Then, thanking Duke Tullio and his sister, the lady Margisia, they departed Beldane for home. The sun was setting as they finally arrived at Belmair's royal castle. Nidhug dropped down onto the flat roof of the battlements, her great wings coming slowly to a stop and folding themselves against her sides. Nidhug immediately shrank herself down.

"I have had enough of flying, Majesty, and will walk the distance between our homes," she said. "Sarabeth will have a most excellent meal for me. The woman is a treasure. But first let me pay my respect to Cinnia, and we shall tell her of our visits to the three dukes."

Together dragon and king descended from the battlements down a staircase into the Great Hall of the castle. Reaching it, they saw there was no fire in the fireplaces, which Dillon thought odd. Even when there was no one in the hall the fires were kept going. There were no servants in sight, either.

"Cinnia will be in the family hall," Dillon said.

But when they reached it the hearth was also cold, and there was no one in sight.

Nidhug experienced a shiver down her back.

"Britto!" Dillon called out. "To me!" His senses were tingling.

Britto came running at the sound of his master's voice. His fat cheeks were pink with the exertion. His blue eyes were red with apparent weeping. "Majesty! Majesty!" he cried, and he flung himself at Dillon's feet sobbing.

"What is the matter?" Dillon demanded to know.

"The Yafir have taken the queen!" his steward sobbed.

"How do you know this?" Dillon asked the man.

"We were here in the little hall last night," Britto began. "After the evening meal the queen had gone to her apothecary to do some work. I went to tell her that we would need a new serving girl in the kitchens, and to ask her permission to hire one. Then *he* appeared. He caught the queen's hand, and they argued but he said, *'Come, Cinnia. You are mine now, for I marked you from your birth.'* And before she could protest they were gone, Your Majesty. There was naught we could do. I swear it!"

"This is all my fault!" the dragon cried, distraught. "I should not have left her!"

"Nay, it is not your fault. Even surrounded by servants, the Yafir were able to take Cinnia. What little magic you taught my queen, my sorceress, was not enough, for your gifts lie in protecting Belmair, Nidhug," Dillon comforted the dragon.

Still the dragon wept large tears in her sorrow.

"Light the fires in both halls, Britto," Dillon said. "Nidhug, cease your caterwauling. It does not help matters. Sit down! The fire is being rebuilt." Dillon drew in several long, deep breaths. This did not bode well for a peaceful solution to the problems between the Belmairans and the Yafir. He watched while the fire sprang up, and soon it was blazing merrily. The room was warming.

"What are we going to do?" Nidhug, who had finally recovered herself, asked.

"I intend to summon that bold Yafir. He has no choice but to answer my call for I am stronger than he. *Ahura Mazda, hear me well. A Shadow-faerie weaves this spell. Come to me! You must obey! Or see your powers melt away.*"

"What do you want, Dillon of the Shadows?" the Yafir's voice asked irritably. But he did not show himself.

"Reveal yourself, sly one!" Dillon commanded him. "Or are you afraid to face me, Ahura Mazda?"

The Yafir laughed. "Why should I be afraid of you?" he said, still cloaked.

"Your childishness wearies me," Dillon replied, and pointing with a single finger he tore away the Yafir's cloak of invisibility.

Revealed, the Yafir looked annoyed. "What do you want of me, king of Belmair?" he said.

"Return my wife immediately," Dillon told him.

"Nay! She was marked from her birth for me," was the surprising reply. "Each female child born in Belmair is marked at birth by one of our own. Then when they are grown if that Yafir wishes to take that female he does. Cinnia was selected to be mine," Ahura Mazda said. "I took only what belonged to me."

"Cinnia and I were joined under the ancient laws of Belmair," Dillon responded.

"The laws of Belmair mean nothing to the Yafir. We have our own codes of honor and behavior to live by," Ahura Mazda said. "Resign yourself to the fact that you will never again see Cinnia."

"Do not force me to destroy the Yafir," Dillon said grimly.

"If you could destroy us you already would have," Ahura Mazda answered him.

"That is where you are wrong, Yafir," Dillon spat. "I prefer the ways of peace to those of war. I would make a long-lasting peace between the Yafir and the Belmairans. I would right the wrongs done to you by that Belmairan king so long ago."

"Do you think I do not know what you have been

doing, what you plan?" Ahura Mazda said angrily. "You seek a spell to keep our women from us! Without the women our race will die. I will not let you do that, king of Belmair!"

"You have grown greedy in your desires, Yafir," Dillon replied. "The women are Belmairan, and without them our race will die. I will not let you do that!"

"You cannot stop me, son of Kaliq! Soon we will outnumber you, and when we do we will take this world and drive you from it as the Belmairans once tried to drive us! You do not even know where we hide ourselves. We come and we go as we choose." He sneered. "You must find us before you can accomplish that which you seek to do. But you will not find us. No one ever has. Force me to face you as many times as you want, king of Belmair. My presence will do naught for you. Cinnia is mine. Soon she will whimper beneath me, begging me for my favors. And if she pleases me I will grant her ecstasy such as she has never known. I have waited long to mate with her. Now let me go! There is no purpose in my remaining here with you, is there?" And Ahura Mazda was gone in a puff of scarlet smoke.

Dillon looked stunned. Not simply by the Yafir's words, but by the fact that he felt helpless. Dillon, son of Kaliq of the Shadows and Lara, daughter of Ilona, queen of the Forest Faeries, felt totally helpless for the first time in a very long while. The last time, the only time he could remember this feeling was when his mother had been stolen by the Twilight Lord. He had only been a boy then, and untrained in the ways of magic. But he was a man now, and considered a great sorcerer. Yet he felt powerless to do anything to help himself, or to help Cinnia.

"Call to your father," Nidhug begged him.

"Nay," Dillon said as suddenly he felt strength flowing back into his veins. "I am a man now, and not a child, Nidhug. Eventually I will ask my father for his aid, and possibly my mother, as well. But not now. Belmair is mine to care for and rule over. Therefore I must find a solution to this puzzle I have been given to solve. What good are my powers if I cannot use them successfully? Cinnia is safe. The worst that can happen to her is that the Yafir overcomes her reluctance to mate with him. He can only do that by working some sort of enchantment. And I must accept that he will and sooner than later. He thinks that like a mortal I will consider my wife soiled, and no longer worthy of my love. But Ahura Mazda is wrong, Nidhug. Cinnia and I are more than husband and wife. We are soul mates. There will be no golden light and crackling of lightning when the Yafir takes her. Of that I am certain," Dillon said with a small smile.

"What if she gives him a child?" Nidhug asked.

"She will not," Dillon said. "I set a silent spell upon her when we were first wed, for I did not want her with child until we had settled this matter. A child might have been used against us in this dispute. Even if the Yafir discovers my spell, he cannot reverse it. Only I can do that. But I need to find an advantage over this bold Yafir lord. I must learn where they dwell, for they know where we dwell. That is their greatest secret, Nidhug."

"How will you do that?" the dragon asked him.

"It will take time," he admitted to her. "I will have to cast any number of spells. One will flow into the other, and the next and the next until the answer is revealed. It is very much like peeling an onion, my dear Nidhug. Now go home, and let Sarabeth feed you, my good dragon. I must go to my tower to begin my work."

"I shall not eat a thing," Nidhug said sadly as she left him. But when she reached her own castle across the gardens, Tavey and Sarabeth, already privy to the news of Cinnia's kidnapping and knowing how distraught their mistress would be, were waiting with her favorite foods, and spent a long evening coaxing some of them into the dragon.

"You need your strength, mistress," Tavey pointed out to her. "Especially if you are to help the young king in his quest."

Nidhug ate, but in truth her appetite had almost disappeared. When she had finished she went to her apartments alone and called out to Kaliq of the Shadows. *"Prince Kaliq, hear my call. Come to me from out yon wall!"*

Kaliq appeared before her. Seeing the dragon, he knew at once that something was very wrong. "What is it, old friend?" he asked her.

"Cinnia has been kidnapped by the Yafir!" Nidhug began, and then she told him all that had happened since she had last seen him. She concluded by saying, "I told the king to call upon you, but he would not."

Kaliq smiled softly. "He is right, Nidhug. This is his problem to solve. He is a man, but would feel less so if his father were to come and make everything all right. He has the intellect and the powers necessary to handle this situation. And Dillon is not a fool. He will call upon me when he needs me. Seeking out the lair of the Yafir is the right first step." Then with a wave of his hand Kaliq enclosed himself and the dragon in a bubble that, while clear within, appeared deep purple and impenetrable to anyone outside of it. "I do not wish to be overheard, and the Yafir enjoy listening, which is why they knew what we were planning. We should have considered it. Cirillo will be here tomorrow. He has found the perfect spell to prevent the Yafir from stealing any more of the Belmairan women. Once we will have cut off their supply of wives and lovers we have our first bargaining chip," Kaliq told the dragon. "Dillon will know just what to do. Now, my dear, I must return to Shunnar. I left a most beautiful lover's side when you called." The bubble about them dissolved, and Kaliq was gone.

There was nothing more to be done, Nidhug realized when she found herself alone again. She climbed into bed and slept until well into the next day when Tavey came with a two-gallon cup of sweet hot chocolate to awaken her.

"The king calls, mistress," her servant said as he handed her the cup.

"I must have a warm oil shower first," Nidhug said. "The travel winds have dried my scales dreadfully, and they are sore."

"I will send a message to the king that you will be there within the hour," Tavey said. "I have already turned on your oil shower, mistress."

Nidhug sighed. "You are truly perfection, dear Tavey," she told him as she rose from her bed and handed him back the now-empty cup.

True to her servant's word the dragon arrived at the royal castle exactly an hour later. To her delight she found Prince Cirillo awaiting her with the king. There was a decidedly lustful look in his eyes as he met her gaze, and she fluttered her purple eyelashes at him playfully. Cirillo grinned as he realized without either of them saying a word that she had missed him as much as he, to his great surprise, had missed her.

"Put a bubble about us while we speak," Nidhug said softly to the two men.

Dillon nodded and enclosed the three of them. "That was clever of you, Nidhug, and a thought worthy of my father. The Yafir have obviously been lurking and listening. Cirillo has the spell. Now we must decide the best way of reaching all of the Belmairan women in danger from the Yafir."

"We must bring all the women together at the same time," Nidhug said. "You have the means to do this. To send me to each duchy will only trumpet our intentions."

"Agreed," Dillon replied. "Best to strike quickly." He looked to his uncle. "The tunnels?"

"Aye, but we will need a fourth person. Nidhug is not strong enough to use my spell. It is woven very tightly, and could injure her if she attempted to use it," Cirillo said. "We can call upon Kaliq or your mother, or my mother."

"I would like to leave my parents out of this," Dillon said.

Cirillo nodded. "I understand," he said. "Mother would probably do it. She's been dying to come to Belmair as I have spoken so highly of it."

"Then I will ask her," Dillon replied. "But let us first plan it all to the last detail."

"Agreed!" Cirillo said. "The tunnels must be opened swiftly. To where?"

"The Great Halls of the three dukes," Nidhug suggested to them.

"Aye," Dillon said. "They are commodious enough for what we need to do."

"And then," Cirillo said, "the spell to bring all the women of childbearing age to each hall must be quickly spoken. They will arrive instantly, and certainly the women will be frightened."

"We set a soothing spell in each hall as we enter it so the women appearing a moment later will not be alarmed," Dillon replied.

"And then my spell must be pronounced immediately," Cirillo responded. "Only then will the women of

Belmair be safe. Once they are, dear nephew, we may move on to learning where the Yafir hide themselves."

"They have taken Cinnia," Dillon informed his uncle.

"I am sorry, Nephew," Cirillo answered. "But you must remember that the Yafir believe that they are fighting for their lives. They will do whatever they must to save themselves and their own world."

"Ahura Mazda said they mark each female born in Belmair, and that Cinnia had been marked for him," Dillon continued.

"How do you feel about this?" Cirillo asked, curious to learn if any of Dillon's mortal nature would reveal itself in this particular matter.

"She is mine," Dillon replied simply.

Cirillo nodded, pleased. "Shall I fetch Mother?" he asked.

"I will go to her," Dillon said. "You know how she enjoys a display of good manners and a bit of groveling." He chuckled.

"At least let me send you," Cirillo answered.

"Aye, I should appreciate that," Dillon responded. "I am weary, for I have spent half the night gathering materials to begin my work."

The faerie prince dissolved the bubble in which they had been standing. Then with a twist of his wrist he pointed to the stone wall before them and a light-filled tunnel opened itself. Without another word Dillon walked into the tunnel and disappeared down its length as the tunnel closed, and the wall became a wall once again. Cirillo turned to Nidhug. "He will be gone for some hours, my pet. Do you think we can find some way to amuse ourselves in the interim?"

The dragon nodded, and suddenly they were in her bedchamber. The faerie prince walked to the chamber door and locked it. Turning back, he smiled at the big-breasted redheaded woman now awaiting him in her bed. She was quite naked, and her milky-white skin aroused him greatly. He walked toward her, his garments falling away as he came. "We shall have a far more amusing time today, my dragon lover," Cirillo said, "than my unfortunate nephew, your earnest young king, will have with my mother." And laughing he flung himself into the bed.

As he did, Dillon found himself at the end of the magical tunnel facing his grandmother, Ilona, queen of the Forest Faeries. "What are you doing here?" she greeted him. "Does your mother know where you are? How could you go off like that to Belmair and marry without us there to give you our faerie blessing? You are an ungrateful boy. When I think of all that I have done for you…" She stopped a moment, and then said, "Why are you grinning at me like that, Dillon?"

Walking up to her, the young king hugged the beautiful faerie. "It is good to see you, too, Grandmother," he told her, and kissed her cheek.

"Pah! You cannot wheedle me, you wretched brat." But Ilona was smiling back at him. "You want something, don't you? You never come to visit your grandmother unless you want something," she accused.

"That isn't entirely true, you beautiful termagant, but

this time I do want something," he admitted. "I need your help, Grandmother. I need it badly."

"Your father made you a king," Ilona said. "What more could you want?"

"May we sit here in your dayroom, Grandmother, so I may tell you all that has happened these last few months?" he asked her.

"You look tired," Ilona said.

"I was up all night bringing together the many materials I will need to create a powerful spell," he answered her.

"Wine! Faerie cakes!" Ilona said, and immediately a servant appeared with a tray bearing the required items. "First you must take a bit of nourishment, my grandson. Then you will tell me everything." And she led him to an upholstered settee, sitting next to him as she fed him faerie cakes and wine. As he ate he felt his eyes growing heavy.

"What have you done, Grandmother?" he asked, even knowing as he inquired.

"You'll only sleep two hours, my darling," she told him. "Then we will speak."

"Do…not call…Mother," he said.

"I won't," she promised him, and with a wave of her hand as she arose the settee turned into a soft bed. Ilona sat quietly watching him sleep.

"Is that Dillon?" Thanos, the queen's consort, came into the room. He was a handsome and dignified faerie man. "What is he doing here?"

"He has come for my help," Ilona said.

"Will you give it to him?" Thanos asked her, curious.

"Of course! He is my grandson, my blood," Ilona replied.

"Is Cirillo's aid not enough?" Thanos said.

"Obviously not," Ilona answered. "And how did you know Cirillo was helping him? I thought only your trees were of interest to you."

"Cirillo is my son, too, my dear Ilona," Thanos remarked drily. "He does speak with me now and again. You are such a jealous creature, Ilona, where your young men are concerned, aren't you?" Bending, Thanos kissed the top of her gilt head. "I will leave you to watch over your grandson, my dear, and go back to my trees. They, too, have their difficulties, but are not as complicated as faeries and mortals tend to be."

In precisely two hours, as Ilona had promised him, Dillon awoke. He felt enormously refreshed and revitalized. There had, of course, been magic in the sleeping potion she had added to his wine. He stretched and sat up. Immediately the bed turned back into a settee, and his grandmother was seated next to him. "Thank you," he said.

"Now tell me what is happening in Belmair, and why you need my help," Ilona said. "Why did you not call your mother?"

"As Belmair's king it is my right to ask for help from whomever I choose to ask," Dillon began. Then he explained everything that had happened to date, concluding, "I need three magical beings to go into the Great Halls of the three dukes to instantly transport all the young women in each duchy, married or unmarried, into those halls, and then to speak the spell that will protect them from the Yafir. You, Cirillo and I will be those magical beings, Grandmother."

"What of the dragon?" Ilona wanted to know.

"She will remain behind in my Great Hall to calm the women who are brought there. She is capable of protecting the hall and the women in it from the Yafir until we return back through the tunnels to work the spell on them ourselves," Dillon said.

"What is she like, this dragon of yours?" Ilona wanted to know.

"Beautiful, kindly, amusing, intelligent," he said.

"Intelligent? That does not sound particularly Belmairan," Ilona observed.

Dillon laughed aloud. "You are jealous of Nidhug," he said wickedly.

"Be careful, you rude boy," his grandmother warned him. "Remember that you need my help. I care not if the Yafir take every female on Belmair for their own. Actually if they did gain control of that world they would be less troublesome."

"I think not," Dillon said. "Remember that for centuries no one in the magic kingdoms has heard or seen the Yafir. They are outcasts, nomads, scorned by all. But give them their own world, Grandmother, and who knows what havoc they will raise with the rest of us." Then he laughed softly at the surprised look upon her face.

"Oh, rude boy, how hot your faerie blood runs! I

am proud of you," Ilona said. "I see cruelty in you you have yet to even tap. I cannot wait to tell your mother!" Then she grew thoughtful a moment. "Why have you not asked for Lara's help?"

"I didn't think a king should run to his mother or father at the first sign of trouble," Dillon told her.

"So you ran to your grandmother instead?" she replied.

"Mortals know you more for *who* you are, Grandmother, than for our blood tie," Dillon said. "Besides, the dragon could not have restored her size quickly enough after coming through the tunnel, and then used the spells necessary in time. She will play her part in my hall. Now, will you help me?"

"Of course I will help you, Dillon," Ilona said.

"Then let us return to Belmair, Grandmother. I only wish my bride could be there to greet you," he said sadly.

"The girl is as protected as she can possibly be," Ilona said. "And if she finally is coerced into entertaining the Yafir lord's cock, she will appreciate yours so much more when she is returned to you. Your reputation as a lover has seeped forth from Shunnar where your loss is bemoaned, and your stamina revered."

Dillon laughed, but then he grew serious. "I did protect Cinnia, but I never considered that the Yafir would touch her. That was not simply foolish of me. It was arrogant. I should have put a spell about the castle. In my eagerness to solve this problem I overlooked the obvious."

"The Yafir are a very difficult faerie race," Ilona told him. "They have become so used to being reviled that they do not recognize kindness or honesty when they see it. They are probably the most selfish of us all, for they think only of themselves all the time. You held out a hand of friendship, and Ahura Mazda spit on it. If you cannot bring him around, Dillon, you will have no choice but to destroy him and send him into Limbo. They are, it seems, their own worst enemy. But you must try to help them in spite of themselves, for like us they are a faerie race," she advised him. "Let us go, rude boy." And with a twist of her delicate wrist and an elegantly pointed finger, she opened a tunnel back to Belmair for them, and together they raced through it from the palace of the Forest Faeries to the Great Hall of the royal castle where Britto almost swooned at the sight of the golden light streaming suddenly into the large chamber as the king of Belmair and his grandmother appeared from out of it.

"Your Majesty!" the steward gasped, swaying upon his feet.

"You'll get used to all this magic eventually, Britto," Dillon replied, laughing. "This great lady is my grandmother, Ilona, queen of the Forest Faeries."

Britto bowed low. "Welcome to Belmair, great lady," he said, his eyes taking in her beauty, and becoming hers in that moment.

"Thank you," Ilona said in her most dulcet tones. She recognized the steward's look of admiration and adoration.

"See that my grandmother has proper quarters and women to serve her," Dillon ordered the steward. "And where is Prince Cirillo?"

"He is with the dragon," Britto answered. "Shall I send for him?"

"Send for them both," Dillon answered.

A serving man came with a tray holding goblets of wine for them.

"Delicious," Ilona said, tasting hers. "My son has spent the hours you have been away seeking my help with his lover," she noted. "A dragon! I would have never considered such a thing. But then Cirillo has always liked older females."

"Nidhug is good magic," Dillon said. "Her heart is a kind one. She is heartbroken that while she carried me to my three duchies Cinnia was stolen away. She raised my queen, and taught her simple magic and healing skills."

"That is why they call your wife the sorceress of Belmair?" Ilona said.

"Yes," Dillon replied. "But she has the ability to be great one day. I will teach her myself. I wish I had already begun her tutelage in stronger magic. Then maybe she might have protected herself from the Yafir lord."

"Hindsight is a fine gift," Ilona noted. "Cease your fretting and concentrate on the task at hand." She looked about her. "This is a good hall, Dillon."

They sat speaking quietly of mundane matters for almost an hour, and then Cirillo entered the hall.

"Mother," he said, coming quickly up to her, kissing her cheek.

"I scent lust upon you, my son," Ilona said wickedly.

"I bathed!" he protested.

"Oh, please," Ilona replied. "Whenever you are in heat you reek of passion. But it pleases me that you are more like me than your father. Where is your dragon?"

"She will be here shortly," Cirillo said. "She thought you might like to see me alone first."

"Ah, she is thoughtful," Ilona remarked.

Nidhug entered the hall quietly, and made her way to where the others were. "Greetings, Your Majesty. Greetings, queen of the Forest Faeries," she said.

Ilona's green eyes moved slowly over the dragon. They narrowed, then opened again. Finally she said, "You are really quite lovely."

"As are you," Nidhug answered. "I can see from where Cirillo gets his beauty."

"Enough!" the prince of the Forest Faeries exclaimed. "We have work to do."

"Do not be rude, Cirillo!" Ilona snapped. "Nidhug and I must become acquainted sooner than later. And I actually believe I might like her."

"Indeed, Grandmother, and we shall all sit together tonight at the high board and speak on all manner of things. Nidhug will remain for the meal. Now, however, my uncle is correct. We have work to do."

"Oh, very well," Ilona agreed. "Just as long as Nidhug and I may become better acquainted," she purred.

"Assuredly, great queen," Nidhug murmured back.

"And I will expect you to tell me all about Cirillo when he was a little lad. I have an egg of my own. Not yet hatched, of course, and I am not even certain yet of its sex, but I can certainly equate with a mother's love." She fluttered her thick purple eyelashes at Ilona.

"You have a dragon mate then?" Ilona said, and she smiled, but the smile quickly faded when Nidhug spoke again.

"Nay, but it is my duty to provide for a successor, and so I allowed one fine young male dragon passing through our world to help me in the creation of that egg. He flew off when he learned he had been fucking the great high dragon of Belmair, and I have not seen him since, nor do I ever expect to see him again," Nidhug said sweetly.

"Later, ladies," Dillon said in what he hoped passed for a stern and firm voice.

Cirillo simply looked relieved when both his mother and the dragon turned to the king with questioning faces. He quickly produced a bubble about them so they might speak in private. "Shall we begin?" he asked them. "You will need to learn my spell," he said. "I will speak it to you now. Memorize it carefully. *Protect the women of Belmair from all harm, and the Yafir. Keep them close within their home. They cannot with a Yafir roam. This spell is an unseen token. It cannot, shall not, ere be broken.*"

"It is a fine spell," Nidhug said.

"A bit simple, perhaps," Ilona noted, "but it should be effective."

"Say it back to me," Cirillo told them, and they did. "Good. Now let us all use the same summoning spell to bring the women into each hall. *Bring all the young women of*—insert the duchy name here—now, *to me, so they may protected be. This hall from Yafir is now sealed. My magic cannot be revealed.* That should do it nicely," Cirillo noted.

"Nidhug," Dillon said to the dragon, "you will remain in this hall to summon all the young women in this section of the kingdom. Count to three before you call them. Then use the protection spell. Each of us will go to a different duchy. I will go to Beltran. Cirillo, you go to Belia, and Grandmother, you will go to Beldane. As soon as you have used the protection spell, return the girls, and come back quickly." He looked at them saying, "Are we ready?"

They nodded, and then turning as one, the faerie trio opened the tunnels to their destinations and raced into the golden light.

"One. Two. Three," Nidhug said. And then, *"Bring all the young women of Belmair to me, so they may protected be. This hall from Yafir is now sealed. My magic cannot be revealed."*

And the hall was filled with all females of childbearing years. They looked about them, startled, and then seeing the dragon gasped with a single collective voice. Nidhug immediately spoke the spell.

*"Protect the women of Belmair from all harm and the Yafir. Keep them close within their home. They can-*

*not with a Yafir roam. This spell is an unseen token. It cannot, shall not, ere be broken."*

There was total silence in the hall. "You are safe now from the Yafir, women of Belmair." Nidhug told them. "Now I will return you to your homes." She did so with a wave of her paw, and was surprised at how strong her magic had suddenly become. It had to be her contact with Cirillo, she thought. About her the tunnels were opened again, and her three companions dashed back into the hall as the tunnels closed behind them. "I have done my part," she told them. "The young women in this section of our world are now safe."

"Alban sends his thanks," Cirillo told Dillon.

"Tullio would send his, but I couldn't remain to wait while he nattered on about whether the spell was foolproof, and asked just exactly how I could be certain," Ilona said. "The man is a pedantic bore, Dillon."

"And Dreng is relieved, but says he wished the spell had been in effect before he lost his granddaughter," Dillon told them.

"And now, rude boy, where is that feast you promised us all?" Ilona stepped up to the high board. "Nidhug, my dear, do come and sit next to me. We have so much to chat about," she told the beautiful dragon. "And the whole evening in which to do so." She smiled brightly.

"There is the real dragon," Cirillo murmured low to Dillon as his lover went to seat herself by his parent.

The king of Belmair laughed.

# 9

WHEN NAPIER IX had pronounced their banishment centuries before, the Yafir had lived in peace with their neighbors, much like them but for the magic they possessed. Told they were to leave Belmair they had made a collective decision to remain. The question was, of course, where they might hide themselves so that they would never be discovered by the Belmairans. Beltran's forests were deep, but because they took up much of the duchy, the forests were active with hunters. Beldane's rolling glens didn't offer enough hidden nooks, and Belia's mountains were too cold. The main province itself, while possessing all the traits of the other three, was too populated. There remained but one place that would allow them to be totally hidden from all of Belmair.

The Yafir had made their new home beneath the seas of Belmair. The land entry into this new world of theirs could be found, if one had known to look for it, in an isolated beach cave on the far side of Belia where the coast was too rough-hewn for settlement and therefore deserted. Using their magic, the Yafir had created towns sealed within great bubbles anchored to the ocean floor. Self-contained, they no longer had any need for the surface world of Belmair above them, except in the matter of females. The sunlight filtered dimly into their new settlements. The sea creatures grew used to them, and their homes were deep enough to ride out the storms.

In the beginning they had taken the one hundred women of childbearing years that Napier IX had refused to give them. The women had come from each of the provinces, including the main one itself. Some of the women had conceived life immediately. Those who had not were then given to other Yafir males until they, too, were with child. Now and again, when a woman could not conceive, she was restored back to her own world. Those women, however, returned without memories that extended beyond the time they were taken. And to punish them for having proved useless to the Yafir, they were returned as old women. The women who were kept by the Yafir were spoiled beyond all mortal women, and lavished with riches each time they bore a child. Those who birthed daughters were the most fortunate, for the matings between Yafir and mortal seemed to produce more males than females. The anomaly only created the need for more and more women.

Cinnia had been in her apothecary grinding lavender into powder to be mixed into soap. Her pestle scraped against the sides of the stone mortar as she worked. The lovely fragrance of the flower rose up to assail her nostrils. It was late in the day, and the sun was low on the horizon. She was hungry, and the scent of the lavender, which was a sleeping aid, was making her drowsy. It was then she sensed she was not alone. Turning about, she saw the Yafir, Ahura Mazda, observing her.

"What do you want?" Cinnia asked him. Her eyes were heavy. She struggled to keep them open even as she realized he was casting a spell upon her.

"Stop!" she cried, her own mind desperately seeking a spell to stop him.

"I marked you for my own at your birth, Cinnia," Ahura Mazda said. "You cannot resist me, for your magic is sweet and simple. Mine is fierce and strong. It is time now for you to come with me." He reached out to take her hand in his.

Cinnia shrank from him. "Leave me be, Yafir! I have a husband, and you are my enemy! Begone!" She flung her pestle at him.

"You have a fiery spirit, Cinnia," Ahura Mazda told her, laughing. "I shall enjoy taming you, and make no mistake about it, tame you I will! But I will not break your great spirit. Now, come!" Stepping forward, he grasped her by her small hand.

His touch rendered her weak, but Cinnia struggled nonetheless to get free of him.

And then she felt as if her entire body was melting away. She had no feeling but for the hand holding hers tightly. She felt herself fading away, her eyes closed despite her desperate attempts to keep them open, and then all was darkness. The cat who kept Cinnia company in her apothecary watched astonished as his mistress and her companion disappeared in a puff of scarlet smoke. The fur went up on his feline back. He yowled, frightened, and then he ran out of the room past Britto, who stared openmouthed.

When Cinnia once more opened her eyes, she found herself lying upon a bed draped with sea-green silks. Confused, she struggled to remember what had happened to her. After several long and frightening minutes, her memory returned. She had been stolen by the Yafir lord, Ahura Mazda. What was it he had said? *I marked you for my own at your birth?* What did he mean? And where was she? Cinnia jumped up from the bed, and immediately collapsed onto the floor. Her legs had simply given out beneath her, she realized, shocked. What was the matter with her? Two women came at once to help her back onto the bed again.

"Where am I?" Cinnia asked them.

"You are in the lord's castle," one of them answered her.

Cinnia attempted to move from the bed again but the woman cautioned her.

"Do not. Your legs have been enchanted to keep you where the lord put you," she explained. "New arrivals are always agitated in one way or another." She smiled.

"I am Cinnia, queen of Belmair," Cinnia told the woman. "Your master has erred by stealing me. My husband, the king, is a great sorcerer. He will destroy Ahura Mazda, and all that belongs to him for this."

"There, there, my dear," the woman said in kindly tones. "You must not be distressed. Yafirdom is a wonderful world in which to live. You will be very happy here, I assure you. And no one from Belmair will ever find you. 'Tis best to put any hope of returning there from your thoughts quickly. I am Arlais, one of Ahura Mazda's wives. My companion is Minau, another of the lord's wives. Are you hungry or thirsty?"

"When will the use of my legs be returned to me?" Cinnia asked them. Arlais was tall with auburn hair that was styled into two braids. Minau was of average height, and had short, white-blond curls.

"I don't know," Arlais said.

"I cannot just sit or lie here forever," Cinnia said impatiently.

"Oh, the lord will be here soon," Arlais responded cheerfully.

"How long have I been here?" Cinnia asked her.

"He put you here several days ago," Arlais told her. "We have been watching over you so you would not be frightened when you awakened. Now surely you are hungry or thirsty," she said again. "What would you like me to get you?"

Cinnia shook her head. "Nothing," she said. "I want nothing but to go home."

Ahura Mazda entered the chamber as Cinnia spoke. He was dressed as always in blue and green silks.

Arlais ran to him with a distressed cry. "Husband,

she has just awakened, but she will neither eat nor drink. What shall we do?"

The Yafir put an arm about his wife and stroked her face gently. "Bring me sweet wine and the lovely little cakes you make, my love. I will feed her myself. Minau, my heavenly one, go along with Arlais and help her." He ushered the two women from the room, but not before kissing each of them tenderly. Then he turned, and coming over to Cinnia, sat upon the bed next to her. "You are confused," he said, and he took her hand in his, turning it to kiss first her wrist, and then her palm. His aquamarine eyes stared into hers, but she saw no menace in them.

"You have kidnapped me and brought me to your world," Cinnia said, trying to free her hand from his grasp.

"Yes," he admitted, "but by rights you belong to me."

"I belong to no one," Cinnia told him.

"You were marked for me at your birth," Ahura Mazda said. "Each female infant born in Belmair is marked by a Yafir male for possible mating at a later date. You bear on your body my mark. A small heart at the top of your cleft is my mark."

Cinnia grew even paler than she naturally was at his words. But she would not admit to her surprise. "Nonsense!" she said.

"Will you deny that you possess this mark?" he asked her.

"I have never in all my life seen such a mark upon

my body," she replied. "Did you examine my person for such a mark, my lord, that you say I have it?"

He laughed. "I have not examined your *person,* I promise you, Cinnia. I intend to very shortly, but when I brought you here I lay you upon this bed we will share, and left you to recover yourself."

"By placing an enchantment upon my legs so I could not escape you," she snapped at him angrily.

"I did that for your protection," Ahura Mazda said. "What was the first thing you did upon awakening? You attempted to leave this bed, didn't you?"

Cinnia flushed guiltily.

"And if you could have left this room you would have, and gone where? You have absolutely no idea where you are, do you?" he said.

*"Where am I?"* she demanded of him.

"You are in the kingdom of Yafirdom. You are in my castle, within the women's quarters," he told her. "You are safe, and will remain so."

"Take me back immediately!" Cinnia ordered him imperiously.

Arlais and Minau reentered the room. One carried a small tray of cakes, and the other a decanter and two goblets.

"Put them on the table, my darlings," Ahura Mazda said. "Then take Cinnia to the baths to be prepared for our mating night."

"*Mating?* I should sooner die," Cinnia cried to him. "I am the wife of Dillon, king of Belmair. How dare you speak of me in such intimate terms, my lord!"

"Under the laws of the Yafir you are not Dillon's wife any longer, for I have claimed you. You have become one of my wives. As lord of the Yafir I am permitted to have six wives, and you are the sixth. I have removed the enchantment from your limbs, Cinnia. Now go with Arlais and Minau. I will feed you cakes and sweet wine when you return." He pushed her gently from the bed, and immediately the two other women took her hands and led her off.

They brought her to a beautiful bath whose walls were covered in pale green tiles, and floors were cream marble veined in gold. They stripped her gown from her, remarking frankly upon the beauty of her body, but gasping in shock at the bush of coal-black curls in the space between her thighs. Working swiftly they slathered the place in a pale pink cream, and when they rinsed it away minutes later Cinnia found herself denuded of the hair. Arlais and Minau smiled, pleased.

But Cinnia's pulse leaped at the sight of a small heart now most prominently displayed at the very top of her cleft. *His mark!* Just as he had said. She could not ever remember having seen that mark when she was a child, but then she had not been seeking it out, had she? They washed her long, night-black hair, and brushed it dry, then rubbed it with silk until it was shining. They massaged her body with fragrant creams that melted into her skin. Finally they pared her fingernails and her toenails before wrapping Cinnia in a pale green silk robe, and leading her back to Ahura Mazda.

"She is ready for you, my lord husband," Arlais said with a smile.

Minau said nothing, but then Cinnia had quickly realized the girl had little to say.

"Come, and give me a kiss, both of you," the Yafir lord said to them, and they each came to his side for a tender kiss. "You have pleased me," he told them. "Now go and spend the remainder of the evening with your sons, my darlings."

When the two women had gone, Ahura Mazda held out a hand to Cinnia. "Come," he said, "and let us drink wine together."

Cinnia shook her head. "Nay, I will take neither food nor drink while I am caught here in your kingdom. We both know that if I do I am bound to this place."

"You will both eat and drink with me," he said softly, but there was menace in his tone. "You are mine, Cinnia, and that mongrel that you married, Belmair's Shadow-faerie-mortal king, will find another wife. Or perhaps if once he learns he cannot find you, his heart will be broken, and he will return to Hetar. Belmair will soon belong to the Yafir anyway. And with you in my arms, and as my wife, perhaps even sooner than I had anticipated. Now, my love, come and join me on our nuptial bed for I should like to become better acquainted with you. Do not be shy. I will be most gentle with you."

*Flea be!* Cinnia said quickly in the silent language of magic.

Ahura Mazda looked amazed as his captive disappeared from before his eyes. "Where have you gone, you Belmairan sorceress?" he called to her. He hadn't heard her spell for she had whispered it too softly.

The tiny flea took several large jumps, and hid itself within the folds of the bed curtains. She was safe for now, but Cinnia knew she could not hold the flea's form forever. She concentrated upon maintaining it, hoping that he would eventually grow angry enough to leave the chamber. But he did not. Instead Ahura Mazda stretched out upon the bed, his hands behind his head as he waited.

"Whatever shape you have taken, you cannot hold it forever," he said. "You are clever, my darling, and have perhaps a bit more skill than I gave you credit for, I fear. I am a patient man, and will be happy to wait until you realize you cannot evade what was meant to be, Cinnia."

Hidden in the folds of the bed curtains, Cinnia waited, and closing her eyes concentrated with all her being on maintaining the flea's form. Several hours passed. Never had she held another form for so long, and she could feel herself growing tired. Then to her relief the man on the bed below arose.

"I will leave you now, my bride, for certainly you must be exhausted at this point," he said, his tone affectionate and amused. "I shall come to you again when you are well rested, and of a more reasonable frame of mind. It was foolish of me to rush our passion, but you are so very beautiful, Cinnia, and I have waited for you for many years."

His footsteps sounded as he walked across the chamber. The door opened, and then it closed. A key turned in the door's lock with a loud click.

Cinnia clung to the flea's shape listening. Had he really left the chamber? Or was he playing a game with her? The flea dropped down onto the bed, and looking about saw that the room was indeed empty. She sighed, relieved, and almost immediately regained her own form. She was so weakend by her efforts of the past few hours that she could not move. Quiet tears slipped down her cheeks as she lay sobbing softly. If only she had thought to shape-shift when Ahura Mazda had first come into her apothecary she would not be in this difficulty. She had to escape the Yafir lord, but she had absolutely no idea of where she was. *Yafirdom?* She had never heard of it, nor knew its location. Could she keep Ahura Mazda at bay long enough to learn what she needed to know? Long enough to escape this place? She was certainly going to try. Cinnia's eyes kept closing, and at first she struggled to remain awake. But hearing nothing but silence around her, and hearing no noise from beyond the door she decided she had best sleep and regain her strength while she could. Who knew when the very determined Yafir lord would come to her again. She needed to be strong if she was going to continue to defy him. Cinnia realized that the flea had been a very successful shape for her to take, and she had probably been able to hold its form for as long as she did because it was so tiny. The moment she heard that key in the door again she would shape-shift once more.

Over the course of the next few days Cinnia continued to outwit the Yafir lord. If his wives came into her bedchamber she was herself, but the moment he appeared she would disappear from their sight, shape-shifting into a flea that hid itself in the window or the bed curtains. Ahura Mazda was not pleased. He had not expected Cinnia's powers to be that strong. He realized the shape she was taking had to be small for her to be able to hold on to it for hours at a time. But there were any number of small objects within the room, and he could see no change in any of them or unfamiliar additions.

"She has taken neither food nor drink since she has been here," his wife Arlais said to him one evening before he attempted again to catch Cinnia. "She is weakening as each day passes, my lord. Soon she will no longer have the strength to shape-shift. She will be yours then. You have but to be patient."

"Unless she dies first," Minau remarked softly. "She is a very strong-willed female, my lord. I believe she will persist in her resistance until she dies rather than yield willingly to you. If you want this girl you will have to use the Lotus, my lord." Minau did not speak often, but when she did all listened.

"Is it in bloom?" Ahura Mazda asked her.

"It will be tomorrow, my lord," Minau said.

"The effects only last a few hours," the Yafir lord said.

"True," Minau replied. "But in those few hours you can have your way with her. After that she will be yours. One sniff of the Lotus blossom and her memories will grow fuzzy and dim while her desires will rouse themselves. When she comes to herself again it will be too late for her to go back to her old life, for you will have made her your own, my lord, and she will be completely aware of it. Is that not what you want? Every moment in your arms will then be etched into her brain. She will not be able to hide from the truth. And during that time you will also feed her cakes and wine. Once she has eaten of our food she is bound to the Yafir."

"Minau," Ahura Mazda said admiringly, "you are the most delightful schemer." Reaching out, he drew her into his arms and gave her a slow, hot kiss. "I adore you," he said against her mouth, and then he released her.

"And she is perfectly correct, too, my lord," Arlais remarked. She hid her irritation that Minau had solved the thorny problem when she had not.

"You will bring me the Lotus blossom the moment it blooms tomorrow," the Yafir lord said. "Now I will go and observe my reluctant love."

They bowed to him as he moved past them and into a tiny room next to the bedchamber where Cinnia was imprisoned. Seating himself upon a padded stool he said, *"Wall! Reveal all!"* and the stones became transparent so he might look into the bedroom. Cinnia sat in a chair she had placed facing the door. She was even paler than usual, and there were purplish-brown circles beneath her eyes, which stared hard at the portal before her. Her resistance had obviously weakened her terribly. Now and again she would nod off only to jerk awake seconds later, her head snapping back sharply. The Yafir lord had to admit to himself that he admired her bravery and her resourcefulness. He hoped she would give him a daughter as strong as she was. Sons he had aplenty. He wanted daughters, and daughters bred on Cinnia would be worth a fortune as wives one day. With half a dozen or more daughters he could cement alliances with other Yafir families, which would make him a strong king when they took Belmair. *"Wall, close!"* He had seen enough, and his male member needed release.

Returning into the dayroom he glanced about at his five wives. Arlais. Minau. Volupia. Orea and Tyne. All pleased him, and had been with him for various lengths of time. Each had born him one or more sons. Two, Orea and Tyne, were with child again, their rounded bellies already showing beneath their robes. "Volupia, my precious, you will share my bed tonight," he told her with a smile, and held out a hand to her.

She came at once, taking his hand and kissing it, smiling into his eyes. "As my lord wishes," she murmured obediently, and then she followed him from the chamber.

"I don't envy her," Orea said softly.

"Aye," Arlais agreed. "His lust for Cinnia is so great that he will ride Volupia hard this night."

"And still not be satisfied," Minau noted.

Tyne laughed. "Soon enough, however, my sisters, she will be one of us. And she will wonder why she resisted him for so long. He really is an incredible lover, and his seed is potent. The midwife tells me I am so big so early that I may have two babies in my womb. I pray to the Celestial Actuary that one is a daughter."

The other women nodded, and then Arlais arose. Taking the key to Cinnia's bedchamber from her pocket, she went to the door, unlocked and opened it. The girl stared at her from the chair, her fingers gripping its arms, prepared for flight. "He has taken Volupia to his bed," Arlais said. "You need have no fear of him tonight."

"Thank you," Cinnia said.

"Why do you resist him? You are no virgin," Arlais remarked. "He is a wonderful lover. Passionate. Gentle. Tender."

"I have a husband," Cinnia said. "One whom I adore. Am I a Hetarian that I would want another man to be my lover? Surely the Yafir must have infected those exiles with their casual attitudes toward marriage. Your master already has five wives. Why does he need another? In Belmair such a thing would not be tolerated."

"But you are not in Belmair, Cinnia. You are in Yafirdom. Besides, it is only proper that the lord of the Yafir have several wives. Ahura Mazda is not an ordinary being. He is above all others. Now go to sleep, you poor girl. Things will be better tomorrow, I am certain." Turning, she left the chamber, closing and locking the door.

Cinnia began to weep with her despair. She was hungry and she was thirsty. Each time she shape-shifted it weakened her, and especially as she held the flea's form for several hours a day. She was relieved that she would not have to tonight. She didn't know where she was, and she hadn't been out of this room since she had awakened in it except to be taken to the baths. How was she to escape and find her way back to Dillon? She wanted to go home. She wanted her husband, and she wanted Nidhug's comfort. If she could not escape this place, wherever it was, what would the Great Dragon of Belmair do? Would she choose another bride for Dillon? Cinnia wept harder, and finally, utterly exhausted, she fell into a restless sleep. In her dreams she heard her name being called. *Cinnia! Cinnia!* But she fled from the sound of it, for she feared it was Ahura Mazda trying to entrap her in her dreams as he could not in reality.

When she finally awoke she could tell by the odd light outside of her windows that she had slept for a very long time. She felt so weak she could hardly raise her head. Her heart jumped at the sound of the key in the door. She struggled to her feet, swaying, but to her relief it was only Arlais, and she carried a beautiful white flower in her hand as she came forward toward Cinnia.

"Isn't it lovely?" she said as she exhibited the star-shaped flower, "Smell!" And she stuck the blossom beneath Cinnia's nose, smiling.

A seductive fragrance rose up, assailing Cinnia's nostrils with an elusive, but potent scent. Unable to help herself Cinnia breathed deeply, and as she did her eyes slowly closed, and she crumpled to the floor.

"Come, ladies," Arlais called to her companions. "Cinnia must be bathed quickly, and made ready for our dear lord."

The five women carried the unconscious girl to the baths, and bathed her as they had that first day. Then wrapping her in a fresh clean silk robe the color of an apricot they carried her back to her bedchamber where the serving woman had already remade the bed with fresh linens. Cinnia was laid upon the bed, and the five woman hurried out, passing Ahura Mazda as they went.

Arlais closed the bedchamber door behind their husband, smiling, well pleased. "The rest is now up to him," she said to the others.

"He'll do his part," Minau said.

"I can only hope she satisfies him," Volupia said. "I can hardly sit today."

Her companions laughed. They could but imagine what was going on now behind that closed door as Cinnia would just about now be opening her eyes.

"Where am I?" Cinnia asked drowsily.

"In our wedding chamber, my precious," Ahura Mazda said. "You are still exhausted." He bent and pressed a soft kiss upon her lips. "You need some wine, and a bit of nourishment to revive you." A gold goblet studded with rubies appeared in his hand. Cradling her shoulders with one hand he raised her into a seated position and put the goblet to her lips. "Can you drink a little for me, my darling?" he asked gently.

Should she be drinking this wine? The thought flitted across her consciousness, but then she began to sip from the goblet. She was so very thirsty, and the cool, sweet wine slipped down her parched throat. "It's good," she murmured, drinking more.

"Aye, 'tis good, my precious," he murmured. Removing the cup from her, he handed her a small iced cake. "And these are good, too." He fed her the cake, which Cinnia gobbled down, and then another.

She took the goblet from him. "I want more!" she said as she now drank deeply.

"You may have whatever you desire, my precious," he told her, smiling at her.

He was so handsome, Cinnia thought. His aquamarine-blue eyes were beautiful, and went so well with his close-cropped silver-gilt hair. He was naked but for a length of silk wrapped around his loins. Reaching out, she ran her hand over his bare chest. "I am your bride?" she asked him innocently. "And this is our wedding night?"

"You are my bride, Cinnia," he said, "and yes, this is our wedding night." He took her hand, turning it to kiss both her wrist and palm.

A little thrill raced through her. "My mind is clouded," she said.

"It has been an exciting day," he said. "All you need remember with certainty is that I love you. You are mine, Cinnia! Mine alone! Now let me worship you as any bridegroom would." His fingers undid the sash about her silk robe, baring her body to his sight. His look of pleasure touched her.

"Have we taken pleasures before, my lord?" she asked him shyly.

"Nay, but you are not a virgin, my precious. Your first husband is dead," he told her. How much about passion she remembered he didn't know, and so he had told the lie in order to reassure her that everything was well. Reaching out, he cupped one of her breasts. It was the size and shape of a plump autumn apple. He fondled it gently, marveling at the softness of her skin. Unable to help himself he pinched the nipple of the breast, puckering it. Then lowering his head he took the nipple in his mouth and began to suck upon it, now and again nipping at it with his teeth.

"Ohhh, oh!" Cinnia murmured, realizing that she was quite enjoying the sensation of his mouth on her breast, his teeth on her nipple. She squirmed from her robe, and when he pressed her back into the pillows again she reached out and pulled the wrap from his loins. "Let me! Let me!" she cried to him, pushing him away from her breast and onto his back. Then rising to her knees she hovered over him, licking at his nipples.

"Ohh, I like doing that!" she said. "Do you like it, my lord?"

"Aye, very much," he told her. Her eagerness was more than he had dared to anticipate. His heart was thundering in his chest, and his cock was growing harder with each passing minute. Still her memory would be impaired for hours to come. There was no rush to have her. Reaching out he caught her head, and brought it to his. His lips touched hers, and he felt fire. Ahura Mazda kissed Cinnia slowly, deeply. His tongue pushed into her mouth to dance with her tongue.

Cinnia enjoyed his kisses. His mouth was sensual and warm against hers. Somewhere in her thoughts she remembered that she liked taking pleasures very much. Drawing away from him she surprised him by straddling him. Then she began to press kisses across his torso. Her tongue followed her lips. She enjoyed the taste of his flesh. It was intoxicating, and aroused her senses. She nipped playfully at his nipples now, and then moving quickly away she licked and kissed her way down his lean, hard body. Her eyes widened as they gazed upon his cock. It was enormous. Thick and very long. She slid her body past it, and then, her knees on either side of his thighs, she leaned forward and enclosed the manhood with her breasts, rubbing it up and down between them.

He watched her, both astounded and delighted. Cinnia had an obvious gift for passion. He watched her playing with his cock, holding back his own lust briefly. But then he could bear no more without satisfaction of his own. "My precious, your wicked desires have me afire. I must share them with you."

"What would you have me do, my lord?" Cinnia asked him.

"Turn about," he said, and when she did he pulled her back so that her sex was now within easy reach of his tongue. "Now put my cock back between your pretty tits, and continue on while I delight you, and I will," he promised her. Parting her nether lips, which were already swollen and moist, he began to tongue her pleasure jewel as he let her rub his swollen cock between her plump breasts. When she began to lick at the tip of it, however, Ahura Mazda knew he could resist her no longer. Nipping her jewel sharply so that she squealed, he rolled her over onto her back, straddling her.

"You are going to fuck me, aren't you?" Cinnia purred up at him. "You are very big, my lord. I do not think I have ever had bigger than you." She clung to him, drawing his silver-gilt head down to her so that their lips were almost touching.

"You haven't," he said. "This is why little mortal maidens like you want Yafir lovers. Our cocks are much larger than mere mortal men."

"Will it hurt me?" she pouted at him.

"You will receive me nicely, I suspect," he told her, moving closer to the entrance of her sheath. "I will put just the tip of it in you," he said, and he kissed her mouth as he did. She was deliciously wet and hot.

"Ohh, that's nice," Cinnia said. "Give me a little more of your cock, my lord." And he did as she had requested. "Ohh, it is so hard and thick," she whispered against his lips. "I must have more!" And when he pushed farther into her she purred against his ear, her little tongue encircling the whorl of it. "More! More! More! Give me more!"

He was trembling like a maid, for she was the most exciting woman he had ever known. He thrust farther and farther and farther.

*"I want it all!"* Cinnia suddenly cried. *"Give me all of your great cock!"*

With a half cry, half groan, Ahura Mazda drove himself into her as far as he could, and her legs wrapped themselves about him so that he might imbed himself to the hilt of his cock. "There, you adorable sorceress!" he hissed at her. "You have it all!"

*Sorceress.* The world tore at her memory, but she could not quite remember. And she didn't want to at this point. She felt him within her. "Now, my lord," she murmured against his mouth. "Give me your lust! All of it! Hard and deep! Hard and deep!" Her nails clawed down his back. "Give me pleasures! *Give them to me!*" she demanded of him. "Hard and deep! Hard and deep!"

He began to ride her fiercely, and to his delight her own lusts rose up and threatened to overcome his. He drove himself into her as she had demanded of him. Hard and deep! Hard and deep! She screamed beneath him as he pounded against her, encouraging him onward until he felt his manhood growing tighter and tighter, and finally unable to help himself he exploded his juices into her; his big body jerking with ferocious spasms as he emptied his lust into her.

But Cinnia had not had pleasures. She was burning with her lust, and wept, cursing him for a weakling as he lay spent against her. "How could you take your pleasure when you gave me none?" she sobbed, her tone disappointed and angry.

Ahura Mazda was confused and upset by her accusations. "I rode you hard," he protested. "Harder than I have ever ridden any."

"You gave me no pleasures. You only took them for yourself," she told him.

"Leave me if you can do no better, my lord. I am disappointed, and need soothing."

"I must rest," he protested to her.

"Nay! If you have magic then make yourself hard again, and give me the pleasures you denied me while you so selfishly took those pleasures for yourself alone," Cinnia said, weeping with her need.

He arose from the bed, and going to a cabinet, opened it, taking out a decanter of yellow-green liquid. He took down from the cabinet's shelf a small marble jar, and lifted the lid from it. Reaching for a crystal goblet from the same shelf he scooped a spoonful of bloodred powder from the jar into the goblet, pouring in the yellow-green liquid from the decanter atop it. The mixture bubbled, boiled and foamed within the crystal. Then the mixture calmed, becoming as clear as the glass it was in. Ahura Mazda drank it quickly down, and when he turned back to the bed to join her, his manhood was enormous once again. "I can only do this once of an evening," he warned her. Then without further ado he mounted her, thrusting himself deep into her.

"Ohhh, yes! That feels so good, my lord," she told him. "Now fuck me harder and deeper than you did before. I will have my pleasures of you this night!"

And once more he began to use her, but though he rode her hard again, though she met every powerful push of his cock with an equally excited thrust of her loins, though she screamed with delight at his enthusiastic efforts and raked his back with her nails, Cinnia obtained only the barest of pleasures as he emptied his love juices a second time. And Ahura Mazda knew it as he rolled exhausted off her lush body. He was shocked by her reaction to his great efforts. Why had he not been able to give her incredible pleasures as he gave to the other women who were his wives?

He might have blamed Cinnia for being a cold woman, but he knew better. He had stood invisible within her castle bedchamber, and watched as she made love with Belmair's young king. The passion between them was incredible with its golden light and its crackling lightning. There was never any doubt in his mind that she was receiving the greatest of pleasures from Dillon. Why had she not received them from him? Ahura Mazda asked himself. He had never performed better with a woman. Perhaps the magical Lotus flower, whose scent had stolen her memory briefly, had something to do with it. But without it he had not been able to get near her, for she had shape-shifted the moment he entered the bedchamber.

She had been delightfully wanton with him, but she had obtained naught from him. Ahura Mazda decided to spend the entire night in Cinnia's bed. When the effects of the Lotus wore off, and she saw where she was and what he was doing with her, perhaps she would give in to him. Mayhap then he could give her the pleasures she deserved. He heard her weeping softly, and gathered her into his muscled arms.

"I will find a way to give you pleasures, my precious," he promised her. "Now rest so we may begin again."

Together they slept for several hours, and then after several hours Cinnia awoke, and the Yafir lord began to make love to her once more. He caressed her breasts, noting that she was less excessively lewd with him this time. He covered her face with kisses, and stroked her lovely body with a tender hand. And when he was fully aroused once more he put her beneath him. Slowly, slowly, he entered her wet sheath. His thrusts gentle at first grew fiercer with each passing moment. She moaned with her rising excitement, and he knew that this time he would give her what she wanted. What she needed. He thrust harder and deeper with each stroke of his huge cock.

Beneath him Cinnia reveled in the hard length probing her, thrilling her, and she felt the beginning of pleasures as they swiftly rose up to claim her in a blaze of fury. "Ohh! Ohh! Ohh!" She gasped as she reached the peak of the mountain. And then she was overwhelmed by the sweetness and the fire. She bathed in it, swam in it, and then as suddenly as it had overtaken her it began to melt away even as she struggled to maintain it. She was falling into a deep whirlpool. "Dillon!" she cried out. As her heartbeat began to slow she opened her eyes to find Ahura Mazda still buried within her, a smile of pure triumph upon his handsome face.

She began to scream, and he put a hand over her mouth as he rode her fiercely to his own finish. Cinnia bit at the hand stifling her. She tasted his blood in her mouth, but he did not release her until he had completed himself. *"How have you managed to do this to me?"* Cinnia gasped, sobbing, as he released her. She was horrified to find herself naked, her hair in disarray and the Yafir lord by her side.

"I told you, Cinnia. You belong to me. Did you think I was going to wait forever for you? I have spent the night in your bed, using you well, and you are, I am pleased to tell you, a most passionate woman." He pulled her into his arms, fondling her breast.

She struggled against him, hitting him with her fists, trying to claw at his beautiful eyes. "Monster! Seducer! You have spoiled me for my husband! I will never forgive you, Ahura Mazda! *Never!*"

"Aye, I have spoiled you for the young king of Belmair, Cinnia. Do you think a high lord with his impressive bloodlines will want back a wife soiled by a Yafir?" he taunted her. "Would you like to know how many times I have fucked you?" He turned his back to her. "Do you see the marks of your extraordinary passion upon me, Cinnia? You took me into your body eagerly, and never have I ridden a female harder than I have ridden you in these last hours. You cannot go back now. *You belong to me!* Accept the truth of my words, my precious."

Cinnia wept helplessly. She was surely ruined now for Dillon. Even though he loved her, the king of Belmair could never accept back as his queen a woman who had been used by another man. Especially a Yafir lord. A creature even despised by his own magical world. It would dishonor him. Dishonor Belmair. A feeling of utter despair overcame her. To never go home again. To never speak with Nidhug. It was more than she could bear, Cinnia considered.

"Come, my precious beauty," Ahura Mazda said to her. "Do not weep so bitterly. You think your life over, but I tell you it has only just begun, Cinnia. Yafirdom is a safe place. My castle has everything in it you could possibly want. You will have pleasant companions in my other five wives. All came from Belmair, and like you were frightened when they first arrived. Now they are happy and content in my love and in the plenty that they have. Each has given me sons. But you, my precious, give me a daughter, and I will make you my queen. And one day we will return to Belmair. Sooner, my precious, than later, for the Belmairans grow older, and there are few children born to them anymore. There is no hope for them, and when he realizes it, Dillon of the Shadows will return to his own world." He caressed her dark head. "You will forget, my precious. With my love and my passion to sustain you, you will forget all but your life with me," Ahura Mazda told the weeping woman in his arms.

Then he began to kiss and lick the tears from her face while Cinnia lay weak with her helplessness. When he mounted her again and pushed his cock deep inside her, she did not object. What was the use of protesting now? She lay quietly beneath him as he used her. But he would not permit her to resist him. He kissed her, caressed her and used his manhood within her so skillfully that Cinnia was no longer able to withstand his blandishments.

"Say you are mine," he whispered in her ear.

"No!" she sobbed.

He laughed softly. "Say it, or I shall not give you release." His cock plunged hungrily within her, keeping just short of her desires. "Say it, my precious!" he growled.

He drove deeper and harder. *"Say it!"* His mouth tugged upon her nipple.

She was going to explode, Cinnia thought dizzily. Her body ached with its need for pleasures, for release. But if she said it there was no going back. She sobbed. There was no going back anyway. "I am yours," she told Ahura Mazda. Almost instantly she was drowning in pleasures, colors bursting around her, her head spinning, her heart hammering wildly as he met her needs and brought her to fulfillment.

"Aye, you are mine!" he told her triumphantly. "You have been since the moment of your birth when I marked you as such, Cinnia." He kissed her hard. "I will love you, my precious. I will love you forever!" And then the proof of his words flooded her, and Cinnia wondered if she would give him the daughter he wanted one day.

She fell into a deep sleep, and when she finally awoke again she was alone in her bed. Cinnia began to weep again. She struggled to remember everything that had happened. The last thing she recalled before awakening earlier had been Arlais coming in with a beautiful white flower, and sticking it beneath her nose to smell. After that it was all a blank. It did not take a great deal of thought to realize that the flower had been enchanted. But what had happened in those hours she could not remember? Ahura Mazda said he had made love to her many times. She was sore enough to suspect that he was neither lying nor bragging to her.

The flower's scent, which she had breathed in, must have dulled her memory so that she permitted him to have his way with her. Cinnia shook her head sadly. No one could say that she had not fought to keep the Yafir lord from having his way. She had held him at bay for several days by shape-shifting into the persona of the tiny flea. Why had she been so foolish as to smell that white flower? But the truth was that Arlais was hardly a threatening figure. It just hadn't occurred to Cinnia that the flower would be magic. She could not remember anything like that in Belmair.

The door to her bedchamber opened, and five women trooped into the room led by Arlais. "Come, Cinnia, dearest, 'tis time for the baths. We go together at the same time each day. We are all Ahura Mazda's wives. You have met Minau, of course. This is Volupia." Arlais drew forward a tall girl with red hair and eyes like black cherries. "And this is Orea." Orea had dark gold hair, and brown eyes. "And Tyne." This last girl had rich chestnut-brown hair and lovely gray eyes.

"He has used you well, I can see," Volupia said. "Good! Now perhaps he will be content with the rest of us. He has been eager for your arrival for months now."

"I don't want to be here," Cinnia said to them.

"Of course you don't," Orea said. "None of us did

at first. And then we realized there was no going back, and that our husband was kind and loving. We are fortunate. Not all of the Yafir have so even a temper as Ahura Mazda. Some we have seen are downright mean. My sister, who was stolen when I was, has a husband who beats her."

"I have a husband," Cinnia said softly. "Dillon, king of Belmair. He is handsome and kind, and I love him with all my heart."

"Put him from your memory," Tyne told her. "He will never take you back now that you have lain with a Yafir. You are now the wife of Yafirdom's most powerful lord. You are very fortunate that you were not put in the Mating Market."

"Tyne, do not frighten, Cinnia," Arlais scolded gently.

"What is the Mating Market?" Cinnia wanted to know.

"Our husband has told you how each female infant born in Belmair is marked by a Yafir male for possible harvesting one day. Girls who are claimed by their husbands have six months in which to prove fertile. If they do not, and their husbands choose to do so, they are brought to the Mating Market. There they are chosen by another single Yafir male who mates with them regularly for three months. If they become with child then the Yafir takes the woman for his wife. If she does not then she is mated by another and another and another until she has a child. When she reaches the end of her breeding cycle and is no longer fertile, she is returned to Belmair. That only happens rarely. It is every Yafir man's duty to produce children else the race die," Tyne said primly.

"Our good lord has given all of us children," Volupia noted. "I have two sons. Arlais has three. Minau, two. Tyne and Orea have one each, and are both with child again as you can see. Alas, none of us has produced the desired daughters. It is to be hoped that you will do that for him."

"We can chatter in the baths, Sisters," Arlais said. Walking to the bed, she took Cinnia by the hand. "Come along now, dearest. A wash, a soak in the tub and a massage will make you feel ever so much better." She kissed Cinnia upon her cheek. "You've been weeping, and you must not. You will be very happy here, I promise you."

When they reached the baths Cinnia was surprised to see servants. The first she had seen within the castle. "Why are they all men?" she asked.

"They are gelded men," Arlais told her. "We have a surfeit of males born, and so those from among our lower class sometimes sell their sons to be gelded and sent into service. There aren't enough women to go around, and of course there are fewer and fewer females born in Belmair now to be marked for harvesting."

Cinnia had been naked to begin with. Now the eunuchs took their garments from the other women. They were led into the first bath chamber where each of them stood patiently in a rounded-out depression in the marble floor while a eunuch took up a large sea sponge, filled it with soap, scrubbed them and rinsed them. Then together they trooped into a second room where a large square scented pale green marble pool awaited them. Its water was covered with rose petals. Beneath the water were benches about three sides of the pool. Seating themselves in the warm water, the women began to chatter. They were quite curious as to how Cinnia had enjoyed pleasures with Ahura Mazda. Avidly they leaned forward to hear what she would say.

"I remember nothing until this morning," Cinnia told them.

"The Lotus flower can do that," Minau spoke for the first time. "Did it make you wanton? It can have that effect on the most proper woman."

"She was very wanton," Volupia said mischievously. "I overheard our husband speaking with Arlais when he left her bedchamber. She demanded pleasures of him over and over again. He was forced to take a restorative so he might continue fucking her until she was well satisfied and could sleep."

Cinnia's pale skin flushed bright red. "I remember nothing until I awoke and found Ahura Mazda using me. I did fight him!"

"But that big skillful cock of his gave you pleasures nonetheless," Volupia laughed. "Our husband has a magnificent weapon, and he wields it well."

"You belong to him. We all belong to him," Arlais said. "We are so fortunate."

"How long have you been here?" Cinnia asked Arlais. The woman looked no older than twenty-five.

Arlais thought, and then she said, "Several hundred

years at least. I was twenty-seven when Ahura Mazda took me. We do not age here in Yafirdom. They say that those who are sent from here grow old immediately."

"That is true. The stolen women who have been returned are crones," Cinnia noted, thinking that here was another reason she could not leave Yafirdom now.

"I am the first woman Ahura Mazda took to wife," Arlais said. "In the many years before he spent his time struggling for the leadership of the Yafir. Once he had a Yafir wife. She died giving birth to his twin sons. They were grown before he took me to wife. Minau has been here for almost three hundred years. Volupia came but seventy years back. Orea and Tyne have been with us over a hundred and fifty years. We all remain the ages we were when we came to Yafirdom. Minau is twenty-three, Volupia, nineteen, Orea, twenty, and Tyne is also twenty. How old are you, Cinnia?"

"I had just celebrated my eighteenth birthday," she answer Arlais.

"So you are the youngest among us," Arlais noted, smiling. "Those born Yafir, or with Yafir blood, grow to adulthood, and then do not show their ages for many centuries. Ahura Mazda is at least two aeons old. He is just reaching the prime of his life for which I am very grateful. If I must remain twenty-seven for the rest of my existence I want a vigorous lover in my husband."

The others nodded in agreement.

"It does not disturb you to share a single husband among you?" Cinnia asked.

"Why would it?" Minau responded.

"Ahura Mazda is kind," Orea said.

"He is generous to all of us," Tyne noted.

"And he is certainly Arlais's vigorous lover with us all," Volupia said, grinning. "We are glad to have someone else with whom to share his lusty nature. He has been known to exhaust two of us at a time."

The other women giggled.

"How do you share him?" Cinnia was curious in spite of herself.

"He visits each of us at least once a week," Arlais explained. "But because you are his new bride, he will spend the next few weeks with you alone. He will want to get you with child quickly so your fertility may be assured. With Orea and Tyne both so great with child, Minau, Volupia and I have had to share the burden of our husband these past two months. We will be delighted for the rest." She smiled at Cinnia.

After a time a signal was given by Arlais, and they left the scented water to be dried with large warm towels by the impassive eunuchs. Then each woman stretched herself out upon a marble bench and received a thorough massage. At last they departed the baths and returned to their large apartment. Cinnia noticed as they sat together in the dayroom that it was a circular chamber with seven doors. One that led out into the corridor of their quarters, and the six others that led into each woman's bedchamber.

A silent serving man brought cakes and a crystal decanter filled with a pale gold liquid. He placed the tray carefully on the table around which the six women were now sprawled upon large colorful cushions.

"You have already eaten cakes and drunk wine with Ahura Mazda," Arlais told Cinnia as she handed her a goblet. "I do not lie to you."

"It makes no difference now," Cinnia replied sadly. "I cannot go back even though I long to do so." She took a deep draught of the liquid in the goblet, and found it oddly soothing. Still she sighed.

Arlais caught the others' eyes, and they nodded understanding to each other. Every newcomer to Yafirdom felt like this in the beginning. But although Cinnia did not realize it, her sorrow would soon pass, and she would be happy and content once more. She took a tiny iced cake and handed it to Cinnia, smiling. "Eat," she said. And Cinnia did.

# 10

THE YAFIR HAD been stopped from stealing any more of Belmair's women. But the young queen was among the missing. Soon all of Belmair knew it, and would have mourned but that Dillon would not permit it. He sent Nidhug with messages to all three dukes, telling them that now the real battle would begin. They had to find where the Yafir were hiding themselves and Belmair's queen.

After having convinced the dragon that even she could not have been in two places at the same time, and was with her king, which was only right and proper, Nidhug ceased her weeping to everyone's relief as she had caused her own moat to overflow in her guilt and grief, temporarily flooding a third of the gardens that separated the two castles. Cirillo's company had helped. He soothed her with especially delicious faerie cakes iced in gold that he conjured from the air, and with his magical kisses, which seemed to melt away her sorrow.

The three dukes were called to the royal castle to discuss the crisis. On this bright late-autumn morning they sat about a rectangular table within a small room with tall windows that looked out over the hills now dressed in scarlet, orange, purple, yellow and several shades of gold and brown against a bright blue sky. A fire in the large hearth warmed the room, the large logs crackling as the flames leaped high up the chimney. At each participant's place there was a chased silver goblet decorated with green malachite.

In the table's center was a large decanter of dark red wine.

Dukes Alban, Dreng and Tullio looked curiously, and perhaps a bit nervously, at Kaliq of the Shadows and Prince Cirillo. They had grown quickly familiar with the young king, and they all knew Nidhug well. There was much magic to be found about the table and the dukes were frankly a little bit afraid if the truth had been known. They waited for Dillon to speak first.

"We have contained the Yafir as you know," he began. "Now we must find them, and take back those women who wish to be repatriated to Belmair. And we must rescue the queen, my wife."

"Surely, my lord, many of the women stolen over the years are now dead," Dreng said. "And as for the others it is unlikely their families will want them returned now that they have been tainted by the Yafir. The threat is contained. It is no more, and our women are safe again."

"The women stolen over these last centuries are very much alive, my lord," Dillon told him. "Mortals living in the faerie world do not age. They remain as they were when they were stolen away. These are women of childbearing age. Many were married. Those stolen in the past few years may well wish to return to their husbands and homes. As for the others, the families that they knew are long gone. They will undoubtedly remain with their Yafir husbands and children."

"It is unlikely their families will receive them back," Duke Alban said quietly. "Dreng is sadly right. Those kidnapped will be considered tainted. I will, however, welcome back any citizen of my duchy of Belia who wishes to return. And I will provide for them if their family do not want them."

"I want my wife back," Dillon said quietly.

"My lord!" Now it was Duke Tullio who spoke. "You cannot accept Fflergant's daughter back as your wife, as your queen. She has been taken by the Yafir. She is tainted! It is all well and good of Alban to offer sanctuary to those from Belia who wish to return. Those women are for the most part the wives and daughters of fishermen and herdsmen. But Cinnia was a king's daughter, a king's wife. You cannot take her back! Belmair's queen must be above reproach, and even a minute spent in the Yafir lord's custody makes her unfit to be our queen. I am sorry for I know you had come to love her, but this is not Hetar where a woman may dabble with many lovers, and still be considered a proper matron. This is Belmair. Dreng, Alban and I will carefully make up a list of maidens from among our families who would be suitable as your queen."

"Do not bother," Dillon said coldly. "I will have no one but Cinnia for my queen. I know, my lords, that you mean well. But I want no other but Cinnia to be my wife."

"What if the Yafir gets a child on her?" Dreng asked in a tight voice.

"I cast a spell on my wife when we were first wed to prevent her from conceiving a child until this business with the Yafir could be settled," Dillon told them. "Our child could have been used against us, against Belmair," he explained. "My spell cannot be broken or reversed by any but me, my lords. She will not give Ahura Mazda a child."

"My lords," Kaliq said quietly, "you argue about something that can be settled at a later date. Let the king continue on with the purpose of this meeting."

Dillon nodded a thanks to his father. "Our first goal is to ferret out the Yafir's hiding place. Every inch of each duchy must be searched carefully, thoroughly. They will probably have set up their world in a maze of connecting caves, or beneath the earth, or perhaps inside the hills themselves. They will be hidden where you would not expect them to hide. Once we have found their hidden place we will decide how to approach them. This business between Belmair and the Yafir does not have to end badly."

"They were told to leave aeons ago," Dreng said belligerently. "They have remained in defiance of our laws. The Yafir need to be wiped from the face of Belmair!"

"If my ancestor, Napier IX, had let them have one hundred women to help them survive, none of this would have happened. As I understand it, the Yafir were good neighbors, Dreng," Alban said. He enjoyed reminding the duke of Beltran that his ancestor had been a king of Belmair, for Dreng could make no such claim. No king of Belmair had ever come from Beltran, and Alban couldn't resist reminding his fellow duke of that.

"It is true," Tullio said thoughtfully, "that they lived peaceably here for many years, but they were also called the *wicked ones,* for they loved playing tricks on those who offended them. Still, Dreng, if we may come to an understanding with the Yafir it would be better for us all. Since being visited by our king I have considered this matter most carefully. I do not want to see our young men lost to war."

"If we are not firm with the Yafir," Dreng said, "they will think us weak!"

"We need not fight a war to convince them of our strength," Dillon told the trio of dukes. "First we find them. Then we deliver a single hard blow that will gain their attention, and bring them to the bargaining table. With the decline in population that has occurred on both sides perhaps living together peaceably is better than perishing. But make no mistake about it, I can and I will win this struggle."

"I still think we should find them and wipe them out like a nest of hornets," Dreng said. "But I will obey your directive, Your Majesty. I will return home, and set my people to seeking out the place where the Yafir hide."

Dillon nodded. "I appreciate your cooperation," he told Duke Dreng. *But,* he thought, *I do not trust you, Dreng of Beltran. I will be watching you to make certain you stir up no more trouble than we already have.* He turned to the others. "Will you also return to your homes and send your people out to search for the Yafir?"

"I will, Your Majesty," Alban said.

"And I also, Your Majesty," Tullio promised. "I am comforted that you would seek peace over war. The people of Hetar are not usually a peaceable folk."

"Indeed, in the land called Hetar, there has been much war until ten years ago," Dillon said. "But there has been peace ever since."

"We will return you to your homes by means of our magic," Kaliq said, and then before the dukes might speak further he did just that.

"You have said nothing while we met," Dillon said to Nidhug.

"I had naught to say," the dragon answered him.

"You do not like Dreng, do you?" Cirillo said to her.

"It was all I could do not to scorch him with my fire," the dragon admitted, and her nostrils glowed a dark red. "How dare he say my precious Cinnia is a tainted woman! We will find her, bring her back and all will be as it was. She is queen of Belmair. Does Dreng not realize that I know he has two granddaughters of marriageable age? He will set neither of them in my Cinnia's place!"

"Nay, he will not," Dillon told her. "For now she is safe, and I have already set our own people to searching every nook and cranny of Belmair province for answers as to where the Yafir have hidden their world."

In Belmair the trees remained full and bright with color for two full months. And then on the morning of the new year Belmairans would awaken to find the leaves gone, and the trees bare. During those two months the people of Belmair's world searched and searched and searched for the hiding place of the Yafir, but they could not find it. Finally the icy season was upon them with its heavy snows, bitter winds and brutal cold. The search had to be suspended until the spring.

Both Kaliq and Cirillo remained in Belmair. Queen Ilona had departed soon after she had helped her grandson and his companions set the spell about Belmair's young women. She said nothing of her son's obvious affection for the dragon. In time it would pass, and it would pass quicker if she did not disapprove it.

"Send for your mother," was her last bit of advice to Dillon before she hurried through the glowing tunnel back to her own forest home.

But Dillon did not send for Lara. Instead he grew sadder and sadder as each day passed without finding Cinnia. Cirillo was little help. It was obvious to all but the most foolish of fools that the faerie prince and the dragon were besotted with one another.

Kaliq finally took it upon himself to seek out Lara's help. One night while Dillon sat staring silently into the flames of the hearth in the little hall, the Shadow

Prince took himself to Lara's home in Terah, appearing in her hall on a winter's afternoon.

"Kaliq!" It was Lara's husband, Magnus Hauk, who saw him first. "It has been some time since you have visited us. Welcome to Terah!" The tall, golden-haired man came forward, smiling, his hand held out in friendship, his turquoise eyes warm.

"Thank you, my lord Dominus," Kaliq responded, grasping the hand with his own. "I have come to bring Lara word of Dillon, in Belmair."

"Send for the Domina," Magnus Hauk said to a servant. "Bring wine for our guest. Come, old friend, and sit with me by the fire."

Kaliq murmured his thanks, thinking that his absence from Terah these last years had mellowed Magnus Hauk's attitude toward him. He took the wine offered him, and sat with the Dominus of Terah. "It is a complicated tale I have to tell," he said pleasantly, "and so I hope you will forgive me if I wait until Lara comes so I need tell it but once. How are the children? Have you found a husband yet for Anoush?"

Magnus Hauk rolled his eyes at the mention of his stepdaughter. "Nay. She has been quite outspoken in that matter. It seems she does not wish to wed, or so she says. Lara has suggested, and I agree, that we leave her be for now. One day she may meet a man she can love. Her mystical sight becomes stronger and stronger. Her healing powers are wonderful and other than in the matter of marriage she is a good daughter to us."

"You are wise to let her be," Kaliq said. "And the others?"

"Zagiri is interested in the young men, but she is still too young for me to consider matching. As for Taj and Marzina, they are yet children, thank the Great Creator! We took your advice, and turned down the proposed marriage alliance between Marzina and the son of Hetar's rulers. They have not accepted our refusal, however, and say they will ask again in two more years. That in itself disturbs me."

Kaliq nodded, and then sensing her entry into the hall he turned to see Lara coming toward them. He rose and went forward to greet her, taking her hands in his and kissing them. Their eyes met quickly, briefly. "You are lovely as always."

"Thank you, my lord," she said in even tones, withdrawing her hands from him.

Together they rejoined Magnus Hauk, who said, "Kaliq brings us word of Dillon."

"Tell me." Lara said the two words sharply.

"He is totally in love with his wife, Cinnia, but Belmair is beset by an enemy who must be made into a friend," Kaliq began. "Unfortunately this Yafir has escalated the problem." He continued on, telling them everything that had happened to date.

"The Yafir haven't been heard of in centuries," Lara said.

"Because they had hidden themselves somewhere in Belmair," Kaliq responded. "Dillon planned to negotiate with their leader, Ahura Mazda, in order to bring the Yafir back into Belmair's society. It would have allowed Belmairan and Yafir to mingle once more on a daily basis, in a normal fashion. There would have been no need to steal women away. But Ahura Mazda believes he can shortly claim Belmair for the Yafir as his numbers grow while Belmair's do not due to the lack of females. And just to emphasize the strength of his position he has stolen Cinnia away."

"Dillon is all right?" Lara asked the Shadow Prince.

"Yes and no," Kaliq answered her. "While he knows with his intellect that Cinnia is safe with the Yafir lord, and that he will regain her, he misses her terribly. His heart pines for her in the midst of a dark and cold winter."

"Do you know where the Yafir secret themselves?" Lara asked.

Kaliq shook his head. "The strongest of my powers are confined to the world of Hetar," he told her. "I retain certain other powers when I am in Belmair, but I cannot tell Dillon where the Yafir hide. And if I could I would not for this is his puzzle to unravel. Belmair is his world now, and as its ruler he must use his own powers to see to his people, their safety and their well-being. He has the skills, Lara, to do it."

"Then why have you come to me?" she asked candidly.

"I think a visit from his mother might ease the sadness he is feeling right now," Kaliq told her.

"He has not invited me to come to this new world of his," Lara said, and there was just the hint of anger in her voice. "Dillon is my eldest child, and we have always had a closeness that others envied. But you took him to Belmair, Kaliq. You saw him wed to a girl I have not even seen yet, let alone met. It has been almost a year now since he was gone, and I have not seen him since that last visit to Shunnar well over a year ago. After you told me of his marriage I expected him to wait a short while in order to become better acquainted with his new wife, his new responsibilities. But after several months had passed, he had still not invited me. Now you say he wants me to come?"

"Nay," Kaliq told her bluntly. "I did not say he wanted you to come. I said—"

"I know what you said!" Lara answered. "Then he has not asked for me."

"Lara, my love, you cannot possibly believe that Dillon would call out for his *mama* in his difficulties," Magnus Hauk said. "In the name of the Great Creator, my stepson is a grown man! He has his pride, as does his mother. If I know Dillon, he will sink into the darkest depths of his sorrow and die before he will ask anyone for help."

"He could have invited me, invited us, to visit Belmair," Lara said.

"Woman, be reasonable!" Magnus Hauk said and he turned to Kaliq. "Is the bride beautiful, my lord? Does she please him?" And when Kaliq nodded with a smile, the Dominus said to his wife, "Were either of us eager to have our in-laws as guests in the earliest days of our marriage?" he asked her. "Even now, do we seek out visitors?"

"You and your mother have never had the closeness that Dillon and I share," Lara replied stubbornly. But there was just the faintest smile playing at the corners of her mouth. They had built the Dominus's mother, the Lady Persis, a home near their own rather than have her living with them.

"There was no time for the niceties from what Kaliq has said," Magnus Hauk said, defending the stepson with whom he had become friends. "Ruling is never easy, Lara, and well you know it. Dillon had little time to settle in before this difficulty with the Yafir arose. Why is it that I never heard you mention them?"

"They have been thought to be extinct," Lara said. "They haven't been seen here in our world for thousands of years. Do you really think Dillon needs me, Kaliq?"

"I think it would boost his spirits, Lara," the Shadow lord answered her. "Did your mother tell you that she helped us when we cast the spell protecting Belmair's remaining women from the Yafir?"

"Aye, she did, which is another reason for my irritation. Why did not Dillon call upon me instead of my mother?" Lara wanted to know. Then she sighed. "Of course. He didn't want to ask his mother, did he? And he didn't ask you, either, Kaliq, did he?"

"Nay, he didn't. Just your brother, your mother and the dragon aided in casting the spell. It was quite masterfully done I must say. The timing was precise and perfect."

"Speaking of my brother, what is this I hear from Ilona? My brother is courting a dragon? To what purpose?" Lara laughed at her own question. "He has always been adventurous in the lists of love, hasn't he? My mother thinks it will come to nothing."

"What is in Cirillo's mind and heart I cannot tell you," Kaliq answered her. "Nidhug, for that is the dragon's name, is beautiful, clever and a female of great common sense. She understands duty, but she is, I fear, a little bit in love with Cirillo."

"You like her," Lara said.

"You will like her, too, when you meet her, and you will meet her if you will return to Belmair with me," Kaliq said.

Lara looked to her husband, and Magnus Hauk laughed.

"Go," he said. "It has been quite a while since you left my side for very long. Remain as long as you need to remain. When you were gone from me all those years ago it was Dillon who stayed by my side and kept my courage up, Lara. I owe him an equal courtesy."

Lara caught her husband's hand and kissed it. "Thank you," she said. "Let me go and find Anoush, and tell her so she will look after her sisters and brother for me." Lara arose from her place by the fire and hurried off to find her eldest daughter.

Anoush was in her apothecary making a salve for toothache with goose grease and ground cloves. "Mama," she said looking up. "When will you be going?"

Because of her daughter's gift of second sight Lara was not at all surprised by the query. "I will leave now," she said.

"I'll watch over Zagiri, Marzina and Taj," Anoush said. "I'm making this salve for him. He is going to suffer a toothache in a day or two. Bring my dearest love to Dillon. Tell him that he will regain his bride. I have seen it."

"Have you been able to see where she is?" Lara asked, curious.

"Not really," Anoush said. "I can tell you it is a world of dim or shaded sunlight." She sighed. "But nothing more, really, except that Dillon's bride is unhappy although she has female companions who seek to cheer her."

Lara nodded. "I will tell your brother that when I see him. Perhaps it will help to narrow their field of search. Thank you for taking my place. Magnus says to stay as long as I am needed so I do not know when I will return." She kissed her daughter upon both of her cheeks, and returned to the Great Hall where her husband and Kaliq awaited. "I am ready to go now," she told them.

"I will return her as soon as I can," Kaliq told the Dominus of Terah.

"I know you will," Magnus Hauk said. How odd, he thought. For the first time in all the years he had known the great Shadow Prince he felt no jealousy toward him. He watched as Kaliq opened the golden tunnel that would serve as their means of transport.

Lara and the Shadow lord stepped into the tunnel

and as they disappeared down its length it closed behind them. At its end they stepped into Dillon's hall in Belmair. She saw her son sitting by his hearth, his head in his hands. Lara immediately went to him, placing a gentle hand on his shoulder as she said, "Why did you not call for me?"

He did not even look up, but his hand reached up to clasp hers. "Because I wanted it all perfect for you," he said. "I wanted my kingdom at peace. I wanted Cinnia by my side. And nothing now is what I wanted it to be, Mother. My wife is gone, caught in carnal bondage to a Yafir lord who threatens the stability of all of Belmair." He drew her around to face him, and Lara sat upon a settee opposite her son while Kaliq remained partially cloaked by the shadows within the hall on this winter's night. Outside, a snowstorm howled relentlessly.

"Did I ever teach you, did Kaliq ever teach you, that everything could be perfect?" Lara demanded to know. "Belmair is your destiny, and you were not brought here to fail, my son. As for your wife, she will return with a greater appreciation for her husband."

"The Belmairan dukes say I cannot take her back. That she is tainted by the Yafir," Dillon told his mother.

"And what did you answer them?" Lara asked.

"I told them I would have her back no matter!" Dillon said.

"Then you are the son I raised you to be," Lara replied. "Do not fret, my son. The winter weather has forced you to cease your search, I know. But the winter will soon be gone, and you will begin again. Anoush wanted you to know that Cinnia is in a place of dim and shaded light. She is sad, but surrounded by women who seek to cheer her. She could tell me nothing more, but I thought it a great deal considering the distance between our world and yours. Your sister sends you her love."

"A place of dim and shaded light?" Dillon considered. "I cannot imagine where that would be. It cannot be inside the hills then. Perhaps within caves? But so far no sign of the Yafir have been found even in caves. Nidhug herself searched the mountain caves on Belia. You must tell her what you have told me, Mother. Perhaps she can help with that small clue. I will send for her tomorrow."

"Where is she now?" Lara wanted to know.

"Within her own castle across the gardens," he said.

"With my brother?" Lara said.

Dillon smiled a small smile. "My uncle is as enchanted with Nidhug as she is with him, Mother. Sometimes Cirillo takes the form of a male dragon, and other times he gives Nidhug a mortal female's body. She has red hair, and breasts like melons, according to Kaliq." The chuckle he emitted cheered Lara greatly although she sent a curious look toward the Shadow Prince, who now stepped forth into the light of the hall.

"You copulated with a dragon?" she said to him.

"They invited me to join them one evening in the beginning of their relationship," he said, his bright blue eyes dancing mischievously. "Nidhug was in her mortal guise so it was actually a woman I fucked, and not a dragon."

"And she has breasts like melons," Lara said.

"Your brother seems to have a fascination with large breasts," he replied, shrugging. "I must admit that the mortal body he has given Nidhug is most voluptuous."

Lara laughed. "And you could never resist a voluptuous female, Kaliq, could you?" she teased him. "But Cirillo has not invited you to join them since?"

Kaliq shook his head. "Nay, he hasn't."

"Dillon, my son," Lara spoke quietly. "I should like to remain with you for a time. But this is your kingdom, not mine. The decision is yours to make as to whether you want me as a guest or not."

*"Stay!"* he said with more urgency in his voice than he had meant there to be. Then he flushed. "You do not think me a weakling?" he asked her.

"Nay, my son. I think you are a good king for Belmair, and will one day be a great king," Lara said. "Now, I am exhausted for it was coming on evening in Terah when we departed."

"I will have our steward, Britto, show you to a guest chamber, Mother," Dillon said, and then he asked her, "Magnus? Does he know you are here? Will remain?"

"Aye, and he was insistent that I come. He sends you his affections and respect," Lara told Dillon.

Britto, hearing his name, had come forward, and waited for the king's instructions. He bowed to the king, and his guests.

"Britto," Dillon said, "this is my mother, Lady Lara. She is the Domina, the queen, of her own land, Terah. She will be staying with me. Will you see she has the best guest rooms we have to offer, and tell Anke she is to serve my mother until my own queen comes home."

"If Your Majesties will grant me a little time to see the Domina's quarters prepared properly, I shall see to it. And I will tell Anke of your desire, my lord," Britto said as he bowed again. "I will prepare a place for the Lord Kaliq as well." He bowed to them once more, and then hurried from the hall.

"A well-trained man," Lara noted. "I am pleased to see your servants know their duties. Would you like me to oversee your hall while Cinnia is away?" She spoke as if the young queen of Belmair were off visiting, and not enslaved in some secret location.

He nodded. "I would be grateful, and so, I suspect, will Britto."

Lara settled into her son's home. She was given a lovely apartment of rooms facing both south and west. Anke was happy to serve her, and Britto relieved to have a woman once again in charge of the household. The day after her arrival Lara met Nidhug, and the two females became friends immediately. Cirillo was not certain he wanted his older sister being friends with his lover. His passion for the dragon was far greater than any he had ever felt for any female before. He did not like sharing her. But it would seem he had no choice, and when he discovered that Lara had no prejudice as he sensed in his mother, he became less distrustful of the relationship Nidhug and Lara had forged.

The winter passed, and spring came quickly to Belmair. Having his mother in the castle seemed to balance his emotions, and Dillon felt his strength returning. The search for the Yafir began again. One afternoon a small procession wound its way up the hillside to the royal castle. Their horses clumped across the drawbridge, coming to a stop in the cobbled courtyard.

Dismounting, Duke Dreng said to the servant who came from the castle, "Inform King Dillon that Duke Dreng is here with family."

Britto, looking out from the main door, recognized the duke, and turning, ran back into the family hall where Lara sat weaving. "My lady, Duke Dreng has just arrived unannounced. I recognized his wife with him, and two young women, as well as several servants. What shall I do? Where shall I put them?"

"Have the servants prepare one of the larger apartments. We will put him and his family, for the young women will be his granddaughters, I suspect, in a single suite. Then run and warn the king. Duke Dreng should not be left waiting in the courtyard. I will go and greet him, and lead him into the Great Hall," Lara said.

Britto dashed off as Lara arose, smoothing her long sky-blue gown, and tucking a stray lock beneath her gold caul. Leaving the hall, she hurried out into the courtyard.

"My lord duke," she said as she approached Dreng and his family. "I am Lara, Domina of Terah in the world of Hetar. I am the king's mother. Welcome to Belmair. Would that you had warned us of your coming your welcome would certainly have been a more gracious one." She smiled at him, and then turned to his wife. "You will be the lady Amata. My son remembers your hospitality fondly." She hooked her arm through Amata's. "Come along. We shall go into the hall. I have sent word to the king of your arrival. Is there some purpose to this visit?"

She led them from the courtyard and into the Great Hall of the castle, where the servants came immediately bearing trays holding goblets of sweet wine.

"You are aware of the tragedy that has befallen Belmair's queen, Domina," Duke Dreng began, and as Lara turned and fixed him with a cold gaze, he stopped.

"My lord, I can only hope you have not come to attempt to persuade my son to reject Cinnia when she returns. It would be a dreadful mistake on your part," Lara said.

"Domina, the king cannot take her back. She is defiled by the Yafir. Belmair's queen must be above reproach. Sooner or later he must choose another queen," Dreng responded. "I have brought two of my granddaughters, Lina and Panya, for his consideration. He need not choose now, but sooner than later he must."

Lara shook her head. "Are you so dense that you do not understand what this is really about, my lord? It is not that the Yafir stole Cinnia. Or that the Yafir have been stopped from stealing more of Belmair's females. This is about the survival of both Belmair and the Yafir. You are at war, my lord, but you refuse to recognize it!"

The duke of Beltran was very surprised by Lara's words. He stared at her as if attempting to see through her. She was very beautiful, and looked far too young to be the king's mother, he thought.

"You are too ambitious, my lord," Lara remarked, "and it is unfortunate."

The young king entered the hall. Coming up to his mother, he kissed her cheek.

*What have we here?* he spoke to her in the silent language of magic. *Two fair prime virgins for my delectation? I can see you have already discovered that Dreng is a fool.* He turned. "My lord duke, welcome to Belmair. Lady Amata, welcome." He kissed her hand with a smile. "And who have we here, my lord?"

"Two of my granddaughters," Dreng said pridefully. "This is Lina." He pulled the girl forward. She had dark gold hair and light blue eyes. "And this is Panya." The second girl had rich auburn hair and gray eyes.

"My ladies." Dillon bowed politely, but touched neither of the girls.

There was a long silence that Lara mercifully broke, feeling sorry for the women. "Let us sit by the fire. It is spring, I know, but the late afternoons grow chill. Was your trip pleasant? You have sailed from Beltran, I assume."

"You know our geography then, Domina," Lady Amata said.

"I have been with my son for much of the winter, and have spent my time learning all I could of Belmair," Lara told them.

"You will remain?" Dreng asked.

"Until my daughter-in-law is found and brought

safely home," Lara replied. "We have narrowed the search as you know." She smiled.

"To some place shaded and dim?" Dreng said scornfully. "It is hardly a clue that will lead to any success, I fear."

"I must differ with you, my lord duke," Lara said. "It eliminates the interior of the hills. The caves will be searched more carefully, especially those with access to light."

"How goes the search on Beltran?" Dillon asked the duke.

"We've finished searching. There is nothing to be found," the duke said brusquely. "We had fields to plant and deer herds to cull. We have done what we could. Why do you persist in seeking Fflergant's daughter, Majesty? She is gone. The Yafir have, thanks to you and your allies, been stopped in their tracks. They can steal no more of our women. Our women are protected."

"Only those who were in the halls that day," Dillon told them. "Those born after that day are not protected. The danger is far from over."

"Oh, gracious!" the lady Amata said.

Duke Dreng shot his wife a ferocious look.

"What is it?" Lara asked the woman.

"Be silent!" the duke ordered Amata.

"Nay, lady, you will tell me what it is that has distressed you, and you, my lord, will be the one remaining silent," Dillon said.

Amata shook her head in distress, looking from her husband to the king. But then she sighed deeply and said, "Several female infants born this winter on Beltran have disappeared from their cradles in the night over the last few weeks. And my brother has written to me that the same thing has happened on Belia."

"They are stealing the unprotected infants," Lara said softly, "to raise within their own world. This is a clever and ruthless enemy."

"I don't want to destroy the Yafir," Dillon said.

"You may have to destroy Ahura Mazda," Lara replied. "He has spent centuries simmering his hate for Belmair and its people. It is unlikely you will be able to save him from himself. I cannot believe that all Yafir think as he does. There have to be others who are more reasonable, and with whom you can deal."

"They have to be wiped out!" Duke Dreng said. "They are a dangerous race, and have taken every opportunity to do us wrong. Why do you persist in believing they can be saved, Majesty? They are ravening beasts! Destroy them! Destroy all that is theirs! Belmair is ours. Our world is for Belmairans, not strangers."

Lara was amazed by her son's response to this tirade.

"If it takes me a century, Dreng, I will teach you that nothing remains stagnant in any world. Belmair is not a perfect world despite the efforts your past kings have made to excise all that did not conform to their thinking. Hetar is not perfect, either. Nor my mother's domain of Terah. Life is vibrant, my lord, and constantly changing, evolving. Sometimes those changes come slowly, so slowly that we barely notice them, if we notice them at all. And other times changes comes so swiftly that we cannot keep up with them, and it frightens us. The only magic native to Belmair is that which the dragon possesses. But once when the Yafir lived peaceably among you there was magic both good and bad in Belmair, for there must always be balance in life. You have forgotten that, Dreng, if indeed you ever knew it. But I am going to educate you in spite of yourself," Dillon, king of Belmair said. "Perhaps my mother is right, and the Yafir lord cannot be saved. If that is the truth then so be it. But the Yafir people may not be filled with such hate as is their ruler, and we can welcome them back into our world to live in peace together. The Belmairans want it, and I am certain the Yafir want it, too. With all the women they have stolen over the years your bloodlines are now well mixed."

"My family's blood is untainted," Dreng said stubbornly.

"What of the granddaughter who was stolen?" Dillon reminded him.

"My sister," Lina said softly.

"She is dead to us now," the duke replied. He sent a fierce look at the young girl. "We do not speak her name now. She is no longer one of us."

"This debate, while fascinating, goes nowhere," Lara said quietly. "I see the servants are bringing in the evening meal. Shall we go to the high board?" She stepped up upon the dais, pulling the queen's chair forward so no one might sit in it. "Will you sit on my son's left, my lord duke?" she invited him. Then she directed Dreng's two granddaughters next to him, seating herself and the lady Amata on the other side of the empty chair where they might speak with some small measure of privacy.

"Your granddaughters are lovely," Lara told the duke's wife.

"They are mine by marriage only," Amata explained, "for they are the children of Dreng's first wife's children. I asked him not to do this," she said softly.

Lara smiled. "My son says you are a sensible woman. He takes no offense."

"Dreng is a man who follows tradition scrupulously," Amata explained. "He will not tolerate change, and everything around us is changing, isn't it?"

Lara nodded. "Yes," she said, "Belmair is in flux right now, but so is every world. In Hetar during the last ten years the women have slowly been gaining political power. Soon they will be stronger than the men. The Lord High Ruler of Hetar is not pleased with this, but so many men were killed in Hetar's wars that there are more women now than men, and they are seizing power."

Amata's eyes were wide with amazement at this revelation. "But women," she said, "should be in their homes, seeing to the needs of their men, caring for their children. But then Hetar and its people descend from those we exiled so long ago for the very sins of being much too independent. There must be an order to life or all becomes chaos."

"The Hetar in which I spent my early years was indeed an orderly place," Lara said. "But the truth, my dear Amata, is that while the men of Hetar took the higher place in that society it was their women who actually did most of the work. And with so many of the men gone it was time for the women to control their own lives. Ten years ago all the Pleasure Houses were owned by men who did naught but collect their profits. It was the house's Pleasure Mistress who managed it all, selected the women, paid the merchants who supplied the foods, wines, garments for the women, and the furnishings. The men who owned the houses did nothing. Several years ago a law was passed that set a price upon each house, and permitted the Pleasure Mistress of each house to purchase it for herself. Over half of the houses were bought up by the women running them. And while many women continued managing their merchant husband's shops and stalls after their death, under the law this had been forbidden for centuries. Three years ago it was made legal for them to inherit and own their own shops."

"But were there not men who could take over for them?" Amata asked.

"Many of these women were indeed forced to relinquish their shops and stalls. The High Council mandated a price be set upon each shop or stall by the Merchant's Guild, which was in the pocket of the emperor, and later the Lord High Ruler. Pay a bribe, and gain a profitable shop for a pittance. And the widow and her children were then put out onto the streets with little to show. It was a small group of men who sought these businesses so they might control prices. Women seeing other women homeless with their children, women taking in sisters and their families began to take note, and heed the call of a small movement seeking change. Hetar is in flux, too."

"What of your lands, my lady Domina?" Amata asked shrewdly.

"Things are changing in Terah, too, but our ways were never as rigid as those in Hetar. Our people are artisans, and those beyond the Emerald mountains, the Outlands clan families, are farmers and herders. Our way of life has always been less structured. But women have always held positions of power among the clan families, and even among the artisans. Terah now has its own governing council which advises my husband, and several of its members are female. Women are important to the development of any society. Even here in Belmair the guardian of your world is a female."

"I never thought of that," Amata said. "You are right!"

Lara smiled at her. "Then I have enlightened you," she noted.

"You have encouraged me to think again," Amata told Lara.

After the meal had been concluded, the minstrel who lived in the castle came with his lute to entertain them. Encouraged by their grandfather, Lina and Panya danced gracefully together to the music as the minstrel played.

"Are they not charming?" Dreng murmured to the king. "Each a perfect example of Belmairan girlhood. They know how to manage a large house, can converse on subjects conducive to the female mind, and are certain to be very fertile. Both have mothers who have delivered between them fifteen grandchildren for our family."

"Virgins, of course," Dillon said drily.

"Of course!" Dreng replied, not noticing the king's tone. "I should never offer Your Majesty used goods. Lina is the more submissive. Panya has a bit more spirit, but is obedient, and needs only the slightest touch of the whip now and again."

"That is good to know," Dillon replied wondering when this foolish duke would cease attempting to peddle his granddaughters to him.

"I will allow you time alone with each of them, Majesty, so you may kiss and fondle them to see which one would please you the most," Dreng continued. "Lina has larger breasts, but Panya's are particularly well rounded if you will note them. But both have good plump bottoms for smacking. I've always liked a woman with a plump bottom," he said, grinning. "It was the first thing that attracted me to Amata."

"Duke, let me tell you once again. I have a wife. I neither need nor want another," Dillon said coldly. He arose from the chair in which he had been sitting. "I will bid you all good-night now," he told his mother and his guests.

"What did you say to him?" Amata, suddenly bold, demanded to know of her husband. "I recognize a man running away."

"I was merely pointing out our granddaughters assets and liabilities to His Majesty," Dreng said, sounding slightly irritated.

"Which caused him to leave the hall," Amata said with a sigh. "When will you learn, Dreng? At this moment the king does not seek another bride. He wants the one he has back. I know that cannot be, but until he knows it you have no chance of making a match. And you will but damage the girls chances with the king if you annoy him again."

"At least we got here before Tullio and his candidate. As we passed by Beldane I saw his sailing ship being readied. Where else would he be coming but here?"

*The Great Creator help us,* Lara thought as she overheard. But before she went to her own apartment for the night she spoke with Britto. "We may have more visitors tomorrow. Duke Tullio, and I don't know who else."

"Duke Tullio is a widower, my lady Domina. He will probably travel with his widowed sister, Margisia, and her only daughter. I will see everything is in readiness."

Lara nodded. "Thank you," she said, and went to her son's apartments to warn him of the new visitors who would arrive on the morrow.

Dillon shook his head. "I want my wife back," he said.

Lara sat down upon a small stool by her son's chair. "But what," she said, "if you cannot regain Cinnia?" she asked him. "Or what if you cannot make Belmair accept as their queen a woman who has been held captive by the Yafir?"

"Then I will leave Belmair," Dillon answered.

"You cannot," Lara told him quietly. "This is not why Nidhug chose you. This is not why Kaliq brought you here. As my final destiny lies in Hetar, so your destiny lies here in Belmair. You were meant to be its king, and meant to bring the changes that need to be brought here. You can, you will, overcome the Yafir, Dillon. I know this in my heart. You are discouraged tonight, and I am not surprised. One day you might have to take another wife. You cannot blame either Dreng or Tullio for putting forth their candidates, my son." She giggled mischievously. "It is really quite amusing."

"It is not!" he said, but he laughed. "Dreng told me that both girls had plump bottoms, good for smacking, Mother. He says he likes a woman with a plump bottom."

"Then I am safe from him," Lara remarked drolly as she stood up. "I must seek my own bed now if I am to be ready to greet your new guests tomorrow."

"I shall go with Nidhug to Belia, and search the caves there again," Dillon said.

"You most certainly will not," Lara told him. "You may go the day after to escape your guests, but you must be here tomorrow to greet Duke Tullio and his family."

From the roof of the castle the following morning, Lara looked the distance to the sea, and saw a great sailing ship coming into port. She smiled, amused. In midafternoon a small procession made its way up the road to the castle. Lara was waiting, and greeted Duke Tullio and his sister, Margisia. The young woman who traveled with them was modestly garbed in rich garments, her head covered by a beautiful shawl of red-and-gold silk. Eyes lowered, she bowed low to Lara.

*Beware! Warn the king to beware of this maiden!* The voice of Ethne, Lara's spirit guardian, murmured to her mistress, and the crystal star about the Domina's neck glowed briefly with Ethne's urgency.

*Why?* Lara asked in the silent speech.

*There is darkness in her, my child.* Ethne advised.

"My lady Domina," Duke Tullio said, "may I introduce to you my sister, the lady Margisia, and her daughter, my niece, Sapphira."

The two women greeted each other, and then drawn forward, Sapphira raised her eyes to Lara, softly murmuring a greeting. They were green eyes. Green like emeralds. But Lara saw that the eyes held no emotion at all. Interesting, she thought to herself as she led the visitors into the hall.

"We have other guests," she said as they walked.

"Aye, I saw Dreng's vessel in the harbor," Duke Tullio replied.

"Is he alone?" Lady Margisia asked none too tactfully.

"He travels with his wife and two of his granddaughters," Lara said. "They are most charming girls, too. The hall was so merry last night when they danced for us." She wished Kaliq were here for he would so enjoy this game that was being played. But the Shadow Prince had returned to his home weeks before, promising to return when he was needed. Dillon had his mother, and Kaliq knew that would lighten his mood until the spring came.

"Greetings, Dreng," Duke Tullio called as they entered the Great Hall.

"Greetings, Tullio," was his reply.

The women all greeted each other, but Sapphira remained modestly in the background until brought forward. She did not raise her eyes again.

"My son is searching in the hills today," Lara said, "but he will be returning in time for the evening meal."

"You didn't go with him, Dreng?" Tullio asked.

"Why? It's useless," Duke Dreng replied.

As the spring sun was setting, Dillon returned to his castle in the company of Nidhug and Cirillo. He greeted his new guests, and almost immediately they adjourned to the high board for the evening meal. The king was charming, but distant. Cirillo made the dragon jealous by flirting with Dreng's granddaughters.

Nidhug eyed Sapphira suspiciously, finally saying bluntly, "Why is it, Duke Tullio, that your niece hides herself from us? Is she scarred that she keeps her shawl over her head and turns her face from us?"

"Nay, Great Dragon," Duke Tullio replied. "But King Fflergant and I were related by blood. My niece and Queen Cinnia are distant cousins. I did not wish the king startled by Sapphira's appearance, for she very much resembles our lost queen." He turned to Dillon. "Majesty, with your permission my niece will reveal herself."

Fascinated in spite of himself, Dillon nodded his approval. "Stand up, lady," he said, "and let me see you."

Sapphira rose from her place, and stepping from the dais stood directly before the young king. Slowly she dropped the shawl covering her head, revealing a swath of ebony-black hair. Then Sapphira raised her face up to look straight at the king.

Dillon grew pale. He clutched the wine goblet in his hand, and the silver crumpled in his hand. *"Cinnia!"* he whispered unable to take his eyes from the girl.

"Nay, my lord. I am Sapphira of Beldane, and I am the king's to command."

"Let my daughter dance for you, Majesty," the lady Margisia said. "I have heard that Duke Dreng's granddaughters danced for you last night."

"Yes," Dillon said, never taking his eyes from Sapphira. "Dance for me! Minstrel! Where is the minstrel?" he called.

*The Great Creator help us,* Lara thought. *He is bewitched by this girl.* She looked to the dragon, who also appeared somewhat shocked.

The king's minstrel came forth, and bowing to Sapphira said, "What shall I play for you, lady?"

"Not your lute," Sapphira replied. "Do you have a reed pipe?"

The minstrel nodded, drawing it forth from his garment. Putting it to his lips he began to play a sweet but temporal tune. As he did, Sapphira kicked off her dainty slippers and began to dance. She was light on her feet and very graceful. She moved easily, and then as she began to discard bits of her gown they saw that it was actually made up of many red silk scarves. Her body twisted sensuously and lithely. Her long arms were quickly bared, and shortly her long bare legs were revealed, flashing amid the thin strips of flying scarlet silk.

Duke Dreng's two granddaughters gasped, and looked at each other, shocked. A knowing smile touched Prince Cirillo's lips as he met Lara's eyes. Nidhug's nostrils glowed deep red, and a tiny whiff of smoke came from them as she watched Sapphira through her narrowed eyes. Dillon came down from his chair at the high board, and as the tune ended Duke Tullio's niece flung herself at the king's feet, and then wound herself sinuously up his booted legs, her emerald eyes locking onto his bright blue eyes.

For a moment the hall was swathed in deep silence, and then Dillon bent to raise Sapphira her feet. "You dance well," he said quietly. Bending, he fitted her slippers back upon her feet, and led her back to the high board, draping her shawl about her shoulders. "Thank you."

"Lina! Panya! Now you must dance for the king!" Duke Dreng said.

"I think not, husband," Amata interrupted him. "The lady Sapphira's performance was quite entertaining enough for one evening."

"But…" Dreng began.

"Nay, Grandfather." Panya spoke for her cousin and herself ending the matter.

The minstrel began to play his lute now, singing a song of Belmair's past. The guests came down from the high board, gathering themselves about the fire in chairs and settees. Lara moved to sit next to her son, who was now flanked upon his other side by Nidhug, who was jealously guarding her master. The women chatted amiably. The two dukes played a board game of Herder, which seemed to be common to all the worlds. Prince Cirillo flirted quite outrageously with the three young women, and soon had Lina and Panya giggling. Sapphira, however, sat quietly, stealing looks at the king who found himself unable to keep from looking back.

*She is not your Cinnia,* Lara spoke silently to her son.

*She is her mirror image, Mother!* he answered her.

*That well may be, my son, but it still does not negate the fact that while she may look like Cinnia, she is not Cinnia,* Lara said. *Ethne says there is darkness in her.*

Dillon stood up suddenly. "My lords, my ladies, I must leave you now. My day has been long, and I must begin seeking my queen again tomorrow. I bid you all a good-night." And he hurried from the hall as if he were being pursued by demons.

Almost immediately the others began to rise, bidding their companions a good-night. Then the hall was empty but for Cirillo, Nidhug and Lara.

"What kind of magic does that girl have?" Nidhug demanded.

"There is no magic in her, my darling," Cirillo said, "is there, Lara?"

"Nay, none. Does she look like Cinnia, Nidhug?" Lara wanted to know.

The dragon nodded. "It is uncanny. She does look like my beloved child, and yet there is something dark about her. I sense it."

"Aye, Ethne has already warned me," Lara said, surprising her brother. She explained to Nidhug that Ethne was the faerie spirit who lived in Lara's star pendant, and advised her when necessary. "Tomorrow when you take Dillon out searching again, I shall send Dukes Tullio and Dreng with their families back home. When you return the hall will be quiet once again. Now good night to you both," Lara said and left them. But upstairs in the dimly lit corridor she saw a slender figure slipping into her son's apartments. Quickly Lara ran down the hall, entering the king's chamber to find Sapphira, naked and climbing into the sleeping Dillon's bed. *"Get out!"* she snarled at the girl as Dillon turned murmuring, *"Cinnia!"*

"He wants me," Sapphira said as Dillon cupped her breast in his hand.

"He wants his wife. He wants Cinnia," Lara told the girl.

"I can be his wife, and while I look like my cousin I will soon make him forget her," Sapphira boasted softly turning to kiss Dillon's lips.

Lara argued no longer. *"Begone back from whence you came, and never, ever come again!"* she said, pointing a finger, and Sapphira was gone from the king's bed.

# II

Walking to her son's bedside Lara smoothed his dark hair. There was a tearstain upon his cheek. She shook her head sadly. Dillon was doing his best to be brave, but Lara could see that her son's heart was slowly breaking as the days passed with no sign of his wife, Cinnia. They had to find the girl, and then they had to convince the Belmairans that she was not profaned, and more than fit to be Dillon's queen.

When the morning came, she took Duke Tullio aside, and told him what had happened. "You will find your niece at home when you return. I found it necessary to send her there. I am sorry."

"Nay, my lady Domina," the duke said. "I am ashamed that my niece would behave in such a fashion. I have never understood her. She is like her late father, and I did not like my sister's husband."

"Does he not influence his daughter to good behavior?" Lara asked.

"He deserted my sister when Sapphira was less than a year old," the duke said. "He said he was going to visit his aged mother, and we never saw him again. Inquiries were made, of course, but his mother never received him, and no trace of him was found. My sister likes to believe he was attacked by a wild beast, and killed. She will tell you that is what happened if you ask her. But it is my belief he simply ran off. He was a sly and secretive fellow, and my niece is a secretive girl. One never knows just what Sapphira is thinking. I am not an ambitious man, my lady Domina, but I will admit that my sister is an ambitious woman where her daughter is concerned."

"And had your niece been discovered in my son's bed this morning, he would have been forced to marry her for honor's sake, wouldn't he?" Lara said.

"The young queen is considered unclean now that she has been held captive by the Yafir, and so the king is free to put her aside and remarry," Duke Tullio replied. "And if Sapphira had been found naked in his bed, aye, your son would have been honor bound to make her his wife, my lady Domina."

"How fortunate, then, that that did not happen," Lara answered him with a small smile. "You and your sister will be leaving us today, of course, as will Duke Dreng and his family. I am so glad that we met, my lord."

Duke Tullio bowed gallantly to Lara. "I am glad, too,

my lady Domina. Terah must be a fine land to have so great and gracious a queen."

"And Beldane is fortunate in its duke," Lara responded.

Within the hour Duke Tullio and his sister, Margisia, were riding back down the castle hill toward the coast where their vessel awaited them. Duke Dreng was not quite so easy to be rid of, however. He protested that he had not had the opportunity to speak privately with the king regarding his granddaughters.

"He is going to have to take another wife whether he wants to or not, my lady Domina," Dreng said. "Queen Cinnia is gone, and even if he did manage to recover her she is impure. Either Lina or Panya would make your son a fine wife. Unless the king has made a match with Tullio's niece, who so resembles the queen. Has he?"

"My son wishes no wife but the one he has, Duke Dreng. I believe he would remain a celibate rather than remarry," Lara told him, hoping to discourage the man.

"Celibate? The son of a faerie woman and a Shadow Prince?" Dreng said scornfully. "Such a thing is not possible, my lady Domina. But perhaps you are right, and now is not the right time for me to offer one of my granddaughters to the king. He has seen them. He will remember them when the time comes, for I will remind him. I will go and tell Amata now that we are leaving."

Dillon came late into his little family hall. He looked exhausted, as if he had not slept at all. A look of relief crossed his face when he saw only his mother. "I suppose they were served in the Great Hall," he said.

"Aye, and now they are gone," Lara told him.

"How?" he asked astounded.

"I sent them home," she told him. "I am, after all, the Domina of Terah."

He laughed, and it was a good sound. "Thank you, Mother." He sat down at the board, and immediately a servant was placing a dish of fresh fruit before him along with a goblet of sweet cider, a small round loaf of fresh bread, which was warm, a bowl containing hard-cooked eggs, butter, salt and jam. Dillon began to eat, and when he had consumed much of what he had been given, he said, "I dreamed of Cinnia last night. I felt her weight in the bed next to me, and I thought I heard her call my name."

"It was not Cinnia," Lara said. "As I came up to bed I saw Duke Tullio's niece stealing into your room. When I got to your chamber she was climbing into your bed. She was naked, and she meant to seduce you. Had she succeeded, and she would have if not for me, you should have been forced to wed her. You were half-drunk, Dillon. And her startling resemblance to your wife would have but added to your confusion. I know you will not repudiate Cinnia when we find her. But you must convince the dukes and the people of Belmair to accept your queen again. Their prejudice against the Yafir are very strong. You will have to stand firm against many to gain your way in this matter, Dillon. Had Sapphira of Beldane tricked you into taking her virginity you would have had no chance at all of taking your wife back. You would have had to wed with this girl and make her your queen," Lara said to her son.

"I would have killed her first," Dillon said grimly.

"I told Duke Tullio. He was honestly shocked, and I believe him innocent in this plot. I suspect it is his sister and her daughter who are ambitious. Sapphira was quite bold. When I ordered her from your bed she refused, saying she meant to be your wife. I used magic to send her back to Beldane. And the first liquid to touch her lips this morning will cause a rather unpleasant rash that will affect the skin upon her face for several days with small blue bumps. It won't kill her," Lara said, "but the itching will be very discomfiting. I hope she doesn't scratch those little blue bumps for if she does they will open, and another bump will form immediately atop the first. I trust Sapphira of Beldane has learned a lesson."

"And what lesson would that be, Mother?" Dillon asked mischievously.

"Not to defy a faerie woman, my darling," Lara told him with a grin. "Now, if you are quite finished with your breakfast you must go out to once again seek your queen. I know that Cinnia has not given up hope that you will find her."

AND CINNIA HAD not. But as each day passed it grew harder and harder to believe that she would be found and rescued. She lived in a world of almost total silence. The other wives had taken her into the garden of the castle. It was an odd place with plantings such as she had never seen. Great leaves both broad and narrow in all shades of green, purple and red grew. They were neither trees nor bushes. She saw no beds of flowers or herbs. And the air was moist and warm. Strangest of all there were no birds or butterflies or insects of any kind. Above her the sky appeared to ripple with shades of blues, greens and grays. There was light, but she could see no sun or stars, nor could she see Belmair's two moons except in reflection upon the sky. Finally she grew curious.

"Where are we?" she asked Arlais as they strolled the gardens one afternoon. "And do not, I beg you say, Yafirdom. Just where is Yafirdom?"

"Beneath the seas of Belmair," Arlais answered, surprising Cinnia, for previously she had always offered only the most vague of replies. "The castle exists within a bubble as do the villages and great homes. The Yafir have lived here in safety for centuries. When they decided not to accept Napier IX's ultimatum they looked about for a place where they believed no one could find them, and decided that the lands beneath the sea was their answer. Belmairans do not utilize their sea a great deal. They travel upon it, and they fish locally here and there. But they never venture out into the deep."

"Then your sky is actually the sea above us," Cinnia said slowly.

Arlais nodded. "Aye," she said.

"What a perfectly clever solution," Cinnia noted admiringly. And then she realized with a sinking heart that it was unlikely she would ever be found.

"There are, of course, entrances into our world from the surface. The sea caves on the northwest side of Belia are isolated and deserted. Our men come and go through them when they bring new females to us. They put them in a bubble, and then travel to wherever they wish to go."

"I do not recall being in a bubble," Cinnia remarked.

"Of course you do not," Arlais laughed. "It would be much too frightening a trip for you. You were put to sleep for your travels. When you awoke you were here."

"Why have you returned some women? And why were they old? And why could they recall nothing of where they had been?" Cinnia queried the woman she considered Ahura Mazda's senior wife.

"Women who are taken from Belmair and do not conceive children for their Yafir husbands may be sent to the Mating Market where they are purchased by other men seeking to have children. Sometimes a woman's secret garden will not accept the seed of one man, but will accept that of another. And we do not waste women here having taken them from their other lives. But now and again, no matter how many men mate a particular woman, she simply does not conceive. Those women are returned to Belmair. Of course many, many years will pass before that is done, and when returned the women revert to their natural state and actual age. I have known a few women who have been mated for over twenty-five years before conceiving. But sometimes a man will keep an infertile woman because he has become fond of her." Arlais smiled. "Our husband hopes for a daughter from you. You have been with us for four months now, but you show no signs of being with child. He is disappointed, but not discouraged."

No, he was not discouraged. Ahura Mazda, while having returned to spending the night with each of his wives in turn, was nonetheless taking Cinnia aside at least once each day, mounting her and filling her with his seed. She bore his attentions, ashamed of herself for enjoying the pleasures she took with him, but in light of what Arlais had told her Cinnia was beginning to accept the fact that it was unlikely Dillon would find her. His magic was great, but it was obviously not great enough to learn where she was being hidden. Cinnia knew, too, that Belmair would never again accept her as their queen. She had seen and heard of the few women who had been returned. Some had been shunned and forced from their villages by their own families by those who had been their friends. The stronger of them survived, and the weak died alone.

"Has no woman ever escaped from Yafirdom?" Cinnia asked Arlais.

"A few have tried," Arlais admitted. "But they have died in the sea. The bubble transports can only be powered by magic, and we mortals have no magic. Most never even reach the bubbles. They are caught, and thrust into the waters to drown as a warning to any other women foolish enough to attempt flight."

"A cruel death," Cinnia remarked.

"Indeed it is," Arlais agreed in her soft voice. "Here in Yafirdom everything a woman could want is supplied for her, given to her. Why would you want to be anywhere else? Most Belmairan women understand that once taken by the Yafir there is no going back. And ours is a peaceful world. Eventually we will return to the land, and Belmair will be ours forever then. Ahura Mazda says it will not be long now."

Ahura Mazda, Cinnia thought. A most complex and intense man. He was a strange combination of both love and danger. His other wives adored him with slavish devotion. He was oddly kind, yet Cinnia knew if she crossed him he would turn deadly. And she was not like his other wives. Arlais and Minau had come from noble families. Volupia was a merchant's daughter from Beltran. Orea and Tyne were farmer's daughters. All had been raised to accept without question the decisions made by their men. Cinnia knew she was not like that. Her father had been king of Belmair. The dragon, Nidhug, had raised the king's daughter to think for herself and to use magic.

Cinnia found it difficult to accept that she would never again be Belmair's queen. That she would never again lie in Dillon's arms. But she was now imprisoned beneath Belmair's sea in a world contained within a magical bubble. Arlais had told her that it took every bit of the Yafir's magic to sustain their hidden world. And there was really no escape. If by some miracle she could learn where the bubble boats were kept, where would she go? She was beneath the sea. But where beneath the sea? Off some coast? Which coast? Or deep in the very middle of the sea? She didn't know, but now she understood why no woman ever escaped from Yafirdom.

Cinnia knew that she had two choices. She could accept her plight and begin to make a new life for herself here beneath the sea. Or she could do the honorable Belmairan thing and kill herself having now been soiled by her captor. Cinnia looked about her new world. She socialized with other women outside of the castle when she went out with the others. She saw no misery. No unhappiness. Everywhere she looked Cinnia saw women leading normal lives, keeping their homes, raising their children. Women who obviously loved, or at least liked and respected their Yafir husbands. These women had made peace with themselves and the Yafir. But had they loved their Belmairan husbands and young men as she loved Dillon?

"What are you thinking?" Ahura Mazda came into her bedchamber where Cinnia had been deep in thought. He joined her on the bed, kissing her lips tenderly. "You look both pensive and perhaps a bit sad, my precious."

Cinnia looked into his aquamarine-blue eyes, and then she spoke honestly to him of her thoughts. She concluded, saying, "If you took me back now I believe I would go."

"You probably would," he agreed, "but you would not be accepted ever again by Belmair, and surely have admitted that to yourself, I know. I will tell you now, Cinnia, for as you know I have access to your former world, that the king argues with the dukes that he will have none but you as his wife and his queen. But having accepted the responsibility of Belmair he cannot leave it now except in death," Ahura Mazda reminded her.

"King Dillon's powers are greater than mine, it is true. But unless he can find Yafirdom, his powers are useless against us though he summons me and I must obey.

"In the end the dukes will gain their way. And even the dragon will finally agree that the king must remarry and take a new queen. If your king did not know what he knows, he would eschew his oath and depart Belmair with a broken heart. But Dillon of Shunnar knows that I but await the day when I may take Belmair for myself and my people. He will never give it to me, Cinnia. He will fight to the death before he releases his hold on Belmair. I but await that day, my precious."

"I could end this by killing myself," Cinnia told the Yafir lord.

"Oh, my beautiful love, do not, I beg you, take your own life!" Ahura Mazda said passionately to her. "Is this world into which I have brought you so terrible? Am I so displeasing as a lover then that you would sooner die than be here with me?"

Cinnia sighed. "You are handsome," she admitted softly. "And you are kind."

"How could I be unkind to the one chosen by me at her birth?" he asked her.

"You took me from all I loved!" Cinnia sobbed, tears beginning to come.

"Love me, my precious! I have loved you forever," he declared. "I was not presented with you in order to become a king. I chose you at your birth, and marked you as my own. You never belonged to Dillon of Shunnar, now king of Belmair. You have always belonged to me, Cinnia. You always will." Then Ahura Mazda surprised her by conjuring a small, sharp knife into his hand. He handed it to her. "Open your veins, and mine, Cinnia. If you would die then so will I, by your side, in your arms!"

She stared at the little knife with its well-honed silver blade that reflected the light from the flames in her hearth. When he turned his arm, and held it out to her, the blue veins visible, Cinnia shrank back. *"I cannot!"* she cried out, flinging the knife from her.

Ahura Mazda gathered her into his arms. "You are mine," he said, "and once you declared it to me yourself. I do not think you meant it then, however. You but said it in the throes of your passion." He kissed the top of her head. "I hope that one day soon you will say those words to me again, and mean them, my precious."

"I don't know if I can," she admitted candidly as she listened to his heart beating beneath her ear. Cinnia sighed to herself. The problem with being an educated woman of magic was that you had great difficulty accepting your place in a man's world. It was far easier for all those other stolen women to accept having been taken from their men. They were accepting of the fact that men were in charge. Those women were not used to, nor capable of making decisions. She was.

"What can I do to make you happy?" Ahura Mazda asked her.

"Bring me some earth and plants from Belmair," Cinnia answered him. "I am a sorceress, my lord, but here I have no purpose. With earth and plants I can grow what I need to make my potions and salves. I have no children to care for, nor can I sit all day like the others beautifying myself for your delectation."

"I do not know if I want you practicing your sorcery," he told her.

"I am not like your wives," Cinnia said.

"You are my wife," he replied.

"One of six. The youngest. And assuredly the most bored," Cinnia told him. "If you would have me happy then let me have a little apothecary. Bring me plants to grow."

"Could you not weave?" he inquired.

"I could, but not all day. Besides, weaving does not require great concentration for me, and I will use the time to consider how I may outwit you," Cinnia told him.

"You could make a tapestry for my hall," he suggested.

"I could," she agreed. "Another mindless task, my lord, that will cause me to resent you even further," Cinnia told him. "Why are you afraid of my having a place where I may brew potions and make charms?"

"A woman should not involve herself with magic," he told her.

Cinnia rolled her eyes, very surprised. "You sound more Belmairan than Yafir," she told him. "Do you see women only as a means of breeding your children and keeping your home, my lord? Is that all female creatures mean to you?"

"Yafir women have always been modest and unassuming," he said.

"Then you should not have taken she who is called the sorceress of Belmair for a wife," Cinnia said bluntly.

"The dragon taught you little," Ahura Mazda said. "Oh, you can shape-shift, my precious, and it is most amusing I will admit. But other than that you do nothing more than brew teas and make salves. Do you not know that I watched as you grew up?"

"And did you watch when Dillon and I made love, my lord?" Cinnia asked softly. "Did you not see what happened when we took pleasures together?"

"A trick used by the sorcerer to convince you that you were his!" the Yafir lord said angrily. He had seen them entwined, the light about them golden, the air alive. He hated Dillon for the passion he had, and the passion he brought out in Cinnia. She had shown no such passion for him, Ahura Mazda thought jealously.

"'Twas no trick, my lord," Cinnia said low.

"You belong to me!" he told her.

"If you say so, my lord," Cinnia responded.

"Sorceress, will you defy me?" the Yafir lord demanded.

"Nay, my lord, I am yours to command," Cinnia said dutifully.

He took her mouth in a quick hard kiss, pinioning her beneath him. "Aye, you are mine to command, and I command you kiss me willingly now!"

He would not break her, Cinnia thought. He would take her from the husband she loved. Then she would make this Yafir fall deeper and deeper in love with her. She would break his heart, Cinnia decided. Reaching up she pulled his head back to hers, and began to kiss him slowly, deliberately, with a heated passion that set his blood aboil.

She took his tongue into her mouth, sucking upon it. Her hands roamed his lean body, caressing him with sensuous touches. She arched her body so that her round breasts pushed against him. Then drawing a little away from him, she said, "Is this what you require of me, my lord?" And when he groaned with his longing for her, she continued, "Give me what I want, and you shall have all of me that you desire, my lord Ahura Mazda. I shall hold nothing back from you. *Nothing!*"

"Will you love me?" he asked her.

"Because I am an honest woman I will make no promises to you," Cinnia said. "I hate you for stealing me from Dillon, and from our life together. But I am a Belmairan king's daughter. I know that as much as I desire to return to him and to the life we had, it can never be. From all I have read in the Academy library the Yafir were not always scorned by my people. Once we lived together amicably. And after centuries of interbreeding with Belmairan women you are actually more like us than you would admit.

"I will accept that this must now be the life I live, my lord. I will give you my body, and take pleasures with you. What other choice do I have? It is all well and good to say that you *marked* me as yours when I was born. Until you told me that I knew it not. When my father lay dying I was given to a stranger. I came to love him, and he me. But I do not believe I can ever love you for the injury you have done to me, to Dillon. Still, if you are content to have me knowing how I feel, then I will no longer challenge your authority over me, or over my life. Just give me some Belmairan earth, and some plants of my choosing so I may once again have a purpose. Certainly you have illness in Yafirdom. It will only increase your prestige to have a wife who is a healer, my lord."

"I can have my way with you without concessions," he answered her, a little bit angered by her candor. He was not used to women speaking to him so frankly. His women worshipped and adored him. He was the lord of the Yafir.

"Surely you can, my lord," Cinnia agreed with him pleasantly, "but forcing me to your will will never be as sweet for you as if I give myself to you willingly." Reaching up she brushed his face with the back of her hand. "You know that in your heart, my lord."

"Belmairan sorceress," he growled at her.

And Cinnia smiled into his aquamarine eyes. "Perhaps there is more to my sorcery than you had anticipated, my lord." She drew his head down to hers and kissed him slowly. Releasing him, she whispered against his lips, "Give me what I desire. And I will give you what you desire. I do not ask you for gold or jewels. Just a bit of my native soil and some plants so I may keep busy. Is it truly so much that you would deny me?" Pushing him from her she opened her chamber robe revealing her breasts. He lunged toward her, but Cinnia stopped him with a hard hand. "Promise me you will give me what I want. My earth. My plants."

"I want your breasts," he said angrily, "and I am your lord!"

*"Promise me!"* she hissed at him. And then she murmured a quick silent spell. *Keep me free from all lust. My wish is fair. My need is just.* Her words had been swift, and he did not hear her, for his desires were fully engaged.

Pinioning her down beneath him his silver head lowered to reach her nipple, and he sucked hard on it. After some time had past he transferred his attentions to the other nipple. Cinnia lay still. Frustrated he bit the nipple in his mouth. Nothing. His lips kissed their way down her torso. Cinnia did not move. His head pushed between her thighs, and peeling her nether lips back he licked at her pleasure jewel, sucked desperately upon it. To his shock she made no sound, nor did her love juices release themselves. His cock was as hard as rock, but he knew he would gain no satisfaction even if he fucked her for an hour without stopping. Her small magic was allowing her to deny him pleasures.

In all of his life Ahura Mazda had never been defeated in anything he had undertaken. But now he knew if he was to have what he wanted of Cinnia, he must give her what she wanted. "You shall have your Belmairan earth and your plants," he told her with a groan. "Refuse my passion no longer, my precious."

"I should make you wait until I have what I want,"

Cinnia said cruelly. "But I will not punish you this time. I shall give you a taste of what you want now, my lord, in order to encourage you to good behavior with me. It will not be like our hasty matings each day when you come to get me with child. It will be time filled with fire, and should you attempt to cheat me of my due, Ahura Mazda, it will never again be like this! You will suffer and ache with the memory of what could be. Now let us begin again with my breasts, my lord. Pleasure me well, and you shall be pleasured in return." *Fill me now with heated lust. The debt is paid. My lord is just.* Cinnia said silently as his mouth closed again over a nipple.

Immediately fire flowed through her. She moaned as he sucked and tongued her, his hand kneading her other breast. She could feel her need for him rising slowly, slowly as he moved to her other breast, then finally began to kiss his way down her torso. But this time he did not go directly to her mons. He kissed the length of each slender leg, kissed each dainty foot, sucking seductively upon her toes. Then he surprised her by turning her onto her belly. He licked up her calves, and thighs. He kissed and nibbled her buttocks. Then briefly he lay atop her, kissing the back of her neck, whispering soft words of his love into her ear with a hot breath. Then he rolled off of her, turning her onto her back and looking down into her face.

Cinnia smiled up at him thinking as she did that she would never love him as she did Dillon. Indeed she might never love him at all. But she could see the passion he had for her in his own beautiful eyes. She could never return to Belmair as anything other than an outcast. And like the other women here she would live for who knew how long. She did not think she was meant to be miserable. Dillon would eventually enjoy pleasures with another woman. Why should she not enjoy them, too? Reaching up, she drew his head back down to hers, kissing him slowly, hungrily. "For tonight," she told him, "I am yours, my lord."

Ahura Mazda had seen the slight shift in her emotions within her green eyes. And now he meant to punish her just a little for her strength. Lying upon his hip next to her he pushed two fingers past her nether lips and thrust into her now wet sheath. His fingers moved back and forth until Cinnia was actually squirming upon his hand with her need for pleasures. Withdrawing the fingers he smiled slightly at her hiss of annoyance. "Beg me for it," he said in a cold, hard voice. "Beg me for pleasures, my precious Belmairan sorceress. I have others here to satisfy my cravings. You have only me! Beg! Or I will leave you, and you will go without my cock, which I know you are ready for now." Then he laughed at the look of outrage upon her face. And to tease her further he found her pleasure jewel, and began to worry at it with a wickedly skilled fingertip.

"Just when I think I might begin to at least like you," Cinnia told him, "you show me once more the monster you are!" She strained against his finger, trying to gain some measure of satisfaction, but he cleverly tortured her while refusing her release.

"Beg me!" he told her, grinning, quite pleased with himself.

"To Limbo with you, my lord! Go and fuck one of your willing women who will spread themselves and say thank-you afterward," she taunted him. "We both know that you want only me, Ahura Mazda! That you marked me at my birth to be yours!" Cinnia mocked the Yafir lord. Then she laughed triumphantly as he flung himself atop her, and drove his great cock into her throbbing sheath with a groan. *"Harder! Deeper!"* she cried.

Now it was he who laughed. "You are begging for it after all," he told her. "You shall have what you want, my precious. I will work you harder, go deeper until you are screaming with the pleasures we are sharing." And then he proceeded to do just that.

Cinnia's head spun wildly. Her heart hammered against her ribs. Their mating was utterly incredible. She could feel every inch of his cock as it drove back and forth inside of her. It was massive, stretching the walls of her sheath, pulsing with life as it made its way deeper and deeper within her until she was crying out with the pleasures overwhelming her, overcoming him. "Don't stop! Don't stop!" she whimpered to him. And he didn't until the pleasures overcame them both, and they fell into a half swoon.

And at that same moment Dillon groaned, and awoke from his sleep. He had been dreaming. Dreaming that Cinnia had taken pleasures with the Yafir lord, and enjoyed them. Tears pricked the back of his eyelids. He swallowed hard. Could he, a foreign king of Belmair, cast aside all tradition just to have his wife back? And if Belmairans would not accept her, what was he to do? He could not take Cinnia and depart. The dragon had chosen him to rule Belmair. His father concurred. He had a duty to Belmair. When the morning came he sought out his mother. "What am I to do?" he asked her. "Last night I had a dream. Cinnia lay in the arms of Ahura Mazda and enjoyed pleasures with him. I believe it is true, Mother. I am coming to realize as each day passes that even if I regain my wife, the Belmairans will not accept her. I have tried to hide from this truth, but I can no longer do it. I do not know what to do. They will force me to another marriage sooner or later, I fear."

"I have never before seen you at a loss," Lara said. "You must love Cinnia greatly, my son. If she has taken pleasures with the Yafir lord you know it is because she had no choice in the matter. Why should it distress you? Women are able, even as men, to enjoy pleasures with those other than their mates. She did not seek him out. He took her. She does what she must to survive until you can find her. At least she will not give the Yafir lord a child thanks to the spell you set upon her. We will get her back, Dillon."

"The searchers grow fewer for the fields needed planting, and tending," he told her. "Among the dukes only Alban of Belia truly aids me now. We have sought everywhere, Mother. There is no trace of the Yafir."

"You have searched in all the obvious places," Lara said. "Where have you not looked, Dillon?"

He shrugged. "We have inspected every cave, the hills, the fields, the woodlands, the meadows. We have sought out villages now deserted but we can find nothing at all."

He sighed. "Where else is there to look?" Dillon asked his mother.

Lara considered the answer to her son's question, and then she said, "Have you sought in the sea?" she asked him

"The sea?" Dillon looked surprised. "How could they exist in the sea?"

"I don't know," Lara admitted, "but you should consider it. After Napier IX banished them from Belmair they disappeared never to be seen again. And yet they are still here, and they exist. They are in none of the places that you have looked, but they are somewhere, Dillon. Why not the sea? It's the only place you haven't sought."

"That is true," Dillon agreed, "but how are we to find them? We need Nidhug. She knows all there is to know about Belmair. Britto!" he called to his steward, who came running. "Fetch the dragon to me at once!" he said. "Tell her it is of great import."

Britto hurried off, and within the hour Nidhug came into the hall with Cirillo. "What is it, Majesty? Has some word come about the queen?" she asked him.

"The sea, Nidhug! We have not looked in the sea for Cinnia!" Dillon cried.

Cirillo looked to Lara. "Your thought?" he asked, and when she nodded, he bowed to her in admiration. "Mother should really make you her heir," he said.

"Please, little brother," Lara replied. "Do I not have enough upon my plate?"

"Nay, Majesty," Nidhug said slowly, "we have not looked in the sea."

"How are we to do it then?" Dillon demanded of her. "Are there creatures in Belmair's seas who would aid us, Nidhug?"

The dragon's brow actually furrowed as she considered his request. She thought and she thought. Finally she said, "Once there was a small clan of Merfolk who made their home near Belia, but I do not know if they even still exist, Majesty. They were extremely private creatures and did not seek the company of mortal Belmairans who considered a half mortal, half aquatic people beneath them. The Merfolk kept to themselves. Now and again they would help the fishermen on Belia seeking fish by directing them to where large schools were swimming."

"I will go to Belia at once!" Dillon said.

"Nay, I will go," Lara told her son. "Ahura Mazda watches you, my son. He does not watch me. Better we not alert him to the possibility that we might find him." And before he might argue with him Lara transported herself to Duke Alban's hall.

Ragnild gave a small frightened cry as the beautiful faerie woman suddenly appeared practically in front of her.

"Forgive me for startling you, my lady Ragnild," Lara said. "I forget there is little magic in Belmair. I am the king's mother, the Domina of Terah, and I have been sent to speak with Duke Alban." She smiled.

Ragnild smiled back, relieved. "I wish I could command your mode of travel, Domina," she said. "I rarely leave Belia for I do not enjoy travel upon the sea." She gestured to a servant who had come into her hall. "Fetch Duke Alban at once. Tell him the king's mother is here to speak with him." She turned back to Lara. "May I offer you some refreshment, Domina?"

The two women seated themselves in a window seat that overlooked the sea below, chatting amiably as they sipped fresh fruit juice and nibbled upon cheese wafers.

The duke had hurried to the hall when he had been told of his visitor. He stood before Lara and bowed low. He had been told of this powerful faerie woman. "I welcome you to Belia, Domina," he said.

"I thank you, Duke Alban. My son has told me of your friendship, and now he has sent me to ask for your help."

"The young queen has not been found yet, has she?" Ragnild asked softly.

"Alas, no," Lara told them. "The king has searched every nook and cranny in all of Belmair, but there is no trace of Cinnia. And then we realized that there was one place that we had not searched. We have not searched the sea."

"The sea?" Duke Alban looked surprised, but also puzzled.

"You know that the Yafir are a magic folk," Lara explained. "It is very possible that they have made a world beneath Belmair's seas. My blood is mostly faerie, but it is Forest Faerie, not Water Faerie. And I carry some mortal blood, but mortals are not capable of going safely beneath the sea, either. The dragon tells us that Belia had a small clan of Merfolk. If they still exist perhaps they could help us, and so I am here."

"Aye, they still exist," Duke Alban said. "In fact, they thrive. They make their homes in the sea caves off the southeast coast of Belia. But whether they will help you I do not know, Domina. They do not like legged folk too much. When I took over my father's dukedom one of my first tasks was to go to the caves of the Merfolk and pay my respects. I brought them several baskets of fresh fruit of which they are very fond. Their chief is named Agenor. He was respectful, but cool. I told them if they needed my aid I would always give it, and then I left. They have never called upon me, Domina."

"If you are not afraid to travel by magic," Lara said, "I should like you to come with me to the Merfolk. They have some small magic that they can use."

"I was not fully aware that they had a little magic for their use," Alban replied. "Perhaps by offering my aid to them I offended them. I did not mean to, but we know so little about them. They have always been so insular a people."

"I am certain you did not offend them," Lara reassured Duke Alban. "More than likely it pleased Agenor that you were so deferential toward him and his people.

And perhaps in that light it would be best to send a messenger to the chief of the Merfolk that you would appreciate being granted an audience with him immediately."

"Aye, good manners are a hallmark of the Merfolk," Alban agreed. "But it will take several days to reach the cave in which he resides."

"Nay, we will use magic," Lara told him. "I will change my appearance and go as your messenger." Before his eyes Lara morphed herself into a serious-looking gentleman in his middle years. *To Belia's Merfolk I must go. Take me quick. Do not be slow.*

Alban and his wife were left openmouthed by both the change in Lara's guise and her sudden disappearance, for they had not, of course, been able to hear her silent spell. "I suppose we will eventually get used to this magic," the duke said, and then several minutes later Lara appeared to them again in her own form.

"Agenor will see us now, my lord. Come, and take my hand," she said, holding out her own hand to him. Lara looked to Ragnild. "He will be safe with me, lady. You need have no fear." When the duke came to stand by her side and took her hand in his, she repeated the spell, modifying it just slightly. *To the Merfolk we must go. Take us quick. Do not be slow.*

Again Alban did not hear her simple incantation, but he suddenly found himself in the sea cave hall of Agenor, the chief of the Merfolk. The tide was out, and Agenor lounged upon a large flat rock. He was alone. "Greetings, Agenor of the Merfolk," the duke said. "Are you ageless that you appear no different from the last time we met?"

Agenor laughed heartily. He had the large, broad torso of a mortal man, but from his navel down he was all fish to his broad flat green tail, which was flecked with gold. His scales were green, as were his eyes. He had a well-barbered, short, dark red beard that matched his thick shoulder-length hair. "You have grown older, Alban," he said. "You are no longer the beardless boy who paid me such careful respects all those years ago. And now you travel in the company of a faerie woman. You have come up in the world."

"This is Lara, Domina of Terah, from the world of Hetar," Alban introduced his companion. "She is the new king's mother."

"So," Agenor said, "old Fflergant's sands have finally run out. I did not know. News comes rarely to this side of Belia."

"We could arrange for me to send you word of important events should you wish it, Lord Agenor," Duke Alban said.

"I will think on it," the chief of the Merfolk said. "You know how we value our solitude here. But now tell me how the dragon came to choose a Hetarian king for Belmair? I certainly would have never imagined such a thing."

"King Dillon is also the son of the great Kaliq of the Shadows," Duke Alban said.

"The son of a faerie woman and a Shadow Prince," Agenor mused. "There must be difficult times coming to Belmair that we need so strong a king. Is Fflergant's daughter now queen?"

"Yes," Duke Alban said, "but that is where we need the help of the Merfolk. The young queen has been stolen by the Yafir lord, Ahura Mazda."

"So they are still here," Agenor said. "Where?"

"We believe they have created a civilization beneath the seas of Belmair," Lara told him. "They can be found nowhere else. We have spent the last few months searching the entire kingdom to no avail. The only place we have not searched is beyond our abilities, for it is in the sea. The king is desperate to restore his wife to the kingdom."

"The Belmairans will never allow it," Agenor said. "They are a narrow-minded people who do not trust any who are not like them. They scorned the Yafir. That is why we keep our distance. Duke Alban is the first ruler of Belia ever to come to us, and hold out the hand of friendship to the Merfolk. While we are content as we are, we nonetheless appreciated his generous gesture. And we will reciprocate by helping you if we can. Do you know why the queen was stolen away?"

Lara explained to Agenor about the unjust banishment, and the disappearance of Belmair's women over the last centuries. How the new king wished to end the animosity between Belmair and the Yafir. That Dillon wished the Yafir to be integrated once more into Belmair's society. The response of the Yafir lord had been to steal the young queen.

The chief of the Merfolk listened patiently, and when

Lara had finished he said, "Even knowing that the Belmairans will never accept his wife again the king would have her restored to him? He must love her deeply. Coming from Hetar he has not the prejudice that the Belmairans harbor toward women taken by the Yafir. I already like this king of Belmair, and I do not believe I have ever said that about any king of Belmair in all of my nine hundred and twelve years. I will help him," Agenor said. "You need my Merfolk to learn if the Yafir have made a place for themselves beneath the waters?"

"Aye, that is exactly what we need," Lara said. "Thank you!"

"It will take time," Agenor said. "We are but a small pod of Merfolk, my lady. Some of my clan are too old and frail to travel out into the absolute depths of the sea. But if the Yafir have made a world for themselves beneath the waters, we will eventually find it. When we do we will report the location to you, and we will rescue the queen for you."

"Thank you, my good Agenor," Lara said. "But first find where she is hidden, and then we will discuss regaining her. This must be carefully done, and we do not want the Yafir attacking you in retaliation."

"We can defend ourselves, Domina of Terah," Agenor responded.

"I am told you like fruit," Lara said. "Where would you like me to place these baskets for you?" With a wave of her hand several woven containers appeared on the sand before Agenor's seat of office. One contained fresh apples, another pears, another peaches, another plums, another all manner of berries, and the last, which caused Agenor's eyes to light up with delight, was filled with pineapples. "They will remain fresh and sweet until the last one is eaten," Lara told him.

"There." He pointed to a rock ledge just above the high water mark in the cave. "My thanks!" His eyes went again to the pineapples, and he licked his lips.

One by one she set the woven containers up on the ledge with a carefully pointed finger, elevating each basket and moving it to its proper place. "'Tis but a small token of the king's thanks," Lara said. "His gratitude will be far greater once he has the queen back, Agenor. Now we will leave you for I see the tide returning, and I quite dislike wet feet," she explained. "Again, our thanks!" Reaching for Alban's hand once more Lara returned them to the duke's hall, where Ragnild was awaiting them. "I will return to my son now, and tell him of Agenor's efforts on his behalf," Lara said. "You are free to tell your good lady of our small adventure this day." And Lara was gone from them in a puff of purplish smoke.

"Mother!" Dillon greeted her as she appeared back in his little family hall. "What news do you bring me? Say it is good news!"

"It is!" Lara exclaimed, smiling. "The chief of the Merfolk, Agenor by name, has agreed to help us find the queen. He will set his people to seeking out any civilization beneath the seas, but he begs you be patient. The seas are vast, and their number is small, my son. I liked this fellow, Dillon. We must do something to make the lives of the Merfolk easier once this is all over. What a wondrous place Belmair is, and the Belmairans, alas, know little of what is here other than themselves." Lara continued, explaining in careful detail her entire visit to Agenor.

"Do you like Alban?" Dillon asked her.

"Aye, he is a good man. Both he and his wife would appear to have open minds, but restoring Cinnia will not be an easy thing once we are able to locate her," Lara said.

"I must continue sending out search parties. I do not want Ahura Mazda to consider that I am any less desperate," Dillon replied grimly. "I am going to have to kill him, Mother. I offered my hand in friendship. I offered to right the wrongs done the Yafir all those centuries ago. His response was to steal my wife so that the Belmairans will consider her *defiled,* and I would be forced to renounce her. I do not see how I can make peace with someone like that. Belmair must have a Yafir lord with whom it can deal. Ahura Mazda has lived too long with anger and bitterness in his heart. We cannot change the past. We can change the present and make a better future. But the past is the past. I will not apologize for it, nor should anyone."

"Bringing Belmair to a different frame of mind will not be easy or simple," Lara warned her son.

"If the dragon had wanted everything to remain static in Belmair then she would not have chosen me to be its king," Dillon said. "She did not need the son of a Shadow Prince and a faerie woman to keep Belmair as it was, Mother."

"You have become such a strong man," Lara said. "I hardly know you now."

"Power is both a gift and a curse," Dillon noted. "It must be wielded strongly, yet carefully. And no being should ever believe that in possessing power they are either invincible or inviolate. That is the lesson Ahura Mazda will soon learn. I know that revenging myself on him will not bring me peace, Mother. It will just put an end to the chapter for me, but I will never forget that my beautiful Cinnia has been hurt by this Yafir's selfishness."

"Perhaps her abduction has a greater purpose behind it," Lara said.

"Perhaps," Dillon said. "But what I cannot fathom."

# 12

THE SUMMER CAME, and Dillon had stopped the incidents of female infant snatching by the Yafir, seeing that each expectant mother was given a charm to protect her newborn daughter. Lara had returned to Terah. For now all they could do was wait for the Merfolk to find out if the Yafir had made a kingdom of their own beneath the sea. But with the warm weather the three dukes came to the king, Dreng and Tullio pressing him to take another wife.

To his credit Duke Alban counseled his fellow dukes to be more patient.

"It doesn't matter if she's found or not," Dreng said bluntly. "She is tainted by her time with the Yafir, soiled and tarnished. She can no longer be considered your wife, or the queen of Belmair, nor will we accept her as such."

"We have so many lovely young women of good reputation and family, any one of whom would be a perfect mate for you, Majesty," Duke Tullio added.

"You have already seen two of my granddaughters," Dreng reminded the king. "And there are several other suitable candidates from Beltran. Tullio has his niece, and at least three other young women. But Alban, it seems, has no one to offer you," Dreng concluded a trifle sourly.

"The king has said he is not yet ready to pick another wife," Alban murmured. "When he informs me that he is I will be happy to offer him several young women from my dukedom of Belia. Until then it would be premature to accost him."

"Bah!" Dreng said unpleasantly. "You are a too-careful old woman, Alban."

"Your Majesty," Duke Tullio said, "that you refuse to choose a new wife but frets the people. It keeps the matter of the Yafir in their minds."

Dillon was astounded by this comment. "Do you think," he asked them, "that simply because we have stopped the Yafir from taking our females that this is the end of it? That we can go on with our lives as if nothing happened? The Yafir mean to have Belmair unless we can prevent it. Ahura Mazda must be stopped, and a new Yafir lord chosen with whom we can negotiate a peace. And how dare you refer to the queen as *soiled* and *tarnished!* She will never give her heart to the Yafir. All the other missing women, your own granddaughter, Dreng. Are they impure? The mixing of Yafir and Belmairan blood has been taking place for centuries now. The children born of these unions are as much Belmairan as they are anything else. New blood brings new facets to a culture, and Belmair's is dying even if you cannot admit it. You are stuck in the quicksands of your own selves. Belmair needs to progress, to move forward. And we will, my lords! I promise you that we will!"

The king's angry outburst left the trio of dukes briefly speechless. Dreng stared angrily at Dillon, but both Tullio and Alban looked away. The duke of Beltran would never change in any way, the dukes of Beldane and Belia knew. But they were both aware that change had already come to Belmair in the person of their new king.

Finally Alban spoke up. "I think we should allow the king a full year to mourn his tragic loss. Had our young queen died a natural death we certainly would give him that time. Why do you persist in rushing him, Dreng? The purple sands in his glass have barely drizzled away a grain. The dragon also grieves the loss of Queen Cinnia and she is not ready, either, for the king to remarry. We have had several kings without queens, my lords," Alban reasoned, his words being meant more for Dreng than Tullio.

"I am willing to wait until the autumn," Dreng said, "but only if a Summer Court is held, my lords. There has been no death here. Let the king open the castle to the noble and wealthy families of Belmair. They will bring their unmarried daughters, and while he may sorrow for Fflergant's daughter in private, he will be surrounded by youth and beauty. Surely it will help to ease his grief, and bring him to a more reasonable frame of mind," the duke concluded with a sickly smile.

"We have not had a Summer Court in many years," Tullio noted.

"An excellent idea, Dreng," Duke Alban said, turning to Dillon. "It really is, Majesty," he appealed to the king. Their eyes met, Alban's begging the king to agree.

"Very well," Dillon said quietly. "I will hold a Summer Court." And afterward when he was alone with the duke of Belia, he asked him, "Why did you want me to acquiesce, my lord? You know I will have no other than my Cinnia."

"By agreeing, you have silenced Dreng, my lord. I will speak to my sister, and she will see that Dreng keeps his distance. You will allow yourself to be surrounded by young women, which will give you time to continue your search. It will also prevent Dreng from nagging you. By the time his patience runs out we may have found the queen, and then the difficulty of keeping her by your side will fall to you. However if the queen has not been found by then—" he paused "—I think we must leave the decision not just to you, Majesty, but to the Great Dragon of Belmair, for she will know what must be done. She has known Cinnia longer than you, and will do what is right."

"Would you accept Cinnia back?" Dillon asked Duke Alban.

"I would if you would," Alban replied without hesitation. "You are right when you point out that Yafir and Belmairan blood has been so mixed over the centuries that there is little difference now between us. And if we may unite as one people in another few generations we will all be one."

"How in the name of the Great Creator was a mind like yours born in Belmair?" Dillon wondered aloud. He shook his head.

Alban laughed. "I was the elder of two sons. My brother is more like the average Belmairan. I believe my father would have given him the duchy but for my mother. She told him I would outgrow my foolish thoughts, and I think she believed I would. It is better, I think, that neither of them lived to see I did not. In fact, I have become more liberal in my thinking. There are others like me in Belmair. Mostly we keep silent lest we be accused of being like Hetarians."

Now it was Dillon who chuckled. "To hear Hetarians being called liberal thinkers is most amusing," he said. "They are even worse in their stubborn behavior than Belmairans but for a few differences. We do not eschew passion or pleasures in Hetar. The Hetarians, whose deity is called the Celestial Actuary, have actually made a very profitable enterprise of our mortal lusts and behaviors."

"They are not spoken of except in hushed whispers of disapproval, and the simple folk know little of them except as a threat to bad children," Alban said with a smile. "What are they really like, Majesty, if I might ask?"

"Hetarians are an orderly people with rules and customs. Like Belmairans. They are a people for whom profit and status are everything. My mother's father was a farmer's lad from the Midlands province. One summer's night my grandmother, Ilona, lured him into the woods, and he was not seen again for some months. When he returned he had an infant, my mother, with him. His father had died in his absence, and his elder brother did not want my grandfather, or my mother in what was now his house. So my grandfather took his child into The City, and his mother went with them. My grandfather became a member of the Mercenaries Guild. He was a famous swordsman. Eventually he was allowed admittance into the Crusader Knights. With each step he took he rose socially, and gained in both stature and importance, which is, as I have said, paramount to Hetarians. He was killed in the great battle between darkness and light that was fought over ten years ago before the gates of The City. My mother killed one of the Dark Army's top commanders herself. Like her sire, she is a famous warrior, and a great swordswoman. My stepfather is very proud of her."

"Hetarians allow their women to fight?" Alban was not certain if he should be shocked. Women warriors? He shook his head.

"Nay, Hetarians do not allow their women to fight, but my mother's destiny was to become, among other things, a famed swordswoman. The women of the Outlands clans fought with her. And now in Terah there are small brigades of women who train in the martial arts.

If war should ever come again to Hetar, the females of the Outlands and Terah will not suffer the fate of the women of Hetar," Dillon told his friend.

"I had heard that in Hetar women were now involving themselves in the business of government," Alban said.

Dillon nodded. "Women are intelligent, my friend. Their talents should be utilized, and not just in the Pleasure Houses of The City."

Duke Alban was fascinated by all his king was telling him. He did not know if he himself was ready yet to embrace quite so much change. But Dillon was certainly giving him food for thought. His dukedom being the smallest, he was more aware than most of the decrease in population in recent years. Changes were going to have to be made if Belmair was to survive. Now if he could only convince Duke Tullio to understand this and stand with him and the king. Dreng was a hopeless case, he knew. They would never be able to bring him to reason until the crisis was upon them, and then only very reluctantly.

The king called for a Summer Court, and from all of Belmair the noble families and those with wealth came to fill the royal castle. They brought their young daughters, granddaughters, nieces and other female relations. They were not great in number, however. Dreng's granddaughters, Lina and Panya, were there along with Tullio's niece, Sapphira. Duke Alban had two nieces, Alpina and Carling, his brother's daughters. His granddaughters were too young to be considered.

The Summer Court was lively with games and contests the day long, with feasting and dancing late into the night. The king put in an appearance each evening, and was always surrounded by pretty young women eager to attract his attention. His Shadow and faerie blood was beginning to boil with the warm nights, the sweet wine and the fact that since his wife had disappeared he hadn't had a woman in his bed.

Their long hair, some straight, and some with masses of curls; golden, chestnut, black as night, as red as the sunset; and always perfumed, blew in the light summer breeze as they danced the evenings away. Ripe young bodies brushed against him teasingly. Blushes and soft voices assailed him. Eyes of blue, hazel, brown, black and gray met his, some boldy, some shyly with fluttering lashes that brushed their cheeks like dancing butterflies. Some spoke with intelligence to him. Others, younger and less sophisticated, marveled to him more times than not on Nidhug's prodigious appetite as she sat at the high board devouring whole roasted boars, platters of cream cakes, and drinking down huge goblets of wine. He managed to avoid these fair creatures during the day, but the nights were becoming most difficult.

"What am I to do?" he asked Nidhug one evening when he had escaped to her castle seeking refuge from the gaiety. "I cannot betray Cinnia."

Nidhug sighed. "You love her, I know," she said, "but it is not healthy for a man to be without a woman. Cinnia is certainly in Ahura Mazda's bed, and has been since he took her. He takes pleasures with her, and she with him. But he can only possess her body, Majesty. He will never have her heart. There is no sin, therefore, in you taking a mistress until your queen returns. Just do not give her a child."

"Who?" Dillon said. "The daughters of the noble and those of wealth have been brought to me to choose another queen. I only called a Summer Court in order to silence Dreng and his constant bleating."

"The summer is almost at an end," Nidhug said. "Among those females is one who will give herself to you in hopes of becoming your queen. Seek her out, Majesty."

Dillon nodded, and then he said, "If I take that woman to my bed, is there any law in Belmair that would force me to wed her?"

"Nay, my lord. Not if there is an agreement," the dragon answered. "I would not betray my child. Oh, the parents or the guardians of she you choose will be at first hopeful, and then when they realize you have no intention of wedding anyone they will become angry. But if there is no child, there can be nothing to hold over you."

"You have been with my uncle too long," Dillon said. "You are beginning to speak with the cold heart of a faerie."

"There is much wisdom in your uncle," Nidhug replied.

"Where is he?" Dillon asked her. "I have not seen him of late."

"He was not needed here in Belmair. Queen Ilona

called him home," Nidhug said in a tight voice. "It is better."

Dillon reached out and patted the dainty clawed paw. "Do not love him, I beg you," he told the dragon. "A faerie love will break your heart."

"It is too late," Nidhug answered the king softly. "But he will be back, Majesty, for you see while he has my heart in his keeping, I have his in mine. Now go and find a nubile young mistress for yourself," she advised him.

Dillon announced that the king's Summer Court would be coming to an end in several days. A great feast was planned. Now Dillon prowled among the young women, who were delighted to preen and flirt with the handsome young king. They knew that sooner or later he must take a new wife, a new queen. And they also knew it would probably be one of them. Each did her best to attract Dillon's attention.

Alban's two nieces, Alpina and Carling, were intelligent young women with much charm, but he had too much respect for his friend to consider them seriously. Dreng's granddaughters, Lina and Panya, were a pair of delightful minxes who kept him constantly amused with their antics. But Dreng, he knew, would not countenance his taking either of them for a mistress. The other young women were for the most part typical Belmairan virgins, and they bored him although he never showed it.

Only one woman attracted both his attention and his lust, and that was Sapphira, Duke Tullio's niece. Was it, he wondered, because she was Cinnia's twin in appearance? Or was it because of the slight air of danger that surrounded her? His wife exuded light. Sapphira was darkness, and the truth was he was fascinated by her. He wondered if Cinnia were here if that would be so.

On the night of the last great feast of the Summer Court they danced together, and Dillon asked bluntly as he twirled her about, "Are you a virgin?"

Sapphira never missed a step, nor did she show any sign of shock or fear. "Why?" she demanded of him. And she smiled into his eyes.

"Because I want to take pleasures with you," he replied low.

"When?" she wanted to know.

"Tonight. After the feast has ended," he told her.

"Will you wed me, Majesty?" she inquired coolly of him.

"Nay," he responded without any hesitation. "I am not ready to remarry. I want a mistress for my bed."

"Then you are asking me to be your mistress?" Sapphira said.

"Aye, I am."

"I will ask my uncle and my mother. They will give you my answer." Sapphira curtseyed to him as the music ended, and turning, walked away.

Dillon's heart was pounding. What had ever possessed him to ask Sapphira such a question? And yet she had not been shocked or dismayed. Was it as Alban had said? Did she believe that by giving herself to him she would eventually become his queen? He watched the sway of her hips beneath the violet silk of her gown as she walked, and felt his cock tightening with his desire for her.

Sapphira felt his eyes on her as she left him, and she smiled a little cat's smile. She was shortly going to reap the benefits of a long and most boring summer. She found her uncle first. "I must speak with you, sir," she said, and walking on found her mother. "Mama, my uncle and I must speak with you," she said. "I will meet you in our apartments. Please do not delay." Then Sapphira walked away.

"Girls!" the lady Margisia exclaimed, rolling her eyes to the other women with whom she had been sitting and gossiping.

"She was just dancing with the king," one sharp-eyed woman noted. "You don't think he has approached her, do you?"

"I doubt it," Margisia replied. "My brother says he does not think the king will ever marry again, for he loved Queen Cinnia deeply."

"Your daughter looks just like the queen," another lady spoke up. "We have all noticed it. Do you not think he might wed your daughter for that reason if no other?"

"I had not really considered it," the lady Margisia lied smoothly. Then she arose. "I see Tullio has already left the hall so I had best join my daughter and my brother and see what this is all about. Good night to you all, and may you all have a safe journey home, my dears." Then she left them.

"That daughter of hers is a sly boots," one of the remaining women said, and the others nodded their heads in agreement.

"Do you think the king has approached her?" another asked.

"Well, if he has it was not with marriage in mind," the first lady answered. "He has been celibate, I am told, ever since the queen was stolen away, and I must say I admire him for that. But he is a man, and we all know men need to take pleasures or they become almost impossible to live with. Look at how he has behaved for most of the summer until a few days ago. We did not see him during the day, and he would make but a brief appearance each night, and then disappear. The girls have been so disappointed although several have actually made good matches while being here. The king comes from Hetar, and we all know how carnal Hetarians are. I think he wants Duke Tullio's niece for his mistress, ladies. But we shall soon see if that is it, or something else."

In the apartments that had been assigned to them, Sapphira sat with her uncle and her mother. "The king wants me as his mistress," she told them bluntly.

"Oh, my darling, how wonderful!" the lady Margisia cried, clapping her hands.

"It is an arrangement that does not please me at all," Duke Tullio said. "It must be marriage or nothing, Sapphira, and I am shocked by your words, Sister."

"Uncle, listen to me," Sapphira answered him urgently. "The king is not ready to wed again, but if I can go to his bed, I can make him love me. I look like Cinnia. If I must I will be Cinnia to him. And sooner than later he will want to wed me."

"You are being foolish in your ambition," her uncle said angrily.

"Nay, Brother," the lady Margisia said. "My daughter is being wise. The king desires her enough to have asked her to come to his bed. And as long as she pleases him no other woman will attract him. *Think!* If your niece becomes queen of Belmair, Dreng can no longer lord it over you. The king did not ask his granddaughters or Alban's nieces to warm his bed. He asked *your* niece, *my* daughter. This is a good thing, my brother. We should rejoice in this incredible bit of good fortune."

"Is this Hetar that you would have your daughter behave like a common Pleasure Woman, Sister? Our women marry. They do not spread themselves for any man but their husbands. You would risk Sapphira's greatest marriage value, her virginity, on the gamble that King Dillon might wed her? What if the queen is found and returned?" Duke Tullio asked his sibling. "Do you seriously believe the king will choose your daughter over Queen Cinnia? Or if she is not found, and the king grows weary of Sapphira and sends her away, what happens then?"

"Even if Cinnia is found he cannot take her back," Margisia said. "She is unclean, and will be driven into the wild to die as those few who have returned from the Yafir have. No matter what the king may say, Belmair will not accept a woman who has been with the

Yafir. This is Sapphira's big chance, Brother. I beg you do not forbid it!"

"Please, Uncle!" the girl begged him.

"Do not tell me that you love him, for I will not believe you," the duke said.

Sapphira laughed. "Nay, Uncle, I do not love him. And he certainly does not love me. But I love the thought of the power being his mistress will offer, and if I can eventually persuade him to marry me then my power will be doubled. And when I give him a son..." She smiled archly. "If I give him a son then no one can stop me!"

Duke Tullio shook his head. His niece's behavior went against everything he believed in and held dear. When his wife had died he had asked his sister to become his hostess, for he had no intentions of remarrying. She brought with her her undisciplined daughter, a charming but spoiled girl of eleven. Sapphira was now eighteen, and as determined as ever to have her way. "If I cannot stop you from this precipitous, rash behavior, Sapphira, at least let me make certain provisions for you with the king for your future well-being."

"I do not need them," the girl said confidently.

But then her mother spoke up. "Nay, Daughter, your uncle is right. The king will put a greater value upon you if Tullio negotiates strongly on your behalf. You do not want to be at his mercy for everything. You will need an allowance, and servants, and your own horses and a carriage. You must have beautiful gowns and jewelry that bespeaks to everyone the king's devotion and respect for you."

"Oh," Sapphira said. "I had not considered such things, but you are correct, Mama. Yes, Uncle, you will arrange these things for me with the king."

"I will indeed, Niece," the duke replied. Foolish women, he thought to himself. What they wanted was negligible in the grand scheme of things. He intended arranging a binding agreement with the king that would give his niece both a wealthy husband and a large dower portion when Dillon tired of Sapphira, which he certainly would. After a certain amount of time had passed a man needed more from a woman than just a lush body and a willingness to enjoy pleasures. He needed a woman with whom he might speak with on a variety of subjects. His niece was not that sort of woman. She was totally involved with herself to the exclusion of everything else. She had avoided her small education as much as possible, and was quite ignorant if the truth be told. But she was beautiful and proud, and she looked enough like Cinnia to be her twin. For a brief while that would be enough for the grieving king.

Duke Tullio sought out the king in his apartments. He found Dillon taking his ease out upon a small, tiled terrace, lounging upon a double couch, garbed in a silk robe. The duke bowed respectfully. "We must speak together, Majesty," he began. "My niece tells me you wish her for your mistress, my lord. Is that so?"

"It is," Dillon replied.

"Before I give my consent to such an arrangement,

Majesty, I need to assure myself that Sapphira will be taken care of beautifully. She must have an allowance, clothing, jewelry, servants, horses, a carriage."

"Of course," Dillon said.

"And there is more, Majesty," the duke continued. "By allowing this, my niece loses her greatest value to a future husband—her virginity. She must be compensated for it. An agreement must be drafted that will guarantee her a wealthy husband and a large dower portion when you grow tired of her and send her away."

Dillon refrained from smiling at this. Here was a perfect example of how close in nature the Belmairans and the Hetarians were. Taking Sapphira for a mistress was to be a financial and commercial venture. "You may draft your paper, Duke Tullio," Dillon said, "but know that I should never just cast your niece off when our liaison ends. However I realize that you and your family will feel safer if Sapphira's future is set in stone."

"I thank you for understanding, Majesty. My sister worries about her child as I am sure you know your own mother worries about you," Duke Tullio responded.

"When everything is done to your satisfaction you will turn Sapphira over to me," Dillon told the duke. "I am anxious to enjoy her company."

The duke bowed. "It should be but a few days, Majesty," he said, and backed from the king's presence.

When his niece, however, learned that she was not going to the king this night she grew furious. "He wanted me tonight! What if he changes his mind while you dawdle and fuss over the bits and pieces of your agreement?"

"You, yourself, have said that he is eager for you. He will wait, and you will not seem so much like a loose woman," the duke told her. "The proprieties will be observed."

"You are right, Brother," Margisia spoke up. "Now tell us exactly what you have obtained for our Sapphira." And when he had, she was ecstatic, and turned to her daughter. "Thank your uncle, my child! He has done well for you. And when the king is finished with your company you will have a wealthy man to wed and a large dower. Far larger than we might have provided for you."

"I mean to be his queen," Sapphira said in a hard voice. "Do you think that I do this thing lightly, without thought, Uncle? I will *make* him love me, and he will never want me to leave him, nor will he think of Fflergant's daughter, Cinnia, ever again. I will be queen of Belmair within a year. I swear it!"

"If it should come to that I will negotiate a marriage agreement for you," the duke told her drily. "But for now I have preserved your reputation and your value as best as I might, Niece." Tullio of Beldane doubted Sapphira would obtain her way in the matter but it would be impossible to convince her otherwise. She would learn by hard experience.

"I must go to him now," Sapphira said.

"Nay. Not until the agreement has been written and signed," the duke told her. "Remember, you are not some farmer's daughter to be taken by the lord of the land. You are my niece. You have value. An apartment must be prepared here in the castle especially for you. Your wardrobe must be filled with gowns of the finest silk. The dower portion he has promised must be with my goldsmith. Only then can you go to the king. I will see you treated honorably," the duke told the girl.

Sapphira pouted, but she nodded reluctantly. "I know you are doing what is best for me, Uncle. I am just anxious to be in the king's arms."

And while Sapphira dreamed of her lover, Dillon found himself both reluctant and eager for the girl. "She looks so much like Cinnia," he told the dragon.

"She is not Cinnia," Nidhug said in disapproving tones.

"You do not favor my taking a mistress," he said.

The dragon sighed softly. "I know you are faithful in your heart to Cinnia," she said. "And I know that you are passionate. How can you not be, given your parents? It could not be expected that you would eschew pleasures forever, Majesty."

"But you do not like the lady Sapphira," Dillon replied.

"Nay, I do not. It is not simply that she looks so like my mistress. There is a darkness in her. We have all sensed it. And I know that your mother would not be pleased with your choice. Either of Dreng's granddaughters would have been a more suitable choice."

"Dreng seeks to make one of his granddaughters my queen," Dillon said.

"True, but he would have jumped at the opportunity to put one of them in your bed without a crown. He is an ambitious man or he should not have put those two girls in your path, my lord. I personally favored Panya," Nidhug said.

"Why?" Dillon asked her, amused.

"She is intelligent, and would be able to converse with you on all manner of subjects. All Sapphira can offer you is her body."

"It is a most luscious body," Dillon noted.

"She will bore you to death, my lord," the dragon said.

Dillon laughed. "I have no interest in carrying on a serious conversation with her, Nidhug. I want only to enjoy her body, and sate the months of pent-up lust."

"Thus speaks your cold faerie heart," Nidhug murmured.

"It is my nature," he responded. "My heart belongs only to Cinnia. My cock, however, must be entertained, else it shrivel up and die."

Nidhug tittered but then she grew serious again. "This girl means to be your queen. She is Belmairan from the top of her head to the soles of her feet. Like most of the others she believes Cinnia is despoiled and cannot be queen again even if she were to be found and returned to you. Sapphira wants to be your wife. She believes by climbing into your bed she can accomplish that goal."

"She cannot," Dillon said.

*"I know that!"* Nidhug answered him. "But she does

not. Tell Duke Tullio you have changed your mind, my lord, I beg of you. Find another female for your bed. One who will understand her place is but temporary. Sapphira gives herself to you because she truly believes she can overcome your reluctance to let Cinnia go."

"You are Belmair's Great Dragon," Dillon told her. "You hold the ancestral memories of all the previous dragons. Is there any law written in Belmair that says women taken by the Yafir are unclean, and cannot return to their families?"

"There is such a law, my lord," the dragon said. "It was enacted long ago because the Belmairans did not want to mix their blood with the blood of the Yafir. But laws can be amended, changed or even dispensed with, as you know."

"Then we shall dispense with this law as soon as possible. It has outlived any usefulness it once possessed. While the Yafir may have retained their magic, their blood is now so mixed with the Belmairans that they have become a different race."

"The dukes will fight you on this," Nidhug said.

"Alban will stand with me," Dillon replied confidently.

"Dreng will not, and with Sapphira in your bed it is unlikely that Tullio will, either," the dragon told him.

"I shall do this *before* the girl becomes my mistress," Dillon told the dragon. "Then we shall see just how ambitious that duke really is. It is my feeling that he does not approve of what Sapphira does although he has negotiated with me in good faith in order to protect his niece as best he can. I think he will stand with me in hopes of dissuading her from her course. And if he does Sapphira may choose not to come to my bed."

"She will come anyway," Nidhug said dourly. "The girl is ambitious, and believes she can win your heart."

"Cinnia has my heart," Dillon said, "and Sapphira cannot have what I no longer have. I will have my beloved back if I have to wait a hundred years."

"To be loved like that…" Nidhug said a trifle enviously.

Dillon smiled. "My uncle loves you," he murmured. "And you, my beautiful, scaly friend, love him. It is a most interesting pairing."

"It is an impossible pairing," Nidhug replied, "and I am foolish, like all females in love. But I cannot help myself. I adore him in his faerie form, and when he takes my dragon form he is equally magnificent." She sighed. "I miss him."

"He will return as soon as we have some word from the Merfolk," Dillon reassured her. "He is clever to remain in his mother's forest for now. It allays my grandmother's suspicions that her son has given his fickle faerie heart to a dragon."

Nidhug could not refrain the chuckle that issued forth from her throat. "Ilona of the Forest Faeries is a most formidable creature," she admitted.

"She is indeed," Dillon replied with a smile. "My mother grows more like her than she would want to know."

Using his magic Dillon brought the three dukes to

his castle the following day. They met in a small paneled counsel chamber with Nidhug in attendance. "I am removing from Belmair's laws the one that forbids the return of women taken by the Yafir."

*"Never!"* shouted Duke Dreng jumping up, his face puce with outrage.

"The blood of Yafir and Belmairan is so mixed now that the law is foolish," Dillon said. "I want peace with the Yafir. This is the first step I will take to make that peace a reality."

"I like this proposal," Duke Alban said quietly. "It makes sense. It is hundreds and hundreds of years since Napier IX caused this problem for all of us. Let us end what has been a great mistake. I stand with the king."

"And what of you, Tullio?" Duke Dreng demanded to know. "Will you betray our land at the behest of this *Hetarian* king who has been foisted upon us?" he asked rudely.

Duke Tullio was silent for several long moments. His eyes met Dillon's, and then he said simply, "I, too, stand with the king, for he is right, Dreng, whether you like it or not. Times have changed while we have remained static."

"Traitors! You are all traitors," Dreng yelled at them. "Take the law from the books if you will, but in Beltran the law will stand! No woman taken from my dukedom, even my granddaughter, will be allowed to return to my lands."

"While I do not need your permission to remove this law from our legal books," Dillon said, "I am grateful to you, Alban, and you, Tullio, for your support. As for you, my lord duke—" and Dillon fixed Dreng with a hard look "—do not think because I deal lightly with you now that I will continue to do so. The law of the land will be enforced throughout Belmair even if you do not like it. Do you understand me?"

In response, Duke Dreng angrily threw over his chair, and stalked from the small counsel chamber where they had all been meeting.

"I can see he will take some winning over," Nidhug murmured drily.

"I will tell Sapphira," Duke Tullio said to the king with a small smile.

"Our agreement will stand if she wishes it," Dillon replied. "If she does not I shall pay you damages for your trouble."

Duke Tullio nodded, and then standing, he quietly left the room.

"What agreement?" Duke Alban said. "If I may be so bold as to ask," he amended his query politely.

"I need a mistress, for I have not taken a woman in almost a year now. As a man both Shadow and faerie, this has been difficult for me. Sapphira of Beldane pleases me, for she is so much like Cinnia, and she had indicated her desire to come to my bed. Of course I would not just use her without a proper agreement with her family," Dillon said.

Duke Alban nodded. "My nieces did not please you?"

"Your nieces are hardly the sorts of girls I would ask to be my mistress," Dillon replied. "They are charming, and amusing, but very respectable. Sapphira, on the other hand, is a bold girl. She thinks she can convince me to desert my wife in favor of her. I have been most candid with her. I have said she will not, but she was willing to come into my bed nonetheless. Tullio has not been happy with her decision, and I cannot blame him. Still, now that I have reversed the law concerning captive women, we will see how Sapphira feels."

"If she is as ambitious as you believe her to be then she will come," Alban noted.

Told by her uncle of this new turn of events, Sapphira was furious, even more so than Dreng, but of course for an entirely different reason. But then she said, "It matters not. He will not find her. No one has ever found the Yafir. The king will be mine."

"You speak confidently for a virgin," her uncle remarked. He cast her a sharp look. "You do still retain your virginity, Niece, don't you?"

"Of course I do," Sapphira said, irritated that he would doubt her. "But I have been schooled carefully by my mother in what pleases a man. We used one of her handsome young male servants for me to practice upon. His cock was restrained, and bound with leather so he could not harm me. And Mama was with us at all times. My virtue is as tightly lodged as a cork in a bottle of new wine, Uncle. I shall scream when he first pierces me, and the blood of my innocence will stain the sheets beneath us, as well as his mighty cock. The king will not be cheated. He will have my virginity.

"But I know how to love a man well, Uncle. I know

the places on his body where my kisses and my touches will be irresistible. I know how to suck a reluctant cock to an upright stance, and how to caress a man's seed sac until he is on fire. My kisses are said to be like burning honey. Fflergant's daughter surely never made the king feel the way I will make him feel," Sapphira concluded with a self-satisfied smile.

Tullio shook his head, surprised. Then he looked to his sister. "You are certain, Margisia, that she is still intact? The king will not like being cheated."

"She is as pure physically as the day she came from my womb," the lady replied.

"I am somewhat shocked that you would have imparted so much carnal knowledge to a virgin, even your daughter," the duke told his sister. "Would it not have been best to wait until she was wed? You did not do these things but recently."

"Nay, I did not," Margisia said to him. "When Sapphira turned sixteen two years ago I saw how men were looking at her. I felt she should have all the knowledge I was denied. My wedding night was a horror because of my ignorance. I did not want Sapphira to suffer as I did. And now it seems fortuitous that she is knowing. She will please the king more, and perhaps she will win his heart."

"Send me to him tonight!" Sapphira said eagerly.

"Nay, tomorrow night," the duke told her. "You must appear to have considered carefully once again after the news which I brought you."

"If you think it best, Uncle," Sapphira agreed

docilely, and she smiled her little cat's smile. "Have my apartments been prepared?"

"I did not think to ask," Duke Tullio said honestly.

"Then you and Mama must go tomorrow early to be certain all is in readiness for my arrival tomorrow." Since the end of the Summer Court, the duke and his family had remained discreetly in a guesthouse on the castle grounds while the matter of Sapphira and the king was being arranged.

"I really think we must, Brother," Margisia said earnestly.

"Very well," Duke Tullio said. The whole thing was becoming very distasteful to him. That his sister had tutored her own daughter in proper sexual behavior shocked him. A woman should be taught this conduct by her husband. He was eager to have the matter settled, and return to Beldane with his sibling. There was a very wealthy merchant in his dukedom who had expressed his interest in Margisia, and had been shyly courting her for several years. It was time, Duke Tullio decided, to make a marriage agreement for his sister. He did not know if he could tolerate her in his household any longer. If he needed a hostess for any event he would call upon one of his five daughters. The truth was he would welcome the privacy of his solitude.

The following morning, he took his sister and went to the castle, where a disapproving Britto ushered them into a beautiful apartment in the south wing of the castle. There was a gracious entry chamber, a comfortable dayroom, a large bedchamber and a private bath.

A small, tiled terrace was set off of the bedchamber. It was furnished with a double couch with a rolled arm at one end, and open at the other. There were pots of rose trees and other flora. The bed was hung with rose velvet. The furniture was white and gold. There were colorful wool carpets upon the wood floor, and tapestries hanging upon the walls. There were hearths in each of the rooms.

*"Oh-h,"* Margisia thrilled, "Sapphira will be so happy here, Brother! Is this apartment not the most exquisite place you have ever seen?" And then she began to weep. "I shall miss my darling girl! I shall!"

"Be silent, Sister," the duke growled at her. "Your daughter is not marrying. She is becoming a king's mistress."

"She will be his queen one day, Brother," Margisia said indiscreetly.

The duke saw the castle steward stiffen with his outrage at his sister's words, and was embarrassed for them both. "You have a serving woman for my niece?" he asked in an attempt to avoid future shame.

"I have chosen my own kinswoman, Tamary," Britto replied. "She is a bit older than the lady Sapphira, and eminently sensible, my lord. She will take good care of your niece, and knows the castle well."

"Thank you," the duke said. Then he turned to his sister. "Are you satisfied now, Margisia?" he asked her.

"Only one servant?" his sister said in an unhappy voice. "How many did the queen have?" she wanted to know.

"One, my lady. Anke, by name," Britto answered her in a tight voice.

"Oh," Margisia responded. One servant seemed so mean, but she would tell her daughter, and there would be time to make changes once Sapphira was safely ensconced.

They returned to the guesthouse, and the duke was relieved that his sister and her daughter spent the entire afternoon together chattering, leaving him in peace. His niece bathed and prepared herself for two hours. Then at sunset a litter came to collect her. By prearrangement the duke and Margisia walked with the litter to the castle. Sapphira was escorted from her litter by a serving man to her apartments. She was surprised that the king had not come to greet her. Duke Tullio was not. She did not bid either her mother or her uncle farewell. Turning her back on them, she hurried off.

Margisia whimpered, the sound cut off by a sharp look from her brother.

"The king is waiting for you," Britto said, and he led them from the courtyard to where Dillon awaited them in the little hall.

The king stepped down from the high board, and came to greet them. "Sapphira is now settled," he said as if he had seen to it himself. "As we sent your vessel home when the Summer Court ended so there would be no gossip, I shall send you both back to Beldane now. Are you ready to go?"

"Thank you, Your Majesty," Duke Tullio said.

"My daughter!" Margisia said. "Am I not to see my daughter before I go?"

"I was told you had already made your farewells, lady," Dillon replied. "Sapphira is safe with me, and shall be well cared for, I promise you. And once she is well settled, perhaps you will return for a visit, if that would please you."

"Aye," Margisia said slowly.

"Then it shall be!" Dillon promised her. "Now stand next to one another." And when they had the king silently said the spell that would transport the duke and his sister back to their own home in Beldane. *Tullio, Margisia, by name. Return now from whence you came.* And they were gone from the king's hall instantly.

"Nicely done, my son," Kaliq of the Shadows said, stepping forth from the darkness at the corner of the chamber. "You are eager to go to the girl."

"Have you ever gone almost a full year without a woman, my lord?" Dillon asked his father sarcastically. "Do not, I beg you, judge me."

Kaliq laughed heartily. "I do not think I have ever gone a day or two without a woman," he admitted not in the least abashed by the revelation. "But bide with me for a few minutes more, and tell me of any progress you may have made."

"None, so far. Agenor has divided the sea into sections, and each section is being searched carefully. So far there is nothing to report. He has not many Merfolk but he is doing his best with the few he has."

Kaliq nodded. "I'll not stay," he said. "You should have a few days of privacy to enjoy your new playmate."

"Do not tell Mother. She does not like Sapphira," Dillon said.

"Lara is right in her dislike, but you are safe for now. In any event, I have no intention of venturing to Terah. Your mother stayed away too long last time, and Magnus Hauk was not happy when she returned. It has been years since Lara went off and left her family. He had forgotten his loneliness without her, for he loves her greatly."

"So do you," Dillon said softly.

"Ah, but your mother is not mine, though I wish it otherwise. For now I am content to amuse myself with other lovers. I am pleased to see you can do the same," the great Shadow Prince said. "I know your heart is Cinnia's, but you are the product of two magical beings. Your lusts run hot, and your juices have been bottled up for too long. Go and enjoy Sapphira of Beldane. Let her passions soothe your troubled spirit."

"She believes by becoming my mistress she can cajole me into a marriage," Dillon told Kaliq. "I have not deceived her or her family in that respect."

"Women faced with what they do not wish to hear often do not hear it," Kaliq said. "They continue to fantasize, and believe that they can make happen what they wish to happen. The girl has been warned, and yet still she has come to you quite eagerly because she insists on believing that she can make so what she cannot. Feel no guilt and enjoy her, Dillon. But do not trust her, for a woman like that is not to be trusted. She will speak soft words to you, but her determination is like rock. Unmoving." Then stepping back into the shadows of the chamber, he said, "Good night, my son." And he was gone.

Dillon left the hall and went to his apartments where Ferrex awaited him.

"I have drawn you a bath, my lord," his serving man said.

"Good," his master said, and then spent a leisurely hour bathing, and another hour being massaged. Putting on a dark blue silk robe he made his way through the castle to Sapphira's apartments, entering without knocking.

"Good evening, my lord," Tamary said, curtseying.

"Where is she?" he asked quietly.

"Awaiting you in the bedchamber, my lord, and quite put out to have been kept waiting I should tell you," Tamary replied.

"It is best she learn her place from the start," Dillon answered.

"I agree, my lord," Tamary said with a small smile.

"Go to bed," the king told her. "Good night."

"Good night, my lord," Tamary responded with another curtsey, and she departed.

The king entered Sapphira's bedchamber. "Good evening," he said.

"Where have you been?" Sapphira demanded to know. "I have been waiting for you forever, my lord! Is this how you mean to treat me?"

"It is your duty to await me, Sapphira," Dillon told her. "You are here for my pleasure, and no other reason. If you wish it I will send you home to Beldane now."

"You are cruel!" She feigned a half sob.

"Aye, I can be," he said. "Are you staying? Or going? If you mean to stay then remove your garment for I wish to see you as you were created."

"You are horrid," Sapphira said, but she complied with his request, shrugging her peach silk robe from her frame.

Dillon smiled a faint smile as he walked slowly around the girl. Her breasts were larger than Cinnia's, but the same round shape. Her belly was flat, her mons plump and smooth, free of any hair. Her buttocks were also slightly larger than his wife's, but they were pleasing to look upon. Reaching out, he ran his hand down her back. Her skin was silky. She did not tremble when he touched her. Dillon shrugged his own garment off, and then moved around to face her. "Now, lady, it is your turn to look your fill," he told her softly.

# 13

SAPPHIRA RAISED HER lowered eyes. They were darker green unlike Cinnia's lighter green ones that were flecked with gold. Her gaze began to travel slowly, assessingly over him, but when it reached his manhood Sapphira moaned low in her throat, and fell to her knees before Dillon. "Oh, it is so beautiful!" she crooned, and she caressed him, running her fingers up and down his length. "I have never seen a manhood so large!"

"I was given to understand you are a virgin by your family, and you told me so yourself," Dillon said. "How is it that you have seen a manhood?"

"My mother has tutored me in the arts of pleasing a man. She has displayed the manhoods of her male servants for me so I should know what they were like. But my virgin's shield is completely intact, my lord. I have never lain with a man, I swear it!"

"I must believe you unless it is proven otherwise, Sapphira," he told her. His hand caressed her dark head. "Do what you will with me, my pet," he said to her.

"I must have it! *I must!*" she cried, and then she took him in her mouth, sucking eagerly upon his flesh, her tongue teasing it, nipping very gently as her fingers slipped beneath him to play with his sac.

Dillon closed his eyes. He remembered the first time he and Cinnia had indulged in this pleasure, and she had been so hesitant and shy. Sapphira was not shy. Relaxing, he let her mouth work its carnal magic, and soon she was gagging slightly as both his length and his girth increased. His fingers tangled in her dark hair, holding her there. He considered releasing his juices in her mouth but decided against it. Instead, he silently spoke the small spell with which he had enchanted Cinnia's womb. *Your little womb will empty be until I give a child to thee.* It was actually just an extra precaution because faerie folk did not give children to those they did not love. He would never love Sapphira. He looked down at her. Her mouth was stretched wide as she sucked him, and her eyes look just a little desperate. He smiled at her. "I think that is enough now, my pet. Release me, and we will move on to other things." When she obeyed he pulled her up, and kissed her slowly. Her lips beneath his were soft, and eager.

"Take me! Take me now!" she begged him. "Your cock is so hard and beautiful. I want it inside of me, my lord! I want to be a woman!"

"Pleasures are best enjoyed with patience. My cock

will remain hard now until I release my juices. You shall be cheated out of nothing, my pet." He led her to the bed with its rose velvet hangings, seating her upon it and pushing her back so that her legs fell over the edge. "Did your mother's serving man suck upon you, Sapphira?" he asked her, and when she hesitated, said, "The truth now, wench, for I shall know if you lie."

"Yes!" she admitted, "but my mother never knew it."

"I thought she was with you at all times during these *lessons,*" he responded.

"Once one of the men lured me off. She did not know it, and I never told. We kissed and cuddled, and he put his finger into me, and then sucked upon me. It was only once, I swear it, my lord! Please believe me! *Please!* I am a virgin!"

"It's all right, Sapphira," he reassured her, standing over her. "I shall soon know if you are telling the truth. If you are not I will have you beaten, and return you to your uncle for a liar and a fraud." He knelt between her outstretched legs, and opened her nether lips to view her jewel. It was well formed. Leaning forward, he licked at it, and Sapphira whimpered. The inner walls of her nether lips, a rich coral in color, were moist already with her lust. The scent of her sex assailed his nostrils, rousing him even further. Leaning closer he took her into his mouth, and began to suck upon the sensitive nub. It took but a few tugs of his lips to send her into a paroxysm of pleasure.

He hadn't even played with her delicious breasts yet, but his need was too great, and she was eager. It would be something for later. He stood, and pulling Sapphira toward him he began to enter her carefully, mindful of a virginity that might or might not exist. She moaned as his great cock began to stretch the tight walls of her sheath. She gasped as it met her virgin's barrier. "You have not lied to me," he said, and then drawing back he thrust swiftly, impaling himself to the hilt.

She screamed, and the sound was genuine. "Please stop!" she heard herself saying to him. But instinct impelled her to wrap her legs about him.

He ignored her because he knew in a brief moment the pain she was suffering would turn to pleasures such as she had never known. He withdrew, thrust again, and yet again and again. He pushed hard and he pushed deep into her. Sapphira moaned, but the sound was no longer one of pain. "You see, my pet, patience is a good thing," he said to her as he increased the tempo of his thrusts until she was screaming with her pleasure, and finally when she swooned he withdrew, looking at the blood upon his cock, and nodding, satisfied. She had not lied, and her eagerness told him she would be an excellent mistress for him. He would smooth out her inexperience, and when he was through with her he would let her have the pleasure of his father's passion before he sent her back to her family to be married.

He took her three times that night before he released his own juices. And then he left her to return to his own apartments where he slept a better sleep than he had in months. When he awoke, Dillon experienced a small qualm of guilt over having been unfaithful to

Cinnia, but then was his wife not being well used by the Yafir lord?

And she was. It had been almost a year since Cinnia had been taken by Ahura Mazda, and his passion for her had not abated at all. And while she felt a deep sadness in her heart, for Cinnia knew she would always love Dillon, she had come to terms with the fact that this place, this man, was to be her life. And she had been able to make herself useful because Ahura Mazda had kept his word to her. Enough soil had been brought from the surface, and she had had square wood boxes constructed, which she placed in the one spot in the gardens that got bright light much of the day. Into these boxes she had planted the many varieties of plants the Yafir lord had found for her.

Within his castle she was given a small chamber for her apothecary. Her plants flowered, ripened and grew. Cinnia harvested the leaves, the berries and specific roots after taking the seeds to plant for the following year. Then she dried certain leaves, berries and roots, and ground the remainder of her crop into powders. Soon the shelves were filled with small jars, which Cinnia carefully labeled. She made salves and unguents for healing, lotions for pleasures and creams for beauty. Some ingredients she rolled into pills. And when she helped ease the pain of childbirth for Orea and Tyne, her usefulness as a healer was established within Ahura Mazda's household.

"If only you could give us a pill to birth daughters,"

the two women had both said to her, for their newborns were healthy sons.

As for her own fertility it appeared that she had none. Though Ahura Mazda came to her almost daily Cinnia showed no signs of being with child at all. He was disappointed, but not discouraged. Cinnia was quietly relieved. Within her there burned a small secret spark of hope that one day Dillon would find her, rescue her and bring her home again. As long as she did not produce a child for the Yafir lord she believed no matter Belmair's laws Dillon's love for her, and hers for him, would prevail over all.

But would he forgive her for yielding to Ahura Mazda's blandishments in those days when her hope had been almost extinguished, and her heart was breaking? She had not thought he would until recently, when Ahura Mazda had taken an almost perverse delight in telling her that Dillon had taken a mistress who was said to be very fair. It was then Cinnia remembered that for Dillon pleasures were a natural thing to be enjoyed. They had been cruelly separated, but their bodies could not be denied. As long as their hearts remained true to one another it would be all right when they were finally reunited.

Oddly it had been the soil and the plants that had banished her deep depression. The feel of the Belmairan dirt between her fingers had renewed her courage. And when her plants began to flourish and grow she had felt her willpower and strength returning. Working her little apothecary had given her life meaning once again.

But Cinnia was not happy, nor would she ever truly be again, she thought sadly. Still the friendship of the other wives was pleasant, for in Belmair she had had no friends but Nidhug. And there seemed no jealousy or animosity among the women. Each loved Ahura Mazda in her own way, and was grateful for his company when he chose to share himself with them.

Then one day as Cinnia walked along in the gardens of the castle she sensed that she was being watched. Turning she realized that she was near the bubble wall, and peeking out from the top of the wall was a creature who had the upper body of a young woman, and she could only assume, the lower body of a fish. Cinnia was enchanted by its beauty. She smiled at it. It had to be a magical creature, of course. *Hello,* she said in the silent language, and then she smiled again.

The creature looked startled, and skittered down behind the wall, peeping out shyly at Cinnia, her long golden hair drifting about her.

*Please don't be afraid,* Cinnia said. *I won't hurt you.*

Still half-hidden, the creature said, *Who are you that you speak the silent tongue? And this dwelling is surely magic made. I have never seen its like before. You cannot be mortal.*

*My name is Cinnia,* she answered. *Do you have a name?*

*I am called Antea.*

*What are you?* Cinnia could not help but ask.

The sea creature laughed lightly. *I am a mermaid, from the race of Merfolk.*

*Of course!* Cinnia exclaimed. *I have studied about your kind.*

*What are you?* Antea asked emboldened.

*I am Belmairan,* Cinnia said, and then she looked about to be certain they were not being observed by anyone else. *These dwellings were created by the Yafir, a magic race. I was stolen by them. Most of the women here have been.*

"Cinnia? Cinnia? Are you out in the gardens? Our husband has come to see us," Volupia called, and Cinnia heard her coming near.

*I come into the gardens each day at this time,* she told the mermaid. *Please come back again, Antea. I must go now or they will see you.*

*I will come back.* Antea swam swiftly away through the thick seaweed that surrounded the magic bubble. She could not wait to find Agenor and tell him of what she had discovered. For weeks the Merfolk had searched the seas in vain looking for something out of the ordinary. And now she, Antea, a mere slip of a mermaid, had discovered something very unusual. She hoped it was what Agenor had been looking for all this time. She, like all the rest of her kind, had been told little. Seek for the unusual beneath the sea, Agenor had instructed them. Well, she had certainly found something unique in the civilization of bubbles that seemed to house small villages, and a very large bubble that held a castle.

It took her several days to reach her destination.

The tide was high, permitting her to swim directly into Agenor's cave. "Father!" she said, calling to him.

The chief of the Merfolk was lounging upon his great rock, peeling and eating a pineapple. His russet-red beard was wet with the fruit's juices. He looked up at the sound of her voice. "Antea, my daughter, you looked exhausted. Here. Have a piece of pineapple, and refresh yourself." He handed her a chunk of the fruit.

Antea popped it into her mouth, chewing, well satisfied. When she had swallowed the piece, she said, "Father, would you consider a community of great bubbles beneath our sea in which are villages, and one with a castle, unique?" Her green eyes were dancing merrily, for from the look upon his face Antea knew she had found whatever it was which her father had been seeking.

"I would indeed consider it odd," Agenor said to his daughter. "You have found such a place? Where is it?"

"It is located in the remote western seas nearer to Beldane than any other land mass. I spoke to a girl within the bubble. She knows the silent language, Father. I think those within the bubble must be magic."

"I believe, my daughter," Agenor said, "that you may have found what we have been looking for, and I must now send for Duke Alban. See if you can find that pesky gull of mine," he told her.

Antea swam to the mouth of the cave, and called, "Nereus! Your master needs you. Come quickly!" As she swam back into the cave, the gull whizzed by her ear, landing itself on a ledge near Agenor's rock.

"Greetings, Agenor! How may I serve you today?" the gull asked.

"Go to Duke Alban, and tell him I may have found what he seeks," Agenor instructed his messenger. "And hurry!"

"Is the duke to await further word from you, Agenor, or is he to come with all possible haste?" the gull wanted to know.

"Ask him to come as soon as possible," Agenor replied.

"I will return with his answer as soon as I can, but it is afternoon now. I suppose you can expect me on the morrow sometime," the seagull said. Then swooping down from the ledge where he had perched himself, Nereus left through the cave entry, his wings stirring up a slight breeze.

Duke Alban was surprised to find himself being addressed by a large seagull in his gardens as the sun set into the western sea. He listened, and then thanked the bird.

"You will remain the night, of course. I will have my servants bring you some fresh herring. Where will you be?"

"The water is calm, and will remain so for a time," the gull replied. "I shall rest here in your little harbor, my lord duke. Your servant may call to me, and I will come for my meal. My name is Nereus."

The seagull remained the night, bobbing upon the gentle swell of the sea by Alban's home. When the duke looked out of his bedchamber window as the sun was coming up the following morning, he saw the gull rising from the harbor on his strong wings, and flying off down the coast to the realm of the Merfolk. Dressing himself, he then turned to face a small blank section of wall within his apartments. He spoke the words that Dillon had given to him. *"King of Belmair, hear my call. Come to me from out yon wall."* Still he was a little startled to see Dillon stepping from the stone wall and into his chamber. He bowed. "Agenor wants us to come with all possible haste. He may have found something for you, Majesty."

"I hope his news is good," Dillon said. "Sapphira is driving me mad. She is beautiful. She is uninhibited, but she is the most boring female I have ever known. Even my littlest sister, Marzina, has more of interest to say than Sapphira. Her only virtue is that she gives me pleasures without complaint."

"It is early," the duke said. "Have you eaten? Would you like breakfast?"

"Let us go and see what Agenor has to say first. I will not enjoy my food otherwise. We will use Shadow magic today. Step beneath my cloak," the king said.

"What if the tide is in?" Alban asked nervously.

Dillon smiled. "A good thought," he paused. "And now it is fixed." He draped his white cloak about them, and when Alban opened his eyes again, for he had instinctively closed them, they were standing upon a crescent of sand before Agenor's rock. "Good morrow, Agenor!" Dillon called to the merman.

"Ah, so 'twas your magic that swept the water back,"

Agenor said. "My messenger isn't even back yet, and here you are. Come up and join me upon my rock, and let the waters flow back in. It is my young daughter, Antea, who brings the news I believe you seek, king of Belmair."

With a casual wave of his hand, Dillon set himself and Duke Alban up upon Agenor's huge flat-topped stone seat of office. He next produced two pillows, and they sat, one on each side of the chief of the Merfolk. "I believe we are ready to hear what it is your daughter has to say to us, Agenor."

"Antea, come into the cave," Agenor called in a booming voice.

They watched as the mermaid swam beneath the crystal blue-green waters and over the pale sugar sands into the cave. When she popped to the surface, they saw a very pretty girl with long, thick, blond hair and bright sea-green eyes. "Good morrow, Father," Antea said. "Good morrow, my lords."

"This is the king, Daughter," Agenor said, gesturing with a hand to Dillon. "Tell him exactly what you saw, and where you saw it."

"Three days ago as I swam beneath the western seas I came upon a group of large bubbles, and within these bubbles were villages, and in one, a castle. I knew at once it was magic. As I watched I observed mortal folk moving back and forth within the village bubbles, living their lives in an ordinary fashion."

"Were some of these folk silver-haired, Antea?" Dillon asked the mermaid.

"Indeed, Majesty, all the men seemed to be and some of the women, but most of the women were dark or fair," Antea said.

"Did you swim near the castle?" Duke Alban inquired.

"I did! It is most beautiful, but it is set within a garden. As I swam closer to view the garden I saw a girl, and she saw me. She smiled, and then she spoke to me in the silent language. I was very surprised, but then I thought that all of it is surely magic-made, my lords, so the folk within, while looking mortal, are nonetheless magic."

"Did the girl tell you who they were?" Dillon asked.

"Nay, we spoke but briefly, but then someone called her. She did not want them to see me, and told me to go. But she asked me to return again. She says she goes to the garden at the same time each day," Antea said.

"Did you hear the girl's name when it was called?" Dillon said.

Antea nodded her head. "But she had already told me her name, and I told her mine. Her name is Cinnia."

Dillon groaned as if he had been injured. Then he took a deep breath, and asked Antea, "Tell me what this girl looked like."

"She was as pale as the moonlight with beautiful long sable-black hair and spring-green eyes. When I first saw her she was digging in a great box of what looked like real earth such as I have seen from the sea. It was not sand."

"It would appear that my daughter has found the queen," Agenor said quietly.

Dillon nodded, and then he said, "Antea, I need you to return to that castle. Will you go for me? I know it is far, but you have already earned a great reward for your discovery. And you will have anything I can give you if you will continue to aid me."

"My lord, I will gladly aid you for naught," Antea said, and Agenor beamed with pride at his daughter's kind heart.

"You must go back to the bubble with the castle, and wait until you see Cinnia again. Let no one else see you. Speak to no one else. Speak only to her," Dillon said.

"What shall I say, Majesty?" Antea asked him.

"Ask her if she is the daughter of Fflergant, and wife to Dillon. If she tells you she is then say to her, *the king counsels you to patience. Now that he has found you, he will find a way to rescue you.* Can you remember that, Antea?"

"I can, my lord," the young mermaid said. "I will go now with your permission, and my father's permission."

"Be careful, Antea," Agenor advised her, "and come back as soon as you have delivered your message."

With a saucy flip of her tail Antea dove beneath the sea and swam swiftly from her father's cave. She left behind her a small spray of golden foam.

"My mermen and I can help to retrieve your wife from beneath the sea," Agenor said to the king. "You will take a sailing vessel to the spot just above this castle. We will then retrieve the queen and bring her to the surface."

"But how can she possibly breathe? She will drown before she reaches the surface," Duke Alban said.

"Not if she is carrying a piece of our magic seaweed. It will enable her to breathe beneath the water as she rises up," Agenor explained. "But how will we get through into the bubble without destroying it and alerting the Yafir? These folk are the Yafir, Majesty, are they not?"

Dillon nodded. "I will give you a spell that will let you pass through the bubble when you need to, and return back, as well. You will leave something in the castle garden when you retrieve my wife." He smiled wickedly and chuckled.

"I will send for Duke Alban, and he will send to you, when my daughter returns again, Majesty," Agenor said.

Dillon nodded, and then standing with Alban he threw his cloak about them, and they were gone. Agenor shook his head in wonder, and then he noticed that where there had been two large silk cushions there were now two baskets of pineapples. He smiled broadly. In the end his aid would cost more than fresh fruit, but then the king was aware of that, he knew.

"WE HAVE FOUND her," Dillon told his father, his uncle and Nidhug as they spoke within a sealed room inside his castle. He had immediately sent for Kaliq and Cirillo when he returned from Duke Alban's. "Agenor has come up with a plan to rescue her." And he explained carefully.

"When Ahura Mazda finds her gone he will come here to retrieve her," Cirillo said. "And then you will have the difficulty of the Belmairans wanting to reject her."

"He will not come if he does not realize that he has not lost her," Dillon said slyly.

They looked at one another and finally to Dillon, confused.

And then the great Shadow Prince began to smile. "It is brilliant!" he said.

"What is brilliant?" Nidhug asked.

"Of course!" Cirillo exclaimed.

"Of course what?" Nidhug demanded to know.

"We will substitute Sapphira for Cinnia," Dillon said.

"He will see through it at once. For one thing her eyes are darker than the queen's," the dragon pointed out. "And she will protest, and tell the Yafir who she is."

"I can change the color of her eyes with my magic," Dillon said. "And I will release her womb from my infertility charm while placing a confusion spell upon her. She will not be certain who she really is at all, and her temporary loss of memories will be put down to the fall she will appear to have taken in the gardens. Sapphira's lustful nature will delight Ahura Mazda, and he will impregnate her. Then he will cosset and spoil her as is his nature with his women when their bellies swell. And he shall have his heart's desire of her. A daughter!

Her memories of who she really is will return then, but I suspect she will not care at that point."

"It is a daring plan," Kaliq said. "And it is well thought out. But you need to do more in this matter than just rescue your wife."

"I am aware of that," Dillon replied. "When I regain possession of my wife I will announce that I am taking Sapphira in marriage. We will plan a great wedding feast for all the kingdom. The false Sapphira will announce she is changing her name to Cinnia in honor of my first wife."

"And you will not set Belmairan against Belmairan over the matter of you taking your old wife back. As far as all of Belmair will be concerned, Cinnia, daughter of Fflergant, was kidnapped by the Yafir, and is lost to you. And King Dillon has taken Sapphira, niece of Tullio of Beldane, as his new wife. Sapphira in a grand gesture to honor her predecessor takes her name. Aye, it is wickedly clever," Nidhug approved.

"The mix of Shadow and faerie blood, it would seem, is a good one," Cirillo noted.

"When I tell Mother she will be so proud."

"I do not mean to allow this incident to thwart my plans to bring Belmairan and Yafir together again as one people," Dillon said. "Ahura Mazda is too filled with bitterness to help me attain my goal. We will have to find another Yafir to become lord. He cannot be the only one capable of negotiation for his people."

"Cinnia may be able to help us when she returns," Nidhug said. "She has been with them for just over a year now, and has surely learned a great deal about them."

"And what is to become of Ahura Mazda?" Kaliq said. "He does not appear to be a man who will step aside for another, even blood kin. We will see he loses favor with the Yafir, and when he has, factions will arise to depose him. When that happens we will choose he who will be the next lord, and see that he gains his people's favor."

"I mean to see him dead," Dillon answered in a cold, deadly voice. "He has taken my wife from me, used her body for his pleasure, stolen a year of our lives from us. For this he will forfeit his life. He will be no loss to either Belmair or Yafirdom."

"He will deserve whatever you give him, Majesty," the dragon said.

Dillon smiled at her. "I have known wickeder," he replied. "The difficulty with Ahura Mazda is that he is resistant to change. Nor will he accept change from others. Actually he is much like Dreng. I honestly do not know if I can ever forgive what he has done to Cinnia, but it is his obdurate nature that will cost him his life. He will always cause dissent, and that dissent can prevent the union of our peoples. Whether or not Ahura Mazda or Dreng likes it, we must share this world. Better we share it in peace. We are different in many ways, alike in many ways. Imagine what we may accomplish united," Dillon said enthusiastically.

"Indeed Belmair can flourish with a great sorcerer as its leader," the dragon said with equal zeal.

"Nothing will prosper for Belmair as it should without its sorceress," Dillon replied. "Cinnia must be restored to her rightful place."

The others murmured their agreement.

"For now we must await word from Agenor," Kaliq reminded them.

"And our plans must be kept secret from all," Nidhug said. "But how will we get to the spot Agenor's Merfolk located without attracting attention?"

"On the day appointed, Sapphira and I will go for a sail. I will transport the vessel by means of my magic to the proper site where Agenor will await me. Sapphira will have already been rendered unconscious, and dressed in a garb matching the one Cinnia will be wearing. The Merfolk will tuck their magical seaweed in her pocket, and take her below the sea to the castle comb where Cinnia should be awaiting. The switch will be made, the seaweed put in Cinnia's pocket, and she will be brought to the surface, where I will await her. I will then bring our little vessel back to our own harbor, explaining to my wife as we travel what has happened, how we have accomplished it and what she must now do to pretend she is Sapphira so none will ever know that we have outwitted the Yafir lord," Dillon explained.

"Will not some be suspicious?" Cirillo asked.

"Perhaps," Dillon said. "But on what will they base their doubts?"

"I will give Cinnia Sapphira's memories up to the day she came to the castle," Kaliq said. "I do not think she would appreciate knowing those memories she gained after arriving," he concluded with a small smile.

Dillon chuckled. "Nay, she would not," he agreed.

"And we can blur the eyes of Sapphira's mother and uncle each time they see her so she appears to them as she has always been," Cirillo added.

"So now we wait for word from Agenor," Dillon said.

"You feel no pity for Sapphira?" Kaliq asked the young king.

Dillon paused, and then he sighed. "Aye, I do," he admitted. "But she will not be harmed by Ahura Mazda. Indeed he will love her above all of his other wives, for she will give him the daughter he so desperately desires. And he will heap many riches upon her. Sapphira is not just greedy for pleasures. She is greedy for treasures of all kinds. Once she gets the lay of the land in which she has been put, she will thrive."

"Does he love the others?" Kaliq asked quietly. "How do you know?"

"Aye, he does," Dillon answered. "With his women the Yafir is gentle and tender. I have watched him in my reflecting bowl. It did not tell me where he was but I could see, and before you ask I did not watch his private moments with them. I could not have borne that. As for Sapphira, she wanted to be my mistress. I did not force her to it. She has done all she could to gain my heart, but I cannot give what I no longer possess. I believe she will be happier where we send her."

Kaliq nodded, satisfied with his son's answer. The older Dillon grew, the more visible and stronger his magical blood became. He would love deeply, passionately, but he was also capable of detaching himself entirely from the mortals around him, and when it became necessary he could exhibit a cold faerie heart. But Dillon was right about mending the rift between the people of Belmair and the Yafir. It had to be done. And Ahura Mazda's bitterness could not be allowed to interfere. The Yafir lord's strength of will and determination had held the Yafir tightly together during the centuries, but now it was time to make changes. As in Hetar, war was not the answer.

They were moving deeper into the autumn now. They had celebrated the end of the year, and the beginning of the new year before word came from Agenor. Keeping their knowledge secret from Sapphira was difficult, for the three men and the dragon were eager to successfully complete their clandestine plot against the Yafir. Dillon was becoming distant with Sapphira, which worried her, for she had not given up on her desire to be queen. She had been unable to conceive a child so far, and now he was spending less and less time in her bed. Sapphira was beginning to feel panic. What if he sent her home, and she had to marry some wealthy man chosen for her?

As they sat eating one evening in the Great Hall—for Dillon would not eat with her in the little family hall he had shared with Cinnia—Sapphira began to whine at him.

"What is it I have done to displease you, my lord?"

"Displease me?" Dillon looked puzzled. "You have

done nothing to displease me, Sapphira. Why would you think it?"

"We do not talk together anymore," Sapphira said.

"We have never talked together, Sapphira," he told her. "Your great skill is giving pleasures. It is not conversation."

"That is cruel!" she cried.

"I did not ask you to be my mistress because of your conversational skills, Sapphira," Dillon told her frankly, "and do not tell me you thought otherwise. Is it cruel to say you are a wonderful lover, and I enjoy the time spent in your bed?"

"It is not enough!" Her eyes were almost black with her outrage.

"I have never lied to you, Sapphira. You knew from the beginning, and your uncle knew, that all I wanted of you was your lovely body."

"It is not enough!" she repeated

"I never hid my desire for you, but I have been very candid from the beginning that all I wanted of you was pleasures," Dillon replied. "Perhaps knowing that you wanted more of me, I was wrong to take you, Sapphira."

"I hate you!" she shrieked at him. "You have a cold faerie heart for all your kindness, my lord. I hate you!" Rising from the high board she ran from the hall.

"She is only angry," Cirillo noted, "for she has been thwarted, and is only now beginning to face that fact. Still, she is not yet ready to give up her quest to be your bride and your queen."

"It makes what we must do easier," Dillon told his

uncle. "The Merfolk are in place and ready. Tomorrow I will take Sapphira, and we will affect the transfer between Yafirdom and Belmair."

"How do you propose to get her to forgive you this night's episode?" Kaliq asked.

"If Sapphira is true to form," Dillon told his father, "a night alone to consider new schemes for entrapping me into marriage will have her disposition sweet and sunny. She will be anxious to please me, and when I suggest that we sail out to enjoy the day she will be most agreeable, my lords."

"You are certain the day will be fair, the winds gentle?" Kaliq said.

"You will assure it for me, my lord, will you not?" Dillon teased the Shadow lord.

Kaliq laughed. "Sometimes," he said, "you remind me of your mother."

"But the day will be fair, and the winds favorable?" Dillon persisted.

"They will," Kaliq agreed with a smile.

The men remained in the hall talking and drinking the excellent Belmairan wine until Britto came to remind them of the late hour. Kaliq, Dillon and Cirillo had spent many years together, and had a great number of memories to share and enjoy. Britto felt almost guilty interrupting them, for there was something warm and wonderful about their laughter that made the mortals in the hall feel safe and comforted; but magical beings or not, he decided, they needed their sleep.

When the morning came and they all gathered for

the first meal of the day, they found Sapphira in the hall before them. As Dillon had predicted she was sunny and even winsome, almost entwining herself about the king in her effort to erase her anger of the previous evening.

"Am I forgiven?" she purred at him, her lips almost touching his, her fingertips playing with his nape.

"Of course you are," he said, giving her a quick kiss on those cherry lips. "And I have taken what you said to heart, Sapphira. So today we shall go down to the sea, and sail down the coast where we shall have a picnic. We shall speak all you wish."

"Oh, how wonderful!" Sapphira cried, clapping her hands. "Just the two of us?"

"Just the two of us," he told her.

She beamed, pleased at him, forgiving him leaving her alone—again—last night after their quarrel. Then Sapphira considered how she would seduce him today and conceive a child with him. When that happened she knew he would wed her, and she would be queen of Belmair as she had planned when Cinnia had been taken by the Yafir. "I must change my gown," she said. And without another word she hurried to her chamber where Tamary helped her into a charming scarlet gown of thin silk with a low neckline, and loose sleeves that fell to her elbows. She wore soft black leather slippers on her slender feet.

"You look lovely, mistress," Tamary said.

"Of course I do," Sapphira replied. "Now make certain to have my bath hot and ready when I return. The king will be visiting my bed tonight."

"You are certain?" Tamary asked, surprised.

"Of course I am certain," Sapphira replied, her tone annoyed. "Why would you even ask such a question of me?"

"But of late the king has not come, mistress," Tamary said.

Sapphira slapped her serving woman hard across her cheek. "Do not dare to spread such falsehoods among your low companions," she warned. "Now be certain to have my bath ready when I come back, or I will have you beaten. Your service of late has been most slack, Tamary."

Sapphira and Dillon went to the castle's courtyard where two horses were saddled and awaiting them. He lifted her into the saddle, smiling to himself at the bold display of her breasts. Sapphira spread her bright red skirts prettily over her horse's flank. Dillon mounted his own animal, and they moved from the courtyard at a leisurely pace down the hill road, through the castle village, finally reaching the small harbor. Taking Sapphira from her horse's back, he helped her into the small vessel moored to the stone quai.

"I thought the boat would be bigger," Sapphira said. "Where is the captain?"

"I am the captain," Dillon told her. "You wanted it to be just the two of us, and so it is," he told her, jumping down into the boat, loosening the rope securing it to the quai.

"I thought you grew up in the desert," Sapphira said nervously.

"I spent my early years in the Outlands, and then in Terah, where my stepfather, Magnus Hauk, taught me to sail," Dillon told her. "I know what I am doing. The day is fair, and the winds gentle, Sapphira. But if you are afraid I will return you back to the castle. As for me, I mean to go sailing."

"No, no!" Sapphira replied. "I will come with you. Oh, look! Here is a lovely willow basket of food and wine for us." She settled herself upon a large silk cushion.

Dillon turned his back to her and raised the small white sail. It caught the wind, and they began to move away from the stone quai. Sapphira sat quietly while he concentrated on sailing them out of the harbor, but once free of it he turned to her, smiling. "You see, Sapphira, I am quite capable of handling our little vessel."

"But if you must spend all your time sailing this ship, when will we have time to talk?" she asked him, pouting just slightly.

"We are talking," he reminded her. "But perhaps you would like to nap in the sunshine until we reach our destination," Dillon suggested.

Sapphira sighed dramatically. "Perhaps I shall nap," she said, curling up and closing her eyes.

*Sleep until you are bidden to waken, with memories but briefly forsaken,* Dillon said silently, and watched as Sapphira slipped into a deep slumber. *Eyes dark will now be light, womb unlock and all be right,* he completed the rest of his spell. It was going to be next to impossible for Ahura Mazda to see any difference between

Cinnia and Sapphira. With his companion now totally unaware, Dillon's little vessel flew quickly, magically over the gentle waves. Ahead of him the Merfolk were leaping and swimming, leading him to his destination. Reaching it, he found Agenor and his pretty daughter.

"A small difficulty has arisen," Agenor said. Then he turned to his daughter. "Tell the king, my child."

"She does not want to return," Antea said softly.

"What?" Dillon was astounded. "What do you mean she doesn't want to return?"

"Can you swim?" Agenor asked.

Dillon nodded.

"Then I think it is best you go and speak with her yourself, Majesty. This is an argument to be decided between husband and wife. And it will be resolved a great deal faster than if we keep going back and forth with your conversation." Agenor reached up, and handed the king a length of seaweed. "Keep this with you at all times, and you will be able to breathe beneath the water," he said. "I will lead you myself."

"Is there some of your magical seaweed for Sapphira? I would take her with us," Dillon told the chief of the Merfolk.

"Aye," he said, and gave Dillon a second piece.

Dillon tucked the greenery in the deep valley between Sapphira's breasts. Then he handed her over the side to Agenor's mermen. Pulling off his boots, he put his own magical seaweed in his shirt pocket and dove into the waters. Agenor at his side, they descended deeper and deeper into the sea. To his amazement he had no difficulty at all in breathing. And then Dillon saw ahead of him the shining bubbles that housed the Yafir.

Agenor and Antea led him to the largest of the bubbles.

*It is almost time for her to come into the garden,* Antea said in the silent tongue.

*Remain hidden within these large plants until I am certain she is alone.*

They waited, and then after several minutes had passed, Cinnia came into view. Dillon's heart contracted with his joy. He watched her smile as Antea swam into Cinnia's sight, and Cinnia smiled, coming forward.

*I will open the wall between the water and the interior of the bubble,* Agenor told him. *We must move quickly, for I have but a few minutes before that wall must be closed, or it will spell disaster for all within the bubble. Take your wife and step swiftly back into the sea, and begin your ascent to the surface. We will place Sapphira in the garden for them to find. Whatever argument you and the queen have must be settled elsewhere. Here is a bit of seaweed for her.*

*I understand,* Dillon answered Agenor.

The chief of the Merfolk pointed with a big finger at the bubble, and without even waiting to be told, Dillon stepped from the plants on the seafloor, and through into the garden of Ahura Mazda's castle, followed by a young merman carrying Sapphira in his arms. Seeing him, joy leaped into Cinnia's eyes, but then she turned to flee him. Dillon jumped forward, catching her by the hand, stuffing the seaweed into her pocket.

"Dillon, no!" she cried softly.

"Cinnia, yes!" he said, and half dragged her back into the sea where, once free of the bubble, they began to rise slowly up toward the surface.

"We'll drown," Cinnia said, and then she realized that not only could she speak, but she was having no difficulty at all breathing. "I can't go back," she said to him.

"We'll discuss this once we are in my boat," he told her.

"How is it I can breathe?" she asked him.

"I'll tell you that, too, when we reach the surface."

Holding hands, they rose up, and Cinnia realized that they were surrounded by smiling Merfolk, including Antea. She looked briefly down, and saw the shadow of Yafirdom fading slowly away until it was entirely gone. Then suddenly their heads broke the surface, and they were bobbing in the sea next to a small boat. He helped her in, and then climbed in himself. *Sapphira in blue. Red to you,* he spoke the simple spell, and Cinnia found herself in a rather revealing red gown.

"What are you doing?" she asked him.

"There was no time below to change your garments since you decided to be difficult," Dillon said. "It would be very odd if they found you unconscious in the garden wearing a totally different dress than the one you had gone out in."

"But I'm not in the garden," she said. "I'm here with you, and I shouldn't be!"

"We had all best return to where we belong now," Agenor said, smiling, as he looked over the edge of the boat. "Welcome home, my queen."

"Swim for but half of an hour, Agenor, and you will find you are in the sea off of your own beach. I would not leave you and your people here to make the long trip home. And in your cave you will find a small token of my appreciation. You already know you have the loyalty and friendship of Belmair's king," Dillon responded.

"Thank you, Your Majesty," Agenor said. Then he said to his people, "The king has made magic for us. We will be home very shortly."

"Goodbye, Cinnia," Antea said, smiling.

"Goodbye," Cinnia replied.

The Merfolk were quickly out of sight, and Cinnia realized that she could see a green coast ahead of them. She remained silent as Dillon sailed their little boat into a small cove. With a wave of his hand he transported them to a sandy beach, along with a willow basket, which she soon saw contained food and wine.

They settled themselves, and after taking a sip of wine she had the courage to ask him, "What have you done, my lord? Surely you know that under our laws I can never again be your wife?"

"The law has been changed, my love," he said, and leaned forward to kiss her lips.

Cinnia drew away from him. "No," she said.

"Have you fallen in love with the Yafir then that you will not kiss me?" he asked.

"No, I do not love the Yafir. But you are Belmair's king. You cannot change the law so you may flout it, Dillon," Cinnia told him.

"The law is not for me," he said. "It is for all the women who would like to live again in Belmair with their Yafir husbands. I still mean to make a peace between us. As far as Belmair will be concerned you are not Cinnia, daughter of Fflergant. You are Sapphira, niece of Duke Tullio of Beldane, and my mistress."

*"What?"* She looked at him as if he had gone mad.

"Sapphira was exactly like you in all ways but her eyes, which were a dark green. They are now light. She will be found unconscious in the Yafir lord's garden, a bump upon her head. Her memories will be muddled and confused, but they will return. But when they do it is to be hoped she is already with child—I believe Ahura Mazda covets a daughter, and he will have one—and she will discover all the wealth she desires can be hers. Sapphira is a very venal and extraordinarily lustful woman. I believe she will be content to be Cinnia instead of herself under those circumstances." He smiled at her, taking her hand and kissing it tenderly. "So you see, as long as you are content to be Sapphira there is little harm done, and Belmair's old laws have not been changed only for you, my love. They have been changed for the public good," Dillon concluded.

She stared at him, the look one of amazement. "You have the mind of a man born into magic," Cinnia said slowly. "Were your father and your uncle involved in this, too?"

"And Nidhug, too," he told her.

Tears filled Cinnia's eyes. "I have missed my dragon," she told him.

"And me? Have you missed me, my love?"

"After the first few days I put you from my mind, for there was no hope that I could see. But I never put you from my heart, Dillon," Cinnia said softly.

"I only took Sapphira to my bed as a means to stop Dreng from insisting I remarry, and give Belmair a new queen," he told her.

"I cannot come back with you," Cinnia told him. "Even hiding behind another woman's name. I took pleasures with the Yafir. And I enjoyed them, my lord."

"I enjoyed pleasures with Sapphira," he replied. "It is meant by the Great Creator of us all that we enjoy each other's bodies, Cinnia. You never knew a man until me. Now you have known two men, and enjoyed them both as they have enjoyed you. You were not unfaithful to me deliberately, nor I to you. I love you, Cinnia. I have never stopped loving you. I loved you so much that I would have given up my throne only to have you back in my arms, my wife."

Cinnia began to cry. "What if this is a dream, and I awaken? And if it is not a dream, what if he comes after me, and drags me down beneath the sea again, Dillon? I am afraid! I am terribly afraid!" And she sobbed without ceasing.

"It will not happen, my love. It will not happen," Dillon swore to her.

# 14

THEY REMAINED TOGETHER upon the beach for some time, Dillon soothing Cinnia and trying to erase her fears. If she was to play the part of Sapphira, she would have to regain a mastery of her emotions again. Cinnia was hard-pressed to believe she was free of Ahura Mazda. "Sapphira did not know you meant to use her in this way, did she?" she said to Dillon, and when he nodded, she continued. "She will tell them who she is, and certainly they will believe her."

"She will say whatever she will say," Dillon replied. "She is your mirror image. Why would they believe her? They will think the fall she has had has addled her wits."

"You have done a cruel thing," Cinnia told him slowly.

"Aye, it would appear I have," he agreed, "but you

will see in the end, my love, that I have not really been cruel. I never lied to Sapphira. From the beginning I told her that the only wife I wanted was the one I had. That the only queen I wanted was the one I had. I am half Shadow, half faerie, and I do not give my heart lightly."

"Do not tell me that she believed you, Dillon," Cinnia said.

"Nay, she did not, but I cannot be blamed for that. I took every opportunity to restate my position. Sapphira is an ambitious woman. She will come to terms quickly with herself when she discovers where she is and who her husband is. She is actually a perfect mate for Ahura Mazda. It is a shame he cannot know so he might thank me," Dillon finished wickedly.

Cinnia laughed in spite of herself, and then she grew more serious. "Ahura Mazda's wives are kind women. They will help Sapphira recover from her fright. Now, tell me how we managed to breathe as we made our way up from the bottom of the sea?"

Reaching out, Dillon drew the small clump of seaweed from her pocket. "Agenor gave it to me," he said. "They do not have much magic, the Merfolk, but they can enchant seaweed so that those of us not water born may breathe beneath the waves when it is necessary. Agenor said to return it to the sea when it had served its purpose."

He stood, and walking to the edge of the water, tossed her seaweed and his, which he withdrew from his pocket, back into the sea.

"Poor Sapphira," Cinnia said sympathetically. "Tonight was my turn to entertain Ahura Mazda, and he is not a man to be denied."

As Sapphira was now finding out. She had been awakened in a garden by the frantic cries of other women. Her head hurt, and she was terribly thirsty. The women had carried her into a room while she frantically attempted to ascertain where she was. But even as her blurred vision came back into focus she could see the chamber in which they had laid her was luxurious. A woman was bathing her forehead.

"Where am I?" Sapphira said.

"In your chamber, Cinnia. We found you in the garden. You had fallen, and there is a small bump with a cut upon your head. Head wounds always bleed copiously, and look more serious than they actually are. The cut is not deep. 'Twill not even leave a scar. You must have hit your head upon a rock. You need to rest."

"Who are you?" Sapphira asked, "And why do you call me Cinnia?"

"I am Arlais, and I call you Cinnia because that is your name," the woman said.

"No, it isn't. My name is Sapphira, and I am the king's mistress. Where am I? What is this place?"

"No, you are Cinnia, daughter of Fflergant, and formerly wife to King Dillon of Belmair, but now you are the sixth wife of the Yafir lord, Ahura Mazda," Arlais said.

A look of great surprise spread over Sapphira's face. Then she said, "No! I am Sapphira, not Cinnia. You cannot keep me here! I want to go back to the castle!"

"The fall has obviously addled your wits, Cinnia," Arlais said. "I think you should sleep a little, and attempt to restore them. It is your night to entertain our husband, and he will not be pleased if you cannot fulfill your duties." Arlais stood up. "I'll leave you now, Cinnia."

When the door had shut behind her Sapphira rose quickly from the bed, and as quickly sat down heavily upon it. She let the dizziness subside, and when it finally had she arose once more and began to explore the chamber. Opening the wardrobe she exclaimed with delight at the magnificent silk and velvet gowns inside. A trunk was filled with beautiful hand-embroidered chemises and night garments. An ebony-and-ivory jewel casket upon a table opened to reveal it was filled to overflowing with beautiful jewelry. Fascinated, Sapphira lifted a rather barbaric necklace of rubies and gold from the case, and slipped it about her neck. Picking up the mirror on the table, she viewed herself. The necklace was beautiful, and it suited her.

Closing the jewel casket, she continued to explore the chamber. Everything was elegant and of the best quality. The bed, hung with coral-colored silks that fell from a brass ring centered directly above it, was enormous. It sat upon a dais. There were great tall vases filled with odd flowers that perfumed the room with an exotic fragrance that Sapphira could not identify. There were tables of shining brass, and those of ebony. There were gaily colored pillows of various sizes strewn about. A small hearth burned brightly. Everything bespoke the refuge of a woman well-loved. Sapphira went to the windows, and looked out upon a strange landscape. The light was soft and multihued. She was suddenly exhausted. Pouring herself a small goblet of wine, she drank it, and lay down upon the bed to sleep. This was an odd dream, she decided, and when she awakened she would be in the little sailing boat upon the sea with the king, her lover.

But when Sapphira awoke it was dark. A small lamp burned on a table near the bed, and turning, she found a man lying next to her, studying her. She screamed, frightened. "Who are you?" she asked him in a trembling voice.

"Arlais said your wits were addled, my precious. I am your husband, Ahura Mazda," he told her.

*"The Yafir lord?"* Sapphira shrank back. "Do not touch me!"

"Cinnia, are we after a year to go through this again?" he asked her patiently.

"My name is Sapphira!" she insisted.

"No, my darling, your name is Cinnia. Sapphira is the king of Belmair's mistress. You are Cinnia, his former wife, and now my precious wife. This is my fault, of course. I should have never teased you about the king's mistress. The blow you took to your head has but brought up old memories, and you are attempting to be Dillon's mistress if you can no longer be his wife," Ahura Mazda said. "Forgive me, my darling."

"I am Sapphira! I am! I am!" she sobbed.

"Nay, Cinnia, you are who I say you are," he told her,

and then he gathered her resisting form into his arms and stroked her dark hair. "You are my beloved wife Cinnia and I adore you." He kissed the top of her head, and then put her gently from him to examine her injury. "The bump is still visible, but the cut is small, and already healing," Ahura Mazda said, his finger running over her injury carefully. "Can you remember how you fell, my darling? The path near the wall where you were found is particularly rough. I shall see it is smoothed so you do not fall again. I know you keep looking for more garden space in which to grow your herbs and other plants. Shall I arrange for more earth to be fetched and more garden boxes built for you?"

"I do not know what you are talking about," Sapphira said. "I do not soil my beautiful hands with common muck."

He took one of her hands up and kissed it. "Your hands, like the rest of you, are always perfection, always beautiful," he told her.

She had not gazed at him until then. Now stealing a careful look, she saw that all the childhood tales of the evil, ugly Yafir were incorrect. He was a tall, slender man with silvery hair and the most beautiful aquamarine-blue eyes. His handsome face was unlined and ageless. Their eyes locked, and Sapphira felt her lust engaged as she stared at him. Her cherry-red lips parted just slightly and her breathing quickened.

He smiled into her face. It was a knowing smile. An elegant hand stroked her jaw. "It is our night for pleasures, my precious," he murmured against her lips, and then his mouth closed over hers. His kisses were slow, deep and sweet. He did not hurry his adoration of her lips. He nibbled at her, and his tongue played with hers.

Sapphira felt herself melting into his embrace, responding eagerly to his blatant adoration. Dillon had not touched her in several months, and his lovemaking, while enthusiastic, had never quite pulsed with the passion that this man did. Sapphira sighed, and with that small sound all of her inhibitions fled. If this was a dream it was a most satisfactory one, but she was beginning to realize that it was not a dream. Briefly she considered she would now be a fallen woman to her own people, but would she ever again see her own kind?

"I do not wish to tire you, my precious," Ahura Mazda said to her, but his hands were already beginning to caress her beneath her silk robe.

Sapphira had a moment of doubt. Should she allow him to continue? Would it matter if he didn't? His mouth closed over a nipple, and he began to suck upon it. She moaned as she felt her own desires beginning to stir and rise. How long it had been since she had enjoyed such delights? She wasn't certain how she came to be in this place, or in the arms of the Yafir lord. There would be time later, she was certain, to consider it, but not now. Not when his mouth was wreaking such havoc with her body. Sapphira wiggled out of her robe, and her hands gently forced his garment from his body, gasping with delight as their naked bodies touched, and she felt the fire between her legs deepen.

He leisurely moved his lips over her lush body,

kissing, tasting, nipping, the soft pale flesh beneath his mouth. She writhed with enjoyment beneath him, murmuring softly as he moved down her torso. As he reached the junction of her thighs they fell open for him. Sliding forward he peeled open her plump nether lips and buried his head between her legs, his tongue eagerly seeking out that sentient bit of flesh. His own excitement was high, for he had never before known her to be so eager, so acquiescent of his attentions. The taste of her was different tonight. She was musk and honey. Her juices flowed eagerly for him. Nipping at that little nub, he smiled as she squealed and shivered. But then she squirmed away from him, and reaching for his manhood, began to caress it.

Sapphira's eyes widened slightly as she looked at the male member she now held in her two small hands. She had never before seen anything as huge. The king's cock has certainly been of a goodly size in comparison with those she had previously seen. But this was enormous. Longer and certainly thicker. Bending, she licked its length several times. She took the tip of it into her mouth, and it filled it. Running her tongue about it she sucked hard. It was much too big, she thought. He would surely split her in two with such a formidable weapon. Releasing him, she looked up. "No," she told him.

"Yes," he said, and mounting her, he began to use her.

At first Sapphira struggled and resisted the Yafir lord who said he was her husband, but then she realized that his massive manhood, while stretching the walls of her sheath was also sending her into a paroxysm of pure delight. *"Deeper!"* she begged him after a few moments had passed. She wrapped her legs about him, clutching him.

He pistoned her enthusiastically.

*"Deeper!"* she cried out again.

Surprised, he stopped. "Unwrap your legs, and raise them up," he instructed her. Then pushing her legs back and over her shoulders, he began to drive into her again.

*"Harder! Harder!"* the woman beneath him whimpered.

He thrust fiercely until her cries of pleasure were so great he could not contain his own juices, and they burst forth to flood her, overflowing, staining her thighs and the bed beneath them. Never had Cinnia given herself so freely, so uninhibitedly to him. He did not withdraw from her deliciousness, but after a few minutes began to ride her again if only to see how far he might drive her.

Her head was spinning. Never had she known pleasures quite like this. "Oh, yes, my lord!" she said to him. *"Again! Do it to me again!"*

Her memory might be slightly confused and impaired, Ahura Mazda thought as he fucked her in a leisurely manner, but the bump she received had certainly unleashed her inhibitions. *Now I will get a child upon her. Now I will have the daughter I so desire!* He fell back briefly.

*"No!"* she shrieked. "I want more!"

"And you shall have it, my precious," he promised her as he turned her over onto her belly. "Get on your hands and knees, Cinnia," he instructed her, and when she had, he slid his great cock into her again. "There," he said as he thrust swiftly back and forth. "Is that not nice, my darling? See how deep I can go?"

"Oh, yes!" she cried to him. "*Yes!* Do not cease, my lord, I beg you! Do not!"

It was a night he would not forget. She was amenable to everything he desired, and her passions were such as he had never known, but had always believed she was capable of giving. At one point as she knelt before him, taking his cock into her fiery sheath, he was even able to slowly push a well-oiled ivory replica of his thumb into her tight little fundament. She squealed wildly, but then spasmed violently, squeezing his manhood completely dry of his love juices in the process.

And finally they slept heavily in each other's arms. When he awoke, surprised to realize he was still in her bed, he also discovered he was in no hurry to leave it. Rolling onto his side he watched her awaken, and when she did, he said, "Give me the daughter that I desire, Cinnia, and I will make you my queen. I will place you above all my other wives. Would you like that, my precious?"

His queen? Sapphira purred with her approval, and reaching up, pulled him into her arms again. This was not a dream. This was real. Somehow, and she could not even imagine how he had done it, Dillon had managed to put her in his wife's place while returning Fflergant's daughter to his side. As she realized what he had done her first instinct was to be furious, but then the Yafir lord began suckling upon her breast again, and promising her extravagances beyond her wildest imaginings. He wanted her. No, he wanted Cinnia, who had obviously not responded to his lusts as she, Sapphira, had. But he believed her to be Cinnia, and if Cinnia she must be, Sapphira thought, then Cinnia she would be. She was surrounded by luxury, adored by this Yafir lord, and the promise of power was enticing. Why did people rail so against the Yafir? She could see little difference between Belmairan and Yafir but for their exotic coloring. "I will gladly give you a daughter, my lord," she promised him. "And then you will gladly make me your queen, and set me above all others, will you not?"

He looked up from her plump breast. "Of course I will," he promised her. "I will make you the queen of Yafirdom, and when I take Belmair for our own, you will rule by my side there, as well. But first you must give me my daughter, my precious." He caressed her soft cheek.

"I will do my best to please you, my lord," Sapphira said to him. What fools her kin were. She was going to be very content living here among the Yafir, wherever here was, Sapphira thought as she drew his head back to her breast.

They remained within her bedchamber for the next three days while on the opposite side of the door Ahura Mazda's five other wives waited and wondered. They did not, however, dare to disturb their lord and master. If they had not heard his roars of pleasure, and her cries of delight now and again, they might have considered that Cinnia had finally murdered him. And when he finally exited her bedchamber he was in an expansive mood such as they had never seen.

"Has the sorceress bewitched him?" Tyne wondered.

"Nay, her magic is small," Arlais said.

"What has happened then?" Volupia asked.

Arlais shook her head. "I do not know."

"I have heard of cases when a bump on the head changes a person," Minau said. "Perhaps that is what has happened. Cinnia has changed, and she is more amenable to our husband, more accepting of him, of our world."

They came to believe that that was what had happened, for the Cinnia they had known for a good year had indeed changed. She was no longer interested in her gardens or her apothecary. Her passion was for more beautiful garments and jewelry with which Ahura Mazda was delighted to gift her. She was imperious and disrespectful of the other women; spoke sharply to the servants, but the Yafir lord would not reprimand her. He was more besotted with her than ever before. He spent several nights a week in her bed, causing annoyance among the other wives who were not pleased to be ignored. And when she began to swell with child she became over proud and even more difficult.

"Have you forgotten about Belmair and King Dillon, then?" Arlais asked her as the wives all sat together one afternoon in their shared dayroom.

Sapphira looked lazily up. "Our lord husband is my reason for living now."

"Not your child?" Minau murmured wickedly.

"Of course," Sapphira said, her tone now slightly irritated. "My daughter is most important to me. She will be a princess."

"How can you be so certain it is a daughter you carry?" Volupia said. "We have all prayed for daughters and been denied. Our husband, it seems, can only throw male children, I fear. Most Yafir do, which is why it is necessary to steal women from Belmair for wives, although now we are unable to ever since an enchantment was put upon them. You are a sorceress, Cinnia. Can you not undo what was done?"

"No," Sapphira said bluntly. "I no longer choose to practice my small magic."

"But if it is not magic, what is it that makes you certain you carry a daughter?" Volupia persisted.

"I just know," Sapphira said. Then she looked to the servant paring her toenails. "Be careful, you clumsy creature! Are you trying to cut my toe off?"

Arlais listened, and suddenly she knew that the girl carrying Ahura Mazda's child was not Cinnia, daughter of Fflergant. Who was she then? Arlais searched her memory, and then she recalled that after they had found her in the gardens the girl had at first insisted that her name was Sapphira. A small smile touched Arlais's lips. She did not know how, but she realized that King Dillon had finally found a way to retrieve his wife, Cinnia, leaving his mistress, Sapphira, behind in her place. It had been masterfully done.

Of all of Ahura Mazda's wives it was Arlais who

was the highest born, although Minau also came from a noble family. But Arlais had been the bride of a duke of Belia. She had been stolen on her wedding day. She understood better than the others the political machinations of Belmair. Ahura Mazda had told her that King Dillon sought peace between the two races. While her husband was a kind man by nature, he had never forgiven the Belmairans for their betrayal of the Yafir, and in his bitterness scorned the young king's desire to reunite the two factions.

Then he had deliberately stolen Cinnia away from the king in an effort to taunt him. And Ahura Mazda had laughed himself sick as the young king had in his pain and despair looked high and low for his wife and for the Yafir. The Yafir lord knew that the Belmairans would never consider looking beneath the vast sea of Belmair. Yet King Dillon had finally sought beneath the seas, and he had obviously found them. What great magic the young king must possess, Arlais thought, to have been able to regain possession of his wife, replacing her with his mistress who was her duplicate.

And Ahura Mazda had not discovered it. Indeed this Cinnia made him happy. She did not want to escape Yafirdom. She was more than content with her place as his wife, and as the expectant mother of his child. It was to be hoped that time would mellow her difficult nature. The birth of one's first child always made certain changes in a woman's demeanor. *I will not tell him of this deception that has been played upon him,* Arlais decided. *He is pleased with this Cinnia. King Dillon is undoubtedly relieved to have his wife back. And he has managed to circumvent the laws of Belmair without the Belmairans knowing.* She smiled again. *Perhaps King Dillon will attempt once more to make peace between us,* Arlais thought. Mayhap she could even get Ahura Mazda to put aside his anger and bitterness for the sake of the Yafir.

She considered the generations that had been born beneath the sea. Was it not past time for them to return to the land? Sometimes, if she concentrated very hard, Arlais could conjure up the fragrance of the freshly ploughed land on her father's estate in a small valley between the mountains in Belia. She wondered if after these several hundred years that estate was still there, and still in her family. She considered if she would ever know the answer to her questions. And if Ahura Mazda scorned any future overtures by King Dillon? Well, Arlais thought, she had born him several sons over the centuries, and she knew that while they said nothing to their father, that they had spoken with her about returning to the land.

Many of the bubbles were getting overcrowded, and it took every bit of male Yafir magic to keep what existed safe for them. Soon they would have no choice but to leave the sea, and if Belmair would not take them back, the Yafir would once again be forced to wander. Arlais wished she had a means of communicating with Belmair, but she did not. She would wait for King Dillon to approach Ahura Mazda once more, and when he did she would use what small influence she possessed with her husband to get him to at least consider what the king had to say. She hoped the real Cinnia was happy once again, safe with her beloved husband.

But Cinnia was not happy. While part of her was glad to have been rescued, her Belmairan conscience worried her terribly. She had been raised to believe that the Yafir were unclean and wicked. That a respectable Belmairan woman touched by them was no longer pure or worthy of the name Belmairan. And while she played the part of Sapphira for love of Dillon, she would not allow him in her bed.

"You're supposed to be my mistress," he said low to her one day as they rode out from the castle and into the hills of Belmair.

"From what Tamary and Anke tell me, you hadn't visited her bed in at least two months, my lord," Cinnia said as softly. "No one sees anything different. You are obviously tiring of Sapphira. End it soon, my lord. Give Sapphira a small home into which to retire, and an allowance. Then find a new wife."

"I cannot do that," Dillon told her. "The agreement between Sapphira's family and me says that if I do not wed with Sapphira and I tire of her, a wealthy husband will be found, and I will pay a generous dower."

"Tell Duke Tullio I do not want a husband. That my love for you is so great I prefer to remain celibate if you will not have me," Cinnia replied.

"Tullio will not accept such a decision on your part. It is his right to marry Sapphira off to someone who can be an advantage to his family. You know this is how marriages among the nobility are arranged. A woman's value to her kin is in the husband she has," Dillon responded, "and the children she bears him. I cannot flout the law."

"You flouted the law when you came after me," Cinnia reminded him tartly.

"The law had been changed when I came after you," he countered.

"Then why not tell all of Belmair?" she demanded wickedly.

"You know the answer to that," he said. He was beginning to get angry.

"Aye, I do," Cinnia said. "You may have changed the law, but you cannot change what has been in the hearts of Belmairans for hundreds of years. They will not accept me, Dillon. And Tullio would probably kill you, or at least attempt to kill you if he learned you had substituted his niece for me in Ahura Mazda's bed."

"Then I shall make Tullio supremely happy by marrying Sapphira, and making her my queen," Dillon replied. "When we return to the castle I shall make the announcement, and you will have until our wedding night to make peace with your narrow little Belmairan heart and mind. We will be husband and wife again, Cinnia." Then he surprised her by putting his horse into a canter and riding away from her.

Cinnia drew her mount to a stop, thinking that she should have been the one to ride off in a temper. Then she laughed. It was the first time she could recall really laughing in many months. Dillon was simply too clever for her. He did nothing he did not carefully consider beforehand. But she was still troubled. How did she put away hundreds of years of ingrained thought? Turning her animal about, Cinnia rode to Nidhug's castle.

Over the few months since her return the dragon had pretended to come around to accepting Sapphira. So it was not considered odd that the king's mistress would visit with Belmair's great guardian. Entering the castle courtyard she dismounted, hardly looking at the groomsman who came to take her horse. She hurried into the small castle and sought out Nidhug who was in her privy chamber reading. Meeting Tavey along the way, Cinnia said to him, "Bring refreshments. Your mistress will shortly need them."

"Nidhug!" Cinnia greeted the dragon as she entered the room.

"Ah, my darling girl, how lovely that you have come to see me," the dragon responded. "You have news! I can see it in your face. Come, sit by me and tell me."

"Dillon has decided it is time to marry *Sapphira* and make her his queen," Cinnia said. "What think you of that?"

"'Tis time," Nidhug responded.

"But, Nidhug, do you not see my problem?"

"Do you still fret yourself over that foolish old law, child?" the dragon asked her.

"I have known a man other than my husband, Nidhug. I am no better than a common creature in some tavern," Cinnia said.

"Nonsense!" the dragon replied. "That law was a

foolish law created by men who did not mind doing what they shouldn't, but penalized Belmair's females for being victimized by the Yafir. The king was right to declare it null and void. You, yourself, have told me that the Yafir never return a woman until it is absolutely certain she cannot produce children, and then only if they chose to return. And how do they return? As frail old women who are then driven out of their families and their communities for being impure. Left to die! This was not a law worthy of our Belmairan hearts, Cinnia."

"I am not an old woman, Nidhug," Cinnia said.

"Nay, you are not. Nor did you bear the Yafir lord a child. Did you ever consider why you seemed to be infertile?" the dragon asked her.

"There is another reason Dillon should send me away!" Cinnia exclaimed. "No matter how often Ahura Mazda used me I did not conceive his child."

"You are not infertile, Cinnia," Nidhug told her. "When you were first wed Dillon enchanted your womb in order to protect you, and any child you would bear him. He feared that until he could make peace with the Yafir a child could be used against Belmair. He wanted to spare you such pain. And a good thing, too," the dragon declared. "We certainly never expected Ahura Mazda to steal you away."

Cinnia was astounded. "Oh, he has saved me from such misery," she cried, but then she said, "Poor Sapphira! Her womb is not closed."

"It was while Dillon kept her, but it is no longer," Nidhug told her.

"Was she really as Dillon has portrayed her, or has he just said those things in hopes of soothing my battered conscience?" Cinnia asked the dragon.

"It was quite odd," Nidhug began. "She looked just like you but for her eyes, which were darker. The king lightened them, however, before he sent her to Yafirdom. But in character she was your opposite. Greedy. Spiteful. Mean-spirited. The servants despised her and feared her."

"So that is why they avoid me," Cinnia noted thoughtfully.

"What of Sapphira's family? I know little of her but that she is Duke Tullio's niece. Who are her parents?" Cinnia wanted to know.

"Her mother is the duke's sister, Margisia. Her father was a wastrel who ran off years ago. She was raised in the duke's household," the dragon said.

"Am I apt to see the duke and his sister? Do they come here often?" Cinnia asked. "Certainly they will know that I am not Sapphira."

"They have not been back since the day Sapphira came to the castle. It is unlikely you will see them often," Nidhug said.

"If Dillon persists in this foolishness to marry *Sapphira* they will surely come," Cinnia said. "I will surely give myself away."

"The king can give you enough of Sapphira's memories temporarily if they come. But of course we can arrange for a great storm to encompass Belmair when you marry the king again. That way few guests can come. I suspect you would like it better that way."

"Dreng would get here no matter," Cinnia muttered.

"Poor Dreng. He paraded two of his granddaughters, sweet girls, I must say, beneath the king's nose, and your husband could see neither of them. Lina and Panya were their names. They liked to dance sedate little dances for the king. And then Sapphira came, and danced a dance stripping off the many scarlet veils she wore, making their dances irrelevant." Nidhug chuckled.

"Sapphira sounds very bold," Cinnia murmured.

"She was bold," Nidhug said. "She made it clear that she wanted the king. That is why I am certain she has settled in quite nicely with the Yafir lord. Once she gained the lay of the land she would come to terms with it, for Sapphira may be venal, but I do not believe anyone could call her stupid."

"That is what Dillon has told me," Cinnia said thoughtfully. "It is true?"

"Of course it is truth," Nidhug responded impatiently. "Why would you doubt the king's word, my child?"

"Because he has manipulated the law to suit his purposes," Cinnia said stubbornly.

"All men are capable of lying," Nidhug remarked. "But I do not believe the king would ever lie to you, Cinnia. His love for you is such that he moved heaven and earth to find you. And then when he found you, he found a way to bring you home. You are a fortunate woman to have such love lavished upon you. True love such as King Dillon has for you, Cinnia, is rare. It should be cherished, not callously tossed aside."

"Have you found love with Prince Cirillo?" Cinnia said slyly.

"He is faerie. I am dragon," Nidhug replied. "And we are speaking of you, not me, my child."

"Is it forbidden somewhere that you cannot love one another simply because of your differences?" Cinnia asked softly.

"We take pleasures together," Nidhug allowed.

"Is not love required for pleasures?" Cinnia probed.

"You know from your own experience that it is not," the dragon said sharply.

"I have heard the rumors since my return. Rumors of a passion shared by both you and my husband's uncle," Cinnia murmured. "Are they truth?"

"We take pleasures together," Nidhug said stubbornly.

"Dragon, answer me! Remember who I am," Cinnia said.

"Sorceress of Belmair, remember 'tis I who have taught you what little you know," the dragon responded. "Now let us return to your problem."

A light knock sounded upon the privy chamber door.

"Come in!" Nidhug called. "Ah, Tavey, bless you. I am just in the mood for a light repast. What has Sarabeth sent us?" The dragon viewed the tray eagerly. "Meat pies! A roasted duck! Fruit jellies and a bowl of baked apples! Did you bring something for my guest, Tavey?"

"I have brought Queen Cinnia a little plate of iced cakes and camomile tea," Tavey said with a little bow.

"The lady Sapphira, Tavey," the dragon corrected her servant.

"If you wish, mistress," Tavey replied.

"What do you mean, *if I wish?*" the dragon demanded to know.

"Mistress, I have served you several hundred years, and I believe I have come to know you well," Tavey said. "Even if you had made your peace with the lady Sapphira you would not allow her the privilege of your privy chamber. Nor would that lady have known you well enough to instruct me to bring refreshment as she entered your house."

"You're a busybody!" Nidhug said.

"I am observant as a good servant should be," Tavey said with a small smile. "And I understand the king's need for secrecy, given the narrow minds in Belmair."

"You are not repelled by me?" Cinnia asked him.

"I see nothing repellent," Tavey replied. "I see only my queen."

"Thank you," Cinnia said, and tears filled her eyes.

"I will withdraw now, and continue my duties," Tavey told them, and departed the dragon's privy chamber.

"You see!" Nidhug said triumphantly.

"He is your dear and loyal retainer, and has known me my whole life," Cinnia responded. "His heart is good, but even he knows the dangerous path we travel."

"And he will keep the secret. Cinnia, my child, aye,

the path is fraught with peril, but believe me when I tell you that there are more folk like Tavey in Belmair than there are those with closed minds. But the king is right. Now is not the time to put them to a test of faith. You are home safe. The king has played the game well with Ahura Mazda. He does not need the world to know it. He wants peace between the two races inhabiting Belmair. If Ahura Mazda will not make that peace then a new lord will be found who will. What is past cannot be changed. We must all move forward, my child."

"You speak to me, don't you?" Cinnia said.

"Aye, I do," Nidhug said. "You are not impure. *You* never gave your heart to the Yafir lord. *He* took your body, but that is all he was able to take from you, Cinnia. It cannot be changed. Now you must move on. Dillon could have deserted you, left you with the Yafir, and no criticism would have been leveled at him. But he did not. He sought for you. Brought you home. Has protected you. Now give him what he needs to know that all is well again between you. Give him your heart, for you have his, my child."

"It is so hard for me to put aside the old ways," Cinnia replied. "I want to, but it is so very, very difficult, Nidhug."

"I know," the dragon agreed. "Sadly there are things that even magic cannot help, change or cure, and your dilemma is one of them. But you are strong, Cinnia, and I know you want to be happy again. You can be if you will let go of the misery surrounding you," Nidhug said.

"Each time it rises up in your memory, force it back with another and more important thought."

"It is so difficult for me to put away the pictures in my head of taking pleasures with Ahura Mazda. He aroused me, Nidhug. I cried with the delight he gave me."

"'Twas only your body responding to the stimulus of his passion," Nidhug said drily. "It was nothing more, my child."

"I feel guilt for the enjoyment I gained with him," Cinnia answered.

"I will wager that Dillon feels no guilt for the enjoyment he gained from Sapphira's ripe body," Nidhug said wickedly. "And do not, my dear child, tell me that because he was a man it was his right but that you must suffer. Or worse yet that women should only enjoy pleasures with their husbands." The dragon made a moue with her mouth and gave a delicate shudder.

"That is the kind of talk that got the Hetarians banished," Cinnia half teased.

"Well," the dragon huffed as she popped a meat pie into her mouth, "I am the Great Dragon of Belmair, and I cannot be banished." Reaching for the duck, she tore it in two and ate half. "Delicious! Sarabeth always flavors her duck with orange and plum." Nidhug smacked her lips, and quickly devoured the other half of the bird.

Cinnia reached for one of the little pink iced cakes and took a bite. Then she sipped at the camomile tea, which had been flavored with honey, and was very soothing. "I suppose since there is really nothing I can do to change any of this I had best accept it, and as you have advised me, move on with my life. But I really do hate being called Sapphira," Cinnia said.

"Before they rescued you, we discussed how you might change your name," Nidhug said. "Just before Sapphira weds the king have her publicly announce she is honoring her predecessor by changing her name to Cinnia Sapphira. It will be considered a grand gesture worthy of a queen, and if Dillon calls you Cinnia in public no one will be the wiser. And by retaining the name that Tullio's family gave Sapphira you will not give rise to any suspicions."

"Convince Dillon to have a small wedding," Cinnia said.

"Nay, you must have a great celebration in the spring, once the winter has left the land," Nidhug said. "It would be very much out of character for Sapphira to want a small, discreet affair. She will want to trumpet her triumph throughout all of Belmair." The dragon reached for the remaining meat pie of the half dozen Tavey had brought her.

"I cannot go about being this woman for the rest of my life," Cinnia complained.

"You must be her until the wedding. Afterward your change in character will be put down to your happiness," the dragon advised. She drained her goblet and licked the last crumb of meat pie from her lips.

"The spring is coming," Cinnia said. "Dillon and I rode out today, and the snows are gone from the hills. We argued, and he rode off."

"He'll be home for dinner," Nidhug said with a chuckle. "They always come home for dinner."

"Does Cirillo?" Cinnia asked mischievously.

"I would not miss a meal at my beautiful dragon's board," Cirillo said as he came without knocking into the room. He took Nidhug's claw up and kissed it tenderly.

"You are outrageously handsome, Uncle," Cinnia told the faerie.

"Do not tell him that!" the dragon cried. "He is vain enough as it is, my child."

But her beautiful eyes were devouring him as she spoke, and the looks he cast at her were just as heated and all encompassing.

"I suppose I had best go home," Cinnia said, but neither of them seemed to notice her at all, and so she departed Nidhug's privy chamber. In the corridor she met Tavey. "Will you have someone bring my horse back to its stable? I think I shall walk home through our gardens."

"At once, my lady," Tavey said, mindful of the other servants bustling about.

Cinnia let herself out through a small door that opened directly into the shared gardens between the two castles. The air was still, and it was quiet. Here and there she noticed that green shoots were making their way through the soil. It all looked dead for the most part, but Cinnia knew within a very few weeks the gardens would be lush and green; that beneath the soil lurked pulsing life in a rainbow of dazzling colors. She had missed this most of all while confined in Yafirdom. From what she had been told of Sapphira she doubted very much that her little garden would be tended.

But it didn't matter now, and she had to put her sojourn from her conscious thoughts. She had to start living her life once again. She had a man who loved her enough to defy everything in order to restore her to his arms. And she had treated him so badly these past weeks, Cinnia thought. Still he had been patient until today when he had ridden off in anger. Well, she would make it right with him tonight, she decided with a smile. The truth was when she thought about it she had missed taking pleasures.

"Where have you been?" he asked her curtly as she came into their little family hall. "I was worried."

She went to him and kissed his lips softly. "I was with Nidhug," she told him.

His arms went about her. "I missed you," he said, his eyes scanning her face.

"'Twas you, my lord, and not I, who rode away in a temper," she reminded him.

"You can sometimes be a difficult woman," he replied. Reaching out, he ran the back of his hand down her cheek.

Cinnia swallowed hard. "It is difficult," she whispered low, "but I am trying. And I believe we must begin preparing for our wedding, my lord."

The joyful light that sprang into his eyes almost brought him to tears. "I will do whatever you want!" he told her.

Cinnia smiled, tears pricking at her own eyelids. "Sapphira of Beldane would want a lavish wedding," she said softly so no other could hear. "It would be out of keeping for it to be any less than grand, my lord. It has not been easy being this woman, but before her happiness turns her into a gentler lady more in keeping with the true Cinnia, she will have her magnificent wedding."

"You are clever, my sorceress," he murmured against her mouth, and he kissed her—a slow, deep kiss that set her heart racing.

"Hush, my lord," she cautioned him. "Do not in your happiness reveal the truth."

"And this time all those I love will surround us," Dillon said. "Belmair's nobility will see a gathering of magical folk such as it has never before seen."

Cinnia laughed aloud. "They will be both fascinated and repelled at the same time, but it is unlikely anyone asked will refuse to attend. Poor Dreng. He will be so disappointed that your bride is not one of his kin."

"He knew he had lost that opportunity the moment he saw Sapphira," Dillon replied wisely. "Still, he is certain to take credit for my giving up Cinnia, and pressing me to take a new wife." Dillon chuckled. "If he only knew, my love. If he only knew."

But of course Dreng of Beltran did not know, and while as predicted he was chagrined by Dillon's choice, he was nonetheless relieved the king had finally made it.

# 15

AHURA MAZDA DEBATED on whether he should tell his pregnant youngest wife that her rival would soon be marrying King Dillon of Belmair. But finally the streak of cruelty in him that he could never suppress brought him to taunt her one day when she had been particularly difficult with his other women and the servants.

"Dillon of Belmair is well rid of you," he told her, sneering. "'Tis to be hoped you can birth me a daughter instead of another son. It took you long enough to get with child. Let us hope Sapphira will prove more fertile when she marries the king next month."

Arlais and Minau looked up, surprised by their husband's words.

"Dillon is marrying Sapphira?" the false Cinnia said in a cold and deadly voice.

"Aye," Ahura Mazda said. "It is to be the finest,

grandest wedding ever seen in Belmair. The king's mother, stepfather, his siblings and the Shadow Prince are all coming. And the faerie prince has convinced his own mother to attend. Belmair's nobility are all agog, and the royal castle will be filled to overflowing with all the guests."

Sapphira was speechless with her outrage.

"I am told the king's sisters are very beautiful. Perhaps I shall steal one of them, and take a seventh wife," Ahura Mazda continued.

"There are seven days in the week," Arlais murmured drily.

The Yafir lord laughed, giving her a wicked wink.

"Take another woman into this house," the false Cinnia said angrily, "and you will never enter my bed again! I should sooner end up in the Mating Market than share you with another, my lord."

"Give me a son, you little witch, and you will," he threatened her.

Reaching out she grabbed a small brass bowl and threw it at him before bursting into tears. "Oh, how could you be so cruel to me?" she sobbed, her hands going to her distended belly as if she were protecting it and the child within.

At once the other women gathered about her, stroking her, comforting her. Arlais gave their husband an arch look that warned him to cease his torture of his youngest wife.

But then the tears stopped, and the false Cinnia said,

"Tell me what you have heard about the wedding. I want to know everything."

"Will it not upset you?" Minau asked. "You do not want to compare it to your own wedding to King Dillon, which must have been wonderful."

"It was hurried, in the presence of the dying Fflergant...my father...and there was nothing magnificent about it. And here again I am a wife without any celebration," she complained bitterly.

"Ceremony is not necessary among us," Ahura Mazda said. "It is enough that I said I took you for my wife. That is how it is among the Yafir."

"Well, there should be more, and believe you me if I give you a daughter there will be! No one is going to tell my child that she is a wife because they said so," the false Cinnia declared. "There is nothing wrong with a little pomp, my lord."

"Pomp," he sneered. "How very Belmairan you are, my precious."

"I did not ask you to steal me away," she cried angrily at him.

"I took you to spite Dillon of the Shadows," he replied with brutal frankness. "That idealistic young fool with his bleating for peace! Does he believe that he can wipe away centuries of intolerance and injustice by merely holding out a hand in supposed friendship? I will never make peace with Belmair. *Never!*"

"I think you are wrong, my lord," Arlais said quietly.

He rounded on her furiously. "You dare to question my decisions, woman?"

"Nay, my lord, you misunderstand me," Arlais responded, not in the least intimidated by her husband. "But it grows more difficult to maintain our bubbles as each year passes. And our bubbles are overcrowded, and we have not the abilities now to enlarge them or build more. Yafir magic has weakened because of the Belmairan blood running through the veins of our children.

"And the Belmairans' population has declined with the loss of their women of childbearing age. We could help each other, and there is more than enough land for all. King Dillon holds out the hand of friendship to the Yafir. Why do you slap it away, my good lord? Will you not at least speak with him?" Arlais asked quietly.

"I know the problems we face," he told her. "But soon we shall be able to take Belmair for ourselves. We will not have to share it. We will drive the remaining Belmairans either into the sea, or to Hetar. I don't care. Be patient, wife. It will eventually all be ours."

Arlais said nothing more. Her husband was wrong. The dragon had brought Dillon to Belmair for a purpose. And that purpose was not to lose Belmair to the Yafir. Sadly, Ahura Mazda's hatred of the Belmairans was such that he could see nothing but his own desires and plans for revenge. King Dillon, however, having decided to bring the Yafir back into Belmair's society, would not be deterred. Arlais decided to speak with her eldest sons, Behrooz and Sohrab, about the situation. It was time that the other Yafir were asked their opinions about a possible peace and her two eldest sons were the men to do it. Both were respected by their fellow Yafir, and neither sought their father's high office, but if it became necessary to replace him, Behrooz and Sohrab would not quarrel over the position. Knowing her sons Arlais knew they would probably play a game of chance, the winner taking all. And they would ask their youngest brother, Nasim, to referee. Nasim was considered a great artist by the Yafir. Politics was the furthest thing from his mind. Arlais felt no guilt over what she proposed doing. She was the first wife, and she had loved her Yafir lord for centuries. She wanted what was best for him. For their people. And she would protect their household. If Cinnia would only give Ahura Mazda the daughter he so desired it would be possible to divert him.

News of the royal wedding to come filtered down into Yafirdom for the Yafir males were always secretly visiting the various corners of Belmair. Sapphira awaited each detail avidly, personally rewarding the bearers of news lavishly. King Dillon had decreed the wedding day to be a holiday for all in Belmair. The wedding guests, other than family, had been limited to only three days at the castle. The day before, the day of and the day after the wedding. Gifts were pouring in from all over Belmair. The king's family had already arrived from Hetar.

Lara had come with her daughters, Anoush, Zagiri and Marzina. Magnus Hauk and his only son and heir, Taj, would remain in Terah, for it was not thought wise for them to leave. Dillon was delighted to see his sisters once again. He was closest to the two elder, for he had shared a life with them before he had gone to Shunnar in the Shadow kingdom to be tutored in the sorcery that came so naturally to him.

Anoush was in her late teens. She showed no inclination toward marriage, but Dillon knew it would take a special man to husband Anoush, who was an amazing healer and had visions of the future. Her talents frightened most men. Several years younger, Zagiri was a golden girl whose greatest desire was to find a husband and wed. She had absolutely no magic in her at all, which was frankly to her mother a great relief. Marzina, his youngest sister, Dillon knew least of all. Dark-haired, violet-eyed, Marzina was a secretive girl, but her nature was one of utter sweetness, according to her mother. She had been born the twin of Magnus Hauk's heir, but she was not his child.

She had been conceived by force upon the Dream Plain, and her father was Kol, the Twilight Lord, now imprisoned deep within his own castle in the Dark Lands for that particular crime. When Lara had seen this unexpected second child spring from her womb she had been shocked, especially given Marzina's exotic coloring. But Ilona had quickly declared the child resembled a relation who was a Nix, a magical water faerie. And no one had questioned her. Kaliq knew, and Dillon knew. Magnus Hauk did not, and he adored having two daughters, one all golden like him, the other dark like a faerie ancestor. But unlike the evil Kol, Marzina exuded light and goodness.

"Where does her talent lie?" Dillon asked his mother curiously.

"I believe she will be like me with her magic," Lara told her eldest son. "She is already doing simple shape-shifting." Her voice was prideful.

"Perhaps it is the influence of her Nix ancestor," Dillon teased his mother.

"Perhaps it is," Lara agreed, her beautiful green eyes twinkling with the shared joke. "She is unique among my daughters," Lara said quietly.

"How is my little brother?" Dillon wanted to know.

"His father's son in all ways. He will be a good Dominus one day," Lara said.

"He is obviously not your favorite," Dillon teased her.

"I love Taj," Lara said, "but I find him almost dull. While Zagiri has no magic in her she is lively and full of fun. Taj is very serious, and his grandmother, the lady Persis, encourages him to self-importance. I have spoken to Magnus on this, but he says Taj will outgrow it. I do not think he will. He is very impressed that his big brother is now a king, and hopes to visit you eventually."

"I will welcome him, and perhaps I can even help him to understand that being a king is not all grandeur, but a great responsibility," Dillon told his mother.

"I like your Cinnia," Lara said. "You were fortunate to be able to retrieve her."

"You know it would have been far more difficult had Sapphira not been her double," Dillon replied. "But even if she hadn't I would have taken my wife back."

"But this way you have avoided conflict with the Yafir until you are ready. When planning a campaign it is always wise to have the advantage," Lara said.

"Ahura Mazda is content believing he has bested you, and you are content because you have Cinnia back. It was a piece of good fortune, and well done, my son."

"I have placed you and my sisters beneath my protection spell. The Yafir lord is bold, and he will learn of the festivities here in Belmair. I understand him well enough to know he would enjoy stealing one of my sisters in order to prove to me once again that he can do whatever he pleases, and I cannot stop him."

"But you can!" Lara said. "You have far more power than any lowly Yafir."

"Aye, Mother, I do," Dillon agreed with her. "But Ahura Mazda is bitter over Belmair's treatment of his people. And it was indeed unfair. I will heal this breach between these two peoples because they need each other. Neither can survive without the other although neither realizes it right now."

The royal castle was filled to capacity by the day before the wedding. Duke Tullio and his sister, Margisia, had arrived. Cinnia had been nervous at their coming, but Dillon had enough of Sapphira's memories he could give to her; and he made certain they had little time with Cinnia. He had darkened her eyes, too, for while no one else was likely to realize it he knew that certainly Sapphira's mother would know her own child had dark green eyes, and not light green ones.

The night before the marriage was to be celebrated the Great Hall was filled to capacity with all the nobility of Belmair and their families. A great feast was served. There was wonderful entertainments. And then the king stood up at the high board, and the hall grew silent. “My bride to be has something to say to all of you,” he said. He offered Cinnia his hand and she stood up to face the hall.

She wore a deep pink silk gown with flowing sleeves that had a wide square neckline. The garment was simple in style, and yet it suited her. Her black hair was contained in a delicate gold caul studded with tiny diamonds. “Tomorrow,” she began, “I, Sapphira of Beldane, will marry the king and become your queen. This should not be but for a tragedy we all know, but I shall not speak of on this happy night. I am said to resemble the good sorceress of Belmair, and so in her honor, that you may never forget her, I have this day added her name to mine. I shall be known from this time forward as Cinnia Sapphira.”

There was a moment of stunned silence, and then the hall erupted with clapping. Smiling, Cinnia sat down, and as she did she saw the looks of complete surprise upon the faces of Duke Tullio and his sister, Margisia. Sapphira’s mother leaned over and hissed at her angrily.

“How could you do such a thing?” she demanded.

“It was the right thing to do, madam,” Cinnia said. “The former queen was not my enemy. I did not even know her although we were distantly related by blood. And it made the king happy. Is it not my duty to make him happy?”

Lady Margisia glared, irritated. “You do your family a disservice by this foolish and emotional action. They will not call you Cinnia Sapphira. You will be remembered as Cinnia! Cinnia, a creature made impure by the Yafir!" She shuddered with her revulsion. "I cannot believe you did not think this through."

"The king wants peace with the Yafir, madam. Is it not better that the unfortunate incident of the king's first wife be forgotten?" Cinnia said quietly.

"He only chose you because you look like *her,*" Margisia said pettily.

"He chose me for a mistress. It is I, Sapphira of Beldane, who has made him love me, madame. It is I, Sapphira of Beldane, who will be married to the king tomorrow, and crowned Belmair's queen. As queen I hold a modicum of power. Be careful you do not offend me lest I banish you from my presence forever. I know who I am, and it matters not to me by what name I am called. Why should it matter to you?"

"You have grown weak," Margisia sneered.

"Nay, I grow stronger each day because of the power of love. You have no love for me, nor does my uncle. I was a thing to be bartered to the highest bidder. Well, madam, you have gotten the highest price for me. Yet you are not satisfied."

"A woman is supposed to be of use to her family, and how else can she be but by making a good marriage," Margisia said.

"Is my marriage to the king not good enough for you, Mother?" Cinnia asked her wickedly. And then she said, "I grow tired of this conversation." She turned away from the lady Margisia and toward Lara, who was seated on her other side.

*Do you speak the silent language?* Lara asked Cinnia.

*Aye, Nidhug taught me when I was a little girl,* Cinnia answered.

*You handled Lady Margisia well. She will soon be gone back to Beldane.*

*The sooner the better,* Ilona chimed in from the other side of Lady Margisia.

Cinnia swallowed a giggle.

*Cease your chatter at once!* Dillon commanded them. *Others will begin to wonder why you have all gone silent. No need to frighten those who do not possess our magic ways.*

*I do not believe I have ever been in a chamber so full of mortals, and quite frankly I find their vibrations disturbing. Too many uncontrolled emotions all boiling beneath the surface,* Ilona declared. Then she said aloud, "The cakes are absolutely delicious, Dillon, my dear. You must give me the recipe to take back with me."

"'Tis not my cook, Grandmother," the king said. "But rather Nidhug's Sarabeth."

"And Sarabeth is an artist where food is concerned," Nidhug told them all.

The evening finally ended with all those in the Great Hall finding their places for a good night's sleep. The wedding was scheduled to take place at dawn in the gardens between the two castles. Lady Margisia joined Tamary and Anke as they finished dressing Cinnia. Her gown was of delicate white silk. The fitted bodice with its square open neckline was embroidered with dainty crystals, as were the edges of the flowing sleeves and the hem of the gown. The gown flowed gracefully down from her hips, about which was a girdle of thin beaten gold decorated with tiny diamond stars. The bride's hair was contained in a delicate golden caul, with two thin braids on either side of her face. She wore no jewelry.

Lady Margisia, in a better frame of mind this morning, could not help but crow. "You have done it, my darling daughter! I wasn't certain that you could, but you have! Your uncle and I are very proud of you."

"Thank you, madam," Cinnia replied. She could not remember her own mother, but she was certain that lady would have been nothing like Margisia of Beldane.

Duke Tullio came to lead her to the ceremony. "The king requests that you carry this," he said, handing her a pure white star lily.

The garden was filled with all the guests who grew silent as the duke brought her to stand before the dragon. Nidhug wore her seal of office about her neck. Her front claws were painted pink this day, and studded with flecks of gold and silver. Dillon awaited her, garbed all in snowy-white, the crown of Belmair upon his dark head.

"Cinnia Sapphira of Beldane," Nidhug began, "will you have King Dillon of Belmair as your husband?"

"I, Cinnia Sapphira of Beldane accept King Dillon of Belmair for my lord and my husband," the bride said.

Nidhug turned to Dillon. "Dillon of Belmair, will you have Cinnia Sapphira of Beldane, as you wife?"

"I will," Dillon answered.

"Then so I pronounce you wed to each other, husband and wife till death," the dragon said. Then Nidhug took a small gold circlet with a bright diamond star upon it, and placed it upon Cinnia's head. "And so I crown you queen of Belmair."

The young couple turned to face their guests who responded with light clapping. At that very moment there was a clap of thunder, and the Yafir lord appeared before them, holding Sapphira by the hand. She was big with child. The guests gasped at this twin of their new queen, and stepped back.

"What think you of your Cinnia now, king of Belmair? She ripens nicely with my child." Reaching out he patted the false Cinnia's belly.

The wedding guests gasped, shocked.

"Perhaps I shall come and steal Sapphira from you one day. They are most alike, and it would be amusing to show them together," Ahura Mazda said. Then he touched Sapphira's cheek, and she was gone, but the Yafir lord remained. Boldly he walked among the guests. He bowed politely to Ilona and Lara, one magical being to another. He looked at Lara's three daughters. "Which one? Which one?" he mused aloud, walking back and forth before the king's sisters, a finger against his lips considering. "One is lovelier than the others. Two dark, one fair. Which one shall I have for myself."

"They are all protected," Dillon said.

"Perhaps I have a spell to overcome yours," Ahura Mazda replied.

"If you did, my lord, you would already be gone," Dillon answered. "Would you like to join us at the wedding feast, Ahura Mazda?"

The Yafir lord looked surprised by the invitation.

It was at that moment that the king's little sister stepped away from her two older sisters. *"We have tired of this game. Now go back from whence you came!"* Marzina said. She pointed a small finger at the Yafir lord as she spoke and to the amazement of all the guests Ahura Mazda disappeared.

"Marzina!" Lara was shocked by her child's actions. "That was very rude. Sensible, but rude." Behind her Lara heard Kaliq chuckle.

"I knew it!" Ilona crowed. "She has the magic in her blood! She must come to me in a few years. Oh, what I can teach her! At last a granddaughter worthy of our faerie blood!" She beamed, well pleased at Marzina.

"Now, Grandmother, you know you love us all," Zagiri said. "And even if I am just plain mortal, Anoush has her special gifts of healing and sight."

"And good gifts they are," Ilona agreed. "But your little sister has just banished a creature back to from where he came. And she is only ten!"

Cinnia looked at the little girl, and she smiled. "Thank you, Sister," she said. "His presence was beginning to spoil our festivities."

"I thought so, too," Marzina said softly. "He was distressing you."

"You shall not attend another wedding like this one again," Dillon said jovially to their guests. And nervous laughter broke out as the guests dispersed to the trestle tables that had been set up below the high board in the gardens. A great feast was served, and the day was spent in eating, dancing, games, music and other jovial pursuits.

Delighted by her discovery, Ilona was in rare form. Even her beloved son's obvious attachment to Belmair's Great Dragon could not distress her. Her grandson had his wife back. Her family had outwitted the Yafir lord and Ilona knew that Dillon would accomplish whatever it was he needed to accomplish. Ilona could not remember ever having seen a Yafir before. They had been gone from Hetar before her birth. She had to admit to herself that Ahura Mazda was handsome in a repellent sort of way. The silvery-blond hair and the azure eyes were very striking. She couldn't help but wonder, surprising herself by the thought, what it would be like to take pleasures with him. She shuddered delicately. It was time to return to Hetar. Perhaps she would go tonight.

As the festivities celebrating the wedding of Belmair's king began to come to an end, the guests began returning to their chambers, preparing for their departure on the morrow.

"I wish we could send Tullio and Margisia home tonight," Cinnia said to Dillon as they cuddled together in their big bed.

"I asked them earlier, but they prefer to travel by sea in the manner in which they came," he answered her.

"Sapphira did not look unhappy," Cinnia noted. "I am happy for it. I hope she will give the Yafir lord his daughter. Her place in his heart and house will then be secure. And he will shower her with all manner of riches."

"Why is it so important that she have a daughter? Most men desire a quiver full of sons," Dillon noted.

"Do you not recall my telling you that? The Yafir men seem to breed up twenty sons for every daughter born. Arlais told me it is a phenomenon that only began occurring after they made their home in the sea. A daughter, even an ugly one, can bring her father great wealth, especially as there are fewer and fewer Belmairan women to steal. And now that our women are protected, a daughter will bring even more gold," Cinnia said. Leaning forward, she kissed a nipple on his bare chest. "When do I get to have a child, my lord? The people will be very disappointed if their new queen does not conceive almost immediately."

"You know I have wanted no child until the danger was passed," Dillon said slowly.

"Can you not protect our child as you have protected the women and the female infants?" she asked him.

"I have expended a great deal of power in those tasks," he said. "Let me speak with my father, and I will see what he advises," Dillon told her.

"Speak with him soon," Cinnia said softly, and she licked his chest with several strokes of her tongue. "While I enjoy taking pleasures with you, my lord, I want a child."

"You enjoy taking pleasures with me?" he said teasingly. He reached out, and squeezed one of her round breasts. Then leaning forward, he licked at the nipple.

Her hand caressed his nape slowly. She would have sworn she could sense his rising excitement through her fingertips. Pulling his head down, she kissed him.

"I love you," she whispered against his lips. "And I have not yet said thank-you for rescuing me. I thought there was no hope for me, and my heart had turned to stone within my chest, Dillon. But you came for me, and I am alive once more. Thank you."

"You are my life," he told her. "From the moment I laid eyes upon you, Cinnia, you had my heart. I want no other wife, no other love. Together we are complete. Apart we are lost souls. I love you." Now it was he who kissed her.

It was a slow, hot kiss that left her feeling weak, and Cinnia sighed, closing her eyes. They were both delightfully naked, and the sensation of his skin upon hers was wonderful. She pulled him closer, shifting beneath him as she both felt and sensed his rising desire. This, Cinnia realized, was the tender passion she needed right now. When he entered her in a smooth glide of hard, throbbing flesh, she cried out softly with her happiness, wrapping herself about him. Together as they rocked back and forth in each other's arms, they shared the deep love they realized was meant to be theirs.

He loved her so much that Dillon found it difficult to control his own nature. He desperately wanted to give her a child, but the war between Belmair and Ahura Mazda had only just begun. And the Yafir lord was a dangerous man who would obviously stop at nothing to gain his goal of total domination of Belmair. If Cinnia had a child then that child was at risk. He willed the life from his juices as they burst forth. And afterward he cradled her within the shelter of his arms while she slept, and he continued to consider what lay ahead for them all, for Belmair.

The war with Ahura Mazda, he realized he had thought. Not the war with the Yafir. He didn't want to battle the Yafir. Dillon knew all too well the brutality and futility of war. He had lived through two wars in his youth, and he did not want to subject the peaceful Belmairans to such tragedy. But then he realized that the Yafir were no more warlike than the people of Belmair. The battle was to be fought within the magic realm, but it could still prove dangerous.

Dillon smiled to himself. The Yafir lord had been so long removed from the reality of the world that he had no idea how powerful Belmair's king really was. And he did not fight in a traditional manner. Rules were all important in the magic realm, but Ahura Mazda appeared to care little for such niceties. His attacks, so sudden and harassing, were always unexpected. It was difficult to anticipate what he would do, and where he would strike next. He voiced these concerns the next day to Kaliq, Lara and Nidhug, who gathered together in the king's library.

"He is erratic in his behavior," Dillon said to them. "But I have come to realize it isn't the Yafir we must contain. It is their wild lord."

"Is he the one who made the decision to remain hidden in Belmair?" Lara wanted to know. "Is he that ancient?"

"It was he was lord then, Cinnia tells me. He had only been lord for fifty years," Dillon replied to her query.

"But he has grown up with a sense of persecution and isolation," Kaliq mused. "And it would seem he has a great need to revenge himself upon Belmair for what he perceives as the wrongs done to his people. But Belmair is not totally at fault in this matter. For centuries the Yafir have been the outcasts of the magical realm, wandering from place to place to place until finally they disappeared. It has been believed that they became extinct. Why no one considered they might have gone into hiding is interesting."

"Why have they been so despised among the magical folk?" Dillon asked.

"No one knows or can remember the reason," Kaliq answered. "Throughout time there have been peoples in all the worlds shunned, scorned, reviled over the centuries. But when asked *why* such a thing should be, no one really knows. The answer from a Belmairan would be *because they are Yafir.*"

"It makes little sense, Dillon," Lara said to him. "But when I was growing up I was ofttimes shunned because I was believed to be half-faerie. My mortal grandmother worked very diligently to make a completely mortal girl of me. She was a loving woman, but she knew the peril of being different for she had eyes to see."

"I wonder what she would think of you now," Dillon said with a smile.

Lara laughed. "I am not so certain that she would be horrified at the life I have led, the heights I have attained and the magic I wield."

"What do you want to do with the Yafir?" Kaliq asked, bringing them back to the problem at hand.

"The problem isn't so much with them as it is with Ahura Mazda. Because he has been successful at snatching women away and building his little kingdom beneath the sea, he believes he is invincible, but he is not. We are aware that I could easily destroy him now that I know where he hides himself. Still I am no fool, and in the end I will probably have no other choice in the matter. But I would win over the Yafir before I must meet that challenge. I do not wish to alienate them and continue the cycle of distrust and hate. I wish to bring them back into our Belmairan society."

"They call themselves Yafir, but the truth is that many of them are of such mixed blood now that they are as much Belmairan as Yafir," Lara noted. "Perhaps all citizens of Belmair, no matter their heritage, should be simply Belmairan. Although this world has four provinces, it is referred to as Belmair, and its people as Belmairans. Should this not also apply to those who are of Yafir descent?"

"I am proud of my heritage, and of the world into which I was born," Dillon said. "But I am now Belmair's king, and consider myself Belmairan, not Hetarian or Terahn. If you live in a world, are part of that world, then you should call yourself by that world's name no matter your heritage," he concluded.

"It would appear that removing Ahura Mazda from his lordship will be a necessity," Kaliq said. "But if you would remove a leader you had best have another waiting or you create a vacuum, which usually provides an opportunity for troublemakers, and it is certain that there will be several of those among the Yafir."

"You should ask Cinnia what, if anything, she may have heard during her stay with the Yafir," Lara suggested to them.

The young queen was called, and came to join them. They told her of their discussion, and asked if she knew anything that might help them reach out to the Yafir.

"Ahura Mazda's first wife, Arlais, has several sons. I do not believe that they are embittered despite their father's emotions. Arlais is a reasonable woman. If I wanted to reach out to the Yafir, I would speak with her before I spoke with anyone else. She will listen to you. She will be truthful. But she will never betray her lord husband. She loves him, you see," Cinnia explained.

"We can reach out to her on the Dream Plain," Dillon said. "I can tell her that I genuinely seek peace, and offer her people a home above the waves once again."

"No, my lord, 'tis I who should go," Cinnia said quietly. "She knows me, and will not be afraid of coming to my call."

"But then she will realize that Sapphira is not you," Dillon said.

"Arlais will not tell Ahura Mazda that you out-magicked him in order to retrieve me," Cinnia responded. "And besides if such a thing became publicly known the Yafir lord would be a laughingstock. She would not do that to him. Besides there is the chance that Sapphira carries a female child."

"Would not a female child make Sapphira supreme to Arlais?" Lara asked.

"He would never put Sapphira or a daughter before Arlais's devotion and loyalty," Cinnia told them. "That is the paradox of this man. He loves his women despite his ambition and his bitterness."

"Then I think Cinnia should be the one to approach Arlais," Kaliq said.

"So be it," Dillon said.

"When shall I do it, my lord?" Cinnia asked them.

"Will she be safe upon the Dream Plain?" Nidhug wanted to know. She had been silent for most of the meeting, listening, evaluating carefully all that was said.

"She will be more than safe for she carries the protection of the king of Belmair, a Shadow Prince and a great faerie woman," Dillon said with a smile. "Do not fret, Nidhug. I swore when I regained my wife that never again would I allow anyone or anything to harm her. I will keep that vow."

"We will wait until evening," Kaliq said. "I think a first visit to the Dream Plain should begin in an ordinary manner, like any evening's preparation for sleep." He took Cinnia's hand, and looked into her face. "You will not be afraid, my daughter, I promise you. About your neck you will wear a medallion of the tree of life. It will protect you in addition to all Dillon, Lara and I will do. Do you believe me, Cinnia?"

"I do!" Cinnia replied, quite surprised by the effect his words and his beautiful penetrating eyes had upon her.

The discussion regarding the problem of the Yafir lord was now over. Dillon and Cinnia went to bid their many guests farewell as they departed to return to the four corners of Belmair. Cinnia was very relieved to see Duke Tullio and his sister, Margisia, depart. She couldn't help but harbor a small guilty feeling for the deception that had been played upon them, and she was frankly uncomfortable in their presence although she masked those emotions well.

"You have made us, made Beldane proud," Duke Tullio said as he bade farewell. He took her by her shoulders, and kissed both of her cheeks. "Be happy, my child," he told her. Then he made a formal bow. "I salute you, queen of Belmair."

"Thank you, my lord uncle," Cinnia replied. "I am content to have pleased you, and brought honor to Beldane."

Margisia enveloped Cinnia in a hug. "I am so proud of you, my darling," she gushed. Then she lowered her voice. "I knew you could do it. Old Dreng is fit to be tied. He's already gone," she giggled. "Now, remember what I have taught you. Gather up as much wealth for yourself as possible. And when you want something special that your husband may not be of a mind to give you, withhold yourself from him while teasing him just enough so he believes you are not. But do not give him your body until you get your way, Sapphira. I hope you garnered a great deal when he forced you to change your name. I know you would have never done it otherwise," she nattered on.

"And do not ruin your figure by bearing him more than one child. Son or daughter, it makes no mind. I would not give your father more than one. A woman's body is destroyed with childbearing, and when it is you will find your husband runs off to a younger woman whose body has not been ravaged and stretched with new life. Men can be so cruel, my darling Sapphira. Remember that you are the only one who will look after you. Trust no other." Then Margisia began to weep. "Oh, my darling daughter! To think I shall never see you again! Oh, I cannot bear it! I cannot!"

"Certainly you will come to visit, Sister," the duke said impatiently. "Now let us take our leave. Our vessel awaits us." Grasping Margisia's upper arm he led her to her horse, and helped to boost her into the saddle.

"Goodbye," Cinnia said. "Travel in safety." She was more than relieved to have Sapphira's mother gone. What a wretched woman. No wonder her daughter had turned out the way she had. Cinnia waved, and tried to look sad.

By late afternoon all the wedding guests were gone. Cinnia spent some time with Dillon's three younger sisters, the oldest of whom was close to her own age. Anoush, daughter of Lara and Vartan of the Fiacre, was a beautiful girl with brown hair and blue eyes. There was a fragility about her partly due to her faerie blood. She was a quiet girl given only to speaking when she had something to say. She was looking forward to returning to Hetar, for she spent her summers in the New Outlands region of Terah with her foster mother, Noss.

"I need to be with my father's people for at least part of the year," she explained to Cinnia. "It renews my spirit, and I do not as often see my visions there as I do in other places. I do not like my gift, but I accept it. Sometimes I wish my blood ran only mortal."

"Yet I owe you a great debt for directing Dillon in the right path so he was able to find me," Cinnia said to the girl.

Anoush smiled sweetly. "That is the best part of my gift. When I am able to help. I am most grateful for my ability to heal, and do not regret that gift at all."

Zagiri, Dillon's middle sister, was a delightful girl with her father's golden looks. She was pure mortal with not an ounce of magic about her. She looked forward to the day when she would find her true love, and marry. "I love my mother," she told Cinnia, "but she has a destiny that has only been partly fulfilled. One day she is certain to go away again as she has done before. It's a good thing I'm nothing like her, and can be here to look after my father and little sister. My father says mother is an amazing and great woman. I suppose she is, but I am glad my faerie blood is dormant. I don't want to be like Anoush, who is so fragile, or Marzina, who already seems to know too much. I just want a husband to love and children to raise. My grandmother, the lady Persis, is teaching me how to cook. She says a husband will appreciate that I can feed him well if our cook falls ill. She says every girl should know how to cook. Anoush can only cook her potions. And Marzina doesn't want to learn," Zagiri concluded.

It was her littlest sister-in-law who delighted Cinnia, however. Marzina was a true faerie child. Dark haired with large violet eyes, she was quick of mind and foot. She was also friendly, impatient and imperious, sometimes all at once. And from the moment she had successfully pronounced her first spell at the wedding feast the previous day, she had become her faerie grandmother's pet, which pleased her well.

"You are a little sorceress," she told Cinnia. "But one day I shall be a great sorceress. My grandmother says it will be."

"Well, your brother has promised he will teach me more," Cinnia said.

"What can you do now?" Marzina asked.

"I do potions, and I can shape-shift," Cinnia said.

"Shape-shifting is easy," Marzina said scornfully. *Anizram, change!* And suddenly a small green-and-violet bird was fluttering before Cinnia's face.

*Ainnic, change!* A tiger cub leaped up to catch the bird between its soft paws.

The bird turned into a bright yellow-and-green butterfly escaping the tiger cub's gentle grip. The tiger then turned into a net that trapped the butterfly. At once the butterfly became a pair of scissors and the net quickly shifted into a beautiful jewel.

*Marzina change!*

*Cinnia change!*

And both the young woman and the girl returned to their own natural forms. Both were laughing.

"You are very good!" Marzina said admiringly. "You shifted quickly enough to counter me. Can we play this game again sometime?" she asked, smiling.

"You are amazing for one so young," Cinnia told her. "I couldn't shape-shift properly until I was twelve."

"We shall become great sorceresses together," Marzina declared.

She had gained a family, Cinnia thought happily. She had never known her mother, who had died shortly after her birth. Her father while kind was still a distant man whose sole concern was for Belmair. Nidhug had been her only family, and the dragon had raised the girl as tenderly as if she had been her own child. Now suddenly Cinnia had three sisters, each of whom was different, yet interesting. She had a mother-in-law, a faerie grandmother, an uncle who was a faerie prince and a Shadow Prince for a father-in-law. And she had still to meet Lara's husband, and Dillon's little brother.

Cinnia realized how truly happy she was. She knew now that had Dillon not been brought to Belmair to be its king, to be her husband, her world would be a very different place. Had she gained her heart's desire and been selected as Belmair's reigning queen she would have never been able to stop Ahura Mazda. But now she had a strong husband, a family, who would stand by her side in the battle ahead.

"Will you all stay with me when I enter the Dream Plain?" she asked them that evening after the meal. "All of you, Anoush, Zagiri, Marzina, too, unless you will not allow it, Lara. I would find it comforting to know I was surrounded by loved ones."

"I do not know if Marzina is old enough for such an experience," Lara mused.

"Oh, please, let her," Cinnia begged. "Her magic, while untutored, is already strong. Unless it would frighten her."

"Please, Mama!"

"I think it would be an excellent experience for her," Ilona, who had not departed the previous night after all, said.

Lara pretended to consider, and then she said, "Yes!" She turned to her two other daughters. "Girls?" she asked.

"I would rather not," Zagiri responded. "Magic makes me uncomfortable, Mama. And Belmair seems to reek of magic, or perhaps it is just because you, Kaliq, Dillon and Grandma are all here at once. Please do not be offended, Cinnia," she said, turning to the older girl with a small smile of apology.

"I understand," Cinnia told her, returning the smile.

"I will remain," Anoush said softly. "If necessary I may be able to help."

"Well," Ilona said pithily, "I suppose three out of five is not a bad tally."

"Mother!" Lara looked askance at her faerie parent who shrugged.

"The chamber has been prepared," Dillon said. "Shall we go?"

Together they exited the family hall where they had eaten their meal. Dillon led them to a chamber high in a tower. The walls were whitewashed, and a large casement window with leaded panes opened to the night sky where Belmair's twin moons, crescents tonight, were just coming into view. Cinnia had stopped in the apartment she shared with her husband just long enough to allow Tamary and Anke to remove her garments, and help her into a plain white silk sleep garment. Entering the chamber, Cinnia saw it had but a single piece of furniture, a bed, the mattress encased in a sheet, a coverlet atop it.

Dillon stepped up before his wife, and opening his raised hand, allowed a gold chain with a golden charm to drop from his closed fist. The charm was fashioned like a tree in full leaf, and each of the leaves was enameled in a slightly different shade of green. He slipped the chain about Cinnia's neck. "The tree of life will keep you safe upon the Dream Plain. Do you know what to expect there?"

She nodded. "Mists which will clear to reveal she whom I seek," Cinnia said.

"You must concentrate upon Arlais, and no other," Dillon warned her. "Think only of her, and call her name. She will come."

"Here," Lara said as she conjured a goblet from the

air. "This is frine, and it will aid you in your efforts to sleep. Drink it, my daughter."

Cinnia took the cup, and drank it all. Then she made herself comfortable upon the bed, which was indeed the most cozy upon which she had ever lain. She looked at the faces of those surrounding her. Dillon. Kaliq. Lara. Ilona. Cirillo. Nidhug. Marzina and Anoush. They crowded about the bed.

"I am going to take us all into the shadows so you will not see us," Kaliq said to her. "That way we will not distract you, Cinnia. But be assured that we are here." His hand languidly encircled the chamber, and they all disappeared from her view, but Cinnia could see two small red-orange spots, which indicated Nidhug's nostrils. The dragon's fire rarely showed unless she was nervous or angry. Cinnia smiled, oddly comforted by that tiny glow. With a sigh she closed her eyes, and began to slip into sleep.

*Arlais.* She pictured the woman who had been one of her companions for a year. Tall. Dark auburn hair and wonderful dark gray eyes. Arlais whose gowns were all in shades of her favorite green. And then to her irritation Cinnia felt awake. She opened her eyes with annoyance, but to her surprise she was not lying in her bed. She was standing in a swirling silvery-gray mist that wrapped itself about her. All was silence. Deep, deep silence. *The Dream Plain,* Cinnia thought excitedly. She had attained the Dream Plain. Now she had to once again put her thoughts upon Arlais.

Closing her eyes briefly to regain her focus, Cinnia

concentrated. Within her mind's eye she saw Arlais in a pale green gown, her heavy, thick braids looped up about her face. "Arlais," Cinnia called. "Come to me upon the Dream Plain, Arlais." She opened her eyes. The mists were thick about her, yet continued to swirl silently. "Arlais, wife to the Yafir lord, come to Cinnia, the sorceress of Belmair. Come to me!"

The mists began to thin until they cleared away to reveal Arlais walking toward her in her pale green gown. When she reached the spot where Cinnia stood, Arlais said, "I knew it! It really is *you.* And it is Sapphira of Beldane who carries our husband's child, is it not?"

# 16

"AYE, IT IS," Cinnia answered the woman. "But you will not tell him, will you?"

Arlais shook her head. "Nay, I will not. He would be shamed to have been outwitted by the king of Belmair. But how?" Arlais was amazed to be standing here in this strange place actually speaking with Cinnia. The magic involved awed her.

"That is not important," Cinnia said. "Ahura Mazda does not understand that my husband is a great sorcerer. Dillon did not act sooner because he could not find me. When he did, however, the switch was made. And Sapphira, being the ambitious girl she is, quickly figured out what had happened, and has obviously decided to be content."

Arlais nodded. "She protested at first, but everyone believed it was a blow to her head that had rendered her memory faulty. Once she had spent a night in his arms she was fully content. They are well matched. Both insatiable for pleasures, and lustful beyond measure. He has high hopes for her child."

"I think he will get his wish," Cinnia advised Arlais.

"Why have you called me here?" Arlais asked quietly, still daunted by this magical place.

"My husband truly wants peace between our two peoples," Cinnia began. "But the Yafir lord's bitterness seems unending."

"It is," Arlais replied. "He will never forgive Belmair."

"But is his attitude that of all the Yafir?" Cinnia asked softly.

Arlais was silent for a long moment as she debated with herself what to tell the young queen of Belmair. Finally she said, "Nay, it is not. The bubbles are overcrowded. The population of women is shrinking, and the men are stopped from stealing others now. There is grumbling, and discontent beginning to arise. But Ahura Mazda hears it not."

"Neither the king nor I seek to foment discontent," Cinnia said, "but is there perhaps a way for us to resolve this that you can consider?"

"What is it that the king seeks to do?" Arlais asked.

"It has been many centuries since the Yafir were told to depart Belmair. In that time the blood of the Yafir has been well mixed with that of the Belmairans. While there are some who will object to those calling themselves Yafir rejoining our society, this is what Dillon wants. He wants us to be one people. We may all hold on to our customs, and sing of our heritage, but we should all be called by one name. Belmairan," Cinnia said. "Your men cannot produce daughters except rarely, living beneath the sea. And both of our societies need female children. Our races are both dying from lack of them."

"Can your people not produce females, either?" Arlais inquired.

"So many females have been taken over the centuries that we have fewer and fewer left each year. Now, of course, Dillon has enchanted our women to keep them safe, but it still does not solve our problem. Nor yours. We need to join together and be one," Cinnia told her companion. "If Ahura Mazda will not listen, is there not someone who will? Is there not some way in which we can save both of our peoples?"

"My sons, Behrooz and Sohrab, would return to Belmair if they could. And there are others like them," Arlais admitted. "But we have been protected from the centuries beneath the sea. We do not know what will happen to us if we return."

"Then this is the beginning of our dialogue," Cinnia said. "Shall we meet again in a few days here upon the Dream Plain? We are both protected here from harm."

Arlais nodded. "Yes, let us meet again. If your husband is the great sorcerer you say he is, then ask him if he knows what will happen to us if we return to Belmair after our centuries in the sea. Will the transition destroy us? What will happen?"

"I will indeed ask him," Cinnia said. "Goodbye." And the mists began to swirl about her once more. She could actually feel herself slipping away as the echo of Arlais's farewell reached her. Cinnia opened her eyes, fully awake.

"Good morning," her husband said, and focusing, she saw the faces about her.

She sat up. "It was amazing," Cinnia declared. "I spoke with Arlais."

Kaliq smiled, as did Lara.

"I wish I could go to the Dream Plain," Marzina said.

"You are too young," her mother told her.

"There is hope," Anoush said softly. They turned to her and could see that her eyes were glazed over with a vision. "But first there will be strife, not war, but strife among the Yafir, and danger for my brother Dillon. He is determined! He does not seek change! He will attempt to kill the king! You must stop him!" And then she slumped against her mother, trembling.

Lara put a firm arm about her eldest daughter's shoulders, supporting her.

"One day those visions will kill her," Ilona said, low. "She is too fragile."

Anoush opened her blue eyes. "Nay, Grandmother, they will not destroy me. I look fragile, but I am strong of heart." She smiled weakly.

"Tell us what happened," Dillon said to Cinnia.

The young queen of Belmair repeated the conversation she had had with Arlais.

"It is difficult for her," Cinnia explained. "She understands there must be a change if we are all to survive. Yet she would not betray Ahura Mazda. It is her two older sons, I think, who will probably aid us. But Arlais has asked a serious question, and you, my lord Kaliq, are probably the one to answer her query."

"Why do you think that?" Kaliq said with a small smile.

"Because you are the most powerful being that I know," Cinnia said candidly.

He smiled again. "Ask your question," Kaliq said.

"Arlais wonders what will happen to the Yafir after centuries beneath the sea. If they return to the land will they become ancient and die? Remember that those who have been returned previously have suffered that fate. How can Belmair make peace with a people who will perish if they come back to our world? But how can we make peace if they remain below the sea, hostile to us? Ahura Mazda promises his folk that he will bring them back, but he has not the magic needed to do such a thing on such a grand scale, and if his people die attempting to live upon the land again then what has been accomplished but the destruction of the Yafir?"

"A most interesting query," Kaliq said slowly. "I must think upon it, Cinnia. It is indeed possible that Ahura Mazda has stopped time because of the mortal blood now flowing with that of the Yafir. How old is Arlais? Do you know?"

"She told me she was twenty-seven," Cinnia said. "And she certainly looks like a young woman in her twenties."

"Could we not create a spell that would allow the Yafir to begin their lives upon the land once more at the age at which they were stolen?" Dillon said aloud.

"What of the children born to them? How do they age?" Lara wanted to know.

"Everyone looks as if they are in their twenties and thirties," Cinnia said. "They seem to age just so far and no more. I saw no ancients at all, even among the servants."

"Fascinating," Kaliq mused. "Yes, Ahura Mazda has some small control over time beneath the sea, but he will not be able to exercise that control upon the land. I wonder if he knows it? It is unusual for a Yafir to have that kind of knowledge. I am curious as to where he obtained it."

"There was a library of what were referred to as forbidden books in a hidden room in the Academy," Cinnia said slowly. "Cirillo helped us discover it, but we were only inside of it briefly when we were forced to flee the place carrying what volumes we could. The library turned in on itself, and disappeared completely. Since Ahura Mazda has the ability to come and go as he chooses, is it possible there was a book there that aided him to increase his magic?"

"Who has the books you managed to retrieve?" Kaliq asked.

"Prentice, the Academy's scholar of magic," Cinnia told Kaliq.

"A hidden room with a guardian that protected it, and caused it to disappear again," Kaliq said. "Whoever did that was more powerful than a Yafir lord. The room is still there. It is just hidden better now."

"Cirillo said the room had gone for good," Dillon remarked.

"Your uncle does not know everything," Kaliq replied drily.

"The key disappeared when the chamber did," Dillon said.

"I will not need a key," Kaliq answered him.

Lara could not help but smile at this. "Let us break our fast, and then you, Dillon and Cinnia may go to the Academy to access the hidden room. After that the rest of us are going to take a nap, for we have been up all night sitting by Cinnia's side as she traversed the Dream Plain."

They all adjourned to the little family hall where the servants were busy setting the board and then bringing in the meal. There were eggs, scrambled into a fluffy, mass along with rashers of crisp bacon, fresh fruit and breads served with little tubs of newly churned butter. Sweet, hot tea was brought. It was not particularly popular in Hetar, but in Belmair it was quite favored. Dillon had developed a great taste for a strong red tea to which he added honey.

"I am going home now," Ilona said when they were finished. "I'll sleep better in my own bed." She looked to her son, but he said nothing. The queen of the Forest Faeries shrugged. "If you need me, Dillon, call to me. I will come."

"Thank you, Grandmother," he told her and he kissed both of her cheeks.

Ilona returned the gesture, reaching up to give his handsome face a loving pat as she disappeared with a smile in a cloud of mauve mist.

"She really is the most elegant faerie," Zagiri sighed, "even if I am not her favorite. Mama, do you think I can attain that elegance one day?"

"I am her favorite," Marzina said smugly with typical ten-year-old candor. "I believe she loves me even more than she loves Dillon."

"I think it is time for both of you to nap," Lara said. "And yes, Zagiri, you will most certainly attain your grandmother's elegance one day. Now come along, girls." And she led them from the chamber.

"You will not need me as you have the great Shadow Prince," Cirillo said quietly. "Come, Nidhug. I believe we should nap, as well." Then hand in paw he and the dragon departed from the chamber.

"An interesting pairing," Kaliq observed. "I am amazed that his faerie heart is genuinely engaged by her." He turned to Cinnia. "Your dragon is quite an amazing female, my dear. I have never known her like before."

"Let us go and regain the hidden chamber, my lord," Dillon said.

"Step within my robes," the Shadow Prince said, and when they did they instantly found themselves in the library of the Academy. As they moved away from him, Kaliq stood very still as if sensing something. Then he said abruptly, "Come!" and led them into the most deserted far section of the archives. Against a wall stood a tall bookcase. *Well concealed as you may be, you may not hide away from me,* he said in the silent language of the magic folk.

To the amazement of his two companions the little door appeared and sprang open for them. Dillon looked to Kaliq, who nodded. Together the trio entered the hidden chamber. He led them to the room's center, and then murmured something to Dillon.

"I am Dillon, son of Kaliq of the Shadows, and Lara, a great faerie woman," the young man began. "I am king of Belmair, and I ask permission of he who guards this chamber to allow us peaceful entry. Reveal yourself to us if you will, great lord."

The eye in the ceiling above them opened, observed, and then suddenly before them a very gnarled and ancient male figure appeared. He was bent, and his hair was the color of pure snow, but his eyes were a startling bright blue. He was garbed all in white.

*"Cronan!"* Kaliq exclaimed, and he bowed respectfully.

"Kaliq," a surprisingly strong voice for one so old came from Cronan.

"When you disappeared it was thought you had gone into the Beyond," Kaliq said.

"This is your son?" Cronan asked, not bothering to offer any explanations to Kaliq though he obviously sought some knowledge.

"Yes, Dillon," Kaliq replied.

"You always were a romantic fool, Kaliq," Cronan said, but his tone was gentle. "Now tell me, young Dillon, king of Belmair, what is it you seek here in the forbidden athenaeum that I guard? Greetings, Cinnia, daughter of Fflergant. You are amazed to find one of my kind here in Belmair, I can see."

*He was a Shadow Prince!* Cinnia had recognized his kind immediately. "I am, my lord," she admitted. "But you do our world great honor by your presence."

Cronan chuckled. "I do," he admitted affably. Then he turned back to Dillon.

"We need to learn how the Yafir lord, Ahura Mazda, manipulates time for his folk. And we need to know what will happen when the Yafir once more walk the land. Will the population die, or can they survive?" Dillon asked.

"Tell me, why do you seek this wisdom?" Cronan asked.

Dillon explained the situation facing both the Belmairans and the Yafir, telling the ancient Shadow Prince, "I wish to bring our peoples together, to live in harmony once again. It has reached the point where neither of us can survive without the other."

"This is a great undertaking," Cronan replied. "And it will not be easy, young king of Belmair. You will have opposition from some, and that opposition will be led by Dreng of Beltran here in Belmair, and by Ahura Mazda himself for the Yafir. Would you start a civil war, young king?"

"Nay! But if we do not unite as one people we stand

in danger of losing both of our races," Dillon said passionately.

"Perhaps that is what is meant to be," Cronan responded.

"Nay! I was not chosen to come from the world of Hetar to oversee the destruction of Belmair's world," Dillon told Cronan firmly. "I was called to unite it."

"He has your confidence, Kaliq," Cronan remarked drily. "I well remember your youth, and teaching you. But he is young yet."

"He is young," Kaliq agreed, "but I believe he can do this, Cronan."

The ancient Shadow Prince nodded. "Very well," he said. "I will help you. The Yafir lord took the knowledge he has from one of the books here. It is called *A Compendium of Time Manipulation.* When that fool, Napier IX, banished the Yafir, and Ahura Mazda was so desperate to save his people I turned a blind eye to him when he entered this place. I let him roam at will, and that is the information he sought and took."

"Can time be maneuvered to protect the Yafir when they come up from the sea?" Dillon asked Cronan. "I would not harm them in any way. I am thinking mostly of those mortals, and those with mixed blood who have lived there the longest."

"It is possible, but it will take a thorough knowledge of time itself, and a very strong magic to make this all happen. You will need that before you can treat with the Yafir," Cronan said sagely. "Those who would return will want to do so immediately once they learn the option is open to them. You will not want to delay for the best way to thwart Ahura Mazda is to destroy his power base, or at least weaken it severely."

"And in the days we are learning about time, and fashioning our spell," Dillon noted, "we can also work toward helping our Belmairans accept what is to happen."

"That, I suspect, will be the most difficult thing of all," Cronan said.

"Duke Alban, I believe, will be open to these changes," Dillon told the ancient.

"Alban descends from the family of the lady Arlais," Cronan remarked. "She was to wed a duke of Belia, but when she was stolen on her wedding day it was her younger sister who wed that duke instead."

"I think it would be a good thing to learn which families lost women to the Yafir, and then bring these two sides, Belmairan and Yafir together eventually," Cinnia suggested boldly. "It might help us in trying to reconcile both folk."

"An excellent idea!" Cronan agreed.

"Do you know where the compendium is?" Dillon asked the ancient.

Cronan smiled. "You must look for it," he said with a small, wicked smile. "Let yourselves out when you are finished. Use your father's spell whenever you wish to enter here. You will be welcome." Then he turned to Kaliq. "Will you join me, my old friend? We have much to catch up on, I think."

Kaliq nodded, and the two Shadow Princes disappeared.

"How did he get here, I wonder?" Cinnia said.

"Perhaps he will tell Kaliq, although Kaliq will not necessarily tell us," Dillon answered her. "Now we had best seek out the compendium."

Together they searched the little library for the next several hours. Each volume upon each shelf was checked for both title and content. Dillon was growing irritated, for the truth was that Cronan probably knew exactly where the book was, and could have told them. He smiled to himself. It was just the sort of thing Kaliq used to do to him when he wanted a lesson firmly imprinted upon his pupil.

Then Cinnia cried out, "Here it is!" She brandished a small leather-bound tome.

Dillon took it from her, and thumbed through it. "I'll take it to read," he said aloud, and he tucked the little book in a pocket within his robes. Putting an arm about Cinnia he returned them to their apartments in their castle. As their personal servants were nowhere to be seen Dillon turned Cinnia to him, and touched her lips with his. "Will you take pleasures with me now, my love?" He caressed her face with a finger. "I missed you last night, Cinnia. Did you miss me?"

"Aye, I missed you," she told him. "How much did you miss me, my lord?"

"Come into our bedchamber, and I will show you," he replied, nuzzling her ear.

Taking his hand she led him from their shared dayroom, and he closed the door behind them, slamming the bolt firmly so they would maintain their privacy while they played. The sun cast dappled shadows upon the stone floor of the chamber and its colorful rugs. He pointed a finger at her, and her gown dissolved. She pointed one at him, and his robes were gone.

Her gaze dropped, and then she said, "I cannot see that you missed me greatly, my lord. Perhaps you were mistaken as to the depth of your affections," Cinnia teased.

Reaching out, he took one of her soft, round breasts in his hand and fondled it. The ball of his thumb rubbed her nipple, which tightened in response.

"Kneel before me," Cinnia said to him, and he did. "Raise your head up, and remember you may not touch me with your hands unless I give you leave. Open your mouth, but do nothing more until I tell you that you may."

He lifted his head, his eyes dancing with delight at the game she was playing with him. He parted his lips for her. Leaning forward Cinnia placed the nipple he had played with into his open mouth. He remained perfectly still, his hands at his sides. She remained silent. He longed to tug upon that nipple, but in obedience to her wishes he did nothing, but he could feel his cock beginning to respond very strongly to this torture.

After a few minutes she said, "You may suckle upon me, my lord." And then she gasped as he pulled strongly upon the tender flesh, mouth, tongue and teeth all working at her. She could see his hands clenching and unclenching themselves.

"Do you want to touch me?" she taunted him.

His eyes, hot with desire, gazed silently up at her as he sucked upon her breast.

"You may fondle my buttocks if you so desire," Cinnia finally told him. "But you will release my nipple if you do so. You must not be too greedy for my flesh, my lord."

His mouth tugged upon her for a short while more, and then nipping fiercely upon the nipple a final time he released it, his hands going immediately to her buttocks, which he kneaded strongly as he slowly, slowly, drew her forward. And when she was exactly where he wanted her, he ran his tongue down her shadowed slip.

"I did not say you could do that!" Cinnia cried. *"Oh!"*

Dillon's tongue pushed between her nether lips, and with unerring aim found her pleasure jewel. He teased at it, and she let him. Her juices were beginning to flow when he released his hold upon her bottom, and swiftly thrust two fingers into her sheath all the while working the sentient nub of swollen flesh beneath his tongue. The fingers moved rhythmically back and forth within her sheath, and she found herself pushing down upon them as she sought to get him deeper.

He laughed. "You're greedy as always."

"You're too good, as always," she managed to murmur.

"Do you want me deep inside of you, my love?"

"Aye! Hurry!" she pleaded with him.

He pulled her down to her knees, and then lay her back, pushing her legs high. "Do you think I am showing you my need now, my love?" he asked, brandishing his manhood, which was now quite swollen and lengthy.

In answer she moaned with her need.

He answered her in a single hard thrust. Then he began to ride her until she was weeping with her delight.

Cinnia felt the length of him plunging forward until he was practically entering the mouth of her womb. He was so hard, and his flesh burned her with his lust. With her legs raised high he could fill her with his full length, and she loved it. She tightened and released, tightened and released the muscles of her wet sheath around him, and he groaned with his delight as, kneeling between her upraised legs, he pleasured her until her head was spinning and she was soaring into the skies above. "Oh, Dillon!" she cried.

And the sound of her sweet voice so filled with ecstasy broke his control. His manhood quivered violently and then exploded his love juices into her. It seemed to him as if his juices would never stop flowing, but finally his big body jerked hard several times, and he collapsed with a gusty sigh. "Cinnia, Cinnia! None has even pleasured me like you do," he told her as he moved to take her into his arms.

"Even she who is said to be my double?" Cinnia asked him wickedly.

"Not even she," he told her honestly.

Hearing the truth in his voice, Cinnia smiled contentedly. "I am glad for that," she said, "though Arlais tells me Sapphira pleases Ahura Mazda well." Then she grew serious. "What will happen to her when he is no more, Dillon? Will Tullio accept her and her child back in Beldane, or will they make them outcasts?"

"I do not know the answer to that," Dillon said. "I cannot be certain if Tullio will accept the changes to come. I know Alban will, and Dreng won't. But I am not certain of Tullio. Only time will give us the answer to that, my love."

Duke Tullio, however, had suffered a great tragedy on his return home. His vessel had been caught in a terrible storm within sight of his own coastline. It had sunk, and only the duke, and four of the sailors aboard had survived to reach the shore. His sister, Margisia, along with everyone else aboard, had drowned. Tullio was devastated, for he had been deeply fond of his only sister. It was the son-in-law who had been designated his heir who had sent word to the king and the queen of the terrible calamity. And because Cinnia was thought to be Sapphira it was necessary for her to put on the mourning white for her *mother.* Perhaps now, she thought, if Tullio ever learned what had become of Sapphira, he would welcome her return. Did Sapphira even know of her mother's terrible end? Cinnia wondered.

She did. Ahura Mazda had learned of the disaster, and considering it a blow against Dillon, trumpeted the news within his own hall. Arlais saw the false Cinnia go pale, and moving discreetly to her side she caught her hand in hers and murmured low.

"Do not show your distress. You can only mourn in secret, my dear."

"Do not speak, I beg you," Sapphira replied, her soft voice trembling.

"I know who you really are, but you make our husband happy, and that is enough for me," Arlais responded.

Sapphira nodded silently, and their eyes met in understanding.

*Poor girl,* Arlais thought. *She is arrogant, rude and selfish, yet I pity her. And what will happen to her when the changes come?* Arlais had spoken to her two eldest sons, Behrooz and Sohrab. They were cautious, but open to her tale of meeting the young queen of Belmair upon the Dream Plain.

"We will not betray our father," they said as one.

"Neither will I," Arlais answered them, "but he will not change. There have been peoples throughout history who have split and gone in different directions when they could no longer live beneath a single rule. Belmair sent those who changed to Hetar. But before any decision is made, before you even speak with your families and adherents, we must learn if we can still survive upon the land. The sorceress has not called me again, but she will when the time is right. We must wait."

It was a difficult time for those looking to change the world. While he studied the small book on time manipulation Dillon also made it his business to speak with the ordinary folk regarding the Yafir. In his own district of Belmair he found the attitudes were mixed.

Some were not averse to sharing Belmair with the Yafir again. Others were strongly opposed to it. The citizens of Belia, like their duke, were more than willing to share their province with the magic folk. The people living in the Beldane sector like those of the Belmair sector were divided, while Dreng of Beltran and his people were diametrically opposed to the Yafir.

"This will take longer than I had anticipated," Dillon said to Kaliq and Cronan one evening as they sat together in the little hall. The ancient Shadow Prince had taken to joining them, and the young king enjoyed his company. It was interesting to see the great Kaliq deferring to another.

"What will you do then?" Cinnia asked her husband.

"If I cannot scatter the Yafir among all four of our provinces, what else can I do but raise another mass of land up from the sea for them?" Dillon replied.

"A most ambitious undertaking," Cronan noted drily. "But will it not defeat your original purpose to bring Belmairan and Yafir together as one people?"

"Perhaps in the beginning," Dillon agreed, "but the most important first step in my plan is to bring them out of hiding. Some will assimilate into Belmairan society immediately. And Belmairans will get to know them through trade between the provinces. There will be more intermarriages between the young people, but these marriages will be negotiated between the families. We will have no more stolen brides."

"First you must solve the problem of stabilizing their

ages so all the Yafir may continue on with reasonable life expectancies," Kaliq said.

"It will not be easy," Dillon said. "I am not certain a mass spell will suffice, and I would do no harm. I believe it may have to be done one by one."

"That is time-consuming," Cronan's ancient voice said.

"You have far greater knowledge than I in this matter," Dillon replied.

"Why do you think that?" Cronan responded.

"You are sympathetic to the Yafir," Dillon said. "Why else would you remain here in Belmair all these centuries? I suspect you have guarded them for all this time. They are magic folk, but of the lower orders, Cronan. They had not the knowledge or power to create the world below the sea in which they live. I think you did that for them."

"You are right, Kaliq. He is very intuitive and clever," the old Shadow Prince said. "Aye, I have been protecting them, but like many races they have become their own worst enemy, and unless something is done they will become Belmair's, as well. Another king in the mold of the previous rulers here would have surely spelled Belmair's doom."

"Then help me to help the Yafir," Dillon replied. "If I raise a new land mass from the sea, can we three together enchant it so that the Yafir may live in safety? I will devise a spell that can be used individually to ply time to our will so some may be dispersed to the other provinces, except Beltran. I have no time to argue with Dreng at this moment. I will deal with him later."

"And what of Ahura Mazda?" Cronan asked.

"I will deal with him later, as well," Dillon said grimly. "First the land must be brought up from the sea. Then it must be made habitable. When that is done then we will approach those among the Yafir who would come up from the sea."

"It is a good plan," Cronan said.

"May I speak to Arlais about it?" Cinnia asked her husband. "That way she can prepare her sons, and their adherents. I think knowing they need not face the immediate hostility of we Belmairans may make their decision an easy one."

"Aye," Kaliq agreed. "It is clever."

"Do I not always achieve my purposes, my lord?" Dillon asked his father.

Cronan chuckled. "He has your ego, I see, old friend. I should like to meet his mother one day. She must be strong to have withstood you, Kaliq, and yet birthed you such a fine son. There is no in-between with these faerie women. They can be either as hard as iron, or soft as butter."

"Lara is a little of both," Kaliq told the ancient. "But the softness is the small bit of mortal blood that flows within her."

The next morning they met in Dillon's library, and spread a great map of Belmair upon a large table. The largest province, Belmair itself, appeared to sit in the very center of the great sea, surrounded by the three smaller provinces of Belia, Beldane and Beltran each set equidistant from each other, and Belmair province itself. To have fit a new province between the others would have destroyed the balance. It was decided to put it in the southern part of the sea away from the others. This way it could be said the Yafir had discovered the place, and had been living there for centuries. No one need ever know about their world beneath the sea if they chose not to speak of it.

The following morning the two Shadow Princes settled themselves upon Nidhug's back, and she flew to the spot where together they would create this new province, which would be called Belbuoy. The dragon hovered over the area as Dillon called forth land from the deep. He stood upon Nidhug's back near the graceful curve of her neck.

*Heed me waters of the sea. Spread yourselves, give way to me. At the calling of my hand, slowly, slowly raise new land. Gentle hills and meadows fair; beaches wide, and harbors there. Soil that's rich and air that's sweet; a place for magic folk to meet. Give way, oh waters of the sea. I ask it of you humbly.*

Dillon raised his hand over the waters, and they began to part. As they did land rose up from beneath the waves lapping at the newly formed shoreline. While he drew the steaming land up both Kaliq and Cronan worked to form hills, and smooth fields and bring golden sands to cover the beaches that surrounded the new land.

*I thank you waters of the sea for your generosity,* Dillon said when it was done.

The trio then set about to make it all fertile. Trees of all kinds sprang up. The meadows were filled with grasses and other growth. And then came animals and birds.

Three large fresh water rivers appeared, along with many brooks and streams. When they had finished Nidhug hovered above it all, marveling at their work.

"It's beautiful," she said.

"Take us home," Dillon said in a weak voice. "We are exhausted."

The dragon flew with them back to the royal castle. The two Shadow Princes, and the young king came down from her back and she was shocked to see how tired and drawn they were. "Are you all right?" she asked them, concerned. "Shall I call someone?"

"Nay," Dillon told her. "We are just worn from our hard work this day."

"We must rest," Kaliq said. He put an arm about Cronan, who could scarcely stand. "Come, old friend. It has been quite a while since we did such work together, and we were both much younger then."

The three men slowly entered the stairwell that would take them back into the castle. The dragon watched them go, and then she rose up and flew across the gardens to her own castle. She found Cirillo awaiting her in her Great Hall. He hurried forward, and taking her paws in his beautiful hands, kissed them tenderly.

"They have done it?" he asked.

"It was the most amazing thing to watch," Nidhug told him as they sat together at the high board, waiting for the servants to bring their meal. "Dillon actually got the seas to part, and give forth new land. They fashioned hills and valleys, conjured up creatures of the air and land, green growth. I have never seen such incredible and strong magic, Cirillo. What little talents I possess pale in comparison. Having seen what I saw today I am almost ashamed to call myself a member of the magic world."

"Do not be, my love," he told her. "You, and your antecedents have kept Belmair safe throughout the aeons. That is great magic. The magic my nephew has is simply different. With his natural talents, and the blood of both faerie and Shadow running in his veins, he should be a strong sorcerer."

"Old Cronan was quite overcome," Nidhug said, her tone concerned.

"It will take more than helping to create a new province in Belmair to send him off into the next life," Cirillo noted. "While you were gone I popped home to tell mother what was happening. She told me Cronan's history. Even among the Shadow Princes he was considered eccentric, she says. She thinks he may be the last of the original Shadow lords, but is not certain. She believes Kaliq would know the answer to that."

"I imagine when the king and his companions are recovered he will want to meet to discuss the next steps we must take," Nidhug observed.

Cirillo nodded. "I expect Cinnia will have to go to

the Dream Plain again," he said. "It will be easier for her this time, I imagine. She will not be afraid."

Cinnia was already preparing herself for another visit to the Dream Plain. Dillon had returned tired, but enthusiastic over their day's work. He had taken a reflecting bowl and filled it with water. Then with a soft word and a wave of his hand he had shown her the new province of Belbuoy.

"You have made it more like this land than like the others," Cinnia noted. "I shall tell Arlais, and she can tell her sons. It will be a good place for the Yafir, and allow our own Belmairans to grow used to them again especially if some of them settle among us to begin with rather than living on Belbuoy. There is so little physical difference between us, Dillon. The males still seem to possess the silvery hair and aquamarine-blue eyes no matter their bloodlines, but few among the women have such coloring."

"Have you seen enough?" he asked, and when she nodded that she had, he emptied the reflecting bowl of its water, and returned it to its place upon a shelf. "Do not go to the Dream Plain tonight," he told her. "I would be near when you do, and I need to rest now to restore my own strength. Come and lie with me, Cinnia. Tomorrow we will speak with Kaliq and Cronan. The plans we make must be foolproof if we are to succeed."

Cinnia took her husband by the hand, and together they lay upon their bed. She wrapped her arms about him, cradling him tenderly, and they slept the night through. When the new day dawned Dillon was refreshed, and his strength had returned. He ate a hearty breakfast, and then in the company of his wife they met with the others.

The great map of Belmair was spread again upon the library table, and with a flick of a finger the new province of Belbuoy appeared upon the parchment. It was then agreed that Cinnia would meet again upon the Dream Plain with Arlais this coming night. Nothing else could be accomplished until then.

"What of dwellings for the Yafir?" Cinnia asked.

"We could do what Lara did when she removed the clan families from the Outlands into the New Outlands," Kaliq suggested.

"I think it too dangerous to move people and dwellings through the sea that same way," Dillon said.

"Move the entire bubble," Cronan told them. "It will protect them, and all within it. Then once it is upon Belbuoy I will remove the bubble."

"But what if all within the bubble do not wish to come?" Cinnia said.

"That is a problem that must be decided among the Yafir," Cronan replied.

Dillon nodded. "If we wish to break Ahura Mazda's hold upon the Yafir they must be given a choice, something they have not had in centuries."

"Then I will go to the Dream Plain tonight," Cinnia told them.

"Take this for Arlais and her sons," Kaliq said, and reaching into his robes he drew forth a small crystal globe. "Tell Arlais that the crystal will show Belbuoy to any who request to see it." He handed the globe to Cinnia.

"But how…?" she began.

"Hold it in your hand as you fall into sleep, Cinnia," Kaliq instructed her. "Because it is magic it will come with you as you journey, and Arlais will be able to carry it back with her when she awakens. That way she can show it to her sons."

Cinnia took the globe, and slipped it into the pocket of her own robes.

"Now we must wait," Dillon said, "and see what will transpire after tonight."

"Then I shall sleep until I am needed again," Cronan said.

"And I will return to Shunnar," Kaliq announced.

"And I will return to my mother's realm then," Cirillo said. "When it is time to act, call me." He turned to the dragon. "Come, my dear," he said to her. "We must talk before I leave you."

"Of course, my lord," Nidhug said, and she fluttered her heavy eyelashes at him as together they left the hall, and began to stroll slowly across the garden.

"There is more between us than just pleasures and passion," the faerie prince said to the dragon as they walked.

"There can be nothing more," Nidhug told him. "You are faerie. I am dragon."

"Knowing the calling of your own heart, do you truly believe that?" Cirillo asked her quietly. "I know that I love you, my lady dragon."

"You are young, Cirillo. You have not even lived a half century yet. I have lived for several centuries now," she told him.

"Age means nothing to those of us in the magic realm, Nidhug. It is nought but a number. *I love you.* If you can tell me that you do not love me then when this matter between Belmair and the Yafir is concluded I will go and never return," Cirillo replied.

*"No!"* the dragon cried, the word slipping from between her lips unbidden. Then she said, "You are cruel, Cirillo."

"Aye, I am cruel. I have a cold faerie heart, and yet it seems to warm for you, and only you. Tell me that you do not love me, Nidhug."

"I cannot," she replied, several large tears slipping down her snout. "I do love you, and it is a most impossible situation, my beautiful faerie prince."

"Nay, it is not. We are magic, Nidhug. If it pleased you I would be that blue-and-gold dragon for as long as we both live," he declared passionately.

"Foolish prince," the dragon replied. "You cannot. You are your mother's only heir. You will one day rule the Forest Faeries, and you must take a faerie wife so you may have an heir to follow you. That is why this is so impossible, Cirillo."

"That time is far in the future, and when that time comes I will do my duty, but my mother has barely reached her prime," Cirillo said. "You are the mate I would have. I will not always be true to you for that is my faerie nature, but I will love no other, Nidhug, but you. You are the keeper of my heart, my darling dragon."

And then the faerie prince took his dragon's form, and together the two soared into the skies above the twin castles. They flew over the sparkling afternoon sea to Belia where they took pleasures together in Nidhug's cave high above the province. Their cries of satisfaction as they mated were so loud that their roars sounded like thunder, and Belia's folk looking to the skies were puzzled by the lack of rain clouds or rain. Finally the two dragons slept until the early evening when they returned to Nidhug's castle. It was there that Cirillo took leave of his lover and returned to Hetar's forests where his mother was awaiting him.

"The scent of lust is upon you," Ilona greeted her son.

Cirillo laughed, but said nothing.

"How goes it in Belmair?" she asked him.

Cirillo told his mother in careful detail, for detail was important to the faerie kingdoms. Detail helped with spells, and other magic to be performed.

"And old Cronan is still useful?" Ilona sounded amazed.

"Did you ever meet him?" Cirillo asked her.

Ilona shook her head. "I know him only by reputation. I wonder what the Shadow Princes will think when Kaliq tells them that he lives."

"I do not know if he will," Cirillo said.

"Aha! Clever creature that he is, aye! Kaliq would keep such information for his own advantage. Well, let him. Had Cronan ever picked a successor it would have undoubtedly been Kaliq or so rumor would have it," Ilona said. Then she turned to her son. "When this is over there will be no need for you to return to Belmair."

"I will always return to Belmair," Cirillo told his mother.

"I think it is time for me to pick a proper faerie bride for you," Ilona told her son.

"Do not, Mother, or you will doom some poor faerie maid to disappointment," he warned her. "My cold faerie heart belongs to the dragon. It is she who warms it. One day I will do as you wish, briefly love another and father an heir or an heiress upon one of our kind. But I love Nidhug, and I will not deny it. Nor will I lie to you about it," Cirillo said.

"You have your father's straightforward manner," Ilona said grudgingly. "Very well, Cirillo, for now I will leave you to your little amusement. If you tell me you will one day take a faerie wife and father an heir then I will trust you to know when the time is right. A dragon! What kind of a son did I raise that he would fall in love with a dragon? I liked it better when you were more like me, flitting from lover to lover."

"I will still take a lover now and again, Mother. I am faerie. Nidhug knows that, and she understands it is my nature," Cirillo said.

Ilona shook her beautiful golden head. "You do know she is older than you?"

"Centuries older." He chuckled, agreeing.

"I shall blame Kaliq for this," Ilona decided. "I

should have never let you study with him for all those years. He has been a bad influence."

"I suspect he would be delighted to know that you think so, Mother," Cirillo teased her, grinning. "Now, if you will excuse me, I shall go and find Father."

She waved him off and, watching him go, she smiled. She had birthed but two children, and each in their way was extraordinary. She was very proud of her daughter, Lara, who while mating with mortals had done her heritage proud. And while she adored her son, the fates were obviously tempting Ilona of the Forest Faeries. A dragon? How had Cirillo lost his faerie heart to a dragon? She wondered if she would ever know.

# 17

"I WILL REMAIN with you while you journey," Dillon told Cinnia as she prepared for her second trip to the Dream Plain. They had gone to the dream chamber, and he handed her the cup of sweet frine that he had prepared. Cinnia drank it down, kissed his lips and then lay down upon the comfortable bed, Kaliq's crystal globe in her hand.

"I feel secure knowing you are there," Cinnia told him. Her head touched the pillow, and it cradled her neck and shoulders. "I love you," she told him, and then she closed her eyes. Slowly, slowly she sank into a deep sleep, and by the look that suddenly touched her face he knew she had reached her destination.

The silvery-gray mists were very thick. Aware of everything about her, Cinnia stood very still. "Arlais," she called softly, and then more insistently, “Arlais! Where are you?” She began to walk through the mists, and then they grew thinner, and she could see Arlais coming toward her.

“I was beginning to think that you had either forgotten or that our first meeting was nothing more than a dream,” Arlais said as they met and embraced warmly.

“Nay, but there has been so much to do,” Cinnia said. “My husband and others have created a new province they have named Belbuoy. He drew the land from the sea, and it is beautiful and fertile. It is to be the Yafir’s new home.” She went on to explain everything to Arlais, who listened intently. And then Cinnia reached into her robes and brought out the crystal globe. “Kaliq of the Shadows has sent this to you,” she said. “You, or whoever holds it has but to ask to see Belbuoy, and they will.” She handed the globe to Arlais. “It is yours to keep. When you awaken it will be with you, and proof of what is happening between us. Have you spoken with your sons?”

“I have. They are cautious, for to trust a Belmairan is not something they have been taught to do,” Arlais said candidly. “But they are also hopeful for a future that will take them back to live upon the land.”

“They are men grown, and yet you are but twenty-seven,” Cinnia said. “Such a thing defies logic, but Dillon says time has been manipulated for the Yafir. Is it not odd to have sons who look your age?”

Arlais laughed. “At first as they grew and grew and

I remained the same it did seem strange. But one grows used to such things. Now, however, there are so many of us. Ahura Mazda kept insisting our men keep stealing Belmairan women, and the women kept having sons, and few daughters." She sighed. "A society peopled mostly by men is not an easy place in which to exist. The men have little to do, and where once we had land beneath the sea where we farmed, now most of that land is taken up with homes for our burgeoning population. The bubbles cannot expand it seems. I have asked Ahura Mazda about this, but he waves my questions away, and will not answer."

"It is not his magic that created the bubbles, or that keeps them safe," Cinnia told Arlais. "The Yafir were saved by an ancient Shadow Prince named Cronan who makes his home on Belmair. I do not know how he became acquainted with Ahura Mazda, but he did. He took pity on the Yafir, for they are considered the lowliest of the magic folk."

Arlais's mouth dropped open in surprise, and then she laughed. "That wicked Yafir," she said softly. "The Yafir had no real lord until Ahura Mazda. When that old Belmairan king banished them from Belmair, they were ready to wander once again. But Ahura Mazda told them he could save them, and they would never have to wander again. With a wave of his hand he took them to the bubbles, dispersing the various families among them. Those who remember that time say that the cottages were already there. In fact everything was there for them. And Ahura Mazda made it possible for them to return to the land to take the women they sought when they wanted them."

"The magic to transport themselves and others is a magic that belongs to the pure-blooded Yafir, but the magic for creating and sustaining the bubbles is not theirs. That is great magic, and only a Shadow Prince has that kind of magic," Cinnia told Arlais.

"So my husband is a fraud." Arlais chuckled wickedly. Then she grew serious. "He will not leave his castle, or his bubble," she told Cinnia.

"In the end he may have to," Cinnia replied. "Cronan is very, very old, Arlais. His strength is waning with each day. Soon he will not be able to sustain the Yafir in their hidden world. He is, I suspect, partly responsible for bringing Dillon to Belmair. He himself has said that none of us, Belmairan or Yafir, could survive with another narrow-minded king. We needed fresh blood. Fresh eyes to see."

Arlais nodded. "I agree," she said.

"You must speak to your sons, and they must speak to their adherents. If the Yafir are to be saved again—if they are to be eventually integrated into Belmairan society, and become one with us—we must move to accomplish this soon," Cinnia told her companion.

"I will speak to them this day," Arlais said.

"Very well," Cinnia replied. "And in two nights time we will meet again here upon the Dream Plain."

Arlais nodded. "I will be here," she said.

And then the two women found themselves being surrounded by the mists of the Dream Plain as they slid away back into consciousness.

Cinnia awoke suddenly to find Dillon dozing in the chair by her side. Looking at her husband, she smiled. He looked so young for a man with such great responsibilities. Rolling onto her side, she reached out and touched his hand. "I'm awake," she said softly, and smiled as his eyes opened. "It is done. We will meet again in two nights' time and hopefully then we will be able to begin to affect the transfer of the Yafir to Belbuoy."

"You are amazing," he told her, and his eyes were filled with his love.

"I could not do this without you," Cinnia responded.

"You are truly my other half," Dillon said. "Where I am weak you are strong. Where you are weak I am strong. I am always amazed that such a perfect match between male and female can be made." He smiled at her. "It is not yet dawn. Let us go to our own bed, my love." He helped her up, and together they departed the dream chamber for their own bedchamber where they slept until past the sunrise.

Beneath the sea, Arlais awoke in her own bedchamber. Ahura Mazda had been with Volupia the previous night but was now gone from her chamber. After she had washed and dressed, Arlais went into the common room, where Minau was already breakfasting. "Good morning," she greeted the second wife, and joined her.

"I think today I shall go and visit my sons," Arlais said. "Do you want to come?"

"Nay, Cinnia is nearing her time, and one of us should be with her," Minau replied. "She is very unpleasant of late, and the others do not want to be near her."

"I am sorry," Arlais replied. "Would you like me to remain instead of visiting?"

"Nay," Minau responded. "You are always taking the heaviest burdens upon yourself. If you wish to see your sons today then go. I can manage Cinnia. She is so difficult of late that even our husband does not wish to be near her." Minau chuckled.

The bubbles of the world called Yafirdom were connected by passageways fashioned from clear crystal quartz. Leaving the small castle Arlais made her way through the corridor that would take her to the bubble community where her sons lived.

She found them in the dwelling that they shared for neither yet had taken a wife.

"Good morning, my sons," she greeted them as she stepped through the door of their cottage. They came forward, kissing her cheeks and leading her to a seat by the stone hearth. "I have brought you a small gift," Arlais said. "But it is delicate, and you must be careful when you handle it." She drew forth the small crystal sphere from the pocket of her robe and held it out. "Take it, Behrooz," she said to her eldest son, "and say aloud, *Show me Belbuoy.*"

Behrooz, a tall young man with the silvery hair and aquamarine eyes of all the Yafir males, took the sphere from his mother. It sat in the palm of his hand. Looking down at it he said, *"Show me Belbuoy, oh sphere."* And then his eyes widened, and a soft gasp of surprise escaped his lips. "What is this, Mother? What is this place?"

"King Dillon and his Shadow Prince companions created this province for us," Arlais said quietly. "He would welcome the Yafir unlike his predecessors."

Her two other sons, Sohrab and Nasim, crowded about their eldest brother, peering down into the crystal in Behrooz's hand.

"Is this a trick?" Sohrab asked his mother.

"It is so beautiful!" Nasim, the artist, murmured.

"Have you and Behrooz not spoken on leaving this world in which we are trapped?" Arlais asked her two elder sons.

"Where would we go? The Belmairans hate and distrust us," Sohrab answered her. "There is no world that will accept the Yafir. Has not our father told us that many times? Is that not why he created this place for us?"

"King Dillon would have us inhabit Belbuoy. And some of our folk may even live in the other provinces except Beltran, for its duke does not want us. Our race is dying. And so are the Belmairans. We need each other to survive. We need to be one people, my sons. At last Belmair has a king, a powerful king, who understands this, and would welcome us. I know that you want to go, for you have said it to me. As for Yafirdom, your father did not create it. Nor does he maintain it. I have learned that the Yafir were saved by a Shadow Prince who took pity on us. It is he who gave us all of this, and keeps it for us. But this great Shadow Prince will not be able to sustain us much longer. He grows weak with the great effort he has been expending for us. We must return to the land, or we will die," Arlais told her three sons.

"There are many who would go, Mother," Behrooz admitted. "But they are afraid of father, and they are afraid of the future. I need more than a crystal sphere that shows me beautiful pictures to convince them."

"And how would we get there?" Sohrab said. "We will drown if we leave the bubbles. We need to know more. How is it that you know these things?"

Arlais smiled. "I have visited with Belmair's queen upon the Dream Plain twice now. Last night was our second meeting, and she gave me the crystal sphere to bring to you so you might see. I will meet with her again in two nights' time."

"We must come with you," Behrooz said. "We must meet this queen and speak with her ourselves. How can we attain the Dream Plain?"

"I do not know," Arlais admitted. "All I can tell you is that I sleep, and the queen calls to me. I follow the sound of her voice through the mists in order to find her. Then we meet face-to-face and speak."

"Ask her to call to us, as well," Sohrab begged his mother. "Before we dare to beard our father we must know more, be certain of these things you tell us and we see."

"If Father has not the magic to have created the bubbles and sustain them, then what magic has he?" Behrooz wanted to know.

"The queen tells me that the Yafir are considered the lowliest of the magic folk. Your father has the power to come and go as he will, to mix potions and to make himself invisible, but that is all he can do. These things I have seen myself. But never have I seen him do great things as he claims he can."

"How can we be certain that this King Dillon is all that he says he is?" Behrooz asked. "Is his magic truly greater than our father's? Remember that our father stole King Dillon's wife away, and has put a child in her belly."

Arlais hesitated a long moment, and then she said, "Your father knows it not, my sons, but King Dillon's magic is so great that he himself came to take his wife back. The girl who will bear your father's child is Queen Cinnia's double, Sapphira of Beldane, who King Dillon took briefly as his mistress. Once King Dillon learned where the Yafir hid themselves he acted immediately to reclaim his wife. But he wanted no direct confrontation with your father because the king is a man of peace. He would solve the problems that exist between us without a war. If the king had taken the queen boldly it would have caused much difficulty between our peoples. You know your father's great pride. He could not have withstood being bested. The wife he calls Cinnia makes him happy, and I am told the child she carries will be the daughter he so desires. There is no need for him to ever know the truth. And the girl is content, as well. She is a creature who enjoys being wed to a powerful male, and loves all the riches he bestows upon her."

Behrooz nodded. "If all you have told us is truth, Mother, then it is time for us to leave the sea and return to the land once more. But ask Belmair's queen to call us to the Dream Plain so we may speak with her, and be reassured." He turned to his brothers. "Do you agree?" he asked them.

Sohrab and Nasim nodded. "We do," they said with one voice.

"To be able to paint in the sunlight," Nasim said softly.

"To be able to farm again," Sohrab replied.

"But how will we get there?" Behrooz asked.

"I do not know," Arlais responded. "That is a question you must ask the queen, my sons. And another question would be how did we get here? Even your father will not say how it was affected."

"Because he does not know," Behrooz said. "If he did not make this all happen, then it is unlikely he knows how it did. He will not want to go, you know."

"He is the leader of his people," Arlais said. "When he sees this is what they want he will relent."

"He will never relent," Behrooz answered her. "His hatred of the Belmairans is too great for him to overcome. As for me, I am tired of hating. I want to live in the full sunlight, and feel the air upon my face. I want to take a wife and have a family. I am tired of living this restricted existence beneath the seas. And so are all of our friends. I know this is all we have ever known, but we know there is more, and we want it."

"You will go even if he forbids it, won't you?" Arlais asked quietly.

Her three sons nodded.

"But first we must speak with Queen Cinnia," Behrooz told her.

"Not tonight, but tomorrow night," Arlais told them. "Drink some wine before you sleep so you will sleep heavily. It is easier to reach the Dream Plain then."

She spent the day with her sons, seeing that their little cottage was cleaned, washing their garments and hanging them to dry in the breezeless garden. Then she fixed them a good meal, eating with them before she returned to the castle. Entering the common room she found the other wives in an uproar and the false Cinnia weeping.

"We cannot calm her," Minau said drily.

"What is the matter with her?" Arlais asked.

"The child does not move!" the false Cinnia sobbed. "Suddenly the child does not move. It is surely dead! He will never forgive me!"

"If the child does not move it is preparing to be

born," Arlais said in a matter-of-fact tone of voice. "Cease your weeping, Cinnia."

"How can you know this is true?" the sobbing woman said.

"Because I have birthed three sons," Arlais responded. Then she turned to Minau. "Is everything ready for the birth?"

"It is," Minau said.

"It is my night with our husband," Orea said. "Is she going to spoil it?"

"Do you only think of yourself?" the false Cinnia shrieked. "When I give our husband his daughter you will be relegated to nothingness!" Then suddenly she turned paler than she normally was, and doubling over, gasped in pain.

"Good," Arlais said. "It is beginning. Keep our husband amused, Orea. I think it will be some hours before the child is born."

"Good!" muttered Volupia beneath her breath.

Arlais and Minau shot the third wife an amused look.

"I will get the herbal draught to help the pain," the sweet-natured Tyne said.

"Why is there such pain?" the false Cinnia cried.

"Birthing is pain," Arlais told her. "Did no one ever tell you that? But then who would have? The daughter of Fflergant lost her mother at an early age, and the dragon who raised Cinnia of Belmair would not have known of mortal pain."

"How long does the pain continue?" the false Cinnia quavered.

"Until the child is birthed," Minau said in a satisfied tone.

"How long will that take?" was the next question.

"Sometimes it is quick. And other children seem to take forever," Volupia murmured sweetly. "It could be several hours, or a day or two."

*"A day or two?"* the false Cinnia's voice screeched.

"Volupia," Arlais said in a stern tone, "go and find our husband. Tell him that Cinnia has gone into her labor. We will keep him informed. And remember it is Orea's turn in his bed. Do not interfere with them."

Volupia grinned wickedly. "I won't," she promised. "I had his company last night." Then she patted the false Cinnia on the shoulder. "I hope it's a boy," she said.

"Bitch!" the laboring woman snarled.

Laughing, Volupia walked away, humming a little tune.

"Bring the birthing chair," Arlais said to a serving man. Then she turned to the others. "Get her up and walking. The sooner the better for all of us. Where is the pain draught? Thank you, Tyne." She took the goblet from the young woman. "Drink now, Cinnia," she instructed and she held the cup to the girl's lips.

Sapphira sipped eagerly at first, but then she pushed Arlais's hand away. "It is bitter," she complained.

"It is medication to ease your pains, but if you do not want it," Arlais said, "you do not have to drink it.

It will help, though." She could see it was going to be a long night. And it would not be an easy one. This was a girl unused to pain of any kind.

The birthing chair was brought. Sapphira whined and sobbed with her growing pain. She complained that Ahura Mazda did not come to her.

"A Yafir man never attends to the birth of a child," Arlais told her. "I was all alone when I had Behrooz. I had only one old nursemaid to help me. You are fortunate."

"You call pain such as I am suffering fortunate?" the false Cinnia groaned.

"You are having a child, and pushing that child from your body will take great effort on your part," Arlais said. "Instead of whining as if you are the only woman in all of creation who has ever gone through this, listen to me, and I will help you. Remember that if this child is a female Ahura Mazda will be eternally grateful to you. Your place in his heart and his household will always be secure. You will need that security, especially if he learns the truth of who you really are," the older woman murmured low.

The false one groaned again. "What if the child is male?" she said.

"You will need all your clever wiles to keep him from selling you into the Mating Market then," Arlais said. "You have made no friends among the others here. They would be glad to see you go."

"Would you?" Sapphira asked nervously.

"Oddly you make our husband happy, and as I am perfectly confident in my own place in Ahura Mazda's heart I do not resent you. I just find you rude and arrogant," Arlais said frankly. "Perhaps you will change when you are more certain of your own place. For your sake I hope so. Now get into the birthing chair so I may examine you, and see what lies ahead this night."

The laboring woman obeyed, seating herself carefully. The chair, which had an opening in its center, was ratchetted up so that Arlais was able to stand beneath it and clearly see the birthing orifice. To her surprise it was well open although not quite where it should be yet, nor could she see the child's head. She stepped from beneath the chair.

"You are doing well," she told her patient.

Throughout the nighttime hours the false Cinnia labored to bring forth her child. As the time of the birth grew closer, thick padded clothes were spread beneath the opening of the chair. Finally the top of the infant's head became visible, and Arlais was excited to see not a bald pate, or one with a covering of light down, but dark, thick hair. She and the serving woman with her encouraged their patient as she struggled to birth the child. The head and shoulders were pushed forth accompanied by a great scream of anguish. In her chair Sapphira gasped for breath, perspiration pouring down her naked body. But she listened carefully to Arlais's instructions, and giving another great push she felt the child free of her body, and heard its cry.

"A female!" Arlais said triumphantly. "You have given our husband a healthy daughter! Tyne," she called to the fourth wife. "Run and tell our husband of the good fortune Cinnia has brought us!"

By the time Ahura Mazda had been told, and put on his robe and hurried to the common room, mother and child were clean and ready for him. He took the swaddled infant from Arlais, and unwrapping it stared at its tiny pink groin. There was no manhood. He finally had a daughter. Rewrapping the baby he took it up in his arms. "I name her Gemma, which means *treasured.* She is, and she will be." Handing the baby back to Arlais, he walked over to where his youngest wife now lay upon a couch. "You have done well, Cinnia. I will expect another from you in a year or two. You will have six weeks of freedom from my bed. Then we shall begin anew. I am pleased with you."

Arlais had a difficult time not laughing at the look upon the new mother's face at their husband's words. The false Cinnia would earn everything she gained from Ahura Mazda. And she would work hard for it all. Arlais knew her lord well. He would not be content until he had two or three daughters now. "You must sleep now," she told the girl.

"The child has a nursemaid to care for it, and another to suckle it."

"I would suckle my own child," Sapphira replied, surprising Arlais.

"For a month then, but no more. He will take you

back into his bed in six weeks, Cinnia, and he will want your breasts for himself, not the infant," Arlais told her.

"He has other breasts to fondle," Sapphira said. "This is his daughter, and I will not have my lord's daughter nursing on the teats of a servant."

"That is a matter you will decide between you," Arlais said. "Rest now."

It was just dawn, and the Yafir lord's first wife sought her own bed for a brief nap. She dared not sleep long, for she must sleep well tonight when she once again joined Belmair's queen upon the Dream Plain. Her servant awakened her after two hours. Arlais made certain word was spread throughout Yafirdom that the lord's youngest wife had borne him a daughter. She soothed the two younger wives who feared their place in the household would be usurped by the sixth wife, now the mother of a daughter.

"It is just one child," Volupia said to Tyne and Orea. "Another of us is bound to have a female infant, and then Cinnia will no longer be the special one. I am certain he has seeded me again. He is delightfully lustful these days."

"He was not so lustful with me last night," Orea complained. "After you came and told him of Cinnia's labor he was distracted. He used me but twice."

"Then he will be doubly lustful tonight," Tyne said with a little smile, "for twice in a single night is never enough for him."

They chattered on throughout the day. The younger

children came to visit their mothers. Arlais was the only one with fully grown sons. The evening meal was served, and afterward Ahura Mazda's first wife excused herself from the group.

"I got no sleep last night with Cinnia's labor. Minau, will you watch over her this evening, and see to the baby? I am going to bed." She stood up from her seat by the fire.

Ahura Mazda entered the common room, and after a quick visit with Sapphira and a peek at his daughter, looked to Tyne, and beckoned to her. With a grin at her fellow wives, Tyne led their husband into her bedchamber and firmly closed the door.

Arlais entered her own bedchamber, washed, and changing into a sleep robe, lay down. She could scarcely keep her eyes open, and wondered if she would even hear the young queen of Belmair's call, but of course she did. The silvery-gray mists swirled about her as she walked toward Cinnia's voice. And then the mists parted, and the two women met. "Sapphira had her daughter early today," she told Cinnia. "Both are well."

"I am happy for her," Cinnia replied. "Have you spoken with your sons?"

"I have," Arlais responded. "They beg you to call them to the Dream Plain tonight so they may speak with you themselves. I humbly ask that you do this for me."

"What is it they seek from me?" Cinnia asked her, surprised.

"Reassurance," Arlais said. "They are young men.

Yafirdom beneath the sea is all they have ever known. And yet they long for the land. It is almost as if it calls to them," she explained. "But they need to know from you, Belmair's queen, that they are welcome. They must eventually beard their father and his authority in this matter. It will not be easy for them. The Yafir grow restless for the bubbles are full, and cannot expand any farther. There is no room for growing or grazing. When asked for more, Ahura Mazda refuses to even consider the requests."

"That is because none of it is of his making," Cinnia told her. "Cronan made a place for the Yafir to hide themselves, to live their lives. Then he left them to themselves but times have changed."

"Call to my sons then, and let them hear this from your lips," Arlais pleaded.

"Behrooz, son of Arlais. Sohrab, son of Arlais. Nasim, son of Arlais. Come to me upon the Dream Plain," Cinnia intoned three times.

The mists again swirled around the two women, and when it began to clear the three sons of Arlais could be seen coming toward them. They looked both amazed and perhaps a little frightened as they came. When they had reached their mother and Cinnia, they bowed politely, Behrooz speaking for them.

"We greet you, Cinnia, queen of Belmair."

"I greet the sons of Arlais," she responded. "What is it you desire from me?"

"Forgive us for our concerns, but did you speak truth

to our mother? Is there really a new province that has been created for us, for the Yafir?" Behrooz asked her.

"There is. I have not been there myself, but my husband showed it to me in a reflecting bowl. Nidhug, Belmair's Great Dragon, was with the Shadow Princes when Belbuoy was fashioned. She says the land is a perfect paradise," Cinnia answered him.

"I lived in your world, sons of Arlais. It is gloomy and dank. Come and live in your province of Belbuoy, and you will live again in the sunlight. You will feel the breeze and you will feel the rain upon your faces. Your animals will grow fat upon its sweet grasses, and your crops will thrive in its rich soil."

"And the king will truly welcome us back to Belmair?" Behrooz inquired.

"My husband desires peace for all of Belmair's peoples, and the Yafir have lived in this world for aeons. You are a part of us as we are of you," Cinnia replied to him. "He will welcome you, and there will be others who do, too. But there will be some who will not welcome you. This is why Belbuoy was created. So that the Yafir have a place of safety until that day when our differences no longer matter, and we accept each other for who we are and nothing more."

"How will you accomplish this?" Behrooz asked Cinnia.

"The Shadow Prince Cronan will make it happen. It was he who gave you Yafirdom all those centuries ago. Here is the tale he told us. He had just come to Belmair from Hetar when Napier IX decided to banish the Yafir. Such an action angered him, for the Shadow Princes believe that all life is precious and sacred no matter the form it takes. He knew, of course, how the Yafir have gone from world to world over the years. He knew their place in the magic realms was lowly, and not greatly respected. But still he felt sorry for them, for they were being driven out of existence, and had nowhere to go. Cronan does not believe that one people has the right to destroy another people. He studied the Yafir, and chose Ahura Mazda as the one to lead the them.

"He brought your father to his own dwelling place. He told him what he would do to protect the Yafir. Then one night while they slept a drugged sleep he surrounded the Yafir, which he had divided into small groups, with the bubbles. The bubbles were already individual self-contained worlds with their villages, and the lord's castle. These he transported beneath the seas of Belmair. When the Yafir awoke the following morning they were in their new world of Yafirdom. Ahura Mazda told them it was his magic that had done all of this. That it was he who had led them to safety, and would now rule over them. This was as Cronan wanted, and for the first time the Yafir were living as normal folk do, and not being driven from place to place."

"So our father has no magic," Behrooz said.

"Nay, that is not so. Ahura Mazda has magic. It is just not great magic as he claims. He can transport himself from place to place easily, and do other small enchantments. But the Yafir have never had the greatest powers of necromancy," Cinnia explained to Arlais's three sons.

"We have been taught nothing. The ability to move from here to there seems inbred in us, but we can do no wizardry, nor can any that we know. Only our father seems capable of magic. Or so he has claimed," Behrooz told her. "We have never been witness to anything exceptional. Tell us, though, what will happen to us when we come up from the sea? Many of us are centuries old. We reach our maturity beneath the sea, and then remain there. Those among us who once lived in Belmair remained the same ages beneath the sea as they were upon the land, and are the eldest among us. Will this moving from sea to land kill our elders?"

"Nay, I have been told they will not. A spell has been fashioned and put into amulets for each of the Yafir so they will begin to age again from the age they are now. When you awaken upon Belbuoy you will all have your amulets, and you will be safe. Have you asked all your questions of me, then?" Cinnia inquired of them.

"We have," Behrooz said, "but for one. When will Yafirdom be transported to our new province of Belbuoy?"

"I know you must speak with your people first," Cinnia said.

Behrooz looked to his brothers, and they nodded. "We have already consulted with our friends," he told her. "We are ready. The Yafir are ready. Take us all.

We will deal with our father ourselves when it is done, my queen."

Cinnia smiled at him. She had not missed his respect. "I will speak with Cronan on the morrow," she told them. "I believe the sooner this is accomplished the better for all. Your father seeks to provoke a war between our peoples. Help us to stop it, sons of Arlais. There is no need for war between us."

"As you help us," Behrooz said, "so we shall aid you, my queen." He bowed to her. "It is time for us to go, my brothers." And suddenly Arlais's three sons were fading away back into the mists.

"Belbuoy will need a duke," Cinnia told Arlais. "Your eldest son, Behrooz, would make a fine lord for his people."

"What of Ahura Mazda?" Arlais asked softly.

Cinnia shook her head. "He will never accept what is to happen, Arlais, and you know it. I think it will end badly for him, though I would wish it not."

Tears sprang into Arlais's eyes. She nodded, unable to speak at first. "I love him," she finally said. "He was not always as he is now, Cinnia. After the Yafir were driven from Belmair his grandfather and father filled him with anger and bitterness. Perhaps you should leave the bubble with the castle and its village beneath the sea."

Cinnia shook her head. "Nay. All must come. It is better that way."

"Ahura Mazda is no fool, Cinnia. We have not spoken to those within our bubble yet for fear of my husband learning of our little plot. But many are old, and long to see the land again. They will not be unhappy to awaken and find themselves upon the land once more," Arlais said.

"It is time for us to go," Cinnia said, feeling a tug of wakefulness.

"Will we meet again?" Arlais asked as she felt the same pull.

"I am sure we will," Cinnia responded, and then she felt herself slipping away. Opening her eyes she saw her husband dozing in the chair by her side. She stretched and sighed, reaching out to touch his arm. "I am returned," she told him.

"Tell me," he said, and Cinnia did. When she had concluded her tale, Dillon said, "We must call upon Kaliq and Cronan to return to us. Now that it has been decided it must be done swiftly before any whisper reaches Ahura Mazda's pointed ears."

"Is it morning yet?" Cinnia asked him sleepily.

"It is just daybreak," Dillon told her.

"Then let us do what must be done, my lord husband," Cinnia replied, and she arose from the small bed in the dream chamber.

Together they returned through the castle corridors to their own apartments where they bathed, dressed in fresh garments and readied themselves for the day ahead. They had a great deal to do once the two Shadow Princes were called upon to return to the castle. Most important of all were the amulets that would have to be fashioned to protect the Yafir from the effects of their centuries beneath the seas of Belmair. Dillon had finally managed to fashion a spell that implanted within the little amulets would protect those who returned to the land, and allow them to begin the aging process from where they had left off.

It was Cinnia who had created the amulets. The star symbol of Belmair, which was made from Belmairan red-gold, and would be inculcated into the left shoulder of each Yafir except those who had not yet reached their maturity, would not need the amulets. They would simply age naturally as if they had always lived upon Belbuoy.

The amulets were brought into the Great Hall, and spread out upon the stone floor. There were several thousand of them. Dillon now came to speak the spell that would protect each Yafir who wore the star of Belmair. Raising his hands he moved them over the little golden stars spread across the Great Hall of his castle.

"This magic star will keep you free,
From your years beneath the sea.
Time be twisted, turn away,
From the Yafir from this day.
Age from now as you will,
Let none this spell turn ill.
This Shadow-faerie lord has spoken,
And this spell shall ne'er be broken."

Cinnia had watched, fascinated, as her husband incanted his spell. The little stars had glittered and glowed as Dillon's words flowed over them. When the sound of his voice had died Cinnia could almost swear she heard the stars sigh. Carefully she gathered them up into soft velvet pouches. Tonight they would be distributed by magic to protect the Yafir as they were brought to Belbuoy.

Now Dillon called to Kaliq and to Cronan to join them. The two Shadow Princes stepped shortly from the shadows. Both he and Cinnia went forward to greet them. Servants came forth with sweet frine to welcome them. Dillon explained all that had happened in the last few weeks. "We are now ready to proceed tonight."

"How will you keep the Yafir safe from the centuries?" Cronan wanted to know.

Cinnia brought forth one of the velvet bags, and drew out one of the tiny red-gold stars. "Each Yafir, but for those who have not yet reached their maturity, will have this star implanted into a shoulder. The spell rests within each star."

Cronan took the star from her, examining it carefully. "So I see," he said. "It is a good spell, my boy. A very powerful spell, and by making the stars part of each Yafir you keep them from losing their protection. Well done! Well done!" He handed Cinnia back the star, and as he did he smiled at her. "The crafting of the stars is quite excellent, sorceress of Belmair," Cronan told her. Then he turned to Kaliq. "They are a well-matched couple, old friend."

"You will not go away now, will you?" Cinnia asked the ancient Shadow Prince. "You will stay with us here in Belmair? Our world is honored to be home to one of your kind. What can we do to make you more comfortable, my lord?"

Cronan smiled again. "Do you know where I live?" he asked her mischievously.

Cinnia shook her head. "No, my lord, I do not, but wherever it may be we will do whatever we can to make it better," she replied earnestly.

"I live at the top of the round tower on the north side of the castle," he said.

*"Our castle?"* Cinnia was astounded.

"No one has bothered with the north tower for centuries," he said with a chuckle. "I thought as it was unused I would take it for my own. Now and again one of your servants stumbles across it, but I gently wipe their memory of it, and send them on their way again. That is how I have lived there undetected for centuries. I have watched you grow up from the shadows of the rooms where you have lived, daughter of Fflergant. I knew at your birth that you were meant for greater things and so with your proper mate I have watched you becoming what you must eventually be. A sorceress almost equal to your husband, Dillon, son of Kaliq and Lara."

"Teach me!" Cinnia said to him.

The old Shadow Prince smiled and nodded. "I will

teach you," he said. "Your first lesson will come tonight as you watch us bring the Yafir from beneath the sea to their new home. But before then I shall teach you how to implant the stars of Belmair within each Yafir. It is only right that you do this, for you are Belmair born." He looked to Dillon and to Kaliq. Both nodded in agreement.

"When will we do it?" Cinnia asked.

"We shall bring the bubbles up from the sea floor one by one, and set them about Belbuoy. As long as the Yafir remain within the bubbles they will continue to be protected from time. We will enter each bubble, and you will go from cottage to cottage implanting the stars in each Yafir who needs one. Once that is done the Yafir are safe from the ravages of time, and we may move on to bring up the next bubble," Cronan said.

"Why not bring all the bubbles up at one time?" Cinnia inquired.

"The bubbles cannot sustain themselves for too long within the sunlight and the air," Cronan said. "That is why we must all work quickly."

"I see," Cinnia said. "Yes, it makes sense, doesn't it? But can I get all the stars for each bubble implanted in time?"

"You can," Kaliq told her. "That is why we only bring one bubble at a time up from the sea. It will take the three of us to maintain the bubble's integrity while you work to implant the stars in the Yafir so that they are protected."

"I have the spell!" Cinnia said excitedly. *"This star of Belmair I thee give, so you upon the land may live. Time begin from whence it ceased. Time be knit no longer pieced."*

"Excellent, sorceress!" Cronan approved. "Now give me your hand."

Cinnia put her small hand within that of the ancient Shadow Prince, and looked up into his startlingly bright blue eyes. Her own eyes widened as she experienced what felt like a heated bolt of energy flowing from his hand into hers.

"All you need do," he told her, still holding her hand, "is place each star in the front of each Yafir's left shoulder. They will feel a tiny surge of the energy I am giving to you. The star will adhere to their skin, and cannot be removed. Upon their death the star will dissolve into their flesh to be burned with their body," Cronan explained. He released his hold upon Cinnia's hand.

She swayed slightly. "Oh, my!" she exclaimed. "Your power is overwhelming, my lord Cronan."

Dillon put an arm about his wife. "Are you all right?" he asked her.

"I will be in a moment. I am so filled with power, and I am not used to it," Cinnia responded to his concern.

"Do not fear, young king," the ancient Shadow Prince said. "Your wife is stronger than you can possibly imagine. Perhaps one day she will be your equal."

"You are old, Cronan," Kaliq chided his friend. "Do not promise what you may not be able to give."

"Old I may be, but not powerless by any means, Kaliq. I think you are jealous for your son." Cronan chuckled. "Or is it for yourself? You have grown used to being the most powerful among the powerful."

"My lords, cease this bickering," Dillon said. "If Cinnia were indeed as powerful as she might be think of all the good we could accomplish here in Belmair."

"The young king is wise," Cronan said.

"Shall we send for Cirillo and Nidhug to join us?" Cinnia asked them.

"Aye," Dillon said. "We will need their help, as well. Cirillo's magic can also help to sustain each bubble as we work to integrate the Yafir. Nidhug will aid Cinnia."

"Britto," Cinnia called to her steward. "Send for Prince Cirillo and the dragon. They will join us for our evening meal. Tell cook to prepare for Nidhug's appetite."

"At once, my queen," Britto said, and hurried off.

As the day finally came to an end, the faerie prince and his lover, the dragon, joined them in the family hall. There they learned all that had transpired this day.

"You have everything well in hand," Cirillo said.

"But we need you and Nidhug, as well," Cinnia told him. "Nidhug will, of course, help me while I transfer the stars to each Yafir. You must help to sustain the bubble until all are protected."

"Gladly," Cirillo said. "And then I shall make each village appear to be newly constructed with painted shutters and doors, as well as dooryard gardens. The villages' beauty should match the province's beauty."

"Oh, thank you!" Cinnia exclaimed. "I want the Yafir to feel welcomed."

The meal was a trifle late in coming, for learning that the dragon would be joining them, the cook had had to roast a lamb over the hearth spit, and stuck a dozen more capons into the oven. She took a pan of artichokes from her pantry, brushed them with oil and set them to baking. Then, knowing Nidhug's sweet tooth, she sent to Sarabeth at the dragon's castle for the desserts. Finally the meal was served up, and well appreciated by the guests. The dragon ate daintily, Cirillo popping whole capons into her wide mouth and wiping the juices from her jaw.

Kaliq watched, fascinated by the pair. He was a man for whom love was all, and he could not help but wonder what the attraction between a faerie and a dragon was like. Finally the meal was concluded. Servants brought basins of scented water, and small linen towels so the diners might wash their hands and faces free of any traces of the meal.

The clock on the hall's hearth mantel chimed twenty-two, and the young king arose from his place at the high board. "It is time," he said. "Are you all ready?"

And as one the other heads in the hall nodded.

"We are ready," Cinnia said, "to begin a new chapter in Belmair's history."

# 18

AHURA MAZDA WALKED back and forth in the circular common room of his wives. In his arms he cradled his week-old daughter, Gemma. "Is she not perfect?" he asked for what was surely the fiftieth time. "She is pure Yafir, are you not, my darling?" he cooed at the baby. "Look at that hair! Silver! Do you know how rare it is nowadays for a Yafir female to have silver hair? And her eyes are already the clearest aquamarine." He turned to Gemma's mother. "Thank you, my precious Cinnia."

"I am not Cinnia, and I am tired of being called by her name," Sapphira said loudly. "I want my daughter to know who I am, and the true heritage she has on my side." She was tired of being ignored, and Ahura Mazda had not been nearly as generous with her as she had hoped he would be. She wanted her own apartments in which to raise her daughter. She wanted to keep nursing the child, and not turn her over to a wet nurse. She did not want to sit about with these other women waiting for the Yafir lord to pay her a visit. Sapphira was not happy at all right now, and her behavior became foolishly rash.

The other women looked up, surprised, all but Arlais who waited for the explosion to come. Sapphira was a truly stupid creature. Did she not understand that her value was in her ability to give their husband a daughter, which she had, but also in being Cinnia, daughter of Fflergant, and queen of Belmair? Sapphira had only one value. Her daughter, and there were five other women who could raise that child.

"What do you mean you are not Cinnia?" Ahura Mazda demanded.

"I look like her, don't I?" Sapphira said with a giggle. "I certainly fooled you, didn't I? You never realized that King Dillon retrieved his wife months ago, putting me in her place. I am Sapphira of Beldane, who was his mistress. I meant to be queen of Belmair, but instead woke up to find myself in your household, and believed to be Cinnia. Since there was nothing I could do about it I decided to be Cinnia, especially since you are such a vigorous lover to me."

Ahura Mazda handed his daughter to Arlais. He walked across the chamber and looked into Sapphira's face. "You are not Cinnia?" he said in a hard voice.

"No, I am Sapphira, niece of Duke Tullio," she replied.

"Who else knows this?" he demanded of her. His eyes were cold.

"Arlais guessed," Sapphira said.

Ahura Mazda turned to look at Arlais angrily.

"Aye, I knew," Arlais said, "but I would not hurt you, my lord, by telling you, for I love you. And, too, my lord, you have been happy with this woman. She is your equal in passion, and she has given you your precious daughter. It is likely she will give you more daughters if you want them."

"The king of Belmair bested me, and you did not tell me," Ahura Mazda said.

"Of course he bested you," Sapphira said. "He is a very powerful man with a faerie mother and a Shadow Prince father. You are only a Yafir."

*Will she not shut her silly mouth?* Arlais thought wearily.

Ahura Mazda whirled back to face Sapphira. His hand reached out to grasp her long black hair. Yanking her to him he forced her to her knees and slapped her face hard. "Belmairan whore, be silent! You yet live only because of your child."

And finally Sapphira realized the extent of her own foolishness. Her strong instinct for her own survival was awakened. She wrapped her arms about his legs, and began to weep. "Do not hate me because I wanted you to love me, and not her!" she whimpered piteously. "You are my beloved, and I but sought to hear my name upon your lips when you made love to me, and not hers. Forgive me the deception I have played upon you, but remember I did say I was Sapphira in the beginning, but none would listen to me. And then after I had lain in your arms the thought of being sent away was too terrible to even contemplate, my lord. Forgive me, I beg of you!"

"I should have you taken to the castle square, bound and spread wide. I should invite any man who wants to to take pleasures with you to do so. You should be left there to be publicly used for a week and a day," Ahura Mazda growled.

The women in the room paled at his words.

"My lord, I beg you, pardon Sapphira's errors in judgment," Arlais said.

"Instead," Ahura Mazda continued, ignoring his first wife, "I will beat you myself as punishment for your lies. And you shall not have my company for pleasures for three, no, for six months. But each night you shall watch for one hour while I take pleasures with my other wives. And when the six months are up you will service my lusts for seven days after which time you had best find yourself with child again. I will require another daughter from you before you are completely forgiven, Sapphira, my precious. Now, kiss my feet, and thank me for my kindness to you."

She did not hesitate, lowering herself to kiss the velvet slippers he wore. "Thank you, my lord, thank you!" she half sobbed. Then gasped as he yanked her up by her long hair, and seeing the anger still upon his face she trembled.

"Fetch the Chastizer, Arlais," the Yafir lord commanded, and Arlais hurried to obey him, returning with a slender, flexible rod. "Ready her," he said in a cold voice.

Arlais handed the baby she had been holding to Volupia. Then she and Minau tore the back of Sapphira's gown open, pulled her forward into a bent position, and held her firmly between them. The room was soon filled with Sapphira's cries as the Yafir lord plied his rod across her back and her buttocks. When he had finished with her punishment he flung the Chastizer aside, and taking Tyne by the hand led her to her bedchamber, closing the door behind them.

Sapphira was sobbing with the pain that had been inflicted upon her person. "I hate him! I hate him!" she whimpered.

"Best he not hear you say it," Arlais remarked as she helped Sapphira up. "You are fortunate he did not kill you, stupid girl. His delight in you was that you were the wife of Belmair's king, and he had stolen you thereby besting that king. Now he knows he did not triumph over Dillon, and he will be looking for a way to get back at him. There are two things of supreme worth to every man, Sapphira. One is his self-esteem, and the other his cock. You have hurt our husband's self-worth. Be glad you still appeal to his cock. It is what has saved you. Any of us could have raised little Gemma."

Sapphira grew even paler than she normally was.

"Just keep telling him how much you love him, and how fine a lover he is," Minau advised.

"Let us get you cleaned up now, and put some salve

on your welts," Arlais said. "Volupia, take the baby to her nursemaid. Then let us all retire for the night. Who knows what the morrow will bring us."

"It will bring the same thing every new day brings," Minau said drily.

But Minau was wrong. She awoke the following day to bright sunlight streaming in through her bedchamber windows. Startled, she arose and went to peer outside. She could see the walls of the bubble but beyond it there were…trees! Hills! Fields! Sights she had not seen in centuries. Was she dreaming? If she was she had not had such dreams in years because she had long given up hope of ever living upon the land again.

But they were certainly upon the land now! Minau ran to her door, and opening it saw Arlais and Orea were awake, as well.

"What has happened?" she asked them.

They shook their heads.

Volupia came sleepily from her chamber. "What is going on?" she asked.

"Someone fetch Sapphira," Arlais said, and Orea ran off returning a few minutes later with the girl. "Where is our husband?"

"Still with Tyne," came the answer.

"Fetch Tyne," Arlais said, "but if he is not awake do not waken him yet."

Tyne came. She looked worn. "He exhausted himself, and will sleep long," she told them. "What has happened?"

"Show yourselves," Arlais called softly.

Her companions gasped as suddenly Cinnia and Nidhug appeared.

"This is the queen of Belmair," Arlais said, "and our Great Dragon. They will explain, but first the queen has a gift for each of us."

"Magic has created a new province to be named Belbuoy," Cinnia began. "It is here that the Yafir will make their home. Some of you may decide to return to the other provinces, and that is permissible. Belmairan and Yafir are to be one now. As soon as we have protected all within your castle we will dissolve the bubble. Please step forward one by one," she told them.

"From what do you protect us?" Minau asked.

"You have lived beneath the sea for aeons, and there you have been protected from time. Without magical protection you would all die but for Sapphira and her child, and any other who has been in Yafirdom too long," Cinnia said.

"I will go first," Arlais said.

"Bare your shoulder for me," the young queen said.

Arlais did as she was bid, watching as Cinnia drew forth from a velvet bag held by the dragon a small red-gold star. The young queen pressed the star against the front of Arlais's shoulder, and Arlais felt the cool metal melting into her skin as Cinnia intoned the spell that had been devised.

"This magic star will keep you free,
From your years beneath the sea.
Time be twisted, turn away,

From the Yafir from this day.
Age from now as you will,
Let none this spell turn ill.
This Shadow-faerie lord has spoken,
And this spell shall ne'er be broken."

Cinnia stepped back. "There," she said. "Who will be next?"

Each of Ahura Mazda's wives came and received the star with its magic spell. Sapphira, however, did not need such protection for the time in which she now stood was her own. Standing before Cinnia, she asked her, "Does my uncle know the truth of all of this?"

"Nay," Cinnia replied. "Do you want him to know?"

Sapphira considered, and then she said, "How will it affect you?"

"In very much the same way it will affect you," Cinnia replied. "The law has been changed, but changing a law and changing people's hearts and minds are two different things, Sapphira. But we have both been wronged. I, by Ahura Mazda, and you by King Dillon. I will gladly do whatever you want me to do."

Sapphira was silent, and then she said, "For the sake of Belmair and its people I think it best we leave things as they are. As I have lived among those who are called Yafir, I can see no real differences among us. But it will take time for all of Belmair to come to that same conclusion." She glanced at their surprised faces. "I am sure you are all surprised by this change that has overcome me." She smiled wryly. "Circumstances and my fellow wives are the good influences my poor mother never was."

"Be warned," Arlais told Cinnia, "that Ahura Mazda now knows the truth, for Sapphira told him last night. If I know our husband, and I do, he will eventually seek revenge although when he awakens to find us now on dry land once more that will be his main concern, and take most of his thoughts and energy."

"I understand," Cinnia responded. "Now, will you come with me so I may protect the rest of the castle's inhabitants? Those others living within this bubble, the villagers, the servants who live away from the castle have already been given their star and their enchantment."

"What of Ahura Mazda?" Arlais asked softly as she led Cinnia and Nidhug from the common room. "Will he be given a star to protect him?"

"Your husband is pure Yafir. He is magic, and does not need our protection," Cinnia said. "That is why his coming and going from our world never affected him. There were not many Yafir of pure blood left when they fled to their world beneath the sea. Those centuries there will not have aged them any more than if they had been here."

Arlais nodded, and took Cinnia and the dragon to the Great Hall where all the servants and other inhabitants in the castle had been assembled. There the young Belmairan queen and Nidhug worked the magic of Dillon's spell and Cinnia's stars for each person in the room. Many wept with joy to be once again in Belmair, upon the land. They kissed Cinnia's hands, and bowed to the Great Dragon, thanking them.

Then Arlais went outside with her guests, and Cinnia looked up and said, *"Shadow Princes, all is well. Would you please remove the spell?"*

To Arlais's amazement and delight, the bubble that had shielded them for so many centuries slowly dissolved in a final rainbow burst of color. A soft breeze touched her rosy cheek, and Ahura Mazda's first wife herself wept as the warm air caressed her face. "Ah," she said softly, "never did I think to feel the wind again. Thank you, my queen!" And catching Cinnia's two hands up in her own she kissed them reverently.

"Your queen, aye," Cinnia replied, "but your friend, too, Arlais. In the time I spent in your household you were kind, and thoughtful. And when you realized the deception played upon the Yafir lord, you did not expose it. I have had time and peace with my own beloved husband, and for that I thank you."

"I was protecting Ahura," Arlais admitted.

Cinnia nodded. "I understand," she told the woman.

Dillon, Kaliq, Cronan and Cirillo were suddenly coming toward them, and Cinnia smiled. She drew Arlais forward and introduced her to the magical quartet.

"You are he who saved the Yafir," Arlais said as she curtseyed to Cronan.

"I am he," Cronan admitted.

"I have never before met a Shadow Prince although we had certainly heard of your kind, and their great magic," Arlais said shyly.

"How pretty you are," Cirillo murmured, and Nidhug growled low, her nostrils glowing orange-red.

"Thank you," Arlais told him. "And you are very bold, but then it is said that faerie men are forward."

Kaliq chuckled at Cirillo's surprise, for the young faerie prince was not used to being scolded by any other than his mother.

"Quite right, faerie men are much too bold," Nidhug agreed.

Arlais curtseyed to the king. "You truly seek peace between my people and the Belmairans?" she asked him.

"I do," he said, "and we shall have it, my lady, if it takes a thousand years although I hope we may come to be one people sooner. Speak with your lord, and tell him that we would be friends. That I hold no ill will toward him, but I will not tolerate rebellion from him. When he is ready to speak with me I will be ready to listen."

Then before Arlais's eyes the king and his party disappeared in a great puff of bright blue smoke. Arlais stood where she was for several long minutes as she realized that Ahura Mazda had to make his peace with the Belmairan king. He really had no other choice for these were powerful beings, and the young sorcerer now ruling Belmair would brook no interference with his plans. She had seen that in his eyes. She walked slowly back into the castle. Within she found something she had not known in years. Happiness. The servants were smiling. The children and their nurses made their way past her, going into the gardens to play in the warm sunshine. She found her way to the common room.

"Is he awake yet?" she asked of no one in particular as she entered.

"Not yet," Minau answered.

Arlais took a long, deep breath, and then went into Tyne's bedchamber where Ahura Mazda lay sprawled upon the bed, sleeping. Quietly she walked across the room and opened the lead-paned casement windows. The sun was just coming around to these particular windows. A soft breeze blew gently, fluttering the bed curtains. Arlais sat down in a small chair by the cold hearth, and waited for her husband to awaken.

And eventually he did. Slowly Ahura Mazda came to himself. He stretched his long limbs and sighed. Then his beautiful eyes opened, and gazed sleepily about. The light from the sun told him it must be close to noon. It was very bright and warm. The breeze blowing through the windows was scented with a garden full of flowers. He could not remember a more pleasant awakening. And then the reality slammed into him. *Bright sunlight? A warm breeze? The smell of flowers?* The lord of the Yafir sat up with a roar, and saw Arlais sitting in the room.

"What is going on?" he demanded, leaping from the bed, and going to the open windows. He looked out upon a beautiful garden filled with flowers. Birds sang. Gaily colored butterflies fluttered about. His younger children ran shrieking with glee along the graveled pathways, followed by their laughing nursemaids. His eyes almost jumped from his skull at the sight. "What is going on?" he repeated, and turned toward Arlais.

"We are no longer beneath the sea," Arlais said quietly. "Put some clothing on, my lord, and we will talk."

"Tell me now," he said, but he was gathering up his garments, and dressing himself as he spoke. "I can see we are no longer beneath the waters. Where are we, and how has this happened?"

"We are in Belmair's newest province, which has been created especially for us," Arlais began. "It is called Belbuoy."

"And you know this because...?" he asked.

"I have spoken with King Dillon and Queen Cinnia. I have spoken with the two great Shadow Princes, Kaliq and Cronan. I have met a faerie prince and Belmair's Great Dragon, the lady Nidhug. They each had a part in all of this, my lord," Arlais told him.

The Yafir lord's mouth tightened, and his eyes darkened with his rage. "They dared to usurp my authority?" he said. "And now we have been put in *this* place? Why? We were told we were not welcome in Belmair. Have we been brought here then to be slaughtered by these Belmairans? And you knew, but did not tell me, Arlais? You are my first wife. The woman I trust above all others. Why have you betrayed me?" He stood before her now fully clothed.

"I have not betrayed you, my lord, and my heart breaks that you would utter such words to me," Arlais said to him. "The Yafir were banished centuries ago. That king is long dead, and the many who followed him since. The king who now rules Belmair is not of this world. He has no preconceived notions regarding the Yafir. He seeks peace with us. Why do you rebuff his overtures? The time for bitterness is in the past, my dear lord."

"I will never make peace with Belmair!" Ahura Mazda declared.

"Which is why this was done without your permission, my lord," Arlais told him. "Most of the folk calling themselves Yafir have more Belmairan blood in their veins. There are few pure Yafir, as you are, my lord, remaining among our people. Even your children's blood is evenly mixed, for all of your wives come from Belmair. We have not forgotten the history of the Yafir, but the Belmairans were not the first to banish the Yafir from their world. The Yafir have been exiled from many worlds."

"Aye, but here we created a safe haven beneath the sea for ourselves!" Ahura Mazda declared. "It is I who have kept our people safe for most of the centuries that have passed, and now you would bring us back to the brink of extinction and danger!"

"The Yafir did not create Yafirdom, my lord," Arlais said. "The Shadow Prince Cronan took pity on your people, and made your continued existence possible through his great magic. That is why as our population grew you could not give us more bubbles for them to live in, and more sea land in which to graze our poor flocks and grow our crops."

"Blasphemy!" he shouted.

Arlais stood up. "Nay, my lord, truth."

"You have never spoken to me with such disrespect," he said to her.

"It is not disrespect, my lord. It is truth I speak to you, and I will tell you more truth. The Yafir are weary of living in the gloom of the sea bottom, the stale air of the bubbles. We would exist in the sunlight, and fresh air of the land. If you are able to create a world beneath the sea then put us back there now! But you cannot. Yafir magic is little magic."

He slapped her, and without another word Arlais turned and left the chamber. "Come back!" he shouted, but she did not. And when he finally went into the common room he found it empty. None of his women were anywhere in sight. Ahura Mazda went to his own apartments, and sat brooding over Arlais's words. What did she mean the people wanted to live upon the land once more? They were *his* people. They did what *he* wanted. What was this rebellion that Belmair was trying to foment among the Yafir? He would not have it! He would have his revenge upon them, and they would think twice before interfering with him again.

Ahura Mazda remained within his own apartments for the next several days. He did not come out even at night to visit his wives. And they did not come to him. Cheerful servants—he was growing to dislike their happy faces—brought him his meals, and saw to all of his needs. But no one came to see if he was all right. Even the ambitious Sapphira. He watched them stealthily from his windows as they sat in the gardens and talked among themselves. He viewed Sapphira in direct defiance of his orders nursing their daughter, whose silvery hair was getting just the faintest touch of gold in it. His anger grew with each passing day. He could feel himself losing control of everything around him, and briefly he was frightened. Then the fear subsided, and his anger against Belmair, its king and queen and the damned dragon who had brought Dillon of Shunnar to Belmair, grew hotter. At last he had a visitor.

"Your three oldest sons have come to see you," Minau told him.

"Where is Arlais?" he asked her.

Minau shrugged. "She will not forgive you for striking her until you apologize," was the reply he got.

"*Apologize?* She was disrespectful of her lord," Ahura Mazda said irritably. He had not meant to strike Arlais. Surely she knew that. He had never before struck her.

"I can only tell you what I know," Minau said. "Your sons await you in the Great Hall, my lord husband. Will you come or no?"

He debated a moment with himself, but then he said, "I will come." Reaching the hall he greeted his three oldest sons, but they did not smile back at him. They offered him no warmth at all, and he was angry at himself for coming.

"As you know," Behrooz said, "each province of Belmair has a duke who is its central local authority, and acts at a counselor to the king when he asks for advice."

"I will not be one of the Belmairan king's flunkeys," Ahura Mazda said loftily.

"We know that, Father," Sohrab said. "And so another candidate was put forth and offered to the people of Belbuoy, which is this province's name. That candidate was accepted by both our people, and King Dillon."

"I am the lord of the Yafir," Ahura Mazda said to his sons.

"Indeed, Father, you are. No one will dispute that," Nasim, his third son, said. "You are the lord of the Yafir, but Behrooz is Belbuoy's ducal authority."

Ahura Mazda could not believe what he was hearing. His oldest sons in rebellion! The Yafir in rebellion! The direction of his anger now narrowed. This, all of it, was the Great Dragon's fault. If that wretched creature had simply chosen Duke Dreng's grandson to be king none of this would have happened. He could have stolen Cinnia away, and no one would have cared. But the dragon had instead chosen a foreigner to rule Belmair. And she had chosen the son of a Shadow Prince and a faerie woman.

Dillon of Shunnar was powerful. Although he would not admit it aloud to anyone else, Ahura Mazda recognized the plain truth before his face. The king's magic was strong. Far greater than his own. And now that king had challenged Ahura Mazda's authority by bringing the Yafir to this pleasant land he had created for them. It infuriated the Yafir lord that the king had been able to do this when he could not. What was worse, Ahura Mazda had been exposed as a fraud before his people by the king and his associates. But in the end it all went back to the dragon Nidhug. The Yafir lord held her responsible for bringing Dillon to Belmair.

*"Father."* Behrooz was speaking to him.

Ahura Mazda focused his gaze about the young man.

"Do you understand what has happened, Father? Your authority among our people is not diminished for you are respected as our leader. I am simply the king's liaison for Belbuoy," Behrooz said quietly.

"You will remain in your own castle with our mothers and siblings," Sohrab said.

"Everything has changed," Ahura Mazda finally said. "My authority is weakened. I am publicly revealed as an imposter by these Belmairans. How can I be lord of the Yafir with no real power to wield?"

"But, Father," Nasim said innocently, "you never had any real power like King Dillon's or the Shadow Princes'."

Ahura Mazda glowered at Arlais's youngest son. "You have your mother's evil tongue," he snarled. "I have certain small powers, Nasim, and I do not believe I have lost them in spite of all of this. I am still competent to move from place to place by magic, and work a spell or two of my own."

"Father, the king would make peace with you," Behrooz said. "He has been kind and fair with the Yafir. He says we must all be one people. We want that."

"Then you are as big a fool as the king," Ahura Mazda said. "If the Belmairans wanted peace then why was it necessary to create this province for us? We will not be accepted by them. They have merely put us in a place where they may watch us closely. And how did they find where we were hidden after all these aeons? Their clever king ferreted us out with his magic, of course."

"Nay," Behrooz said. "The Merfolk found us, and told him."

The Yafir lord hissed. "Agenor! I thought that fish-tailed devil was oblivious to our existence beneath the sea."

"In answer to your question the Belmairans must make peace with our shared history even as we must, which is why King Dillon gave us our own province. Dreng of Beltran will never accept the Yafir, but Alban of Belia and his people will. Tullio of Beldane may welcome some of our folk. Perhaps if he knew the truth of your sixth wife our path would be easier, for our baby sister, Gemma, binds us to Beldane by blood," Behrooz pointed out.

"You do not think making public that the king managed to snatch his wife back and set Sapphira in her place will make me more of a laughingstock?" Ahura Mazda growled, annoyed. "That the big-bellied woman I paraded before the king and his guests at his wedding was not his wife, but another? All of Belmair will laugh themselves to tears, and the king's reputation will be even more enhanced. And none of this would have happened had it not been for that ridiculous dragon! In the end it all boils down to her. Without her none of this would be, and Yafirdom would yet exist beneath the sea."

"Whatever has been responsible for bringing us all to this place, Father, is of no matter. It is what it is, and will not be altered," Behrooz said. "Your folk are content with this great change. They are happy. My brothers and I saw our younger siblings playing in the gardens as we came. Never had we heard such shouts of happiness. Belbuoy is a good place, and it is ours. I beg you to make your peace with King Dillon."

*"Never!"* Ahura Mazda shouted at the trio. "Now, my traitorous sons, get you gone from my sight. Do not return. I never want to see any of you again!"

The three said not another word. They bowed respectfully to their father, and departed the Great Hall of his castle. Ahura Mazda sat brooding by the big hearth, drinking wine for what remained of the day. The evening meal was served, and he saw that Arlais was not in her place. He said nothing. Tonight was his night in her bed. The thought of her anger toward him fueled his lustful nature. He would probably have to force her to pleasures, and he would enjoy every minute of it, he thought grimly. Arlais was a passionate woman, and after he had taken his fill of her he would punish her words to him this day by torturing her sexually. His member hardened beneath his robes with the thought, and looking to Sapphira he ordered her beneath the high board to ease his desires. Of all his wives she had the most skillful mouth and a divinely wicked tongue. He leaned back with a sigh, sipping his wine as, kneeling between his thighs, she took him between her lips and began to suck upon his member.

But when the time came and he entered Arlais's bedchamber he found it empty. He called to Minau, who he knew to be her best friend. "Where is Arlais?"

"She has gone, my lord," Minau said quietly.

*"Gone?"* He looked surprised. "Where has she gone?"

"With her sons, my lord," Minau replied.

"Get out!" he said to Minau in a hard voice, and when she had gone he shut the door to Arlais's bedchamber, and sat down. Gone. Arlais was gone. She had left him without so much as a word. He could not believe it. Standing up, he opened her wardrobe and looked inside. It was empty, and her trunk was nowhere in sight. He sat back down again. He was stunned. Gone. She was gone.

Arlais was the first of his wives. He remembered with delight the day he had stolen her. It had been her wedding day to a duke of Belia. How she had fought him! But he had persisted, and eventually he had won her over. She loved him. He was never certain about the others. But he knew that Arlais loved him. And he loved her. So much so that he had waited to take another wife until she had given him three sons. And now she had left him without so much as a word. He did not know if he could ever forgive her. He would not ask her to return. It was beneath his dignity. Let her live out her life, grow old, without him. He had the others, and perhaps he would take another woman, but then no. The Belmairan women were now protected from the Yafir.

Another mark against the dragon, Ahura Mazda thought grimly. Everything always came back to that creature they called Nidhug. He wished he had the power to kill her, but he did not. Did she have an heir? He knew Great Dragons never revealed their successors until they were within a few hundred years of death. Then they brought them forth to teach. But she had not revealed her heir yet. But surely there would be an egg hidden away somewhere that contained her heir. A dragon who had been around for as long as he knew Nidhug had been would have an egg. And he would find it, he vowed. It became a burning necessity for him. Each day he left Belbuoy, and searched high and low, far and wide for the place the dragon had secreted her egg.

The Yafir settled happily into the new province of Belbuoy. Their farms and their flocks flourished. Within the year a few trading ships began calling at the small harborside town they had built. It was called Yafiri. Cautious at first the captains and crew of these vessels discovered not an odd folk, but people much like themselves. They were quick to speak of it in the other provinces, returning again to Yafiri to trade for their fine leatherwork.

Duke Alban paid a visit, and invited any Yafir, particularly those with Belian roots to come and settle in his province. He was warmly greeted by Duke Behrooz and his mother, the lady Arlais. Both were surprised to see they had similar features. And those who investigated the possibility of emigrating to Belia were delighted when they were warmly welcomed by families to whom they were related by blood.

Curious, and encouraged by Alban, Duke Tullio came to Belbuoy. Like other Belmairans who had previously visited he was surprised to find the Yafir so much like his own people that he was ashamed to have been filled with disdain and bigotry. He, too, opened his province to any with Beldanean blood who would come. "I have many men anxious to wed," he told Behrooz.

"I think your lads will have to share the women for now until we can both replenish our populations," Belbuoy's duke answered.

Tullio could see the wisdom in that. "We will build a house for the women," he said. "They may choose partners and mate until they are with child. And after each child is weaned they will return to the House of Women to mate again."

"One day such desperate measures will not be necessary," Behrooz said.

While visiting Belbuoy, Tullio learned in confidence from its duke the deception that had caused Cinnia and his niece, Sapphira, to exchange places. She had wanted to know if one day she decided to return to Beldane she would be welcome. Tullio embraced his deceased sister's only child, and assured Sapphira that she would always be welcome in Beldane. Then he admired his great-niece, Gemma, tears in his eyes as he did, for she much resembled his dead sister in her features.

Dreng of Beltran remained intransigent. He could not be convinced that the Yafir were a people like himself.

He would not see his granddaughter who was among the stolen females. But if Dreng would not change one day, it was clear his people would, for they came to visit Belbuoy out of curiosity and returned to their own province to preach the truth of the current-day Yafir.

Dillon and Cinnia, monitoring all of this, were pleased. Their magical companions had returned to their own homes. Kaliq to Shunnar and Cronan to his castle tower. Cirillo came and went from the forest kingdom of his mother on Hetar with great regularity, and Nidhug was a happy dragon, content to be with her lover, sleeping in between his visits for she was no longer needed. Belmair was peaceful.

But then Nidhug awakened one night, her great heart pounding against her ribs in terror, an emotion of which she was not closely familiar. She lay quiet, listening, and then she faintly heard a shout of triumph. The dragon arose from her bed, and went to the windows. Outside all was quiet, but she could see in the garden below outlined in the moonlight of the twin moons someone coming toward her castle holding a lamp to guide them. Opening the casements she called down, "Who is there?"

"It is I, Cinnia," came the reply.

"I will come down," Nidhug called, and she hurried from her bedchamber.

Tavey was already opening the door when she got downstairs.

"Do you not sleep?" she demanded of him.

"Something awakened me, mistress," he said. "I know not what it was."

Cinnia entered, and Tavey took her lantern from her. "I was awakened with the terrible feeling of impending doom," Cinnia said. "Something is wrong, but what?"

As she spoke Nidhug felt as if something had gripped and released her heart, and she said, "I must go to Belia!"

"I will go with you," Cinnia replied in a tone that brooked no argument.

Together they hurried outside, and Nidhug lifted Cinnia up onto her back. The young queen snuggled down into the pouch upon the dragon's back as Nidhug grew to her full height and size. Unfolding her lacy golden wings, she rose into the air and turned toward Belia. Using her magic, the dragon flew so swiftly that they arrived at their destination on Belia's heights within a few short minutes. There in the mouth of Nidhug's nursery cave they saw Ahura Mazda. Nidhug let out a shriek of fury for the Yafir lord held in his hands the egg containing her successor.

"Your maternal instinct is strong, Great Dragon," he mocked her cruelly. "It did not take you long to sense your offspring's terror." He laughed.

Nidhug was speechless with her own concern for her egg.

Cinnia crept from the pouch upon the dragon's back, and standing, she called to Ahura Mazda, "Why do you wish to harm Belmair's Great Dragon, my lord? What harm has she done you? She is a benevolent creature who protects us all."

"What harm has she done?" Ahura Mazda snarled. *"What harm?"* His aquamarine-blue eyes were almost white now with an anger Cinnia could not fathom.

"She is responsible for Belmair, is she not? And what does she do when your father dies? She brings a stranger to Belmair to rule, to wed with you! You should have been mine. I marked you at your birth. The stranger the dragon brings to Belmair is a great and a powerful wizard. Together with his kind he seeks out my world, sets himself up to destroy me and dismantles my authority among the Yafir. None of this would have happened had the dragon simply chosen another Belmairan to rule. Now my sons have defied my jurisdiction over the Yafir. My first wife has left me. All because of the dragon's decision I have lost everything I hold dear."

"Your bubbles were overcrowded, and your people restless," Cinnia reminded him. "My husband offered you peace. He created a beautiful place for you and the Yafir to live. An opportunity to rejoin our world, my lord. He has done you no harm. Without Dillon's foresight both of our worlds stood in danger of extinction. Do you not understand that? If Arlais has left you I do not doubt it was with good cause. And if your sons prefer peace and a life upon the land to living beneath the sea, is that not their choice. For they are men, not children. The Shadow Prince who created the bubbles and who has sustained them over the years is very old now. He no longer had the strength to keep you safe beneath the sea. Were my husband not a benevolent man he would have let those bubbles burst. Then you and your people would have died beneath the sea. But he did not. For that you owe the dragon a great debt of gratitude. Had she not brought Dillon to Belmair, who knows what would have happened to all of us."

"I will tell you what would have happened," Ahura Mazda said, enraged by her words. "The Yafir would have come from the sea, and taken Belmair for themselves."

"Can you manipulate time, my lord?" Cinnia asked him sarcastically.

"What has time got to do with this?" he shouted at her.

"Have you forgotten that it was the bubbles that kept you from aging naturally?" Cinnia asked him. "How could you have brought the Yafir up from the sea? Even with the knowledge from *A Compendium of Time Manipulation,* had you been able to bring them from the bubbles most would have died within a few days as their years caught up with them, and in many cases passed them. You had not the power to do what you sought to do, Ahura Mazda."

"I did not age when I traveled back and forth between Belmair and Yafirdom," he said.

"Because those of you who are still pure Yafir have some magic about you," Cinnia explained to him. "But most of your folk are now of mixed blood. They could not have survived your plans."

"You are confusing me!" he shouted at her. "My

world has been destroyed, and it is all because of your damned dragon! Now, Nidhug, I will destroy your world!" And raising the dragon's egg high above his head Ahura Mazda smashed it to pieces on the rocks before the cave. "There!" he exulted. "There will never again be another like you to harm the Yafir!" And his wild laughter echoed throughout the craggy mountain peaks.

Cinnia could hardly believe what happened next. With a shriek of agony Nidhug's body shot forward, and she bit off Ahura Mazda's head. Cinnia could hear his skull crunching as the dragon's teeth ground it into pulp. Nidhug reached up, and lifted Cinnia from her back. Then the dragon rose up into the air, her back claws clutching the decapitated body of her enemy. Flying out over the sea she dropped the headless form into the water, spitting the mash of Ahura Mazda's head after it.

She was weeping uncontrollably when she returned to the ledge of the cave where Cinnia stood. Enormous tears flowed down her face, and then down the mountains. The rivers of Belia began to rise, and overflow as they flooded into the sea, and its waters began to rise. Her great body shook with her grief as she looked at the bits of shell and yolk upon the rocks.

Cinnia was crying, too, but she also had the presence of mind to realize what was happening. "Nidhug, please," she begged the dragon, "shrink yourself to a smaller size. You are causing the sea to rise, and it will flood all of Belmair."

"My child! My child!" Nidhug sobbed. But then she

brought herself down to her everyday size, weeping all the harder.

They remained upon the ledge the night long, the dragon sobbing, Cinnia attempting to offer what comfort that she might. Finally as the sun began to rise Cinnia reached out to call to her husband in the silent language. *Dillon! Bring me home!* "I am going to leave you for a while," she told Nidhug. "But I will be back shortly."

Looking up hollow-eyed, the dragon nodded, and then burst into a fresh round of tears as Cinnia disappeared.

"Where have you been?" Dillon asked his wife as she reappeared in their bedchamber. "I awoke and you were gone. Then I heard you call out to me."

Cinnia told him what had happened. "I suppose I awoke when Nidhug did because I am so aligned with the Great Dragon. Oh, Dillon, she is more than distraught. She is heartbroken beyond measure. I do not know if she can survive this tragedy. It was such a vicious thing for Ahura Mazda to do. I'm glad she killed him though I never thought her capable of such a terrible act. What can we do to ease her sorrow?"

*"Cirillo, Uncle, hear me call, and come to me from out yon wall,"* Dillon spoke the spell aloud.

"It's a bit early to be calling upon me, Nephew," Cirillo of the Forest Faeries said as he stepped into their bedchamber. "Oh," he chortled looking about him. "Am I to join you? I never considered, Dillon, that you might share the beauteous Cinnia with me." He leered mischievously at them.

"I am not sharing my wife, you lecher," Dillon said, grinning. Then he grew serious. "Nidhug has suffered a horrific tragedy. Tell him," he said to Cinnia.

Cinnia once again related the tale to the faerie prince.

Cirillo grew pale with shock as she spoke. When she had finished he said but five words. "I will go to her!" He stepped out onto the balcony of their bedchamber, and as they watched in amazement the handsome faerie man turned himself into the exquisite sky-blue and gold dragon. Unfolding his silver and gold wings he rose up into the morning skies, and in the blink of an eye was gone from their sight.

As he reached the mountains of Belia and hovered above her nursery cave he saw her crumpled and weeping before the entrance. She was almost gray with her misery, and Cirillo's cold faerie heart almost broke to see her so. Setting himself down, he walked over to her, and touched her gently with his paw. "Nidhug," he said. "I am here."

The dragon looked up at him with sorrowful eyes. "Cirillo! Oh, Cirillo, my heart is destroyed. My child! My child is gone." And she wept afresh.

He gathered her up, and held her close. "I cannot bear to see you like this, my love," he told her. "I cannot change what has been done to you, Nidhug, but perhaps I can make it better for you."

"How?" She sniffled, nestling against the blue and gold scales of his chest.

"You are required by the magic world of which you are a part to replenish your kind," he said. "I will give you a child if you will let me," Cirillo told her.

"But faeries only give children to those they truly love," Nidhug said softly.

"And I love you," he told her. "Oh, one day I will wed with some pretty faerie girl, and to please my mother love her enough to have an heir for the Forest Kingdom. But you are she to whom my cold faerie heart truly belongs. Will always belong. I would sire your child, and when that egg hatches, I will indeed be father to it. Together we will create a Great Dragon such as Belmair has never seen!"

Nidhug began to cry again. But this time her tears were tears of happiness. Theirs was a love that should not be. Yet it was. A faerie prince and a Great Dragon of Belmair. And together they would create her heir.

"Come," she said, and she led him within her cave where as they mated passionately their roars of joy thundered throughout the mountains of Belia, bringing the rains that washed away all evidence of the murder done.

Nidhug laid her new egg, setting it into a fresh nest of willow and swansdown that Cirillo had fashioned for it. He blessed the egg and, this time, added a protection spell. This egg would remain safe and hatch in its time.

As the glorious sunset spread its myriad of reds, oranges, golds, purples and greens across the Belmairan skies, Nidhug and her faerie mate stood watching, filled with happiness. Above them the great star that was called Hetar rose to blaze across the night skies, settling between Belmair's silver and gold twin moons. Their world had begun a new era. Dillon and Cinnia would rule in peace for a thousand or more years to come. And there would always be a Great Dragon of Belmair to guide them and their descendants.

* * * * *

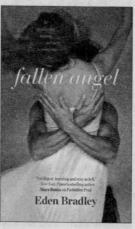

**A long-lost sword**

**A willing heroine**

**A quest to prevent humanity's sacred secrets from falling into the wrong hands**

# ROGUE ANGEL™

Share the daring adventures of archaeologist Annja Creed as she travels the world in search of forgotten treasures and hidden truths. Will her journey end in triumph...or tragedy?

Available Now

Available September 2012

GOLD EAGLE®

Read Annja's adventures six times a year!

Look out for Rogue Angel™, available wherever books are sold.

**www.readgoldeagle.blogspot.com**

RA62157R

**From *New York Times* bestselling author**

# HEATHER GRAHAM

**A tantalizing trilogy**
**from the Krewe of Hunters series**

Available now!

Coming July 31.

Coming August 28.

Pick up your copy wherever books are sold!

HARLEQUIN® MIRA®
www.Harlequin.com

MHGTRI12